PAGE THREE

The older woman gave Johanna a pitying glance. "Haven't you heard?"

"Heard what?" Johanna pressed.

Arlene was carrying a local tabloid put out by Fleet Street irregulars, the ones who dealt in sensationalism and voyeurism. She held up the paper. "Harry's on page three if you'd like to see what he's been up to."

Johanna snatched the paper. "Are you out of your mind?" she cried.

"No," Arlene said. "But you are if you don't divorce him."

SAPPHIRE AND SHADOW

◆

MARIE FERRARELLA

Published by arrangement with
Palace Books Inc.

HarperPaperbacks
A Division of HarperCollinsPublishers

This is a work of fiction. The characters, incidents and dialogues are products of the author's imagination and are not to be construed as real. Any resemblance to actual events or persons, living or dead, is entirely coincidental.

HarperPaperbacks   *A Division of* HarperCollins*Publishers*
10 East 53rd Street, New York, N.Y. 10022

Copyright © 1991 by HarperCollins*Publishers*

Cover photo by Herman Estevez

First printing: September 1991

Printed in the United States of America

HarperPaperbacks and colophon are trademarks of HarperCollins*Publishers*

10 9 8 7 6 5 4 3 2 1

Chapter One

It wasn't where she wanted to be.

Johanna Whitney impatiently ran a hand through her straight blond hair. She shifted in the very expensive, very uncomfortable Louis the Fourteenth chair, watching thin women with fantastic bone structure, small waists and no breasts parade before her wearing designer dresses that would cost the average man two months' salary. She could easily buy several without so much as a second thought. It didn't matter. It hadn't mattered for a long time now.

The chair's intricately carved design hurt her back and forced her to sit up straight. It made her empathize with West Point cadets standing at attention. Their lives were beyond their control, too, at the mercy of the nebulous powers that ran things.

Just the way hers was.

Johanna crossed and uncrossed her legs, trying to support herself by balancing her weight on the armrests but to no avail. The pain in her lower back was spreading to the base of her neck.

This wasn't where she wanted to be. It wasn't where she had hoped to be.

At thirty-four, Johanna knew her world was the kind that women daydreamed about as they did the laundry or shopped with a wagon load of squabbling children. They fantasized about things that she actually possessed as they sat, stuck in traffic, squeezed in subways, jostled in buses. Hers was a fairy tale world, a dream come true. At least, she thought with an unconscious curl of her lip, from the outside.

She felt lonely, useless, unfulfilled.

Along the back wall was a huge mirror to enable patrons to see both sides of dresses that were paraded before them. Johanna looked at her reflection and stared at the woman who was gazing back at her. Who was this woman? Who *was* she? What was all this going on around her?

Her thoughts became jumbled.

Like her life.

For a moment, she became detached from herself, from all that was going on around her. It was almost as if she was having an out-of-body experience. She hovered high above the ongoing procession of women in the room. She floated above it, seeing the models, the boutique owner who stood behind her chair like an obsequious servant, everything in short staccato clips, flickering before her eyes. Unreal. It was all unreal. Like her life had become.

The thin lipped, carefully made-up woman who was attending Johanna frowned behind her back, careful not to let the mirror capture the annoyance on her face. This was taking too long. The fashionably dressed director's wife hadn't shown the slightest bit of interest in any of her best creations thus far. Americans never knew what they wanted, only what they didn't want. Her native British patrons pleased her far more.

She touched Johanna's arm lightly. "Would madam be interested in something else?"

Yes, Johanna thought. I'd like to go back into the past, back fifteen years and start all over. Maybe I could do it better this time.

Better? How could she possibly do it better? How could she correct her error when she didn't know what had gone wrong in the first place?

Johanna ran her fingers across her lips. She was thirsty. Actually, more like dehydrated from the last headache tablets she had taken.

A woman in her position should be happy, Johanna thought sadly. She shouldn't dwell on what was missing. She should concentrate on what she had. And what she had made her the envy of so many. She had prestige, money, servants, two homes—no, two houses, she corrected herself. A home was something very different. A home had been that apartment on Seventy-second street in New York when Harold was just starting out, when they had lived on love, dreams and sardine sandwiches until she thought she'd developed gills. It was a tiny apartment crammed with secondhand furniture and first hand love. Wonderful, exquisite, soul wrenching love. Somewhere along the line, a trade had been made. Their furniture had been upscaled and their love had deteriorated until there were moments now when she didn't think it was there, that it had ever been there at all. Perhaps she had imagined it all. Perhaps she had wanted it so badly that she had created it all in her mind. Maybe it never existed. In any case, right now it was just a distant dream, far beyond her reach. But it was something she wanted to experience again. She *needed* to feel it again, to live that dream once more instead of being trapped in this waking nightmare.

Was it normal to feel so dead at thirty-four? So empty? Her life was full of glitter, her photograph appearing in newspapers and magazines as she graced Harold's arm and elegantly bestowed her presence on his movie premieres. And yet, it was all meaningless.

Her life was full of emptiness.

"Madam?"

Johanna roused herself. It was time to get out of this damned chair before her legs permanently atrophied.

"I'll take the rose one."

What did it matter, anyway? Harold never noticed anything she wore anymore. He never noticed *her* any more, except to make some sort of snide remark.

"The Givency?" the boutique owner asked, her hands folded across the flat expanse where a bosom should have been.

Johanna wondered if the woman had ever been a model herself. She had the structure for it. "The beaded one," she answered absently.

"The Givency." She offered her most approving smile. "An excellent choice."

Johanna knew that the woman would have said those exact same words even if she had opted to buy the curtain that hung in the background and had asked for a gown to be fashioned out of that, Scarlett O'Hara style. Everyone was always saying things they didn't mean, she thought hopelessly.

Johanna rose, smoothing her skirt absently. "Thank you."

The other woman waved back the next model, signaling an end to the private show. "When will madam be available for alterations?"

You don't have to talk about me in the third person, I'm not dead yet, Johanna thought, annoyed at the woman's subservient manner. I just feel that way.

She shrugged her shoulders carelessly. "Now's as good a time as any." Megan had taken Jocelyn for a tour of one of the museums. There was no reason to hurry back to the suite. No reason at all.

"Yes, of course." The woman studied Johanna's figure.

Her eyes rested on Johanna's breasts. They were high and firm and made for complications. "We shall have to make allowances for madam's—"

"Cleavage?" Johanna supplied, amused.

Cleavage. Harold had had another name for it, Johanna thought suddenly, her mind gravitating back to the sun-filled little apartment. He had hardly been able to keep his hands off her then, had stirred her, and made her body sing just for him. There had been no money and they had spent a lot of time dreaming, the radio playing softly in the background. And a lot of time making love on a bed whose mattress insisted on folding inward. They hadn't minded. They had slept together, their bodies as entwined as their lives had been.

Now they were two strangers living beneath the same last name, sharing a daughter and a past and not much else.

Johanna allowed herself to be ushered into a dressing room that was decorated in soothing mint. A heavyset woman who moved with amazing agility fluttered around her, making nips and tucks and murmuring under her breath, supposedly making conversation but obviously satisfied to work without any response from her.

Johanna closed her eyes, drifting back. Oh God, she wanted to go back.

Harold had dreamed such big dreams for them that she had almost felt overwhelmed. She had put aside her own budding career as an artist and devoted herself to him, only him. He had had that kind of magnetism then, that kind of charisma. She had adored him as only an idealistic nineteen-year-old could. Who would have thought that when those dreams began coming true, they would go on to ruin everything else for them?

She opened her eyes and looked down at the top of the woman's head as she did something with pins to the front hem. There was the tiniest barren spot at the crown. "What month is it?"

The woman looked up at Johanna, a flicker of curiosity in the close-set brown eyes. Was this thin-boned woman on something, she wondered. Everyone knew what month it was. "August."

"August." It had been August then too.

"You know what I want, Jo?" Harold had asked, stroking her body slowly in the aftermath of lovemaking.

The pre-dawn air had been hot, humid, with the promise of more unbearable weather as soon as the sun came up.

She had tried not to let her mind flow away from her as it always did when he touched her that way. "No, what?" She moved restlessly under his hand.

He raised himself up on his elbow and looked into her eyes. He moved his palm against her erect nipple. It excited both of them. "To marry you and make love like this forever."

"Ask me," she had coaxed.

His sandy brown hair had fallen over his forehead and into his eyes the way she always loved. It made him look so boyish. It stirred protective feelings within her. A whole cauldron of feelings, protective, sexual, everything.

"Will you?"

"Will I what, Harry?" She remembered fluttering her lashes and trying to look coy, as coy as she could with nothing on but the gold ring she always wore. It had been her mother's.

With a laugh and an oath, Harold had rolled over on top of her and her body had immediately responded to the long, lean frame that she had come to know better than her own. "Marry me, you shameless flirt."

"Well," she pretended to consider, "I guess I'd better. I never argue with a naked man just before he's about to make love to me."

"Am I?"

"You'd better, or I'll be forced to rape you."

He had brushed the silver-blond hair made damp by the

sizzling New York heat from her face, his tongue glazing the pulse at her throat.

"Sounds interesting. Show me."

And she had, wildly, deliriously, joyfully. They made excruciatingly wonderful love. He had been her first lover. Her only lover, but she hadn't had to have others to know that this was something rare, something very, very special.

They had gotten married the next weekend in Maryland. Her father and two sisters had rushed out to be with her and they had all gone out for Chinese food afterwards. Her fortune cookie had promised her a happily-ever-after existence and she had hung onto that for all she was worth, wanting to believe it, wanting to believe anything that promised her that what she had would never end.

Just goes to show you, never trust a fortune cookie, she thought cynically.

When had it started to go wrong? When the Hollywood lions had nodded their sage heads in approval at his efforts? When each success had become that much more terrifying to him because he felt he had to meet it, to best it, with his next effort? She didn't know. She only knew that she had lost him and a part of herself, a part of herself that she missed fiercely.

I'm dead, she thought as she looked at her reflection in the mirror, seeing the thin frame, the ample breasts, the sad, faraway china blue eyes cast in a pale face that had once served as an artist's inspiration. I just haven't lain down yet.

"Is this for a special occasion, Mrs. Whitney?" The manager peered into the dressing room to satisfy herself that all was going well. The dressmaker looked up at her for a moment, then continued to flit about Johanna, working with unobtrusive hands.

"My husband and I are invited to a production party," Johanna said absently. A party used to mean a few intimate friends, or even better, just the two of them. Now it meant a host of people she didn't know and didn't want to know but was expected to be nice to for Harry's sake. She hated attending them.

"It must be so exciting, being the wife of such a famous director."

"Must be," Johanna answered softly. *But you can't tell by me.*

Damn it, she loved him, didn't he realize that? Didn't that cocaine-addled brain of his remember the same things she did? The same wonderful memories?

No, she knew better. All Harry remembered was the last trade figures on his films. And the figures weren't good anymore. That was all that mattered. Johanna balled her hands into clenched fists.

The dressmaker looked at her oddly, a pin suspended between her fingers and the fabric.

Enough, Johanna thought. *I've got to get out of here.*

"What are you doing?" the plump woman asked, clearly upset as Johanna suddenly started shrugging out of the gown. Pins scattered and the dressmaker muttered something to herself, her accent making it almost impossible to understand the fast, soft flow of words.

"I don't have time for a fitting," Johanna said suddenly. "I just remembered an appointment." There was no appointment, she just wanted to get away, to get out, to breathe. "Let me pay for this and I'll make arrangements to come back for another fitting."

The manager folded her hands before her and nodded. "Very good, madam."

I'm not "madam," Johanna wanted to cry. *I'm Joey Lindsey from Connecticut and I want my happiness back.*

But she said nothing. Composure, control, had been drilled into her from early on. You had everything when you had control. Now she simply slipped on her own clothes and hunted through her purse for the American Express card she carried, the card that had replaced a good many old, familiar things in her life with expensive new ones she hardly noticed after they arrived from the store. Image. It was all part of the image, part of what Harold wanted. It had nothing to do with them, with her.

"Anything wrong?" Discreetly the store manager, who towered over Johanna by five inches, looked down into the chaotic gray leather purse that Paul had purchased for her last birthday and tried to pass off as a gift from Harry. Paul, she thought, was loyal to the way they had once been.

"I can't seem to find my charge card."

The manager shrugged slightly. "Madam needn't trouble herself. It can be taken care of when she returns for the next fitt—"

"Damn it, don't you get tired of talking to people as if they weren't in the same room with you?"

Johanna turned and looked into the mirror that ran along the west wall. She didn't know who looked more surprised at her outburst, the boutique owner or her.

"I'm sorry. I think I'm a little overwrought." No, I'm a lot overwrought. And I never used to be.

The other woman nodded benevolently. "No need to explain. As to the card—"

Johanna wanted no favors because of Harry. "Wait, let me call my hotel suite. I'm sure I must have left it there. My husband can bring it over."

If he's straight, Johanna added silently.

Chapter Two

"**Damn it,** it doesn't last long enough. Why doesn't it last long enough?" Harold Whitney ran a thin, nervous hand over his haggard face.

Before him, on the glass top of a coffee table in a suite on the twelfth floor of the Hyatt Carlton Tower Hotel, were two short, narrow white lines.

"How much of this shit do I have to put up my nose before things get better?"

It was a rhetorical question meant for him, not for the blond-haired man standing behind him. But since he was the only other person in the room, Paul Chamberlaine felt a need to respond. The answer was blunt, direct. It was the only way Paul knew how to operate, unless it came to matters involving Johanna. In the fast-paced, double-dealing world of filmmaking, she was his only weak spot. He would have gone to great lengths to shield her. She was the reason he was still here. He looked at Harry with barely suppressed loathing.

"I don't think there's enough coke in the country to do that."

"Ever the optimist."

Harry took the reed straw in his shaking hand. A little more and it would be better. Just a little more and then things wouldn't look so hopeless, wouldn't feel like they were closing in on him, wouldn't haunt him the way they did these days.

Everybody was always trying to get a piece of him, dig a segment out of him. Paul, Johanna, the production company. Those shitheads in Hollywood. Why couldn't they all just leave him the hell alone? Why couldn't they have a little faith in him? He could work another miracle. He had done it before, taking a nothing film and making it into the blockbuster of the year, to be cheered by the public and critics alike.

He could do it again. He *would* do it again. He just needed another hit to make it all clear to him, that was all.

Paul lit a cigarette and exhaled slowly. He had given up smoking twice this year. Working with Harry always made him start again. He watched the man he had once admired lean over the coffee table, hovering over the crooked white lines.

"That garbage is destroying your brain."

Harry snorted. "A hell of a lot you know. This is the only thing that keeps my brain going."

Paul debated throwing in the proverbial towel, packing up and going home to Denise, to his kids and to his sanity. It was getting to the point where he didn't know why he was staying on, why Johanna was staying on. The man on the sofa bore little resemblance to the man they had both once known, both once loved.

"If you believe that, you're in worse shape than I thought."

Harry was sick of people talking at him, telling him what to do, what not to do. Who the hell did they think they were, anyway? "Don't knock it until you try it."

"I don't have to try pointing a gun to my head to know it's suicide to pull the trigger."

"Nice line. Save it for your next script."

Paul crushed his cigarette out in the ashtray on the table with an irritated movement. "I'd like to save *you* for my next script."

Harold looked up slowly at him and malevolence spread across his face. All the support that Paul had given him through this difficult project was totally forgotten. This latest slight encompassed his whole being. He didn't remember that Paul had come to his rescue and taken a cut just to help out. He remembered only that Paul had written the last film he had produced. And it had sunk like a lead balloon.

"Write a good one and we'll see."

It was everyone else's fault he was going through this. He blamed everyone else for the awful spate of bad luck he was having with his films. It was just bad luck, that's all. Nothing more. He hadn't changed. He was still as capable as ever.

God knew, he tried, but everyone kept failing him. Paul, Johanna, Sam, everyone. And they all expected so much, so damn much out of him. A pound of flesh wasn't enough anymore. His soul wasn't enough. He had nothing left to give and still they cried: more, more, make it better.

Well, he would, he'd show them. He'd show them all. Harold B. Whitney wasn't meant to be a has-been, a failure. He was a genius.

The white powder went into the straw and exploded inside his nose. For a moment, just for a moment, he was at peace and yet vitally alive. Bits and pieces of projects flashed through his brain. All star-studded, all wonderful. He was wonderful. It was going to work. It was going to be all right.

It was going to be more than all right.

Somewhere in the distance, he heard a bell ringing, but couldn't place it, couldn't place himself. All he wanted was for the rush to go on, to take him spiraling to lands that lesser people only dreamed of. To places that were getting harder and harder to reach.

"It's Johanna."

Harold blinked. Reality was calling him. With extreme difficulty, he tried to focus his mind. "Where?" He looked around the suite. It swam before him, but he didn't see her.

"On the phone." Paul held it up.

"She wants to talk to me?" His tongue felt thick and he didn't want to talk. He wanted to feel. There were things to do, projects to conquer. And he was equal to all of it!

Damn, Johanna was always interfering with his life, his space. Johanna had left in tears this morning. She was always leaving in tears these days. Woman was all water, no substance.

"No," Paul covered the receiver, instinctively feeling that Johanna wasn't going to want to hear this, "she wants her charge card."

"Why, is London for sale?"

Harold laughed hysterically at his own joke, his voice cracking. The sound of his laughter filled his head and reverberated back. The room sounded as if it were full of laughter.

Laughter at him.

No, damn it, they wouldn't laugh at him. He'd pull this off. He *had* to pull this off. And then they'd all come crawling back to him. As they should.

Paul shook his head. "She's at a boutique on Regent Street and she forgot her wallet."

"So? What does she want from me? I'm not her errand boy."

You're not her husband lately, either, Paul was tempted to say, but let it pass. He had been with Harold's production company for eleven years now, coming in when Harold had been riding the high, heady crest of success and adulation. He had seen the man once thought of as a boy genius descend into his own private hell, dragging his family with him. The fawning cheers had turned to ill-concealed smirks and Harold had sought inspiration and solace in drugs, in starlets eager for attention, giving him the attention he sought so desperately. He sought support in everything except the right things.

Paul gave up. He turned from the pathetic sight on the sofa and spoke quietly into the receiver. "I don't think he can come to the phone right now, Johanna."

She kept her smile in place. She knew that the boutique owner was straining to hear. People loved gossip the world over. She shielded the phone with her hand and turned her back.

"Is he stoned, Paul?" The question was whispered.

Paul felt for her. "He's his usual self." Though silence met his statement, he heard the pain, the defeat. "Look, exactly where are you? I can bring the card over to you."

"You don't have to—"

"Look, I want to get out of this hotel room."

He looked over to where Harold sat, nodding and humming to himself. His legs were moving up and down, as if some unseen puppeteer was pulling strings.

Poor damn fool, he thought. Harold was humming the theme from his first picture, the one that had been such a rousing success. The one he could never match.

"I don't know of anywhere where I can find a beautiful woman to talk to me for a few minutes. Have a little pity, fair lady."

Johanna laughed. Paul could always make her laugh and she was grateful to him. "I left my wallet in my room on the bureau. The shop's on Regent Street, near Piccadilly Circus."

"I'll be right there," Paul promised.

"And Paul?"

"Yeah?"

"Thanks."

"Don't mention it." He replaced the receiver and went to get her wallet.

Harold raised his bleary eyes in Paul's direction when Paul walked out of the second bedroom. "So, she's made you into her errand boy instead, huh?"

Paul didn't miss the trace of jealousy in Harold's voice. He made light of the situation. "Can't leave her stranded."

"Why not? You're leaving me stranded. Everyone leaves me stranded."

He had heard this refrain before. There was no point in commenting. Harold was beyond hearing anyway. Paul pocketed Johanna's wallet and crossed to the door.

"You don't want her to be embarrassed in public, Harry. Think of what it would look like in the press, the wife of Harold Whitney without funds."

Harold sank back in the sofa. "She's always buying things."

Paul was tempted to keep walking, but he had never run off from confrontations. "Women who feel neglected buy things, Harry."

Harold smirked at the watery figure in front of him. "Been reading Cosmopolitan again?"

"Just being a student of human nature, Harry," Paul said easily. "It comes in handy in my line of work."

"Yeah? Well, save it for your scripts and leave Johanna to me."

"I'd like nothing better, just let me know when you're back in town."

He hadn't the strength to raise himself up from the sofa, even though energy seemed to be boiling in his chest. "What's that supposed to mean?"

"Figure it out." Paul slammed the door behind him. Waste, he hated to see waste. And Harry was quickly disintegrating right before his eyes.

"Ass," Harold shot out vehemently, then closed his eyes as another wild rush came. He was pathetically grateful and his hand gripped the arm of the sofa as he hung on for the ride.

It was over before Paul reached the elevator.

"Harry in?" The owlish man who stepped off the elevator nodded toward the suite behind Paul. He was Harold's production assistant. One of many who had come and gone. Garrison Hatheway was determined to stay, one way or another.

Paul got into the elevator and hit the open button as he answered. "Yeah, he's in. See that he doesn't hurt himself, Gar."

Garrison jammed his fists into the pockets of his baggy corduroy trousers. "Oh shit, is he—?"

"Isn't he always?"

"Hell, I don't know why I hang around."

"Same question plagues us all, Gar, same question plagues us all." Paul lifted his hand from the button and pressed for the first floor. "Guess we're all hoping for a renaissance." The elevator doors closed on him. "Most of all, Johanna, I'd bet."

"Do you want me to come in with you?" Paul asked an hour later as he stood by the suite door again.

Johanna shook her head. She liked Paul's company, but she couldn't use him as a shield. Harold was her husband, her problem. She couldn't solve it by hiding behind other people.

"No, there's no need." She stood up on her toes and kissed his cheek. "Thanks for riding to my rescue."

Paul leaned into the kiss. Damn Harry, didn't he know what he had, what he could lose? "What's a shining knight for?" Paul laughed.

She saw the pity in his eyes and turned away.

The hostility hit her like a hot, hard hand as soon as she walked into the suite.

"Where are all the packages?"

She simply walked straight to her room. "There are no packages, just one dress."

Harold rose on unsteady legs. He took two steps toward her, holding onto the back of the sofa for support. "Just one dress," he mimicked her voice. "How many thousands did it cost?"

She turned on him, her hurt spilling out. "Less than the

money you spent on Alexandra King in the Bahamas last month."

She had read about it in the tabloids. It seemed that lately it was the only way to keep abreast of what he was doing, by reading about it in the papers along with the rest of the world.

Harold kept on gripping the back of the sofa to steady himself. He couldn't pass up a challenge. "She wasn't a bitch."

Why, why are you arguing with me? Why won't you become the man I married again? "Is that what I am?"

He saw the hurt in her face and felt oddly triumphant. He could still evoke emotion as he chose. That was all part of being a director. And he was the best. "That's what you've become."

"If I am, you made me that way."

"I can't take all the credit."

"No, maybe not, but you certainly had a featured role." She hated this, hated arguing. The only time they spoke to each other lately was in raised voices. She took a deep breath and tried to clear her head.

"Why aren't you working?"

"I *am* working." He tapped his temple. "Right here, the greatest work goes on right here."

"How? There aren't any brain cells left. You've burnt them all away." She took hold of his arm. "Harry, please, can't you stop doing that?"

"Doing what?"

She shut her eyes. "Never mind. I'm going to my room."

Harold watched her go and wondered what had happened to the cocaine he had put out for himself. Paul. Paul must have taken it. Dirty rotten bastard, helped himself to everything around here, helped himself to Johanna too, more than likely.

Johanna heard Harold's voice go up as he hurled a stream of curses through the locked door. She squeezed her eyes tight. How much more she could put up with before she broke down completely?

Chapter Three

Johanna didn't know how long she sat on her bed, wadding a section of the bedspread beneath her hand, trying to pull herself together. She needed something to take her mind off Harry, off her life. Forcing herself up off the bed she found a tape that Denise, Paul's wife had given her. She had put it away in her bureau and forgotten about it. It was a tape of the sound of rain falling. Denise found it invaluable when she was feeling tense. She said it always worked for her.

But it didn't work for Johanna. She was too keyed up for it to penetrate to her inner soul. With a defeated sigh, Johanna shut off the tape. It was no use. She felt as if she was coming apart. This couldn't be happening to her. This couldn't be *her* life. And yet it was.

Finally, to block out the sound of Harry's voice in the other room, the sound of the words of past arguments that echoed in her head, she decided to take a shower.

She stripped and left her clothes lying in a heap on the

bedroom floor. Walking into the bathroom, she reached into the shower stall and adjusted the temperature until it was just hot enough for her to bear. She stepped in and let the water hit her full force. Johanna closed her eyes and tried to clear her mind, hoping that the steady, pulsating beat of the water coming from the shower head would somehow wipe out the residue of the last scene with Harry.

She stood there a long time, just letting the water wash over her, waiting to be cleansed. There was nowhere for her to go today and nothing to do, nothing that she felt like doing. Once she had grabbed every nuance that life had to offer with both hands, savoring everything. Now there was only a deepening malaise that reached out, attempting to take away her soul.

Johanna knew she should be doing something, anything, to shake the grip of this awful depression that threatened to engulf her permanently. Perhaps irreversibly.

A shudder passed over her body. Imagine how awful it would be to feel this way all the time. Even her first love, art, the thing that had been the sole most powerful driving force in her life before she had married Harold, no longer held an allure for her. At one time she had dreamed of holding her own shows, of sharing herself with the world through her paintings. Now she couldn't even work up the enthusiasm to visit the nearby Tate Gallery. It was as if everything she held dear had died or was in the stages of dying around her. Within her.

She felt so alien, so unlike herself. She hardly recognized the person she had become. With a pang she remembered how she had always greeted each day with such enthusiasm, such zest. How she had felt so wonderful just being alive, anticipating the incredible things that were waiting for her around the next corner. But that had been when she was nineteen, twenty, twenty-one, a hundred years ago and in another life.

Life held nothing for her now.

With a jerk of her hand, she turned off the water and

stepped out of the shower, heedlessly dripping on the pearl gray mat on the tiled floor. Naked, she leaned over the sink and wiped the steam from the bathroom mirror. The reflection that stared back at her looked almost gaunt.

No, damn it, she wasn't down yet. She was going to find a solution to this mess that her life had become. Somehow, somewhere, there had to be a way to get them back to where they once had been. Life *was* worth living. She wouldn't let go of that. She *couldn't* let go of that. If she did, Johanna knew she would die.

She took the huge bath towel from the rack on the wall and slowly began to blot her body. She looked at herself critically. She was still young, still blessed with a good figure. She was still the same person she had been inside. She could make it work.

Besides, there was Jocelyn.

At the thought of her twelve-year-old daughter, the tiny lines etched by sadness about her mouth began to soften. Jocelyn was her pride and joy, the embodiment of everything good in her life. She was everything that a mother could want, bright, sunny, pretty, with the promise of startling beauty just a few years away. Whatever happened between her and Harry, right or wrong, at least they had created this one sweet life. Perhaps that would have to be enough.

She looked at herself again and raised her chin. *C'mon, Joey, no one said life was going to be fair. Or easy. You're only down and out when you give up. Don't give up!*

"Terrific." Johanna drew away. "Now I'm giving myself pep talks in the mirror."

She laughed, but the laugh rang hollow. She had never felt this empty, this hollow before. All her rationalizations, all her logic were failing her now. She knew she was hanging on by her fingertips and they were beginning to grow numb. But hang on she was bound to do until she found a way to make it right again.

What else could she do? She couldn't give up totally.

That wasn't her. Her father, a gentle-voiced man with infinite patience, had taught her never, ever to give up. And so she was bound to try again.

With a sigh, Johanna wrapped the towel around her body. Taking a second towel, she fashioned a terry cloth turban for her hair. She was going to go to Harry and ask for a truce, to tell him that they had to start over again. It wouldn't be the first time she had said those words, but maybe this time they would stick. Maybe he was reaching bottom, just like she was, feeling just as desperate. Maybe he wanted a change and didn't know how to go about it. And maybe, she prayed, together they could regain what they had once had.

She squared her shoulders and opened the bathroom door.

She heard movement in the next room. "Harry?" she called out. "Harry, I want to talk to you."

But when she walked out into the area that served as a sitting room for the suite, Harold wasn't there. Instead, she saw Megan, the young woman she had hired to help take care of Jocelyn while they were in London. Ariel Natwik had resigned her position as nanny, citing the fact that she was getting on in years. But Johanna knew better. She knew that the old woman left them because she disapproved of Harold and the lifestyle that he lived.

Jocelyn had protested that she was too old for a nanny, so Megan was hired as a compromise.

A compromise, Johanna thought dryly, in more ways than one.

Large brown eyes swept over Johanna's towel-clad body.

Comparing us, Megan, dear? Johanna thought. I'm not ready for the glue factory yet, even if I am twelve years older.

Instinctively, Johanna moved regally into the room. She had learned long ago how to deal with uncomfortable situations and keep the other person from knowing just what she felt.

"Harry, um, Mr. Whitney's left for the studio, Mrs. Whitney," Megan told her, her eyes not meeting Johanna's.

"I see."

And what would I see if our eyes met, little girl, Johanna thought. Guilt, remorse? Or a smugness? Don't you think I know?

The dark-haired, sloe-eyed Megan had been to bed with Harry. Probably more than once. He could still be very, very charming when he wanted to be.

It seemed, Johanna thought, that Harry was having an affair with everyone these days, everyone but her. Even though she had insisted on coming along with him on this trip to London despite his assertions that he was going to be busy with the film, nothing had changed between them. They were still occupying separate rooms, where once separate beds would have been unthinkable. She laid awake at night, missing him, missing the intimacy that had once been hers alone, feeling sorry for herself, feeling angry with him and cursing the fate that had fulfilled his fantasies beyond his wildest dreams and done this to them.

"Where's Jocelyn?" Johanna asked.

"Right here, Mom."

Johanna turned around as the young girl came up behind her. At twelve, she was up to Johanna's shoulder, her young body strong and hard, just beginning to reach out to the ripening that was to be. She had long, shimmery silver-blond hair just like her mother and looked, just as Johanna did, much taller than she really was. At the moment, her hair was pulled back from her face and neatly arranged in a French twist.

"How do you like it?" Jocelyn twirled around, hand on hip, showing off her new look.

Johanna's mouth hardened as she shot Megan a disapproving glare. Megan raised her chin defiantly, but said nothing.

"I don't," Johanna said.

Jocelyn was wearing designer clothes meant for someone

much older than she. The dress adhered to her young body almost provocatively. Her fresh face was carefully painted with blush and shadow and lipstick, creating an illusion of a child-woman.

"Take it off." Johanna's voice was deadly still. "The dress, the make-up, take it all off."

Jocelyn's wide smile turned into a petulant pout instantly. She took a step closer to the *au pair* girl. "But Megan said I looked sophisticated."

"Twelve-year-olds don't need to look sophisticated. They need to look clean."

Jocelyn dug in. "I'm not a baby any more."

To lose her temper would gain her nothing. Johanna smiled, tempering her words. "No, but you're not a grown-up either, my love." She took her chin in her hand. When Jocelyn attempted to retreat, she tightened her hold, though careful not to hurt her. "I'm afraid you're in that valley betwixt and between right now. You'll be old soon enough. Enjoy all this while you can."

"You don't let me enjoy anything!" Jocelyn snapped back, pulling away. She played her ace card triumphantly. "Daddy said he liked it."

"Daddy likes strolling hostesses of the evening," Johanna murmured under her breath, looking pointedly at Megan, "and has very little taste left anymore. There's the bathroom sink, Jocelyn," she pointed behind her. "Use it."

Jocelyn flounced out of the room and slammed the bathroom door behind her.

"Mrs. Whitney," Megan began, folding her hands before her, "I didn't think—"

Johanna whirled around. The smile was still on her face, but it had hardened. "No, I'm sure you didn't," Johanna said. "Next time, please do. Her name is Jocelyn, not Lolita."

Megan stared at her, confused. "What?"

Johanna waved her hand at the younger woman. "Before your time, I imagine. An old movie. An even older book."

She remembered sneaking into the theater her best friend's father owned to see it. Forbidden fruit at the time. Her mother had had a fit and called to upbraid Mr. Wyatt for his careless lack of supervision. She had been embarrassed for days. "Might seem tame by today's standards," she mused. "But it goes without saying that I want Jocelyn to stay twelve until she reaches thirteen." By which time, you'll be gone, Johanna promised herself. "And so on. One step at a time, understood?"

"Yes, ma'am." Megan's smile, as well as the polite tone she used, was forced.

Ma'am. God, that word made her feel old. Old and ugly and unloved. It seemed as if there was very little these days that didn't.

Johanna went to her room to get dressed.

When she emerged again, Jocelyn's door was still closed. She hesitated before it, debating whether to give the young girl her space or talk to her. No, there was too much space giving and not enough communication these days, Johanna thought. Space was just another term for emptiness. Nothing was solved with emptiness. She tapped on the door lightly.

"Jocelyn?" There was no answer. She knocked again. "Jocelyn, can I come in?"

"If I said no would you stay out?" her daughter asked defiantly.

"Probably not."

"Then come in."

She opened the door and found her daughter sitting on her bed. Her face was scrubbed, the french twist gone, replaced by loose hair that hung down to her shoulders. She was wearing jeans and a tee-shirt that bore the face of Jon Bon Jovi. She was Jocelyn again.

Johanna glanced over at the heap in the corner. The new dress with its accompanying patterned stockings and high heels were all tangled into a ball and lying on the plush rug like a toy that had garnered disfavor.

Johanna tested the waters. "Jocelyn, I didn't mean to sound cruel." Easily, she sat down on the edge of the bed. She watched Jocelyn pull back a fraction of an inch in an act of defiance.

"Then why did you?"

Johanna folded her hands in her lap. She had always been honest with Jocelyn. She cared too much to be anything else. "Because being a parent sometimes means you have to be."

Jocelyn sat up, tucking her legs under her. "Daddy never is."

"No," Johanna echoed, "Daddy never is. But Daddy doesn't always know what's best for you, honey."

"Why?"

"Because he's so busy with other things and he doesn't want you to be mad at him, so he says yes a lot."

Jocelyn tilted her head, her hair spilling over her shoulder. "And you want me to be mad at you?"

"No, baby, I don't." Johanna moved to put her arm around Jocelyn. Jocelyn stiffened. The argument wasn't over yet and Johanna knew that Jocelyn wasn't through trying to win.

"Let me hold you, Jocey. I need to hold you."

Tentatively, the girl moved forward, wanting the contact as well, even though she feared the battle lost.

Johanna laid her cheek against the top of her daughter's head as she put her arm around her.

"Sometimes, you've got to accept 'no,' got to accept waiting for things. If you have everything right away, then there's nothing to reach out for, nothing to look forward to." She stroked her daughter's head. "It'll all happen for you someday, Jocelyn, I promise. But don't rush it. Make memories, honey, make lots and lots of memories at each stage of your life." She raised her head and looked into the eyes that mirrored Harry's so well. "It helps during the bad times."

"Well, okay." Jocelyn's voice was low and grudging, but

the stiffness in her young body had disappeared as she leaned into her mother.

"And you can keep the dress."

Jocelyn sat up. "I can?" The eyes grew bright again.

"You can." Johanna grinned. "You'll grow into it."

"But it fits me now."

Johanna laughed fondly and ran her hand along Jocelyn's cheek. "You'll grow into it, trust me." She rose and crossed to the window. Far below, people were milling about, living lives, being happy. She envied them. Turning, she leaned her hands behind her on the window sill. "I feel like an ice cream soda."

"Strawberry?" Jocelyn asked hopefully.

It was both their favorite. "What else is there?"

Johanna put out her hand to her daughter. Jocelyn bounced off the bed, the argument and the dress temporarily forgotten. For the moment she was twelve once more, and the lines of communication had opened. Johanna knew they would shut down again, and again, but as long as there was a wedge, she'd make use of it.

For now, she would enjoy the afternoon and several hundred forbidden calories with the only person who meant anything to her.

Chapter Four

Harry didn't come back to the hotel that evening.

Johanna waited up for him until past midnight, wanting to talk, wanting to bridge the widening chasm that was separating them, making them strangers. She was more than eager to do whatever it took to get them back together. Fair means or foul, she didn't care. She was determined to use anything at her disposal. All she cared about was that they become a family again. She was willing to overlook how badly he had treated her, how awful he had made her life, if only he'd make an effort to gain some self-control, to become the man he once was.

She wanted the pain that haunted her to be a thing of the past.

As the minutes slipped into hours, Johanna began to pace restlessly about the suite. She hated waiting. She had rehearsed what she was going to say to Harry over and over again. But now, her initial confidence was fading with the passing time. She'd tried to discuss their problems with him before and had gotten nowhere. What made her think she'd succeed this time?

It was late and she had given up hope. Jocelyn had fallen asleep on the couch and had to be roused in order to be put to bed. Megan retired shortly after that, at eleven. The young woman hadn't bothered trying to hide her hurt over Harry's absence.

Poor little fool, she probably thinks Harry's world rises and sets around her, Johanna thought. Harry would have told her that, told her endless lies that she would cling to. Johanna felt oddly sympathetic for the woman who had betrayed her trust. She was young and naive and not the first who had gotten herself entangled, however briefly, with the larger than life Harold T. Whitney. And not the last, Johanna thought ruefully.

Yet she could forgive him that, forgive him a great deal more if only he would make amends, come back, just be the Harry she knew and loved.

Moving slowly, she crossed to the window and drew the drapes, shutting out the dark night with its oppressive shadows. But Harry didn't think there was anything wrong with the way he was, Johanna thought sadly. It was everyone else who was changing, who was different.

How in God's name did she begin to untangle that and make it right?

The colorful silk kimono opened and closed about her long, slender legs as she roamed the suite, unable to find a place for herself. Harold had rented half the floor when he and his entourage descended upon London and on the famed suburban Pinewood Studios where he would direct his newest movie. Somehow it seemed appropriately titled *New Faces, Old Lies*. That was the story of their lives lately. It was hard to keep track of the truth these days.

When she had stood packing in her blue and gray bedroom in Beverly Hills, she'd told herself this trip was going to be different. She was getting good at lying to herself, she thought sadly. Pinewood was best known for its James Bond pictures; and Harold, what was he best known for these days? His debauchery? His penchant for blaming others? His past history of blockbuster movies that refused to repeat itself?

"Stop it."

Johanna massaged her temples. She had another headache. She was driving herself crazy analyzing and reanalyzing her situation. There was nothing to go over. It was all very simple, she told herself. She wanted to talk to Harry, to offer a truce, to do whatever needed doing to hold the family together and make it work again. That was why she had trailed along to London when she would have been happier staying in the States. Foolishly, she had hoped, prayed that something akin to an epiphany would happen to Harold. Something that would bring him back to his senses, make him see that he was destroying the best part of his life. Not his film career but his wife and his daughter. Lives were so much more precious than things, than careers. She wished he could understand that. She'd leave the mansions, the jewels and the furs without so much as a backward glance. At one time she had reveled in them, but then they became a symbol of how far she had come— how far away from Harry she was.

Harry was now notorious for his womanizing. Some of them lasted longer than others, but most of the women were just bodies to be sought in the night. His mistress more than any other was Success and the whimsical muse had turned her back on Harry, hurling him into the black depths of despair and wedding him to drugs in his search for a catalyst to bring back the glory of his past.

But she still loved him, or the Harry she felt existed trapped beneath the stranger he had become.

Where *was* he?

She bit her lip as she looked at the clock. It was past one. Her hand hovered over the telephone before she made up her mind. Finally, in frustration, she called Paul. Her guilt at waking him didn't wipe out her need to know where Harry was *this* time.

You're becoming a masochist.

She heard the phone being scraped off the receiver on the other end and dropped before she heard a groggy voice mumble, "Hello?"

"Paul, it's Johanna." She swallowed. This was humiliating, even with a friend as good as Paul. "Do you know where Harry is?"

Paul picked up the clock on his night stand and struggled to focus in on the dark red numbers. He had dropped into bed an hour ago, exhausted. Sleep had taken hold of him in a vise-like grip immediately and had blotted out everything else. It took a minute to pull himself into the present.

"He was at the studio when I left."

"Working?"

There was a pause. "Yeah."

Even though she expected it, her heart sank anyway. "Paul, you never could lie well."

He laughed awkwardly as he cursed Harold silently. If he had married Johanna first, life would have been a great deal different for her. "You'd think I'd have learned after all these years."

"What's her name?"

Paul sat up in bed, awake now. He ran a hand over his disheveled hair. "I honestly don't know."

She sat down on the sofa, feeling oddly numb.

"I didn't mean to bother you." Her voice trailed off.

He heard the pain in her voice and fervently wished there was something he could do. "Johanna, why do you stay?"

She shrugged helplessly, even though he wasn't there to see. "Because I love him."

"Really?"

"Really."

He couldn't understand. Harry treated her abominably. He would have left a long time ago if he had been in her place. "Why?"

"Why's the sky blue?"

"This isn't philosophy, Johanna. This is your life." He shifted, pulling the sheet around his waist. "You deserve better."

"Yes," she agreed, "I do. And he used to be better. A lot better."

"I remember."

"Maybe what I'm waiting for, staying for, is because," her voice became thick as she fought back tears, "I keep hoping he'll be like that again. That this is just some sort of madness he's going through. It's as if he had a personality transplant."

"Cocaine does that to you."

"Don't patronize me, Paul. I know drugs do that, but he doesn't have to do drugs." She ran a hand over her mouth and took a deep breath to steady her nerves. "Sorry, I didn't mean to snap. I'm not myself lately."

"You have cause."

She smiled. Good old Paul, always in her corner. "Maybe when this picture is over—"

He couldn't let her nurture an illusion. It was best if she just faced the truth. "It's not going to be over."

"What?"

"Johanna, the movie's a mess. He can't seem to get it together anymore."

"Then help him," she begged. "You've always managed to help him before."

It was too late for that. "I can't play Svengali to his Trilby any longer, Johanna. I'm worn out. Burnt out. He fired me today."

"He's always firing you, Paul. It doesn't mean anything, you know that."

"Maybe." He paused, wondering how he could phrase this. Now that he had done it, he was free. But letting Johanna know was the hardest part. He knew it would be. Paul had planned to stop by her suite in the morning to tell her. Now that she had called, there was no putting it off. "Johanna, I'm leaving tomorrow."

"What?" Her hand tightened on the phone. "Where are you going?"

"I'm leaving for the U.S. For my own sanity. It's all settled. I'm booked on flight number 59. Come with me," he coaxed suddenly, seriously.

"Why Paul," amusement came from somewhere, but she had no idea where, "is this an indecent proposal?"

"I only wish." He laughed as he reached for the pack of cigarettes by his bed. "But I'm a monogamous kind of guy." He shook out a cigarette. It fell on his bedspread as he leaned over for a match. He lit it and inhaled deeply. The smoke felt hot going into his lungs. It didn't help.

"And kind."

"That too, on occasion."

"On every occasion with me. I'll miss you." Without Paul, there was no one to turn to, besides Arlene and Arlene was little more than an acquaintance. Suddenly, the room felt colder, lonelier than it had a moment before. Johanna felt like the last person left alive on a raft adrift in the ocean.

"Yeah, me too." The whole business left a bad taste in his mouth. "Sure you don't want to come home?"

More than anything. "Harry's my home, Paul. You know that."

"Yeah, I know. Too bad he doesn't know it. You're one hell of a girl, Johanna."

"Promise you'll tell me that when I call you in the middle of the night again."

"Promise."

She didn't want to hang up. It was as if she was breaking the last link she had to the real world. "Need a ride to the airport tomorrow?" She looked at the clock on the stand next to the telephone. It said one-thirty. "Today," she corrected herself.

"Greg's taking me. But thanks."

He thought about staying, but he wasn't accomplishing

any good and Denise had called, telling him she missed him. It was time to go, to move on. He had stayed at the funeral too long, he thought.

"Take care of yourself, Johanna."

"Always. 'Bye."

Slowly, she replaced the phone in the cradle.

She rose and ran her hands up and down the sleeves of her kimono. The chill she felt refused to leave her. She had leaned on Paul and now he was going. Maybe it was an omen. Maybe she should leave too.

But she couldn't leave. Without Paul, Harry'd be lost. He had come to depend on the man heavily, even though he never admitted it. She forgot about Harry's infidelity, forgave him without even thinking about it and made up her mind to come to the studio tomorrow.

If the mountain won't come to Mohammed, then Mohammed had damn well better come to the mountain. She had gone through too much to stand on ceremony. And pride was for people who had something to lose. She no longer had. Besides, it was their anniversary. The smile that twisted her lips was a sad one.

Just six miles north of Heathrow airport, Pinewood Studio sat like a fairy princess dropped in the middle of a forest. It was known as the largest studio in Europe and Johanna could well agree as she drove through the grounds, trying to find her way to the big white sound stage where once the epic movie *Cleopatra* had been filmed. Her nerve-wracking drive from the hotel had left her in a poor mood to confront Harry. But she hadn't come this far just to turn around and go home.

Determined, she parked the leased vehicle behind the huge building and slipped inside the sound stage. The dimness enveloped her and she took a moment to let her eyes adjust before finding someone to give her directions.

Johanna saw him from a distance, his head bent close to the script girl's and she couldn't help wondering if the buxomy redhead had entertained her husband last night. The woman wore a tight skirt and looked like his type. Young and eager and available.

With deliberate force, Johanna pushed the thought out of her mind. She hadn't driven here on a journey that confused her in a car she detested to confront her husband with accusations and recriminations. She had come with her heart in her hand to start out fresh, to be the supportive wife the way she always felt she was. Paul was somewhere over the ocean, flying home and Harry had lost his best man. He was going to need her now more than ever. Maybe he'd finally realize that.

The sound stage was thick with people all hurrying off somewhere else. Carefully, Johanna tried to pick her way through the tangle of cable wires that snaked their way across the huge floor. The area was humming with carpenters and technicians getting in each others' way. Sets were being created out of nothing, illusions formed that lived and died in a moment. There was a vitality here. It was, she thought, not unlike the very act of creation. Something would come from all this, something large and full with a beginning and an end and people would pay to see it. She was proud of what her husband did, proud of him. At least, she had been.

Johanna kept her eyes on Harry as she made her way forward. Suddenly, there was a shout behind her and a rumbling noise. Johanna felt herself being physically thrown against the wall. Her body was pressed hard against it and there was no room for movement, scarcely room for breath. She was surrounded by a tall, hard male body. Startled, disoriented, hardly knowing what to say or think, Johanna tried to raise her head up. The wind was almost gone from her lungs, but she managed to gasp out. "Just what the hell do you think you're doing?"

"Sorry, luv, but your head's far too pretty to be separated from your shoulders."

And then Johanna did look up, up into the softest brown

eyes she had ever seen. The stranger made absolutely no movement to back away and she felt his rather intense reaction to her. It was startling and at the same time, oddly exhilarating. The grin on his face told her that he wasn't embarrassed by it.

She knew she should have been, but she wasn't either. That in itself embarrassed her.

Chapter Five

There was something forceful and yet gentle in the way he held her. She felt protected, yet there was a tingling, alert sensation running through her entire body that definitely didn't allow her to relax. Something was happening here.

Johanna gathered her wits about her and looked up at the stranger's face. She thought his manner was at odds with the impression the rest of him created. The dichotomy she sensed in his actions was intensified by what she saw in his face. Overall, it was a strong, manly face. But the eyes, the eyes gave him a kind, sensual appearance. He had large, expressive, inquisitive brown eyes framed with long dark lashes. Amused eyes. Dangerous eyes. And yet, somehow, young eyes.

But even with those eyes, he appeared to be someone powerful, someone strong. Someone who would always stand his ground. It was in the square cut of his jaw, the wide, sturdy planes and angles of his face. The confident air of his body.

"Wouldn't want you to be hurtin' yourself, luv," he repeated. The definite lilt of a cockney accent flirted with the deep strains of his voice. There was a definite appreciation of the situation—and of her—as well as a concern in his eyes.

A crowd was quickly forming around them. Johanna was just beginning to realize how close she had come to being seriously injured by a piece of scenery as it was lowered into place.

Her eyes grew wide as she looked at it now and the near miss settled into her awareness. "Oh," was all she could manage. She just stood there, unable to think of anything else to say. She didn't know if her reaction was caused by the fear of being hurt, or the sensation of having his body pressed so closely up against hers.

"Would've been a mite more than the word 'oh' if that thing had hit you, luv."

He inclined his head as he spoke, but made no effort to release her. There was a twinkle in his eyes. On someone else, it might have been interpreted as a leer. But on this man it qualified as a twinkle. Whether it was harmless or not she had yet to determine.

"You ought to know better than to be walkin' round without lookin', luv." The open face sported a huge smile as he looked at her, one of his hands braced on the wall above her head. "I haven't seen you around before. You new?"

Johanna put her hands on his arms and with a bit of reluctance created some space between them. Hard. Firm. Something apart from her consciousness was pleasured. "I'm—"

"What the hell do you think you're doing, pawing my wife!" Harold bellowed. Oblivious to what had almost happened to her, he came charging at them.

Johanna immediately felt a pain in her temples. Harry made her feel so tense lately. With a sinking feeling, she knew a scene was coming.

The stranger took a cautious step back, his hands raised high in the air. It was clear that he was surprised and that he would leave the explaining up to her. But there was no sign of intimidation in his manner. She liked that. Harry, she knew, didn't. If he couldn't frighten, couldn't bully, he took the absence of these reactions as a threat to his position.

"He just saved my life," Johanna answered quickly, the nervous agitation still in her voice. "That backdrop—" She pointed at it as she let her voice trail off. It was still swaying.

"Well, what are you doing wandering around here anyway?" Harry raged. He was annoyed at having his set disrupted in this manner. It seemed harder and harder to get things together these days.

She had gotten more attention, more expression of concern from a stranger, she thought. She felt color rise to her face and she damned Harry for it.

"Looking for a way to make you a widower," Johanna snapped before she knew she was going to say anything. The crowd had stepped back, clearing room for the three main players in the center.

Johanna turned slightly and saw the look the young props carpenter gave her. She wasn't sure if there was sympathy or pity in his eyes, but she wanted neither. Johanna ignored Harold and put her hand out to the stranger. "Thank you, Mr. —?"

"Reed." The grin was wide, guileless and strictly for her. "Tommy Reed. Just Tommy."

Johanna was looking at Harry, yet sensed Tommy's long, appraising, approving look as it touched all parts of her. For a moment, just for a moment, she forgot that Harold was there, or rather, that he was already walking off, leaving her behind. Perhaps that was why she appreciated Tommy's look so much. It had been a long time since she had felt so feminine, so much like a woman. Harold made her feel like a beggar, old, haggard, and unappealing.

The look in Tommy's eyes was not one reserved for a

haggard old woman. It was clearly sexual, even if he had no idea that it was there, and she suspected that he might. She nestled the kernel of pleasure it created to her breast and smiled at him again.

"Thank you, 'just Tommy.'"

"My pleasure, luv." He nodded his head and returned to work. The others in the crowd gradually melted away and the din of work resumed.

She stood still a moment. She had come to talk to Harry and should be following him. Yet she watched the tall, muscular young man as he picked up the tool box he had dropped when he had hurled himself against her and pressed her to the wall. The muscles of his shoulders rippled beneath the washed out blue tee-shirt.

Abruptly, she turned and walked after Harold, taking much more care as she picked her way across the heavily littered stage. Harold looked unapproachable, angry, not like a man whose wife had just been saved from injury but a man who was annoyed at the very reminder that he *had* a wife.

Johanna wet her lips. "Harry?"

"I'll talk to you later, Michelle," he said to the script girl.

The redhead literally glided away. Johanna didn't miss the guilty look Michelle had on her face.

"Are you through ogling the hired help?" Harold demanded coldly, his voice low, but not low enough. He jerked his thumb in Tommy's direction.

She opened her mouth to defend herself, but knew it would be useless. Better to ignore his remark. Otherwise they would be involved in another circuitous argument that had no resolution, no end. Besides, she knew that he was only trying to divert her attention, accusing her of what he was guilty of himself.

"I didn't come all the way out here to argue with you, Harold."

He glared in Tommy's direction. "No, it looked like you came here to take your pick of the litter."

The words hurt, even after all this time, even though he hadn't touched her in so many long, lonely months. How could he have once loved her and think that of her now?

"He just saved me from getting hurt, that's all. Can't you be grateful for that?"

His eyes cut her to ribbons. "I think you're grateful enough for both of us."

He began to walk away. The two leads were rehearsing a scene and he wanted to listen in. He had no doubts that it wouldn't go right without him.

Momentarily, she thought of giving it all up. But she hadn't come all this way, hadn't flown over the ocean to begin with, to run off now with her tail between her legs. She put her hand on his arm, taking a firm hold. "Harry, I want to talk to you."

He stood still, enduring her hold, enduring her. "Can't it wait until I get back to the hotel?"

She hated that tone he used. "It *was* waiting until you got back to the hotel. Except you never *got* back to the hotel last night."

"So you brought your fight here." He threw up his hands, ever on the defensive. "That's all I need, for you to act the part of the irate wife."

Johanna gritted her teeth together, keeping her voice down. She hated scenes, hated people looking at them so knowingly.

"No one has more cause than I do."

Damn, this wasn't going the way she wanted it to.

Johanna saw hatred in Harry's face. He gestured toward the back where Tommy was working. "So go throw yourself into young Galahad's arms and get your revenge. I don't doubt you've been doing that with enough other men behind my back."

She wanted to strike him and curled her fingers into her

hands. "There have been no men behind your back or anywhere else. That's what I came to tell you, damn you. I love you." He was doing it to her again, making her lose control, stoking her anger when all she wanted to do was to forge a truce.

The condescending look on his face told her that he didn't believe her. "A wife who's been faithful doesn't have to go reassuring her husband that she hasn't done anything." He was twisting things around. He always was good with words.

The words poured out before she could stop them. "She does if her husband's a paranoid coke snorting son of a bitch."

He turned his back on her, rigid, cold. "I've got work to do."

Again she took hold of him, but this time, he shook her hand from his arm. "This is more important, Harry. This is about us."

He whirled around, fire in his eyes. She didn't know him. "There's nothing more important than the success of this film, do you hear me? Nothing!"

Johanna closed her eyes and let the air out of her lungs slowly as she slid down into a seat. If she didn't sit, she'd fall. It was as if she had just lost the power to move.

"I guess that just about says it all." Her voice was distant, lost. Slowly, she began to accept defeat.

He looked at her in silence for a moment, still wondering why she was bothering him this way. A nuisance. She had become nothing more than a nuisance to him.

"No, no it doesn't. There'll be a lot more said once I get back to the hotel. Do what you want on your own time, but don't come wiggling your hips, flirting with my crew and embarrassing me in public."

"Embarrassing you?" Her head snapped up. She gripped the arms of the seat and rose to her feet. "Embarrassing you? What about me? What about all the times you've embarrassed me in public, flaunting those—those tramps, so that everyone knew?"

"Shut up, you're hysterical." He looked around, but everyone seemed to suddenly become busy with something else.

"Damn right I'm hysterical. And you made me that way." Suddenly, it came home to her, the waste, the terrible, terrible waste this all was. One more time. Maybe, just maybe—

"Harry." She buried her pride and forced her voice to stay calm. "Please, can't we just forget about everything and start over?"

He was already watching the rehearsal and making mental notes he hoped he could remember when the time came. Nothing seemed to stay put in his mind anymore. "What do you mean, over?"

"I mean, forget about the arguments, forget about—" She didn't want to go into details. Details made it harder to forget. And she wanted to forget, desperately, wanted to forget everything that had happened these last ten years. "—about everything. I love you, Harry."

Funny how forced the words sounded to her ear as she said them. She still loved him. Didn't she? Or was she only waltzing with shadows of what had once been, afraid to admit that the music was over, afraid to sit down?

The words sounded a little forced from lack of usage, she decided. There was a time she said it every day. As did he.

"We need to rebuild what we had."

He had wasted enough time with her. He began to walk away, sparing her words only as he moved. "There's nothing wrong between us."

She stared at him, wondering if he was so far gone into his own world that he actually believed what he was saying. "How can you say that?"

"Very easily. If there's something wrong, then you've created it. You weren't supportive enough of me to—"

The dam broke. All the thing she had endured, all the

hurts, humiliations she had put up with, she had done because she felt that somehow, someday, he would stop and realize all that she had gone through. For him to say that she wasn't supportive told her that everything she believed to be true was not. Someday wasn't coming. He remembered nothing, was grateful for nothing, would never feel any contrition for his hurtful words and horrible behavior.

"Not supportive of you? I sublimated my entire life for you!" she cried.

He reached over and ran his fingers over the five carat diamond bracelet on her wrist. "Must have been very hard on you."

She stared down at the bracelet as if it was something she had never seen before, something ugly. And, in a way, it was. It marked the schism between them. He had given that to her at the premiere of his first film. His biggest success.

"These were trinkets you gave me, not things I asked for." She shook the bracelet in his face angrily. "The only thing I ever asked for was you."

"But you didn't say no when the 'trinkets' came." His tone was scornful.

"You'll never understand, will you?"

"The only thing I understand is that you're getting in my way here, Johanna. I have a picture that is already falling behind schedule and those damned bastards back in Hollywood are going to have me cut up and served as an appetizer at their next gathering if I don't deliver a blockbuster."

She picked up her purse. There was no point in staying here and arguing with him. There was no talking to him. Maybe he was right. Maybe it was her fault somehow. Maybe he would be more receptive once he came home, came back from England, had this picture wrapped. There was nothing else she could hope for.

"I'll see you at the hotel," she said quietly. "By the way, happy anniversary."

"What?"

"Never mind."

He didn't even bother to watch her walk away. He was relieved that she was going. She was crowding him, all the time crowding him, wanting pieces, just as everyone else did. And he had none to spare. He needed to concentrate on getting this picture done. And he had such trouble concentrating these days.

He began to look around the set for Garrison. Garrison had promised him that he would score this morning and if he didn't have a hit soon, he knew he couldn't hold himself together much longer.

Chapter Six

The noise on the set elevated to a roar, swirling all around her as she walked away from Harry. Johanna wanted to cry, needed to cry, but no tears came to her eyes. She was utterly empty inside. There were no tears left for Harold and none for herself. Her marriage, if that was what it could be called, was beginning to make her feel physically ill as well as emotionally drained.

She had to do something else in order to take her mind off this horrible situation. Her marriage had to be denigrated to an insignificant thing if she was going to preserve herself.

She'd go to the Tate Gallery with Jocelyn. Yes, they'd make a day of it. Today. Johanna knew she was grasping at straws, but she had nothing else and maybe one of those straws would lead her out of this valley of despair.

Lifting her chin, she felt a little better. She passed Tommy on her way to the exit and he smiled at her. There was no reason in the world why the smile of an almost perfect stranger should buoy her up and make her feel human again, but it certainly did. After being stripped down and mentally beaten by Harold, it felt good to have someone else look at her as a desirable woman. There was no mistaking the look in the prop carpenter's eyes. She blessed him for it.

"Hey!" someone yelled behind her. "Did you hear? Those goddamn terrorists did it again! They blew up another plane."

She had no idea why she knew, but she did. Instantly. Something went cold inside of her. Slowly, she turned around and looked at a square-jawed, tall man shouting the news to a friend of his up in the rafters.

"What flight was it?" The words left her lips in slow motion.

The man looked at her curiously. "Flight 59 out of London."

For a moment she stood frozen, wooden, and then the rapid beating of her heart overwhelmed everything and blacked it out. She felt hot. The world grew progressively smaller and then disappeared altogether.

When she came to, she was laying on a hard leather couch in a crammed office. Something cold and wet was on her forehead. She looked up into Harold's very annoyed face.

"Are you pregnant?" he snapped out.

When she had been carrying Jocelyn, there had been a period of time, early in the pregnancy, when she had fainted a lot. Other than that, she had always been sinfully healthy. She didn't feel very healthy right now. She felt ill, desperately ill.

"Paul," she managed to get out.

"I knew it." Harry began to pace, raging at the betrayal, raging not because it was his wife, but because it was his friend who had been the one to do it, to misuse his trust. "I knew that rutting bastard was just hanging around to sniff at your skirts."

She shut her eyes tight as the tears she had been unable

to shed earlier came, sliding through her lids, slipping down her cheeks to her temples. She couldn't manage the strength to brush them aside.

"No." The single word was forced out through a throat that tears had managed to tightened. "Paul was—he was on that flight."

Harold blew out an impatient breath. "What flight, for Chrissakes? I've got a picture to film."

Shakily, she drew in air, forcing herself to pull her thoughts together. Everything in her mind felt like it was tangled with everything else. She couldn't make sense of anything.

"The one that was just blown up. Someone, someone on the set just came shouting that the terrorists blew up flight—Oh God, poor Denise." She covered her mouth with her hands to keep a sob back. "Poor Paul."

She felt bereft, as if she had been irrevocably stripped of her last means of defense. Paul was the closest thing she had to a best friend and she knew that if she needed a word of support, of encouragement, or just a shoulder to lean on, he would be there. There was no need to say anything to him. He understood. The two of them had been there in the beginning with Harry and they shared that between them.

And now he was dead.

And so was she. It kept coming back to that. Always to that.

She looked up at Harry. He looked stricken, lost. Forgetting her own pain, she reached out and squeezed his hand. And for just a moment, Harry held on to her. He sank down on the couch as if his legs couldn't support him any longer.

"What do you mean Paul was on that flight? He's right here."

Slowly she shook her head. "No, Paul left England this morning."

"But he can't leave. He's the writer. This is his story.

He always hangs around the set when we're filming his stories."

She wished it was true. She wished that when she turned around, she could see Paul, tall, angular Paul, with his hands in his pockets, shaking the shaggy mane of blond hair and biding his time until he could form the right words with which to ease Harry along in the right direction. But she knew she never would again.

"You fired him."

Harry rose, agitated, lost. "I didn't fire him," he shouted, a child denying an accusation for an action he couldn't remember. He ripped both hands through his hair, tugging so hard he pulled several strands out, then dragged his hands over his face.

In defeat, he let them drop. They hung at his sides, useless. There was nothing to hold onto anymore. Paul had been his rock, his steadying force. They had fought, he had railed, but there was always Paul to make things safe. Paul was home base.

"And even if I did, I was always firing him."

"This time, it stuck."

He dropped down beside her on the couch again. The voice was small, hopeful in the midst of hopelessness. "Maybe he missed the flight."

She shook her head slowly. "No, he was on it. I feel it."

Johanna reached out for his shoulder to support herself as she tried to rise, but Harry had shifted away from her, away in his frustrated confusion. She sighed and let her hand fall. Bracing herself, she swung her legs off the couch and tested to see if they had regained their strength. Her legs felt shaky, but this was no time to think of herself. She had to call the airline, find out if there were any survivors. She already knew that there weren't, but a small part of her always remained infinitely hopeful. Her sisters had always teased her about her optimism and called her Pollyanna.

Well, Polly had just about reached the end of her road, she thought sadly.

Smoothing back her hair, she looked down at her husband. He was sitting there, looking like a broken man. She hardly knew him. She lived on memories the last few years but what she saw before her over and over was transforming those memories into nothing more than self-deluding fantasies, something that had never been, had never happened.

"I'm going to call Denise as soon as I hear all the details. She's—she's going to want to have someone to talk to."

Harry nodded, not hearing what Johanna said, only the drone of her voice.

Johanna eased herself out of the room. She turned as she closed the door and saw Harry huddled on the couch. She felt sorry for him, but had no words to offer. The loss she felt choked them off.

She had reached her car when someone called out her name. She turned and saw the props carpenter who had saved her life striding toward her. He moved with the sure, light stride of someone who was master of the world in which he lived. She envied him that, envied him the illusion. There were no masters. She thought of Paul. There were only victims in the end.

"Are you all right, Mrs. Whitney?" Tommy asked when he was beside her.

She forced a smile to her lips. "Yes, you saw to that."

"No, I meant that I saw that you had fainted. Was it just the shock of almost getting beamed?" When she didn't answer right away, he looked at her car. "Do you need someone to drive you home?"

She looked back at the sound stage door. "Don't you have work to do?" She didn't want to talk about Paul with anyone. His death was too personal, too hurtful. God, she hadn't felt this awful since her mother had died.

"Always, but I'm ahead of myself at the moment. If you don't mind me saying so, you're a bit pale looking at the moment."

She touched her cheek. "Pale's my natural color," she said, trying to maintain the painful smile. How could she smile, talk, when Paul was dead? "There are usually seven little men following me wherever I go."

"Then you're all right?"

No, I'm far from that. I've just lost my best friend and now I have to call and tell his wife that he won't be coming back to her.

"Yes, I'm all right. Thank you for being so kind, Tommy."

"No hardship when the lady's one the likes of you."

Was he flirting with her? Or was he too open to realize that he was doing it? She didn't know. She only knew that she liked him instantly, liked his kind, open manner. She always responded well to kindness. It gave her hope for the world, for herself.

She even managed to wave goodbye after he helped her into the car and closed the door for her.

Chapter Seven

"Telephone, Mrs. Whitney," Megan said in a sing-song voice as she held the telephone receiver aloft and waved it from side to side.

She was becoming more irritating with each passing day. Megan was dressed in a vivid purple spandex skirt and white tee-shirt top. The neckline dipped low, bringing attention to her breasts. The shirt was one size too small and Megan wore no bra. Johanna frowned. Megan was Jocelyn's idol. She wished Megan would keep that in mind. As it stood, Johanna definitely didn't want Jocelyn emulating the young woman.

Johanna pushed the newspaper she was paging through aside on the sofa, registering annoyance. Megan constantly addressed her in that irritating voice. She had already brought it to Megan's attention several times to no avail. The *au pair* girl had just stared at her and nodded and gone on doing it. Johanna felt that this was Megan's childish way of letting her know that she held one over her.

Well, Johanna thought, if going to bed with my husband makes you feel superior to me, you have a low threshold of superiority.

She couldn't wait until this "holiday" was over and Megan was a thing of the past.

"Who is it, Megan?"

"It's that boutique where you bought your gown." Her voice barely hid her insolence. "They say they need to know when you're coming in for another fitting. Otherwise the gown won't to be ready by Friday."

The party. Johanna had totally forgotten about the party she and Harry were supposed to attend. Of course they would go. Harry wouldn't allow a small thing like the death of his closest friend and associate to interfere with business.

No, he hurt, she relented. She had seen that look in his eyes. Somewhere, beneath that veneer of false bravado, he did hurt over the loss of Paul. But it wouldn't stop him from attending Alicia's party. Business, however dirty, was business.

"Tell them I'll wear it as is." The fit had been good enough, she remembered. Besides, what did it matter, anyway? It was all meaningless. "It doesn't have to look as if I was poured into it."

She saw Megan's long, lazy appraisal as the young woman's hazel eyes slid over her from head to foot. For a split second, Johanna was tempted to look away, then something refused to let her. She returned the girl's look and it was Megan who finally dropped her gaze, her lower lip curling.

"She said never mind," Megan told the woman on the other end. "Send it over as is. Yes, I see." Megan hung up. "They're not happy about this, Mrs. Whitney."

"That makes two of us," Johanna answered. She glanced at her wrist watch, as she had done a half a dozen times in as many minutes. There was no more putting it off. If she did, she would be late.

Johanna squared her shoulders. It was time to leave. A

wave of panic hit her stomach and she unconsciously pressed her hand there.

"Sure you won't change your mind about coming with me, Jocey?"

She looked toward her daughter. Jocelyn was sitting on the floor, paging through a fashion magazine Megan had gotten for her. In the background, the television played on. No one was bothering to watch it.

Jocelyn gave her mother an impatient look. The question had been put to her before. "No, Megan and I are going out." She giggled behind her hand before she managed to compose herself.

She was behaving very oddly lately, Johanna thought. Maybe it was all a phase. Maybe it was because they had taken her away from her friends and forced her to spend her summer in a foreign country with only eight channels, Johanna thought.

She might have read more into it, had she not felt ashamed for wanting to hide behind her daughter, to use her as a shield of sorts in this awful ordeal she was going to have to face.

"All right. I don't know how long I'll be gone," she said as she crossed to the door. She looked back, but Megan and her daughter were oblivious to what she was saying. She gave up. "Goodbye." There was no response. No one seemed to have even heard her. Johanna raised her voice. "Goodbye."

"Huh? Oh, yes, goodbye," Jocelyn answered, then turned her attention toward Megan and more important matters.

Hero worship, Johanna thought as she rode down the elevator. Jocelyn had a bad case of hero worship. It was easy to see why. Megan was tall and pretty and seemed to have everything. Certainly clothes and a sharp, flashing wit. But the shallow streak that Johanna detected within Megan made her wish that she hadn't chosen her to come along with them. There hadn't been enough time to make a proper choice. The woman they had used and relied on all these years had quit, only two days before the trip to London. Johanna had frantically accepted the first civilized person who had arrived from the agency with no communicable diseases.

Just goes to show you, you can't go by first impressions. Well, it would pass. They'd be going home soon. In the fall school would start and Megan would be gone. They had a housekeeper at home and that was sufficient.

The tall, burly doorman snapped to life when he saw her walk through the revolving door and approach him. His name was Masterson and Johanna had made his acquaintance the first day they had arrived. He unconsciously approved of the white two-piece suit she wore. The single strand of pearls at her throat was just the right accent. A lady, through and through. There were so few of them these days.

"Good afternoon, Mrs. Whitney. It looks like a very pleasant day for you. Shall I have someone bring your car around?"

She smiled and shook her head. "No, I think I'd rather have a cab this afternoon. I really don't know my way around London that well and driving on the wrong side of the street always confuses me."

"The wrong side, ma'am?" Masterson's tone was amused as he beckoned for a cab to break free of its formation and pull over to the curb.

Johanna smiled up at the man. "I guess you don't consider it the wrong side."

"No, madam, we don't." He held the door open for her and tried not to admire her legs too much as she slid into the cab.

Johanna leaned forward. She glanced at the rearview mirror. The cab driver had small, squinty eyes, set in a pockmarked, lined face that had seen more than its share of the rough side of life. It sent a slight chill down her spine. She was just being unduly jumpy of late, she thought.

"Heathrow airport, please. Pan Am terminal."

The wiry cab driver nodded as he pulled the handle of the meter down. "Pan Am terminal it is, mum."

Johanna tried to settle back in the seat but found that she was too tense. Maybe she should have driven, she thought. That way, on the way back, she would have had something to occupy herself with, to fill in the silences. A reason to lapse into silence herself. God, what was she going to *say* to Denise? What words were possible in this kind of a situation?

"I had a friend on the plane those terrorists bombed," Johanna said, suddenly wanting to talk, to talk to a stranger because it didn't hurt so much to tell a stranger things. "And I would have been on it, too."

She said the last sentence softly, half to herself in wonder, abruptly remembering Paul's urgings to leave London and fly home with him. If Paul had convinced her, she and Jocelyn would have been on that flight with him. And now it would be Harry collecting bits and pieces of them. Would he have wept? Would he have even cared? She thought of telling him, and then rejected the idea. The plain truth was that Harry didn't care, not in his present state. It was useless to try and force him to be something other than what he was now. Nothing she had done thus far had accomplished anything to make him change.

She saw the cab driver's eyes looking at her sympathetically in the rearview mirror.

"Oh, it's sorry I am to hear that, mum."

"That's all right. I'm going to meet his widow now."

"Then the meter'll be off," Gallegher said, gently but firmly.

Johanna rested her head against the back of the seat and closed her eyes as the cab wove its way through midday traffic.

Chapter Eight

"I won't take no for an answer, Johanna. You need to get out."

Johanna held the telephone receiver in her hand as she paced about her bedroom. She was alone in the large suite. She had planned to spend the afternoon with her daughter only to find that the girl had gone, leaving a note in her wake. Not even so much as a verbal communication.

She felt completely useless. The meeting with Denise at Heathrow Airport had been dreadful. At least it accomplished Denise's need to confirm that Paul's body was missing without hope. But on a face-to-face basis it was agonizing. She loved Denise and felt for her, but it was a relief for Johanna finally to return to the apartment. But Harry was back on the set, and now she was left alone in the apartment with no one to talk to and only her own thoughts to contend with. And her thoughts were all too bleak.

Still, she felt a reticence about going out to lunch with

Arlene. It wasn't that she didn't like the older woman. She did. And, in the right mood, Johanna found her company amusing. Arlene, ten years her senior, knew everything about everyone—Harry most definitely included. Her privileged information came by way of her marriage to Sam Baker and through the entertainment world connections she nurtured almost zealously. Bawdy, loquacious, she was born to gossip. Not to malign, but to share in whatever there was to share about other people's lives.

And for what it was worth, she had, without warning, appointed herself Johanna's guardian angel.

"You can't stay locked up in that hotel room forever, sweetie." For a moment, only for a moment, the woman's voice softened. "I know how you must feel about the accident."

"But—"

"No buts. At least," Arlene laughed lustily, "none worth a second glance these days. Now, I'll be by in half an hour. Sam's busy with work Harry dumped on him today, so I'm totally fancy free and I intend to make you my fancy. Get dressed to the teeth, sweetie. I'm taking you out to lunch."

She didn't want to go, didn't want to see anyone. "Arlene—"

"Fine, I take that as a yes. See you." The line went dead.

Johanna hung up. A small smile curved her lips. Arlene was right, she had to get out, to do something, however meaningless, before she became dubbed the madwoman of the Hyatt Carlton Towers Hotel. Johanna glanced down at the plush carpet beneath her slippered feet. She had roamed her bedroom so much these last couple of days that she was surprised there weren't worn paths in the rug.

With a sigh, half in resignation, half in anticipation, Johanna turned toward her closet.

True to her promise, Arlene was at her suite within half an hour. It never ceased to amaze Johanna that Arlene was always punctual. Women of her acquaintance were notorious about disregarding time. To be late was to be fashionable. Arlene was always afraid she'd miss something crucial if she wasn't there on time.

Arlene breezed into the hotel suite, dressed in pearls, a fur stole haphazardly thrown about her shoulders and a designer dress at least one size too small for her ample frame. Arlene was always just about to go a diet. Tomorrow. Today there was always too much good food to be sampled.

The petite woman made Johanna turn around as she studied her critically.

"Well, you look none the worse for this beastly weather." She stopped to consider her words. " 'Beastly.' My God, I'm beginning to talk like them. Any day now, I'll be asking for tea instead of a coffee and tonic." She leaned over and pressed her hand to Johanna's arm, as if imparting an important confidence. "When that happens, I want your word that you'll shoot me."

Johanna couldn't help smiling. "If it'll make you happy."

"What'll make me happy," Arlene answered, easily linking her arm with Johanna's—it didn't seem to trouble her that Johanna, slender, with a model's bone structure, made her look like a comic foil—"is if that leading man they've picked for this little so-called 'epic' of Harry's would give me a tumble and take me off for a weekend in the Cotwolds."

"Where?"

"Ready?"

Without waiting for an answer, Arlene pressed Johanna's purse into her hands. Johanna tucked it under her arm and nodded.

"The Cotwolds, sweetie. The country made by God when He was practicing for the rolling hills of Ireland." She grinned wickedly, nudging Johanna out the door and to the elevator.

Johanna knew that the only time Arlene let her native chauvinism come to the fore was when she felt she was confronted with British snobbery. Arlene Baker had been born Annie Mahoney of some county in Ireland that Johanna never could remember. Her flaming red hair had been real once. Now it needed a helping hand from a well-known bottle of hair rinse. But nothing could dilute the fire in the woman's eye or in her soul.

"You find Dale Kincaid attractive?" Johanna asked as they walked into the elevator. She thought that he was far too pretty to be labeled as masculine.

"Attractive?" Arlene rolled her eyes and heaved a big sigh, her hand to her ample bosom. "He makes me forget to breathe. Where are your eyes, girl?" She jabbed at the first floor button.

Johanna shrugged, her shoulders moving restlessly. "I guess I don't notice things like that."

Arlene pressed her fingers to Johanna's wrist. "There's a pulse there, so you must be alive."

"Am I?" Johanna couldn't resist asking, a smile playing on her lips.

The doors yawned open, exposing the plush furnishings of the opulent lobby. Arlene, as always, led the way out. "Oh, now we come to the heart of it. Tell Aunt Arlene all about it, sweetie," she coaxed.

"Just baiting you," Johanna dismissed her momentary slip coolly.

Arlene was far from convinced, but she let the matter drop.

Until cocktails.

Seated at a prominent table in the Cafe Royal, breathing in the ambience where once Oscar Wilde had roamed freely, Arlene subtly urged a cocktail on Johanna. And then another. She had herself a well-earned reputation for being able to hold her liquor with the best of them, but Arlene knew that Johanna needed little more than white wine before her edge slipped away. She wanted the younger woman to relax. She looked far too tense for her own good, although considering what Johanna had to put up with, Arlene could hardly blame her for being tense.

"Now then," Arlene began, leaning over the small, white

linen-draped round table and covering Johanna's small hand with her own, "spill it. What's really been bothering you, Johanna?"

She knew without hearing the words, but felt that Johanna needed to verbalize the matter. Getting things off your chest always helped, Arlene thought.

Johanna played with the stem of her glass. The overhead light was caught in the fluted crystal, shattering into a rainbow of colors. There were no rainbows anymore, she thought sadly. Not for her.

"It'd take less time to tell you what wasn't."

"But that would be boring."

Arlene smiled up at the young, slim-hipped waiter who came to serve them their main course of sinfully delicious french cuisine. Johanna thought the woman would devour the young man with her eyes.

"Another round, please," Arlene gestured to the two glasses. She gazed after the waiter until he disappeared, then turned back to look at Johanna. "Do I embarrass you, Johanna?"

Johanna watched the amber liquid coat the sides of the glass as she moved it. "No."

Arlene laughed. "You don't lie well after one whisky sour."

Johanna looked up at her and shrugged, grinning. "Sorry."

"I like to look. They won't let me touch." Arlene sighed deeply. "Besides, I probably wouldn't know what to do with it if they did." She frowned down at her broiled halibut. "It's been a long, long time since Sam found his way into my bed for anything more than a good night's sleep." The impish smile was gone and her blue eyes were serious as she regarded Johanna. "The same, I take it is true with you."

"I—"

The waiter appeared with their drinks and Johanna fell silent.

"Here." Arlene pressed the new glass on her. "Take a good sip of this and then tell me."

Johanna started to protest and realized that she really didn't want to. Why not? Just this once, why not loosen up a little and admit what was wrong? She probably wouldn't say anything that Arlene and the immediate world didn't already know. She tossed back the drink and closed her eyes as she felt it slip, warm and comforting, to her belly.

She opened her eyes to see Arlene looking at her, waiting. "I think Harry's made love to every woman in a ten mile radius in the last nine months but me."

Poor kid. "By last tally, other than skipping me, you're probably right."

Even in her present semi-euphoric state, shame began to lick at her. "Does everyone know?"

Arlene shrugged as she drained the last of her glass and looked wistfully at it. "I don't know. The prime minister might still be in the dark, but as for everyone else, they know." She raised her eyes to Johanna's, wondering how a louse like Harry had won a woman of breeding like her. "He thinks with his pants first."

"When he bothers to think at all." It surprised Johanna that she could sound so vehement about Harry's faults in someone else's presence. Usually, she played the loyal, forgiving wife, suffering in silence. Except to Paul, she had hardly ever voiced her unhappiness. It appeared now that she didn't have to.

Johanna took another long swallow. The drink was strong and soothing. She felt warm and oddly happy. The details of the plush surroundings and lavishly painted ceilings were now lost on her. They all kind of blurred together. She knew the mild, contented feeling she was experiencing was temporary, but it was here now, and that was all that mattered.

"You know, Arlene," Johanna confided, "the Amazons really had the right idea about men."

"How's that?"

"You fooled around with them, and then you killed them. No ties, no pain."

Arlene nodded, the mound of fluffy red curls bouncing around her head like springs that had suddenly been compressed and then released.

"Truer words were never spoken. If I had left Sam on a high point instead of wallowing in this valley of neglect, I might be thirty pounds lighter." She helped herself to a slice of French bread and buttered it generously as she continued to philosophize. "Food isn't as good as sex, but at least it stays with you a while." She patted her hip and laughed lustily. "A long while. C'mon, Johanna," she lifted the younger woman's chin with her finger tip, "no man is worth brooding over. With the lights out, they're all the same."

"I wouldn't know."

Arlene drew her carefully penciled eyebrows together. "You mean you never—?"

Johanna shook her head. It wasn't chic to admit it, but Johanna had never cared to be chic. "Never."

Arlene stared at her as if she was trying to comprehend this information. Food and gossip were temporarily forgotten. "Really?"

"Really."

"Oh my God, I could be dining with the last of a dying breed. You're practically extinct, sweetie. A virgin wife." She giggled, then saw that Johanna was hurt. Arlene hurried her next words. "That's rather refreshing, actually, considering the jaded world we find ourselves living in." She leaned closer, scrutinizing Johanna's face. She knew of several men in their immediate sphere who would have wanted this woman in their beds, whatever the price. "Never even once?"

Johanna raised her head. "No."

"My dear, how do you stand it?"

"I don't need 'it.'" She tried to curb her annoyance. She

knew Arlene meant no harm. "I need Harry. I need the way he was. I want love, Arlene, not sex."

"Well—" Arlene drew out the word as she considered Johanna's statement. "When you can't get what you want, you take what you can." She caught their waiter's eye and lifted her empty glass aloft. The young man nodded and retreated.

Johanna suddenly felt sober as she shook her head. At least her mind was clear. The rest of her body wasn't in focus yet. "Sorry, that would be selling out, settling for it. And I don't do that kind of thing."

"No, apparently not. A pity. When you want your sheets warmed, let me know. I know of at least three candidates who would offer you a good size chunk of the moon to be able to nibble on your, um, ear," Arlene amended when she took stock of who she was talking to. "And other parts thereof," she couldn't resist adding.

Johanna had the last of her drink, then set the glass down. "You take them."

"Oh, I would if I could, Johanna, I most certainly would if I could, but with me, they only want the ear, to talk, to complain and to get sympathy. I'd switch with you in a minute."

She paused to consider her last statement. She thought of Harry in place of Sam. Sam might not be loving, but he wasn't unkind. And there was something brutal about Harry. "Well, maybe not."

Johanna laughed sadly as she played with her salad. "I didn't think so."

Chapter Nine

There had been a time when she looked forward to attending parties like this one, Johanna thought. Then it had been an experience akin to stepping into Wonderland. She had been fascinated by the glitter, the wealth, the power that churned within these gatherings of the finely dressed chosen few. The beautiful people. But she had found all too soon that they weren't so beautiful after all, not beneath their carefully made-up faces and their expensive designer clothes. They were greedy, grasping and cruel. Not all of them, but enough.

Perhaps it was like this everywhere, although she couldn't remember feeling this way in the little town where she had grown up. Perhaps, she mused, that was the problem. She had been too cocooned, too sheltered, too untrained to be able to handle the sort of life she was living now.

Maybe these types of goings-on did exist elsewhere, but they seemed more pronounced when they involved Hollywood persona because the people were all larger than life, or so their publicists would have wanted the rest of the world to believe.

Johanna glanced at her husband as they entered, together for once. She smiled but felt like a hypocrite. Everyone there, she felt, knew that their union was a sham.

Harry still cut a resplendent figure in his tuxedo. Ten pounds lighter than his sparse frame should actually be carrying and with a haunted look to his eyes, he was still a very good-looking man. And charm, when he wanted it, could ooze through his very fingertips. There was a magnetism in his eyes, when they weren't glazed over, she thought cynically, that held his audience, male or female, right where he wanted them.

She supposed it was the memory of that, and nights of tenderness and pleasure, that kept her where she was, hoping, praying. Johanna alternated between despair and optimism when she thought of the future. Mostly, she thought, despair.

Johanna saw people staring at them as they entered the vast hotel ballroom. Harry knew how to make an entrance, she thought, even when he walked silently into a room. Heads would turn, conversations would pause. Once that had been because he was the bright young director, the lightning-witted genius who could make a turnip cry or laugh at will, let alone a performer. Everyone wanted him to direct their picture, everyone wanted to be seen with him.

Now, Johanna knew, the conversations stopped because fresh speculation would begin. Was he straight tonight? Would he make a fool of himself? How long before he'd fall on his face, or find a woman to seduce? And how long would it be before he destroyed himself completely? She had no doubts that bets were made as to the length of time it would take.

Part of her heart ached for Harry, her Harry, the old Harry. And part of her felt that he was getting no less than he deserved. She prayed that perhaps the scorn of his peers and sub-peers, as he had begun to call them, would finally shake him up like nothing else could.

Alicia Martin, her hair done up in a winged hairdo that seemed to wantonly defy gravity, her bosom nearly exposed in its entirety in a sapphire blue gown that bore a designer's name and price, glided toward them like a shark cutting through the water to get to its prey. In her cool, regal manner she simultaneously nodded at Johanna and dismissed her. Her attention, for whatever reason, was entirely on Harry. She offered him both cheeks to be kissed.

As he kissed her, she took hold of both of his hands in hers. "Harold, darling, we were beginning to think that perhaps you weren't going to come."

His gaze lingered over her exposed breasts, then he cast a belittling glance at Johanna.

Johanna wondered if he had managed to do a line or two of powder before they came, even though he had promised her, contemptuously enough, that he wouldn't.

"Johanna," Harry informed Alicia, "was having second thoughts about coming tonight."

"Second thoughts?" The scarlet nails fanned out along the tanned expanse of breast.

Harry was talking about her and staring at Alicia. Johanna felt her temper rising.

"Second thoughts?" Alicia repeated, pouting prettily. "Should I be offended?"

Johanna knew Alicia didn't give a damn what she thought about the woman or her party. She wasn't in the business of caring what wives thought. Only studio hierarchy mattered and it seemed that Alicia hadn't decided whether or not Harry was down for the count.

She'd be damned if she'd stand there like a mute. "It's just that Paul—" Johanna began.

"Yes, yes, terrible tragedy, wasn't it?" The dead did not matter. They didn't make policy or money. Alicia linked her arm through Harry's and was already leading him away. "But life is for the living, isn't it?" she laughed wickedly into Harry's face as she slowly rubbed her bosom against his arm.

"—has only been dead a couple of days and I thought it wasn't appropriate to attend a party just yet," Johanna finished, determined to get the words out. For whatever good it did, she thought ruefully. She hated Alicia Martin, hated this party and hated herself for not saying no to Harry. He certainly wouldn't have missed her if she hadn't attended.

Maybe that was why she had decided to come after all.

"Talking to yourself, sweetie?" Arlene came up behind her. She was dressed in a black sequined floor length gown that made her bear a striking resemblance to a sparkling Franklin stove.

Johanna sighed as she turned toward her friend. "I wasn't when I started out. But it seems no one wants to listen."

She cast a damning look in Alicia's direction. The woman was still clinging to Harry and laughing up into his face as if he was saying something very witty. Johanna had no doubts that Harry probably thought it was.

"Not about anything sad, you know that." Arlene looked around the room, apparently absorbing everything. It was her chosen avocation. There was nowhere that she would rather be than in the center of a party. "They all carry their own little Greek tragedies around with them, or so they think. Much more like pathos or last week's soap opera. 'As The Stomach Churns,' how's that?"

Johanna laughed. "I think I've heard that before."

"Well, I said it with more flair," Arlene declared with conviction. "Now, let's go and ogle some great looking men."

But Johanna made no move to join the woman. "Where's Sam?"

Arlene pretended to frown. A second chin puddled beneath her first. "That's not what I meant."

"Seriously—"

"Seriously," Arlene answered solemnly. Then she relented as she gestured vaguely to a far corner of the banquet room toward a cluster of people who were making more than their share of noise. "He's over there somewhere, probably still with that platinum starlet from *Spanky's Holiday* breathing all over him. Dora McDaniels I think. Poor ditzy thing thinks if she gives Sam a little action, he can get her a part in Harry's film. Life never changes, does it?"

Subtly, Arlene guided Johanna toward a table covered with trays of food. In the center of the long table was a sculpture of a nude female.

"Oh, I don't know." Johanna shifted her eyes from the sculpture and scanned the table. Maybe having an *hors d'oeuvre* wouldn't be a bad idea after all. "I think it does."

"Maybe." Arlene helped herself to a plate full of something that looked like pigs in a blanket. Many pigs. "Trouble is," she popped one into her rounded scarlet mouth, "it changes for the worse."

Johanna shook her head. Beneath her wispy bangs, her brow furrowed. "I don't like to think that."

"Neither do I, but it's true." Arlene stopped eating. "Are you planning to stop the party by breaking into a rendition of *Tomorrow* and making us all weep into our handkerchiefs?" The *hors d'oeuvre* hovered an inch away from her mouth.

Johanna guided Arlene's short fingers to complete the action. Lips met food with satisfaction. "You forgot how to weep a long time ago, Arlene."

"Oh, I don't know." She saw someone across the room and sighed. "I weep every time I see a young guy in tight pants walk by and know I can't have him."

Johanna handed her plate to an attendant behind the table and shook her head when he tried to offer her more. "If he's wearing tight pants," she turned back to Arlene, "then he's probably gay."

"Maybe." Arlene popped two heaping crackers into her mouth and they slid down in an amazingly fast time. "But I'm not prejudiced. Besides," she spread another healthy slab of cheddar cheese over a tiny cracker, "it would certainly be fun finding out. Hold it," she called to the waiter who walked by.

"Arlene, you can't," Johanna hissed, not exactly sure what her friend was capable of.

"I'm just getting another glass of champagne, Johanna," Arlene said innocently, her small eyes disappearing into her face as she grinned. "Relax a little."

The tall, handsome waiter smiled broadly at the two women and lowered the tray to accommodate Johanna's reach. She accepted a glass, winding her slender fingers around the stem, almost for support rather than having something to drink.

Arlene watched the waiter as he moved away from them. "Just look at those hips, will you?" Her sigh was audibly loud. "Where do you think they get all those gorgeous men from to act as waiters?"

"The unemployed actors line," Johanna said simply, sipping her champagne.

The drink was bitter and not at all pleasing. Alicia was skimping again. Quantity instead of quality, Johanna thought. But she didn't set it down. She wanted to have something to do with her hands instead of just knotting them together.

She looked around the huge room for Harry. It wasn't hard to find him He was now in the center of a crowd. Probably pontificating. The crowd was made up mostly of young women. Once, he had been in the center of crowds of men, men who listened when he spoke. Now he talked to women who pretended to listen and hoped that they could get something out of it.

"Has he left you unguarded again?"

Johanna turned as she heard the deep baritone voice to her left. "Hello, Marty." She nodded at the assistant producer her husband had convinced to link his name with this movie. She wondered if her smile looked as forced as it felt.

"You know," Marty slipped an arm around her shoulders, "Harry might be a movie genius—"

"The operative word here is 'might,'" Arlene said into her glass, but loud enough for Johanna to hear.

"—but he certainly doesn't seem to know how to appreciate the finer things in life. Now if you were mine, Johanna—" Lazily, he let his fingertips glide along her bare back.

She raised her eyes to his face. The meaning of his words were very clear. It was an open invitation, any time, any place, anywhere. She felt revolted. "But I'm not, am I?"

"My loss."

She patted the smooth, handsome face. "You'll get over it." She saw the star of Harry's ill-fated fiasco coming their way, a woman with ivory skin, flowing blond hair—her own—and a figure that was only out done by her insatiable appetite for good looking men. "In about five minutes, I'll wager."

Marty looked at her quizzically as she took a step backward, safely away from his arm. Then he saw Tracy and his smile broadened. "Business," he murmured, taking his leave.

"Of the most important kind," Arlene laughed bawdily, drawing glances their way. "You know, sweetie, there's something you could learn from Tracy."

"What?" Johanna watched the couple disappear in the crowd. "How to carry my own penicillin in my purse?"

Arlene wagged a stubby finger at her. "Tacky, tacky, sweetie."

Johanna grinned. "But true."

"No argument. What I was referring to is that Tracy has fun."

"Fun, to paraphrase, my dear Arlene, is in the eyes of the beholder. Having some handsome, sweaty guy strip me of my clothes and—"

"Stop, you're getting me all excited." Arlene fanned herself with her hand as she rolled her eyes up to the ceiling.

Johanna moved away from the buffet table, seeking a quieter space away from the swell of the crowd. "Fooling around just for the sake of doing it is not my idea of fun, Arlene."

Arlene looked as if she thought Johanna was in serious need of help. "What is your idea of fun?"

Her slim bare shoulders moved up and down shyly. "All the corny things you laugh at."

"Maybe I laugh at them because I can't have them," Arlene said quietly.

Arlene's answer wasn't what she had expected and it surprised her. Johanna began to comment on the glimmer of truth she had seen exposed, but Arlene shut it away, her face impassive, her eyes roaming.

"C'mon, I'm going to find you a dance partner. You're not going to stand here like a wallflower when I know that there are at least a dozen men just dying to hold you in their arms."

She knew it was useless to argue, but she thought she'd give it a try. "Arlene, why are you so intent on my having a good time?"

"You'll have it for both of us. Call it vicarious living. I'm a stage mother, okay?"

"You're not old enough to be my mother."

"For that, you gain a place in my will. Now c'mon."

Arlene took Johanna by the hand and led her across the floor. Johanna turned to see Harry pocket something someone had just handed him and then walk quickly toward the bathroom. Her heart sank.

"All right, Arlene, you win. Let's find me a dance partner."

Arlene had seen Harry as well. "Atta girl." She grinned triumphantly.

Chapter Ten

Johanna wasn't wrong.

She wished she was, but it was very evident to her that she wasn't. Harry had scored some cocaine and had snorted it in the men's room. Even if she hadn't overheard two men talking about it later that evening, laughing about how pathetically anxious Harry had been to inhale the white powder, she would have seen it in his frenzied behavior. As did everyone else. She felt embarrassed for him, humiliated for herself. Wasn't he ever going to learn? Wasn't he ever going to come to his senses?

She knew in her heart what the answer to that was.

His behavior, his gestures, were more erratic, more frantic than ever. Supposedly, according to articles that she had read recently, including a well-researched piece in a national magazine with an astronomical readership, cocaine was on the outs. It was no longer popular nor glamorous to be taking it, either as part of a group activity or alone. Johanna knew that to be a myth. The fact was, she thought dismally, that the drug was still available, that there were still people hooked on it. It was still being done on a daily basis by a lot of people; they were no longer as blatant about it, that was all. Except for Harry. Harry acted as if he could do anything, as if he thought that no one suspected his "secret."

She saw Alicia Martin smirk and cast her a pitying glance. Harry was a joke to her, an amusing monkey with which to entertain her guests. Johanna was torn between wanting to flee and scratching the woman's eyes out. She did neither. She stood her ground and held her head up high. Harry's emotional shortcomings were not going spill out and soil her or Jocelyn. She wouldn't let them. In that, she knew she was stronger than Harry. She could find the will to rise above this. Harry couldn't. He had no chance to break free. There was always someone to get him a hit and no one to wag a reproving finger at him. Except for her. And that made her an ogre in his eyes.

Johanna watched as he poured himself over a woman she didn't recognize. The woman was more than receptive to his blatant overtures. Johanna watched with eyes filled with anger, for Harry, for the woman, for the industry that had made him this way and for herself for staying. The pitying glances from the other women at the party hurt her pride more than watching Harry act the flirtatious lover in search of a willing partner. She wondered why. Maybe because she was finally numb inside. She wasn't sure.

She missed Paul. He would have kept Harry from making a total spectacle of himself. Paul would have managed to do that for her. But Paul was gone and Harry was out of control. There was absolutely nothing she could do. To try to coax him away from the starlet he was devouring with his eyes would have just made her look like a fool and she couldn't bear that. Besides, it would have accomplished nothing.

As the long evening wore on, Johanna mingled, talked, and predominantly, endured.

Finally, mercifully, the party began to break up and it was time to leave. Harry made rounds and bid everyone good night by name, so far gone that he didn't know people were laughing at him and the comical figure he now cut. He didn't know, but Johanna did. It cut pieces out of her soul. She led him outside, holding onto his arm to keep him from falling over his own feet.

"I'll drive," Harry announced when the valet brought their leased Mercedes.

The control she fought all night to maintain finally broke. "The hell you will. Get in on the passenger side, Harry. I'll drive."

Sweeping passed him, she took the keys from the valet, pressing money into his hand. She had her hand on the door when Harry pulled her around.

Harry clamped his fingers around her wrist. He wanted to make her surrender the keys, to surrender the superior tone he felt she used. His face was close to hers and he almost snarled. "You hate to drive in London. You said so, remember?"

"I hate to die even more."

Her eyes were cold, daring him to challenge her. She was aware that the valet had backed away, unwilling to be a witness to the scene. She could hardly blame him.

Harry opened his mouth to curse her, then abruptly shut it, shrugged and grinned foolishly. "Suit yourself."

He walked to the passenger side of the car on rubbery legs and all but fell in. Johanna breathed a sigh of relief. Her eyes met those of a woman she was vaguely acquainted with who stood waiting with her husband for their car. Johanna raised her chin, smoothed the skirt of her gown and slid in behind the wheel.

The party had been held at a hotel not far from their own. Johanna, her teeth clenched, her knuckles white on the steering wheel, made her way through the sparse traffic on King's Road and turned right on Sloane Street. She nearly made a wrong turn on Beauchamp Place, but recovered in time, mentally chastising herself. Next to her, Harry sat, humming, oblivious to everything. His very presence unnerved her. They couldn't reach the hotel fast enough for Johanna.

Wade Masterson snapped to attention as Johanna pulled up to the curb. With agility that didn't seem possible for a man of his bulk, he was at her side and opening the door for her. Two slightly uneven rows of teeth flashed at her as he smiled down into her face. He had already labeled Johanna as one of the most attractive women he had ever seen the moment she had checked in. The most attractive as well as one of the saddest.

Then Wade Masterson looked at Harry and his genial smile froze a little around the edges.

"Good evening, Mrs. Whitney. Mr. Whitney." He turned ever so slightly toward Johanna, his considerable frame cutting Harry off. The snub did not go unnoticed. "Will you be needing any help tonight?"

"No." Johanna smiled her gratitude even though it pained her to have people see what she had to put up with. "I think we can manage very well." She handed the doorman the spare keys to the car. They were enveloped in a pound note. "If you'll just have someone put it away."

"Of course, ma'am." Masterson touched two fingers to his hat. Mrs. Whitney was a lady, a genuine lady. Too bad her husband was just a miscreant.

She took Harry's arm, not because she wanted to, but because she was afraid that if she didn't, he would fall down at her feet.

Harry was busy trying to focus in on the lobby and keep the colors from bleeding into one another. "I can walk, dammit," he hissed at her.

But she refused to let go of his arm as she made her way slowly, deliberately, to the elevator. She felt eyes following them on their path and told herself that it was only curiosity, nothing more. People were always curious about the rich and famous. "Crawl would be more like it," she said between clenched teeth.

He wanted to pull away and found he couldn't quite manage it. But he always had the strength for an icy retort. "You'd like that, wouldn't you? To see me crawl."

She sighed as she pressed for the elevator. Almost immediately, the doors slid open before her. It was empty, thank God. "Not at all."

"Oh," he stumbled as he entered and caught himself against the back wall, "the ice princess is back."

She reached to help him, and then dropped her hand. What was the use? The damn fool would never understand, would he? "I don't play parts, Harry. I am first and foremost, your wife."

"And don't you forget it!"

He drew himself up to his full height. He appeared taller than five ten because of the weight he had lost. He braced himself, holding on to the bar that ran the length of the elevator. Whatever they had given him tonight, it kept coming back in little flashes when he least expected it. He was going to have to ask Garrison to get him more of the same as soon as possible.

"I'm not the one who forgets, Harry." She was weary of it all. With a sigh, Johanna took his arm once more as the elevator came to a halt.

Harry slumped against her. "And neither do they."

He was babbling again, she thought, struggling to make her way down the wide hallway as Harry leaned heavily on her. She propped him up against the wall as she took her key out of her clutch purse.

"Who's 'they,' Harry?"

He looked at her contemptuously. She knew who they were. She was their informant. They smuggled information to the head of the studio. Lies. All lies.

"The guys that were slobbering all over you tonight."

Oh God, not again. "No one slobbered, Harry."

The suite was dark and she turned the light on. She

hated the dark now, hated it because it brought her thoughts into focus so much more clearly. She wanted no thoughts tonight, nothing. She was suddenly beyond being bone weary of it all.

"Don't you think I saw them?"

She refused to even look at him. "The only thing you seem to be seeing are things you insist on fabricating in what's left of your mind." Angry, she threw her purse down on the coffee table and marched toward her bedroom. She wanted nothing more than to shut him out.

He grabbed her arm and spun her around. The effects of the cocaine suddenly disappeared, as they were wont to do, and he came crashing down to earth with a depressing jolt. A moment ago, he had seemed too weak to stand, but now there was almost superhuman strength in his grip. His fingers pressed into her bare flesh, his face loomed inches away from hers. Every inch exuded malevolence.

"The only reason Marty Scoffield and Earl Haywood want to get your pants down is to get close to me."

She tried to jerk away and almost cried out from the pain, but clenched her teeth to keep the sound back. "Then why are they bothering with me? Your pants are *always* down. Not for me, but for everyone else." With another yank, she freed herself and walked into her room. She tried to shut the door, but he pushed his way in. There was sheer fury in his eyes.

"Are you accusing me of being gay?" The veins on his neck stood out.

The look in his eyes told her to back away, but it was too late for that. Too late for a lot of things.

"No, I'm accusing you of being sick, of using sex to feed that starving ego of yours, of using cocaine to tell yourself that you're wonderful instead of finding a way to make it all work again for you."

His face turned a deep shade of purple and his eyes were dark. "I *am* working at it." He backed her up against the wall. "What do you know about the kind of hell I go through?"

And still, she couldn't back down, though her knees were weak and her heart was hammering in her throat. The words had to be said, to be freed, just this once. "I know because I go through it with you."

He laughed into her face. The sound was cruel, cold. "You've got everything. I'm the one who has to sweat it out, I'm the one who has to come up with *it*, that magic formula that brings in the money and makes people cheer."

She shook her head. Pain sliced through her temples. "Who the hell told you you had to be Superman?"

"Me." Harry pounded his chest. "I told me I had to be Superman." There was pure anguish in his face and for a moment, he seemed to forget she was even there. "I had them, dammit, had them in the palm of my hand."

He looked down at it as he squeezed it shut and she knew that was what he wanted to do to the powers he was referring to, the great "them." Squeeze them until they were all lifeless. Dead.

He remembered she was in the room with him, and he hated her. She was part of it, part of his defeat. Perhaps even the cause.

"And now they're making demands on me. But they'll come back crawling." He began to stumble from her room.

She knew he was going in search of more cocaine. She made one last attempt to stop him, to bring him to his senses. "You're the one who's crawling, on your knees, in front of the great white goddess. Can't you see that?"

He turned on his heel. "You don't know what you're talking about!" he shrieked.

Hot tears shimmered in her eyes, tears of anger, of frustration and of sorrow for what was gone and dead. "Don't you think I saw you going into the men's room?"

He sneered at her. "Where did you want me to go, the ladies room?"

"You know what I'm talking about. Somebody gave you some snow and you took it."

"That's what you do with it."

Grinning, he dipped his hand into his pocket and pulled out a tiny packet. It was all he had left tonight. More. He'd need more by tomorrow. He had to remember to call Garrison. That little leech. Why didn't he ever get enough for him?

"No!" Because she caught him by surprise, she managed to snatch the packet away from him. "This is what you do with it."

She ran by him and he knew instantly what was on her mind. It was the only clear thought he had had all evening. She was going to get rid of it. She couldn't! He needed it, needed it more than he needed to breathe. He tried to reach her, to stop her, but the cocaine had made him slow even though it made him believe he was fast. Harry missed when he grabbed for her.

Johanna flushed the packet down the toilet.

Dazed, he saw it disappear. "You bitch! What have you done?" he screamed. In a frenzy of anger, he hit her across the face with the back of his hand.

The blow knocked her backward. It hurt far beyond what the physical impact would have warranted. The blow filtered throughout her whole body.

It was a death knell.

Harry was beside himself and the room was swimming again. His head felt as if it belonged to someone else. "Where the hell am I going to get more tonight?"

The malevolent look in his eyes had her taking a step backward instinctively.

"I could kill you," he snarled, doubling his fists up.

"That too would be only a re-enactment." Her voice was hollow.

She held her hand to her cheek. There was no longer fear in her eyes. Her eyes had gone dead, as had her soul.

Harry had done that to her, she thought. This was only the final step.

He began to stalk out, but then stopped by her bed. He picked up a book. She saw him holding it as she came out of the bathroom on legs that didn't belong to her.

"What's this?" he asked, his voice dangerously low as he held it up for her to see.

"My diary," she said dully.

"You've written things in there about me." It wasn't a question. It was an accusation.

"Yes." She didn't add that writing in her diary helped her get by. It was the only way she could. She needed to write, to pour her heart out on paper the way she couldn't in real life.

He spun around and hurled the book past her head. She ducked in time. "You're spying on me!"

"What?"

"Like that fuckin' little painter who wrote down everything about his friends. You've been spying on me. Who are you selling this to?"

"Selling this to?" She stared at him, too confused to understand his words.

"Don't parrot things back at me. Who's paying you to write this?"

"Nobody. It's for me," she cried, rushing to pick it up. But he pushed her out of the way as he snatched it up. "Give it back to me."

"Nobody," he held it aloft, out of her reach, "nobody is going to read your distorted little tales, you tramp."

He cursed at her again before he slammed the door in his wake.

Johanna crumpled to the floor in a heap, too drained, too paralyzed to move. All she could do was silently weep. The beads of her Givenchy gown cut into her face and neck as she lay there, but she couldn't move. Not for a very, very long time. There was nothing to move for.

She wished for death.

Chapter Eleven

Something, she didn't know what, forced her up to her knees and then to her feet. The simple journey took what seemed like a lifetime to Johanna. She had no idea how long Harry had been gone, how long she had been laying there, huddled in her two thousand dollar gown, her body in a fetal position, sobbing for what was, what wasn't and what could have been. It didn't matter. Time didn't matter. One moment was like another and nothing mattered any more. Nothing.

Except for her daughter.

She felt unsteady, disjointed, like a child taking its first step. On legs that felt as if they belonged to someone else, Johanna moved haltingly, touching walls, furniture, not so much for physical support as for emotional support. The rooms all felt so large, so formless. The suite appeared to be a vast unknown. For a moment, she couldn't remember which of the four bedrooms Jocelyn was in. The suite was used for entertaining visiting dignitaries and millionaires with money to burn. Right now, her lips twisting bitterly, it housed Harry.

No one had any sense of discrimination these days, she thought, detached.

Easing the door to Jocelyn's bedroom open, Johanna stood on the threshold and looked into the dark room. She just wanted to see Jocelyn, to hear the easy breathing of innocent sleep, to touch base with the only good thing left in her life.

The odor that accosted her was distinct. The stale, bittersweet smell of marijuana. She knew it well enough. It had been Harry's mainstay until someone had introduced him to cocaine.

Johanna's heart stopped. Her baby? Her *baby*? Oh God, no.

NO!

She wanted to scream, to rant, to shake Jocelyn awake and hear the denial from her own lips. Johanna's mind raced frantically as she dragged her hand through her hair. Hairpins dangled on errant waves of hair, then fell to the floor, unnoticed.

Maybe Megan had smoked it in Jocelyn's room. Megan. Megan, that was it. But if it were Megan, then the smell would be in her bedroom, not Jocelyn's. She wouldn't blatantly walk through the suite, smoking. Even she had some kind of sense.

But even if it were Megan, it would be Jocelyn too, because Jocelyn aped everything that Megan did.

Tears formed and slid down her cheeks, catching on pearl pink beads before they disappeared.

She had lost, lost everything. Johanna braced herself against the door frame, for a moment too weak to move, too stunned to think, trapped like a fly in amber, real, yet unreal. She felt as if someone had physically hit her. She clutched her stomach, afraid that she would be sick. She had never felt so isolated, so alone in her life.

There was only one thing left to do.

Johanna straightened suddenly, like a soldier whose honor had been stripped from him, a soldier left with only one recourse with which to gain honor back. Honor and peace. Everlasting peace.

As if in a dream, Johanna moved through the shadows of the suite to her own room. The silence mocked her.

The only question that remained was how to do it.

She would kill herself.

There was no gun, so the fastest way was withheld from her. Harry had left, taking every last bit of cocaine with him. She knew all his hiding places now. He had never been very clever about it, afraid he wouldn't find it when he needed it.

She pushed her tear-stained hair from her face. She couldn't do that. Even if Harry hadn't taken it all, she realized that, even in the depths of her despair, she wouldn't have taken drugs to end it all. It would have shown their ultimate triumph over her. And it wasn't drugs that had triumphed over her, but the underside of life, bringing with it shattering despair. She wished now that she had taken that prescription for sleeping pills her doctor had tried to press on her before she left. He had said she was beginning to show signs of fatigue and his way of dealing with problems was to throw pills at it.

But pills were drugs done up in fancy ribbons, she told herself, her mind sliding into the darkest bottom of depression. It felt so black. She couldn't live with this blackness eating away at her. The pain it created was unbearable. There was nothing to live for. Harry was lost, Paul was gone and Jocelyn, she had lost her too. She had lost her to Harry's way of life, to the Megans of the world.

"What's the point?" she cried out into the empty room. "What the hell's the damn point of it all?"

She felt like breaking things, slashing them.

Slashing.

A razor.

She had a razor in the medicine cabinet. Two slashes

and it would all be over. She remembered reading somewhere about a woman who committed suicide in a bathtub because the pain was lessened that way. Two slashes in a hot tub and she could just let life dribble away, no pain, no regrets, only a cocooning warmth beckoning to her, enveloping her in its arms.

In a trance, Johanna walked into the bathroom. The door clicked shut behind her and she pressed the lock. She stripped off her gown, kicking it into a corner. The diamond earrings and matching necklace he had once given her were thrown on top. She wanted nothing to do with Harry's money. It had been the lure of money that had done this to him.

Focusing her mind on only one thing, she took out the razor from the medicine cabinet and placed it on the lip of the sink. Slowly, she began to run the bath water. Steam began to fill the small, rose tiled room. It clouded the mirror.

Mechanically, from some ingrained habit that had been with her before her memory had formed, Johanna cleared off the fog from the glass with the palm of her hand. The woman who stared back at her had haunted eyes. Eyes like her mother's had been.

"What are you doing, Mommy?" she had asked, coming into a bathroom just like this, only half way around the world and a quarter of a century ago.

Her mother had jumped and pulled her hands behind her back. "Nothing, darling, nothing at all. Just go out and play."

And she had.

She hadn't seen the blood dripping down from her mother's wrists onto the bare floor, hadn't returned in time to see her alive again. She could have saved her if she had only *seen*. But she hadn't.

Her mother had had cancer and wanted the dignity to decide where and when she was going to die, not become some pin cushion for doctors, wrenching her family's heart out as they watched her waste away day after day. She hadn't wanted to drain them of their emotion or their money.

She had only succeeded in one goal.

Johanna and her younger sisters had been shattered by her mother's death. Johanna could never bring herself to use the word "suicide." She had been shattered by despair and consumed with anger. She had never totally forgiven her mother for leaving her behind, for not staying and trying anything that science had to offer, searching for a cure. She had never forgiven her for not trying to stay alive. For her.

Ever so slowly, Johanna raised her head and looked back into the mirror, mists fading from her eyes. Was this what Jocelyn was going to think? To feel? Would Jocelyn someday be standing in a bathroom like this one, with the same deadness inside of her, treading the same path? Was she just continuing a cycle that Jocelyn would feel compelled to follow, because her mother had seen no use in fighting, in going on? Would this feeling of defeat be perpetuated by her if she gave in now?

Horrified, Johanna threw down the razor. It clattered down to the tile as she covered her face with her hands. Tears fell, tears of anger, not at herself but at everything that had brought her to this place, to this moment, to this empty hopelessness.

What had she almost allowed Harry to do to her?

She let out a wrenching sob of despair and turned off the water in the tub. She opened the drain and watched the water swirl out.

So the tub was emptied, so would her emptiness go.

Johanna clenched her hands until she felt her nails dig into her flesh. She wanted to live, damn it. If Harry was killing her off by inches, making her feel useless, worthless, then Harry was her cancer, just like her mother had had cancer. Except that she was going to cut it out. Cut it out and live.

It was as if something mystical had happened in that steam-filled bathroom, as if a hand had touched her shoulder and cleared her mind. She was still Johanna Lindsey inside, still the same woman she had always been. But she had woken up to her surroundings. She had just been sleeping, benumbed by a stronger drug than Harry was taking.

No more. She was not going to let herself be a prisoner of love, or of past dreams, or of anything else. She was going to be free of it, no matter what it took.

She was going to take charge of her own life.

Johanna shuddered as she picked up the razor from the floor. What she had almost done came back to her in vivid terms. Suddenly, she saw her mother, her blue bathrobe sprawled out in a half circle around her, discolored with blood, her own blood. She had looked so alive, yet so lifeless.

It wasn't going to happen to her. She was going to fight, goddammit, fight to regain her right to be happy.

She walked back into her room and turned on the light. She wanted light, no more shadows, no more darkness. Sitting down on her bed, she picked up the phone and dialed a familiar number.

A muffled male voice answered. "Hello?"

"Daddy? Daddy, it's me, Johanna."

There was a slight pause as Jim Lindsey collected himself. "Joey?"

She closed her eyes, pulling in strength from his voice. Her father had always been so strong. "Yes."

He sat up, immediately alerted by the strange tone in her voice. It was breathless, as if she had been running a long way.

And she had, she had been running from death.

"Joey, is anything wrong?"

"No," she quickly assured him, "everything is all right. Now. I just wanted to call you, to tell you that I love you."

"Joey, tell me what's wrong."

She couldn't tell him what she had almost done. It

wouldn't be fair. He had lived through so much. He had been the tower of strength for three frightened little girls, hiding his own grief and being both mother and father to them for all these years. In the last part of his life, he deserved only the best. She vowed not to give him any reason to grieve. It was a vow she now knew she could keep. That in itself gave her hope.

"Nothing. I just miss being in the States, miss seeing you."

"You're welcome to come here any time you want, Joey, you know that. I never get enough of seeing you and my only granddaughter."

Johanna smiled. It was so wonderful hearing his calm, deep voice. He had chased away so many fears for her as a child. He had never been impatient, never short with her. His work as a pharmacist in the small town they had lived in had been demanding. But no matter how busy he was, no matter how tired, he always had time for her, time for Mary and for Laura. He was the kind of father she would have wished for Jocelyn.

"I might be home sooner than you think," she told him.

He caught something in her tone, but let it pass. Johanna would tell him in her own time. Although the most cheerful of his three children, she was also stubborn and couldn't be hurried. It was her spirit he had always been proudest of.

"How's Harry doing?"

"The same." She let her voice go flat. "I think it's over, Dad."

She knew it was, but thought to begin gently with her father. Jim Lindsey was old-fashioned and believed in marriages lasting until the end of time, like his own had. He had never remarried after her mother had died. He said he would always have a wife.

"Are you sure?"

She shifted, waiting for the discomfort, for the sorrow to seep in. It didn't.

"Pretty much."

He knew how much Johanna had loved Harry. He had never fully approved, had felt there was something dark within the man his daughter had chosen, something self-centered that didn't make enough room in his life for Johanna, but he had said nothing. His daughter's happiness was everything to him. But now it was different. Now he was free to tell her what he thought.

"About time."

"What?" The shock of her father's answer brought her around like nothing else could.

"I never told you."

"What?"

"That I didn't like him."

"No," she found that she could smile now, "you never did."

Inexplicably, she wanted to cry, to laugh, to hug her father. A door had opened somewhere, a door to her cell. She was free.

There was time enough for details later. Now he needed to know only one thing. "When are you coming home?"

She pressed her lips together, thinking. "I'm not sure yet, but I'll let you know."

"I'll wait to hear your call. And Joey—"

"Yes?"

"I love you." His voice was full, rich. "Remember not to settle. You deserve better than that."

"Yes." She laughed softly, remembering that Paul had said those exact same words to her. "I do. Goodbye, Daddy."

Johanna hung up the phone and stared at it a long time.

Chapter Twelve

"It can't be helped," Harry repeated, his voice rising in agitation, though Johanna hadn't asked for an explanation. "I have to go to Italy for a few weeks, maybe even a month. Something about the locations shot we decided on not working out because of expired work permits and problems with the crew. The pain-in-the-ass art director can't seem to get it through his damn thick head that we're already over budgeted on this."

Annoyed, Harry paced around his bedroom, throwing things haphazardly into his suitcase. Every so often, he snuck a glance at Johanna. He couldn't quite put his finger on it, but she wasn't herself this morning. He had fully expected some sort of scene after last night. He had never hit her before and a part of him did regret it, even though he couldn't bring the words out to tell her. Another part of him, the part he listened to, felt that she deserved it, deserved that and more.

But she didn't seem to expect an apology. Actually, he

got the distinct impression that she didn't care if he apologized. She looked composed, almost serene when he had walked into her room at ten. She was up and dressed while he still had on his robe and pajamas. He had been prepared for tears, for pleas, for hot words. There weren't any. When he had told her of the sudden change in plans, she had met that without so much as a blink of an eye. Though he should feel relieved, it irked him.

As if she had no objections to his departure and to the things they both knew would be occupying him while he was gone, she calmly followed him to his room when he motioned her there.

She tried not to show how relieved she felt that he was leaving, even for a few weeks. "Who'll take your place here?"

"Nobody can, but Sam's going to try and hold the fort together until I get back." He straightened and leveled a look at her. "You can't come with me."

She looked down at her hands to keep from looking at him. Why hadn't she realized before how much she loathed him? How pitiful he had become. She had deluded herself for so long, deluded herself into thinking that this weakness of his, that his maniacal behavior would all somehow pass. But in reality this turmoil between them had lasted longer than the period of time she had held onto so tenaciously. The Harry before her was one she had known for almost eleven years. The Harry in her heart had lasted less than one third that time. The handwriting had been on the wall a long, long time, but she had been trying to put wallpaper over it without seeing.

She saw now.

"I wasn't going to ask."

Harry stopped packing. His sandy brows pulled together as he studied her. What was she up to? "You weren't? Why not?" he asked suspiciously.

She raised her eyes to his and he damned her for what he saw there, for the coolness with which she regarded him.

It made him angry. And he had no idea what he was angry about, or why, only that he was.

Simplicity was best. She didn't want another argument, another scene. That would solve nothing at all. "I thought you'd be happier going off without Jocelyn and me tagging along."

She had a lover. That had to be it. No woman looked that smug, that cool, unless there was a man rolling her in the sheets. Rage filled him.

"Who is it?" He grabbed her arm and jerked her to her feet. "Who the hell is it?"

She wouldn't give him the satisfaction of seeing fear in her eyes. God, she hated him. "Who's what?" She winced as he dug his fingers into her flesh. "Harry, you're twisting my arm."

"I'll do a good deal more than twist your arm if you don't tell me who you're putting out for. Is it that dumb asshole prop carpenter from the set? Is that how your fancy runs these days? Is it?" he demanded, shaking her violently.

Biting off a scream, Johanna managed to yank her arm free and took a step back, away from Harry. He moved to grab her again, but the look in her eyes stopped him.

"Don't you ever, *ever* touch me again." Her voice was low, dangerous.

His face was contorted in a contemptuous sneer. "I'll touch you whenever I want to. You're my wife."

"In name only," she retorted. "And it won't even be that much longer."

"What are you going to do?" He laughed at her, at the idea of her ever leaving. There had been empty threats before. He knew she'd never go. She'd be turning her back on too many comforts. "Get a divorce?"

The look in his eyes was meant to intimidate her, but this time it had no effect. Johanna had been to the depths of hell and back. He was never going to send her there again.

"I'm going to do what I should have done a long time

ago." She turned her back on him and walked out.

"Go ahead, go!" His voice cracked, as did the veneer of control he was displaying.

When she didn't turn around, Harry immediately moved in front of her and blocked her way. He put his hands on her shoulders, but instead of grabbing her roughly, there was a gentleness to his touch that was reminiscent of a long time ago. Johanna had to hold herself in check. She felt her resolve weakening a little.

"I'm sorry, Jo. I'm sorry." The words came from him in a sob.

She was moved for a moment, moved to take him in her arms, to soothe him, to comfort him the way she used to before this awful wall had gone up between them. But the aching love, the need to be needed, was gone from her. It was, she knew, too late for them. If she hadn't been so blind, she would have realized that fact a long time ago. Whoever they might have been fifteen years ago, they were totally wrong for each other now. She wasn't in love with the man who was, but who had been, or who she *thought* had been. In either case, he wasn't here now.

What was before her was a frightened man who saw enemies lurking behind each shadow. There was nothing she could do for him, no solace she could offer. She'd been all through that time and again.

Harry rested his face in her hair, just for one moment, seeking strength. His breathing was labored, as though something was choking him.

"It's just that there's this pressure, this damn pressure." He pulled back, pinching the bridge of his nose, his eyes closed. She could almost see the pain he felt. "Everyone wants something from me, and I don't have it to give. And when they find out—" Desperation filled his voice. She had heard it all before. It was this that kept driving him to cocaine, to seek brilliance where there no longer was any.

"You're still a good director, Harry. Give yourself a

chance. You're choking off your potential, killing it before it has a chance to grow."

He laughed disparagingly. His eyes looked like those of a haunted man. "You sound like Paul did."

"Paul was right." About a lot of things, she added silently.

He crossed back to the bed and the open suitcase and stared at it mutely. He picked up a shirt and just held it in his hands, as if he didn't know what to do with it.

Johanna took it from him. "I'll help you pack." He merely nodded and let her take over.

"Maybe when I get back," he murmured hopefully, to himself more than to her, "it'll be different."

Yes, she thought, it will be. Very different.

He took her silence as agreement. He had to.

She needed time to think, to plan. If she divorced Harry, she would be on her own and the prospect was frightening to her. She had left college just ten credits short of her degree at Harry's insistence. Things had been moving so fast for him then and he had moved with it, taking her along. He had promised her that she could always go back and get her degree later. Much as she had wanted to, she had never found the time to go back to school. There was always something that came up to prevent her. Being Harry's wife had been a fulltime occupation.

She knew that by law she was entitled to half of everything they owned. She didn't want it, didn't want anything to remind her of the hell she had been through. Besides, there wasn't all that much anyway. Harry was mortgaged up to the limit. His money had been lost in films that didn't pay back and in the endless stream of cocaine and women that passed through his life.

But without a degree, there was precious little she could do. Be a saleswoman? A waitress? That wouldn't begin to pay the bills for the two of them and there was Jocelyn to think of. She couldn't just hurl her daughter into poverty after the life she had led.

The life she had led.

The words echoed back in her mind. Johanna thought of last night, of coming into her daughter's room and smelling the stale smoke that clung to the walls and furnishings. Jocelyn was too young and too naive to realize that the air conditioning system would only cause the smell to linger that much longer, trapping the air in the room. She hadn't spoken to Jocelyn about it because she knew her words would be met with resentment and rebellion.

Maybe a good dose of deprivation would be good for the girl after all. Johanna had seen too many privileged children fall victims of their parent's generosity, ending up as shallow human beings, unable to fend for themselves, unable to stand up to life.

That wasn't going to happen to Jocelyn.

If she had even entertained second thoughts about leaving Harry, leaving the jaded world they lived in, seeing what was happening to Jocelyn would have pushed her toward it. It was time to make a break. For both of them.

But to where? Johanna knew she didn't want to go back to Los Angeles. If she lived there, she felt that the cycle would catch up to her again and hurl her back into the center of the hurricane. This time she might not get a second chance to bail out.

Her father would take her in, of course, without a moment's hesitation. She was tempted, sorely tempted. She wouldn't have to shoulder so great a burden if she lived with him, at least in the beginning. She thought of the sleepy college town where her father still worked in the same drugstore as a pharmacist. Everyone knew everyone else and it was comfortable, warm. Safe.

But she had outgrown that. She didn't want safe. Safe didn't challenge her and she would become too placid. Maybe that was what had been wrong in the first place. She had come from that little town too trusting, too naive, to see what was happening to her and Harry. A more savvy woman would have seen the signs a long time ago and either done something about it or left.

She wouldn't think about it yet. Somehow, it would work itself out. She needed time just to float, to appreciate the fact that she wasn't brutally in love with Harry anymore. She needed time to fully realize that she was finally going to heal and find herself at last.

And the first step was to put Megan on notice. She wasn't going to go on putting up with the girl's behavior any longer. Johanna marched into the girl's room after tapping on the door once for form's sake.

"Mrs. Whitney, I'm not dressed," Megan protested, raising a towel in front of her. Behind it, the young woman was totally nude.

Johanna arched a brow. "You're wearing more than you wore for my husband."

Megan opened her mouth to protest, then looked lost for a proper reply. She held the towel tighter around her slim body.

"You don't have to lie and I haven't come to fight you for him. If you're fool enough to win him, that's your problem, not mine." She drew her brows together. "But I will fight you for Jocelyn."

"Jocelyn?" Megan looked at Johanna, completely bewildered.

"I walked into her room last night and smelled something."

The marijuana that Harry had given to her. Megan flushed. "I, um—"

"No excuses, Megan, no denials, no threats." Johanna took a step forward, a lioness intent on protecting her cub. "Consider this only a simple warning. If you ever, *ever* give my daughter that kind of garbage again, I'll have you up on charges of compromising the morals of a minor so fast your head will spin."

Megan raised her chin defiantly, her face rigid. "You can't do that."

Johanna only smiled. It made Megan's blood run cold. "Try me."

Megan's bravado crumbled. "You want me to leave."

Johanna shook her head. "No."

Megan looked surprised. "I don't understand."

"If you leave, Jocelyn will think I sent you away. She'll resent me for it." Johanna thought of the divorce that would come. "There'll be enough for her to resent me for soon enough. You can stay as long as we remain in London. But I want you to serve as the perfect example of young womanhood in flower." The words brought a cryptic smile to Johanna's lips. If Megan could pull that off, she deserved to be in one of Harry's movies. "Do I make myself perfectly clear, Megan?"

Megan looked down at the rug and curled her toes. "I think so," she mumbled.

"Think well," Johanna warned, taking the girl's chin in her hand and raising it until their eyes met. "No wild parties, no dope, no make-overs. Jocelyn is twelve, going on thirteen, that's hard enough. She doesn't have to go on twenty-nine for another seventeen years. You will do things together that are appropriate for someone Jocelyn's age. Movies, museums, sight-seeing, that kind of thing. No boys, no tight clothes, no walks on the wild side. Do we understand each other?"

Megan nodded slowly. "Yes, Mrs. Whitney."

Johanna took her hand away from the girl's chin and extended it to her. "Good."

Megan took her hand hesitantly. Her towel began to slip and she pulled it up with her other hand quickly.

Johanna tried not to let her lips curve. "And you can call me Johanna."

Megan licked her lower lip nervously. "About, about Mr. Whitney—"

Johanna was not about to discuss her husband with Megan. "What happened between the two of you is your own business, and probably, your own loss."

For a moment, there was a touch of compassion in Johanna's eyes, but then she banished it. Compassion had been her downfall with Harry. She had learned that not everyone deserved it.

She glanced at her watch as she heard the door to Jocelyn's room open and close. It was almost noon. Time for a truce of sorts. She turned to see her daughter approaching.

"Now, why don't the three of us go out to lunch at the Chelsea and then you and Megan can plan the rest of your day together?"

"Yes, Mrs. Whit—Johanna," Megan amended.

Jocelyn stood in the doorway, staring at the two of them. It was hard to say which surprised her more, the fact that Megan was wearing only a towel in her mother's presence, or that the three of them were going to be going out together to share a lunch. She smiled uncertainly as her mother put an arm around her shoulder.

"Let's leave Megan to get dressed, Jocey. I'm starved."

Jocelyn merely nodded.

Chapter Thirteen

Before he left, Harry had promised to call Johanna as soon as he reached Italy.

He didn't.

Although she hadn't expected him to, Johanna still marked the incident down in her new diary, labeling it the last promise to her that Harry would break. There would be no more promises because for there to be a promise, the receiver had to believe. Johanna had ceased to believe. That Johanna, the one who took words at their face value, was gone forever.

It both relieved and saddened Johanna to realize that she was no longer trusting, that a certain cynicism had crept into the way she dealt with people and with life itself. In gaining something, she had lost something precious.

In the days that followed Harry's departure, Johanna initially thought that it was that final scene in the bedroom which had transformed her. Actually, the incident had only been the catalyst. All the ingredients for the metamorphosis had been there all along, simmering, waiting for the final push. Harry and his rage had just sent her over the top.

The day was dreary. Harry had been gone a week and there had been plenty of time for her to act, to do something about reorganizing her life. Yet she had made no moves. She felt unsettled. She supposed that perhaps, subconsciously, she was making the final adjustment to this new station in life that she had come to.

The weather wasn't helping her restless mood. There seemed to be no demarcation from early morning, to noon, to late afternoon. The sky was a hazy gray that lightened and darkened whimsically and with no warning, like a frown coming over the face of the sky. Rain fell intermittently and annoyingly.

Johanna felt fidgety, trapped within her hotel room, within her mind. She knew that when Harry returned, whatever shape he was in, she was going to tell him that it was over between them, finally over. She wanted a divorce and nothing more from him than that.

But what came after that? She didn't know yet.

She heard Jocelyn sneeze. Her daughter's cold had been growing steadily worse since Harry left.

"Feeling any better?" Johanna asked as she walked into Jocelyn's bedroom.

Jocelyn sat on her bed, surrounded by magazines, books and cassettes, looking absolutely miserable and displaying no interest in any of the paraphernalia that littered her room. Megan sat over by the window, staring out through the window at the gloomy day. She didn't even bother to turn around as Johanna entered the room.

"No," Jocelyn sniffed, then blew her nose into a tissue. The floor was covered with a myriad of wadded up pink tissues that had missed their target, a wastepaper basket which stood off to the side.

Johanna leaned over and felt Jocelyn's forehead. It seemed to be a little cooler, but the girl was still warm. "Well, your fever seems down."

Jocelyn thumbed through a magazine, its pages flipping by unnoticed. "That's not the only thing," she said glumly.

Johanna looked over toward the dormant television. "Nothing on television?"

"Nothing." It sounded as if she were pronouncing a death sentence.

Johanna crossed to the console and tapped the VCR that stood on top of the set. "Well, the hotel's provided us with all the latest equipment. Why don't I rent a tape for you to watch?"

Jocelyn seemed to come alive at the suggestion. "No cartoons, Mom," she begged.

"No cartoons," Johanna promised. "Any suggestions?"

Johanna looked from Jocelyn to Megan, who looked even more bored and restless than Jocelyn did now that she turned away from the window. It was apparent that in the week since they had had their talk, Megan had turned obedient, though decidedly sullen.

It was as if she had no one to appear bright for, Johanna thought. Probably because Harry wasn't around to notice her in her tight skirts and short shorts.

Just her hormones dying to run wild again, Johanna diagnosed. Besides, Megan wasn't her concern. Her daughter was.

"How about *Summer Fun?*" Jocelyn suggested hopefully. "I love anything with Rick Renfield in it." She cast a side glance at Megan for approval. The dark-haired young woman merely shrugged, as if it was all the same to her.

"I'll see what I can do," Johanna promised.

Johanna returned in half an hour. She had managed to find not one but two videos that were currently out with Jocelyn's newest heartthrob, a young actor with more hair than talent. But it wasn't his acting ability that had Jocelyn sighing. It was his dimple—as well as various other parts, Johanna suspected. The young actor did incredible things to a pair of faded jeans.

No doubt about it, her little girl was growing up, Johanna

decided with a sigh. She thought of storing her in a tower and cutting her long blond hair until she was twenty-five, but knew that did no good. All little girls grew up. She had. Johanna felt a wild desire to protect Jocelyn from all the mistakes that she had embraced with open arms. That too would do no good. Mistakes had to be made in order to learn from them. Miserable idea, she thought cynically.

"Will you ladies be all right alone?" She was trying her hardest to make Jocelyn feel as if she was treating her as an equal and not just as a young child, even though in her heart there was a part of Johanna that wanted to keep her that way.

"Sure." Jocelyn shrugged carelessly. "You going somewhere?"

"Just out to clear my head." She kissed Jocelyn's forehead even as the girl pulled back from the fuss. It felt a little warmer again. Johanna reconsidered. "Maybe I'd better not."

"Go ahead, Mom," Jocelyn muttered moodily. "Quit treating me like a baby."

Johanna held up her hands. "Heaven forbid, Granny." She winked as she picked up her purse. "I won't be too long."

But she had lied. Not intentionally, of course. She hadn't intentionally gotten lost in the maze of traffic that seemed to engulf her, coming out of nowhere and with no warning. She had just wanted the freedom of a ride for half an hour. She should have realized that was impossible in London. She was ensnared in a jam that had police rerouting traffic until she had no idea whether she was still in the country or not.

And then the car died.

Just as the rain started again.

She got out of her car and felt like weeping in frustrated anger. Either that, or shooting the stalled vehicle.

"Damn!" she cried out, kicking a tire. People drove by

without giving her a second glance. The rain fell, pasting her green raw silk blouse against her body.

He saw her from a distance and moved his van into the lane closer to the street. He wanted a better look.

He was right. It *was* her.

Tommy pulled over to the side of the street half a block away. Turning up the collar of his shirt, he hurried toward her, wondering what she was doing there. He had heard that her husband had gone to Italy. He had naturally assumed that she had gone with him. The man had seemed insanely jealous that day on the set.

"What's a nice lady like you doing out here in the rain?" Tommy asked as he approached Johanna.

She stood shivering in the rain, too angry to retreat into her car for shelter. She whirled around at the sound of his voice and then smiled so broadly that she thought she'd laugh. A familiar face. "Getting wet and having a breakdown."

He thought that he had never seen a lovelier face, so frail. She almost looked angelic. To distract himself, he looked at her dormant vehicle. "You mean the car?"

She shook her head. Her hair had turned a dark shade of honey from the rain. "No, I mean me." She ran her hands up and down her arms. "I hate this miserable weather. I hate being in London. I hate Europe. I hate driving on the wrong side of the road." She realized she was beginning to babble and covered her mouth with her hands in a futile gesture. "Oh God, Tommy, I've never been so miserable in my whole life."

He looked embarrassed for her, yet felt protective of her at the same time. "I'm sorry. It's none of my business, Mrs. Whitney."

She hadn't meant to let the note of hysteria break out like that. Composing herself, Johanna went on. "I'm the one who's sorry. There's no need to apologize. Lately, my life has been everyone's business and the name is Johanna." She pushed her hair out of her face. "I have decided to completely disassociate myself from anything that remotely has to do with Harold T. Whitney—except for my daughter, of course."

He grinned now. "Of course. You have a daughter?"

"Yes. Jocelyn. She's twelve." She liked his smile. It seemed so genuine. She had had her share of phony smiles. Everyone in Harry's entourage had one.

"There's O'Hurley's." He pointed to a pub across the street that he frequented. "We'd better get you inside and nursing a hot cup of tea before your daughter's mother comes down with pneumonia." He took her arm.

"No chance of that. I never get sick." But she went with him anyway, because she wanted to get dry, because she wanted to drink something hot and warm. And because she liked the sound of his voice.

"You don't say." He held the door open for her.

"Absolutely." A board creaked under her foot as she crossed the threshold.

"Gerald," Tommy called out to the bartender as he followed Johanna in, "two teas, please."

"One tea and one coffee," Johanna corrected, cupping her hands around her mouth to be heard above the din. "Make that Irish coffee." She turned and saw the amused look Tommy gave her. "Takes the chill out, so they tell me."

"Aye." He grinned and a dimple appeared in one cheek. "So they tell me." He raised his voice again. "You heard the lady. Two Irish coffees it is, Gerald."

Gerald, wearing a multi-stained apron large enough to serve as a tablecloth about his wide middle, grumbled. "Make up your minds, you two, for the love of heaven."

Without giving it a thought, Tommy placed his hand on the small of her back and guided Johanna to a tiny booth off to the side. The small gesture was utterly intimate and Johanna felt herself responding to it. And to Tommy.

Because of its distance from the bar, the booth had a clear view of the room and the dart game that was being seriously played out between two feisty looking old men in worn plaid caps. Each had his own respective cheering section.

Tommy nodded toward Gerald. "He adds charm to the place."

She looked around for the first time. Unlike a bar or a lounge back home, the place Tommy had brought her to was well lit and somehow cozy. She could see that it was a place where people of both sexes could meet and just talk. There was none of the feel of it being a meat market the way singles bars back in the States were. She began to relax a little.

"It *is* charming." She looked back at Tommy, her eyes bright, curious.

"A pub's purpose is to serve warm beer and cool advice," he said.

"Your coffees," Gerald announced, placing two ivory colored mugs before them. Hers had a fine, thin crack running around the side.

Tommy reached into his pocket for his wallet.

Johanna realized what he was doing and placed her hand on his shoulder to stop him. "No, please, allow me." Gerald looked on, amused. "It's the least I can do since you saved me from a king-sized headache on the set."

Tommy shrugged nonchalantly, not thoroughly comfortable with the offer. "Anyone would have done the same. And I'm not used to a woman doing the paying for me."

"And I'm not used to accepting favors without returning them in kind." She smiled at him. "Humor me."

He realized that he wanted to do a lot more than just humor her. "Aye, that would be easy to do."

She didn't know whether he was aware of it, but his gaze made her feel like a woman. "Then we're agreed."

He withdrew his hand from his wallet. "If that's what you want."

She laughed and took a sip of the black coffee. It was hot and the whiskey in it was hotter, but it did a lot to burn away the chill she was feeling. In one fiery moment, it blurred the room and made her oblivious to her wet clothing. "Why are you here?" she asked suddenly.

"Because a lovely lady needed to take the chill out of her bones." He laughed at her.

"No." She shook her head and found that the room tipped a little. They certainly didn't believe in watering down their liquor. "I mean why aren't you with Harry and the others in Italy. Don't they need sets there?" She took another healthy sip. The heat was getting easier and easier to withstand.

Tommy toyed with his mug, watching her. "They might, but that's for the prop carpenters to build."

Johanna blinked, confused. "Oh, did I make a mistake? I thought you were—"

"I was."

Then she didn't understand. Was the whiskey clouding her brain? "But?"

He took a long drink. "Your husband had me fired, I'm afraid, right after you left the set."

She stared at him, appalled. But that sounded just like something Harry would do. Johanna felt both ashamed and angry. "That bastard."

"Aye, that was a word I played with in my mind." Although he sounded as if it hadn't bothered him at all. He struck her as the type that rolled with the punches. Or maybe he hadn't learned yet that they hurt at times.

She was ashamed of her husband, ashamed that Tommy had lost his job because he had helped her. "I'm so sorry." The words sounded hopelessly inadequate.

He hadn't meant for her to feel guilty. "You needn't be. I went back to working with my father. I'm happier that way, actually. Working on the set was a lark, because my friend Jamie thought it might be fun. But I like working for myself better."

Someone cheered and she looked at the game at the dart board. One of the men had won and the loser was chal-

lenging him to another game. Johanna looked back at
Tommy. His eyes were on her and she felt herself fighting
a blush. "What is it you do?"

"I build things."

"Like a contractor?"

"More specifically, like a carpenter. I'm working on a
chest of drawers right now."

"Oh, for whom?"

He finished the rest of his coffee and set the mug down.
"An old couple I know in Gloucestershire."

"Does it pay well?" She knew she shouldn't be asking,
but questions seemed to come so easily with him. The Irish
coffee didn't hurt either.

"Not that particular one, but I'm not doing it for the
money."

"What do you do for money?" Too late, she realized that
the question might be misconstrued.

He grinned a moment, rocking on two legs of the chair.
He liked the blush that colored her face. It made him think
of delicate pink roses painted on a fine piece of china.

Pulling his lips into a serious expression, he addressed
her question. "I'm helping to remodel this old house that
some Americans've bought recently and now want reno-
vated. But for myself, for my gratification, I'm working on
this chest. There's a certain satisfaction to working with
your hands, creating something unique."

She looked at his hands. They were strong hands. Hands
a woman could feel safe in, not the artistic hands she had
felt on her body so long ago. Yet though they were large,
there was nothing clumsy about them. Harry's hands had
been graceful and delicate. And impersonal.

Abruptly, she realized that she was staring and shifted
her gaze. She took another long sip and found her embarrassment waning.

"You know," she told him, leaning forward slightly.
"You're very easy to talk to.

"Right now, Mrs. Whitney—"

"Johanna."

"Johanna," he amended. "I think you'd find an aborigine easy to talk to."

She ran her fingertip along the fine crack on her mug. "You think I'm drunk?"

"I think you are, as the expression goes, feeling no pain."

His choice of words struck a chord. "Oh now, there you're wrong, my friend. I feel pain all right. I feel lots of pain. But it's time to stop just standing there and taking it."

He seemed to understand what she was saying. He had certainly heard enough about Harry during his short stay on the set. "What are you going to do?"

What was she going to do? Suddenly, she knew. "Well, the first thing is that I'm going to leave Harry."

"And the next thing?"

"I don't know," she admitted. "I can't seem to plan that far ahead yet."

"But you will."

She put down her mug, pleased by his answer. "Yes, I will. And you're wrong."

"Am I?"

"Yes."

"About what?"

"An aborigine would be a lot more difficult to talk to than you."

He laughed. The sound created a warm and happy sensation within Johanna.

Chapter Fourteen

The soft murmur of voices in the pub created a soothing effect. Johanna felt as if she could go on talking to Tommy for hours. There were no uneasy long silences, no sense that there was some sort of ritualistic feeling out of male and female going on beneath the words. They were just two people, talking. And enjoying each other's company.

Johanna leaned back in the booth and watched as raindrops lazily slid into one another and then raced down the multi-paned window. Beyond it, a heavyset man in a yellow rain slicker was hooking up the Mercedes that Harry had leased for her. Tommy had called a local towing service for her and had stayed to keep her company while she waited for it to arrive. It was he, not she who had braved the rain and had taken care of the details when the tow truck had finally arrived. At Tommy's insistence, she had remained inside, nursing a third cup of coffee, this one sans the Irish touch. She wanted a clear head when she returned to the hotel.

Now, sitting opposite her, Tommy glanced out the window. He saw that the car had been secured and that the driver was climbing back into the cab of his truck. He turned back to look at Johanna. "It looks like you're going to need a ride back to your hotel, luv."

Johanna picked up her purse. Looking over to the far end of the bar, she saw that the public phone was occupied. She bit her lower lip in frustration. She had every intention of calling a cab, although the idea of going back right now, instead of waiting for a cab to arrive, was tempting.

"Oh, I couldn't put you out any more than I already have." Johanna smiled her thanks. "I really shouldn't have let you wait here with me to begin with."

"Why not? I've nothing else to do this evening." He signalled for the check. "It's been rather nice spending some time with an intelligent lady." A barmaid responded quickly, having eyed him for some time. She took the money he tendered. "Keep the change, darlin'."

The barmaid beamed and moved on, her hips swaying saucily.

Johanna wondered if Tommy knew that he was saying all the right things to her. His words weren't polished or studied. And they seemed to tumble out as soon as he thought of them. There was an honesty to them that meant more than all the flowery lies she had ever heard. He was very sweet and guileless.

And young.

Robbing the cradle, Johanna? As the thought played itself out in her head, she fidgeted slightly with her purse.

But no, it wasn't like that. She was sure that Harry would have seen it in that light. He couldn't conceive of a man and a woman carrying on a conversation for more than a few sentences before they started stripping off each other's clothing. And while she had to admit that she found Tommy exceedingly attractive in a rough, earthy way, she was in no way inclined to carry that attraction to any sort of fruition.

Or so she told herself.

"You're sure I'm not putting you out?" she asked, hesitating. "I can always call a cab."

He cocked his head. He had only worked for Whitney Productions a little more than a month, but in that time he had picked things up and had heard a great deal about the man in charge. Harold T. Whitney was not the kind of man Tommy would have wanted to associate with on his own free time. He thought of him as a bully, a womanizer and a weakling. He especially disliked men who threw their weight around women and Harry was notorious for that. Seeing his wife, Tommy found himself disliking Harry to an even greater degree.

He wondered if she was afraid of being with him because of her husband. Or was it something else? "You can call one if you feel more comfortable—" he began.

"Oh no," she said quickly, not wanting him to think that under any circumstances. "It's not that. I can't think of when I've felt more at ease. You've been nothing but kind—"

Tommy leaned forward and she caught the musty scent of soap, cologne and man. Something within her stirred. "Then let me be a little kinder."

With a touch of nervousness, she licked her lower lip. "If you wish."

Her unconscious reaction was very appealing to him. He wondered what it would be like to kiss her. Tommy rose and pulled back her chair for her. "I wish."

Johanna glanced over her shoulder as she got to her feet. "You know, Tommy, you're going to make some lucky girl a wonderful husband someday."

"Someday," he echoed easily, leading the way to the door.

"But not soon," she surmised from his tone.

"No, not soon."

He held the door open for her. Warm mist hit her face

as she stepped out. London weather was truly awful, she decided.

With an unstudied movement, he put his arm around her shoulders and drew her close as they hurried down the street. "I've a bit of the wanderlust in me yet. It wouldn't be fair to a wife if I wanted to just pick up and leave."

Johanna tried not to think of how good he felt against her. "She might want to pick up and leave with you."

He shook his head as they instinctively drew even closer together, united against the inclement weather. "The car's over there," he pointed. "Women are nesters by and large."

"Are they now?" She laughed now and took his hand as they ran across the street together. She felt breathless and wonderfully alive, more alive than she had in a long, long time.

She stood, brushing rain from her face as he unlocked the passenger door for her. "I know of several who would argue with you on that point." She slid into the van. The interior smelled of lemon drops. She wondered if he was partial to them.

"Then they wouldn't be the ladies for me. I *like* a nester." He put his key into the ignition. "And someday, I hope to find one."

"You won't have to look far."

He turned his gaze on her.

He thinks I mean me, she thought suddenly, embarrassed. "I—I mean that you're an attractive young man and women are always on the look out for attrac—I'm not saying this right, am I?"

He laughed and covered her hand with his own. His hand was large, capable. Hers were small and delicate. He liked the contrast.

"I think I get the drift of it, Johanna. Now then, where are you staying?"

Relieved that things had been cleared up, she gave Tommy the address and he nodded, throwing the van into first gear.

Johanna looked down at the stick shift he handled so effortlessly without even thinking. "If I had to drive that, we'd never get out of the garage. I can't tap dance and drive at the same time."

"Tap dance?"

She pointed to the floor. "Too many pedals."

"Oh." He shrugged. "Like everything else, you get used to it."

She thought of the demise of her marriage and grew serious. Some things one never got used to. "I suppose," she said quietly.

He read her mood and wondered at it, but felt it best to let her have her privacy.

When they pulled up in front of the hotel, the doorman looked surprised to see Johanna alight from the rather sorry looking dark blue van.

"Shall I have the valet park this for you, sir?" he asked Tommy.

Johanna and Tommy exchanged grins at the formal question. Tommy handed the man his keys. "Just for a few minutes, if you don't mind."

Masterson took the car keys into his gloved hand, holding them aloft by his fingertips as if they have leprosy. "Very good, sir."

"I always see a lady to her door," Tommy confided to Johanna when they had passed through the revolving door. "My Dad made that a strict point of honor."

"I wouldn't want you disappointing your father," Johanna laughed.

God, it felt good to laugh. It had been so long since she had felt the desire to laugh. Her accidental run-in with Tommy had been a godsend. The pensive mood that had been haunting her was spent and she no longer entertained any feelings of being sorry for herself. She felt much too good for that.

When they arrived at her door, Tommy took the key

from her and opened it. Turning the doorknob, he handed the key back to her.

"Good night, Tommy." Johanna raise herself up on her toes and brushed his cheek with an affectionate kiss. "It's been a very pleasant evening."

He touched his cheek as she opened her door and smiled to himself. She was a lady, he thought, in every sense of the word. A lady he would like to see more of, if she were so inclined. He wondered if she was.

He saw that her shoulders stiffened slightly as she stood in the doorway. "Anything wrong?"

"I don't know," she murmured, then laughed at herself. "Just a feeling, I guess. Over-active nerves."

She threw open the light switch. There was silence in the suite. A strange, unusual silence that she couldn't quite put her finger on. But it bothered her. It was too early for the girls to be sleeping, she thought. And then she heard it.

A moan.

She went immediately to her daughter's room. Tommy followed without being asked. Jocelyn lay on her bed, flushed and tossing fitfully.

"Jocey?" Johanna knelt down on the floor next to the bed. "Baby, what is it?" Johanna touched her daughter's forehead. It was hot. Her whole body felt hot. Jocelyn was burning up. "Honey, where's Megan?" Why hadn't Megan tried to summon a doctor? Where was she, anyway? Guilt and frustration began to rise up. She shouldn't have left them. "Megan," she called out.

Without a word, Tommy left her side and went to look in the other rooms. He returned within a few moments. "There's no one else here, Johanna."

To Johanna's horror, Jocelyn began to jerk and tremble. Johanna tried to hold her down. "Oh my God, she's going into convulsions."

Tommy edged Johanna out of the way firmly and tucked Jocelyn's blanket around her before lifting her into his arms.

"We need to get her to a hospital emergency room," he told Johanna. "This happened to my younger sister. C'mon."

Johanna scrambled up to her feet, eternally grateful that Tommy had taken charge. Following Tommy out into the hallway, Johanna had to remind herself to lock the door. Impatiently, she jabbed the elevator button then silently willed it to come quickly. When it did, it was empty.

"It's going to be all right, baby," Johanna said soothing. Jocelyn didn't seem to hear her. She squeezed her eyes shut tight against the glare of the light in the elevator. Johanna held her hand tightly as they rode down to the first floor.

People in the lobby stared at the strange threesome, but gave them a wide berth.

"His car, quickly, Masterson," Johanna asked the doorman. "It's the blue—"

"Van," Masterson supplied. "It's not a car one forgets quickly at the Hyatt. What's the matter with the young lady?" he inquired as he signalled for a valet.

A thin young man built like a jockey hustled over and took the keys from Masterson.

"She's running a high fever," Johanna answered, wanting to run after the valet to get him to move faster. Jocelyn moaned again. "Shh, baby. It's going to be all right. We're taking her to the hospital."

"Wait right here," Masterson instructed. He called a second valet over and then dispatched him into the hotel. The couple behind Johanna murmured impatiently. "There's a sick child here," the doorman explained using a tone that was not as gracious as it might have been.

His expression softened to a wreath of compassion as he turned and looked at Johanna. "I've sent Ben to call for the local bobbies. They'll escort you in. Westminster Children's Hospital is your best bet, Mrs. Whitney. It's close by."

She didn't want to wait. She wanted to go now, as soon as the van was brought around. But common sense told her they'd make better time with a police car clearing the way for them. She nodded her thanks, afraid that her voice might break if she spoke. Harry was always telling her that she was a poor excuse for a wife and mother. She blamed herself for this. If she hadn't gone out—if she had stayed in, she would have gotten Jocelyn to a doctor as soon as the fever began to rise.

The valet brought the van to a screeching halt before them, and jumped out, holding the keys out to Tommy. Johanna climbed in first. Tommy settled Jocelyn against Johanna and she put her arms around the girl, rocking slightly, hoping that it would sooth her. Tommy took the keys and hurried around to the driver's side. He swung into the seat, poised and ready, curbing his own impatience to be off. Within moments, the sing-song sound of a siren was heard piercing the night air.

"Hang on," Tommy warned her. Johanna felt the van lunge forward.

She whispered the same words to Jocelyn and bit her lip to keep from crying when she realized that the girl still didn't hear her. Murmuring encouragements, Johanna stroked the girl's head.

As soon as Jocelyn was better, and she told herself that there was no other conclusion that could be reached, Johanna vowed that she was going to find Megan and send her packing immediately.

Or maybe, Johanna told herself, stroking her daughter's forehead and wishing that it was cooler, she'd just kill the irresponsible little witch.

The thought gave her something to consider as she held her daughter in her arms.

Chapter Fifteen

There was something about Tommy that made her put her faith in him. Johanna had no idea why she trusted a person who was for all intents a perfect stranger to her, but she did. She felt better for Tommy just being there with her. It wasn't so much that he took charge of the situation. He didn't. He didn't overwhelm her and make her feel incompetent or more guilty than she already felt. If anything, his manner made her feel as if she wasn't to blame for this. Harry would have been all too quick to point a finger at her while he did nothing to remedy it. Instead, Tommy took the given situation and handled it competently. He made her feel that they were in this together. As a team.

With their police escort, they arrived at Westminster Children's Hospital quickly. Johanna managed to say a quick thank-you to the policeman, then hurried after Tommy as he carried Jocelyn in through doors that bounced opened automatically when he approached.

Jocelyn was still drifting in and out of consciousness.

Johanna caught up to them and took her daughter's limp hand in hers. She held it tightly as she and Tommy walked down the corridor into the emergency room.

There were only a few people seated in the vestibule, each apparently waiting for someone beyond the green doors which separated the well from the ones seeking help. Unconsciously, Johanna gripped Tommy's arm.

"It's goin' to be all right, luv," he whispered.

Johanna hung onto the words like a promise.

A brusque, mannish-looking older woman approached them and without a hint of a smile or a trace of humanity, waved them over to the registration desk. "We'll need some facts before she can be attended to." She pulled out a drawer and removed a stack of forms.

How can she think about paperwork when her daughter was suffering? What was the matter with this woman? Didn't she have any feelings? Angry words rose up to her lips. Johanna fought them back. Shouting wasn't going to get her anywhere.

"I can tell you anything you need to know," she told the woman, "if you'll just get a doctor to take a look at my daughter."

The woman frowned, puckering her dark brows into almost a single line. "We can't go getting ahead of ourselves, now can we? In each situation, there are specific procedures that have to be adhered to."

"Rubbish," Tommy declared. He shifted Jocelyn's weight slightly. His forearms were beginning to ache. "This is a bloody emergency, madam. This little girl needs to be seen *now*."

The woman bristled. But looking at Tommy's unsmiling face had her relinquishing her stand within a few seconds. He looked like someone she didn't want to argue with.

She rose dramatically and matched back to the green doors. "This way." She shoved the doors open with the flat of her hand and they jumped apart. The sign on the left door warned people to keep clear. Tommy wondered if the woman came with the same kind of a warning.

He turned and smiled encouragingly at Johanna as they followed the short, squat woman into a large, antiseptic room. Two sides of the room were lined with cots. There was hardly any space between them. Curtains that had once been stark white but were now a faded eggshell color were the only thing separating one cot from another. It generated a very sterile atmosphere.

That only added to Johanna's anxiety. She began to think that if Tommy wasn't here, she would be falling apart by now. First there had been the stress of her marriage ending, and now this. Alone, it would have been too much for her to bear.

The woman from the registration desk summoned a nurse and then turned her attention to Johanna. "If you're quite content, I'll need to speak to you at the desk now." It was more of a command than a statement.

"Tommy, would you—?" She looked down at Jocelyn.

"Sure, I'll stay with her. Don't you worry none."

Johanna merely nodded and followed the woman out of the room.

Fighting off a mental fog, Johanna managed to give the woman all the necessary information. After she signed the release, she literally bolted from her chair to join Jocelyn. Behind her, she heard the woman hiss out an annoyed sigh. Johanna silently addressed a few choice words in her direction.

To her relief, Tommy was still with Jocelyn, talking to the girl and telling her that it was going to be okay. Jocelyn seemed to have settled down. She was no longer tossing and turning, and she was conscious. That in itself was comforting.

Johanna took her daughter's hand in hers again. "Hi, stranger." She smoothed back Jocelyn's wet bangs.

Jocelyn tried to focus in on her. "Mom, I feel awful," she cried softly.

"I know, honey, I know. It'll be all right soon," she promised.

Jocelyn closed her eyes and fell asleep again.

Johanna recalled a fragment of a prayer from her childhood and silently said it over and over again. Tommy said nothing. But he remained there. It helped.

It took forever for an emergency room physician to finally come and see them. Johanna had begun to despair that they were going to stay the night and well into the next day, waiting. Her hands were icy. She couldn't seem to get warm enough, in contrast to Jocelyn, who continued to run a high fever. Twice Johanna told Tommy that he should go home and twice he ignored her, much to her unspoken relief. Having him with her gave her someone to talk to, someone to share her feelings with. It kept her from imagining the worst.

When the physician and a technician took Jocelyn off to run a few tests, Johanna was left looking down at the empty cot. Looking down and worrying.

"I don't know what it is about being sick in a strange city." Johanna tried to laugh at her fears, but she still couldn't shake the feeling. "But it has you imagining all sorts of things. Back home, this would seem almost routine to me." It wasn't entirely true, but the familiarity of home would have taken some of the fear away. Being in London, thousands of miles from home, made it that much more strange.

As she spoke, she knotted and unknotted her hands. Silently, Tommy took one of her hands in his and held it. She gave him a heartened smile.

"When Jocey was thirteen months old, she ran a high fever and went into convulsions."

"Does she have a history of—" He wasn't certain just how to phrase his question.

"Epilepsy?"

Tommy nodded.

"No. I had her tested. The doctor went along with me,

probably because of the fee I imagine. He owned the clinic and taxes come high in that part of the city. But he did laugh when it was over. Told me I was overreacting. Very high fevers are known to bring on convulsions." She shrugged helplessly, staring at the slightly frayed curtain that bisected the area between them and the next cot. "I knew someone who died from food poisoning. He was staying in a little town in Italy, visiting relatives. If he had been in the States, he'd be alive today—" Her hand moved jerkily over the sheet, worrying it.

Tommy covered her hand again with his own in an effort to reassure her. "We're not entirely barbaric here."

The contact of hand on hand seemed strangely fortifying. She drew strength from it. Johanna smiled her gratitude at him. His brown eyes were soft, comforting. But she felt guilty at detaining him. "Isn't there some girl you should be with?"

He grinned and tilted his head, studying her. He left his hand where it was. He enjoyed touching her, even so virginal a contact as this. "Are you trying to get rid of me?"

Johanna looked down at their joined hands. Odd that it felt so natural. "No, but I feel like I'm taking you away from someone."

"No one that I know of."

"No one special?" She remembered what he had told her earlier, that he wasn't ready to get serious about anyone, but she had thought that was purely for conversation's sake. She found it hard to believe that someone as kind, as handsome as Tommy Reed was unattached.

"Not yet."

His words and the look in his eyes brought a shiver down her spine. If she didn't know any better, she would have said it sounded like a promise.

What was the matter with her? It was precisely her earlier dalliance that had kept her away from Jocelyn until the girl had gotten to this state. How could she even be thinking about someone when Jocelyn was lying in this hospital, deathly ill? And to be thinking about someone younger than she was—? She didn't know exactly how old Tommy was, but she knew he had to be younger than she was. Perhaps as much as ten years. Or was it just that she felt so old lately?

It was the stress she was under, she assured herself. Anyone could crack after what she had been through with Harry. What she needed was a vacation to pull herself together, not a crisis on the heels of her decision to leave him.

"Mrs. Whitney?" A tall, thin-faced man in a white lab coat came into the microcosm created by the white curtains. There was a stethoscope peering out one of his deep pockets. Behind him, an orderly brought Jocelyn back and helped her onto the cot.

Johanna took hold of Jocelyn's hand and squeezed it before she looked up at the doctor. "Yes?"

"I'm Dr. Powell."

"But where's Dr. MacIntire?" There had been a young, shaggy-haired resident attending Jocelyn. He had been the one who had taken her off for the lab tests half an hour ago.

"He's off duty."

Johanna tried to curb her impatience. Didn't anyone stay to see things through? Careful, Joey, you're letting yourself become hysterical. "What about my daughter?"

Dr. Powell drew his cheeks together as he appeared to search for each one of his words. "We've given her something to lower her fever, but I think it's best to keep her here in one of the rooms overnight for observation."

"What about the tests?"

"Nothing conclusive yet," he said impersonally. "As I said, this is just a precautionary measure."

Jocelyn gripped her mother's hand harder. "Mommy?" The voice was young and frightened.

No more pretense at being sophisticated and blase, Johanna thought with a tug at her heart.

"Right here, Jocey." Johanna looked at the doctor. "All right. Can you put a cot into her room so I can stay with her?"

"We don't have accommodations for parents." Though his tone was formal, there was a trace of compassion evident now in his voice. "You may, however, stay in the lobby if you wish. It isn't very comfortable, but it's close." His small, round eyes appraised Tommy. "I would, however, recommend that your husband take you home and you can return tomorrow morning. She's in no apparent danger. We only want to be certain that she won't have a repeat episode."

Johanna opened her mouth to correct the doctor's misunderstanding as to who Tommy was, but she let it go. She was more concerned with Jocelyn than misconceived notions and appearances.

"I think Jocelyn would feel a lot better knowing I'm close by."

Jocelyn smiled weakly. "Thanks, Mom," she mouthed.

Johanna squeezed her hand just as a gurney was rolled into the tiny area. Tommy stepped aside to give the orderly room.

"Up you go, princess," Johanna said, breaking contact.

"You can follow her to her room if you like, Mrs. Whitney," the doctor told her, "but as you must know, visiting hours are long since over."

"I'll go back to the lobby like a good girl," she promised, "once Jocelyn is settled in."

The hospital was a maze of corridors and signs pointing off into all directions, declaring routes to different facilities. Carefully, Johanna traced her way from the fourth floor down to the first until she finally found the lobby. And Tommy. He was sitting in one of the gun metal gray bucket seats. It looked far too small to accommodate his long frame.

"What are you doing here?" she asked, surprised.

He lifted a container of coffee in her direction. "I thought you might need this."

She slid into the chair next to his. "You're an angel." She removed the lid from the container and took a long, deep sip. It tasted terrible, but at the moment the hot liquid fortified her the way nothing else could have. It filled her empty stomach and made her feel almost human again.

As did he, she realized.

But coffee was one thing, this budding feeling for the man next to her was quite another. She had to put a stop to it. After all, she was still a married woman, even if she had been one in name only for the last nine months or so. She still had no right to get involved with anyone. It wasn't fair to the person, or to her. Her emotions were still raw. She couldn't risk anything that might make them break open and bleed again.

On top of that, she felt foolish about her reaction to Tommy. What would he think, she wondered, sneaking a look at him, if he suspected that his kindness had stirred a chord within her, making her susceptible to things of a more intimate nature? He'd undoubtedly have a good laugh with his friends.

She realized that he sensed her looking at him. Nervously, she cleared her throat. "You know, this is the umpteenth time you've come to my rescue in one way or another. If you're not careful, you're going to become a regular hero."

He grinned, shrugging it off casually. "Must be all those nights me father used to read to me from *Ivanhoe* finally bearing fruit."

"*Ivanhoe?*"

"The novel by Sir Walter Scott." He took the empty coffee container from her and put it down on a tiny side table.

Even the small gesture seemed somehow sweet, intimate. "I know who wrote *Ivanhoe*," she answered, "I just pictured something a little lighter for a little boy, like *Winnie The Pooh.*"

"Who said I was a little boy?"

She looked at him, surprised. "You weren't?"

"I was fourteen at the time. A friend of mine offered to let me ride his motorcycle. It was a short trip. I broke my collar bone, not to mention both my legs and a couple of ribs."

"Ouch."

He laughed. "My sentiments exactly. I was stuck in a hospital very similar to this one for six months. My dad came to read to me every night until they chased him out. Fond of that book he was." There was an affectionate smile on his face.

"And your mother?" she couldn't help asking.

"She died when I was three," he told her quietly. There was still a trace of pain lingering within him that he had never really gotten to know the woman who had given him life.

"Well, we have that in common." She wanted to reach out, to touch and comfort him the way he had her. But she didn't. It was too bold a move. "My mother died when I was nine."

"Both half orphans. Small world."

And it felt like it was growing smaller. She pushed the thought from her mind. She was just extremely over-wrought, that was all.

But she knew it was more than that. She knew herself too well to lie. The fact was, she was vulnerable and Tommy was being more than nice to her.

Something within her clutched at the cup of kindness and drank deeply.

Chapter Sixteen

The constant din of unfamiliar sounds and the austere room with its uncomfortable gray vinyl couch, combined with the anxiety she felt at having Jocelyn separated from her, made it impossible for Johanna to sleep. But she felt she had to try. She needed to be rested, if not for herself, at least for Jocelyn.

She was too tense to rest.

Instead, Johanna spent the night talking with Tommy, exchanging confidences, telling him about Harry, about the years that had been good, about the decade that hadn't been. She didn't know why he remained, but somewhere in the night she had stopped questioning his reasons for being kind to her. She was just grateful, fiercely grateful at this show of kindness from a stranger. Because of Harry, she had come not to expect kindness from anyone.

In those hours before dawn, Johanna learned a great deal about the man who had come to her aid more than once. She learned how deeply his love of working with his hands really went. She learned of the work he did by fashioning things out of wood using tools that had been used by craftsmen a century ago. He took a great deal of pride in his work, in his creations, though he didn't speak of it until she prodded him.

In a way, she thought, he was as much of an artist as she had once felt she was, creating beauty out of nothing, beauty to share.

With the same confident, patient way he approached his life and his work, Tommy managed to draw Johanna out about herself.

To Johanna's surprise, she found herself telling him not just about her hurt, but about her dreams. She told him things she hadn't told another living soul. She discovered that they shared a mutual love and respect of art. By the time the first rose colors of dawn began to light the sleepy sky, she had agreed to let him take her to the Tate Gallery once Jocelyn was well.

It almost sounded, she thought, like a date. But of course it wasn't. Dates were for other people, not for her. She had admitted to herself that she no longer felt married to Harry, that she actually hadn't for a long time now. A divorce would be only a technicality, legally declaring something that had been true for too long. So she was really free to date, but she wouldn't, couldn't. This would be just a pleasant outing between two friends, for she considered him that. After sharing the night with him, she felt that she knew him a good deal better than she knew the superficial people who inhabited Harry's circle of acquaintances.

Still, the idea of spending more time alone with him made her feel content in a way she hadn't felt in a long time. She was actually looking forward to something with a sense of delightful anticipation instead of the dread that had been part of her life.

Johanna felt exhilarated despite her lack of sleep. Exhilarated and young again. Silly that a mere conversation in a dimly lit hospital lobby could work such miracles, but it had. She felt as if some of the mental shackles that Harry had chained her with were beginning to fall away. The deadness within her soul, that darkness that had beckoned her on to suicide, had disappeared.

Johanna combed her tangled silvery blond hair with her fingertips. She became conscious of how disheveled she had to look. "Oh God, I must look awful."

Tommy grinned. "Not at all, luv, not at all. You look good in green." He leaned forward and touched her arm under the pretext of feeling the blouse's material. "It feels quite nice."

Her mouth went dry. "It's silk."

"Expensive. Suits you."

She felt foolishly pleased. Her skirt was wrinkled and she realized that one of the shirttails of her blouse had worked itself out of her waistband. She uncurled her legs from beneath her and stood up, tucking the blouse back where it belonged.

"You're being kind again. I must look like a sight," she murmured, embarrassed. She longed for a toothbrush and a few cosmetics. They were all in her bedroom at the hotel. When she had left yesterday afternoon for her ride, she had no idea it was going to turn into an odyssey.

"Yes," Tommy agreed simply, smiling at her. "A sight for sore eyes."

"You *are* good for my ego, Tommy." She laughed, touching his shoulder as she spoke.

The gesture made her stop as she abruptly became cognizant of what she had just done. She had once been a toucher, touching people easily as she spoke. Her hands had been an extension of her, of the way she felt. But life with Harry had curtailed that, making her withdraw until she touched no one at all. She couldn't seem to reach out, bound the way she was by the oppressive life she led as the wife of Harold Whitney. She was just now beginning to realize what a living hell it had all been. Like someone waking from a bad dream, she couldn't understand how she had permitted it to continue for so long.

"I certainly hope I'm good for your ego," Tommy said softly as he tucked an errant strand of her hair behind her ear.

She had to exercise considerable self-control not to react to his touch. She had the strongest desire just to turn her face into the palm of his hand. "Why?"

"Because your husband wasn't. He should never have done that to you, you know."

She couldn't take her eyes away from his. They were soft, brown and hypnotic. They seemed to see things. An artist always saw things beneath the surface, she thought. He had to be able to envision things within a lump of clay, or on an empty canvas. Or visualize completed wholes while handling disjointed pieces of wood.

"Done what?"

"Stripped you of your self-esteem."

"He didn't." As she said it, she knew it was true. "He just buried it."

Tommy cupped her face in his hand and she felt warmth and strength and compassion all in that one simple movement. "He should be horsewhipped."

Because he was an artist, he did see things not evident to the untrained eye. He saw the wide open, hungry gaze in her eyes when she regarded him. With someone else, he would have taken this to be an invitation to sex. But it was different with Johanna. There was something almost innocent there in her eyes. She was like a small child being shown something for the first time. He wanted her, but if something was to develop, he knew that it couldn't be hurried. She needed time. And he would give her all the time she needed.

"I'll keep that in mind the next time I see him."

Someone entered the lobby and Johanna rose to her feet, shifting away from Tommy. "I'd better go find out when I can spring Jocelyn."

He was on his feet in an instant. "I'll come with you."

There was no thought of telling him no. Instead, Johanna linked her arm through his. "All right, let's go, Ivanhoe."

Jocelyn was relieved to see her mother enter the room. Her smile puckered into a confused expression when she saw Tommy enter behind Johanna.

Johanna took her daughter's hand in hers. It felt so much stronger this morning than the limp, hot hand she had held last night.

"Jocey, this is Tommy Reed, the man who was nice enough to drive us here last night. He's also the man responsible for keeping your mother from being flattened by a flying piece of scenery at Pinewood Studios *and* for having our car towed to a local garage to be fixed. It broke down. That was why I was late coming home yesterday."

He's also the man who helped me keep body and soul together all through the night, Johanna added silently.

Jocelyn absorbed all this information the way most twelve-year-olds assimilated data. Quickly, to be filed away and lost among the archives in deference to more important things, like the latest rock star's vital statistics. "Hi."

"Hi," Tommy responded warmly, taking the young girl's hand and shaking it. "Feels pretty firm to me," he observed. "Looks to me like you might be ready to go home today."

Jocelyn brightened immediately, deciding that she liked her mother's friend. "Am I ever."

Jocelyn's manner was bright and lively as she spoke and asked questions. She bore little resemblance to the feverish, convulsed girl they had brought in a little over twelve hours ago.

Tommy volunteered to look for the doctor on duty so that Johanna could talk to him. He returned shortly with the doctor they had originally met in the emergency room.

Quickly reviewing her chart, the physician agreed with their observation that Jocelyn was ready to go home. He wrote out a prescription for Jocelyn to take until it was exhausted and told them that they could leave the hospital at any time.

"But I highly recommend before eleven," he said, pretending to share a confidence, "or else they'll soak you for another full day." He winked at Jocelyn who lost her heart to him totally. She thought he was cute.

"Doctor, what did she have?"

"Just some elusive twenty-four-hour virus that rattled her cage and then disappeared as quickly as it came. It has a long, technical name that will have no bearing on her life whatsoever." The shaggy redheaded young resident ruffled Jocelyn's hair. "She'll be good as new before you know it. Maybe even better. Take care of yourself," he said to Jocelyn, recognizing a full-fledged case of puppy love when he saw it.

"I'll go bring the van around," Tommy told Johanna, "while you get her ready."

Johanna nodded, watching him go. He seemed to take on responsibility so easily, she thought, without being asked. Harry wouldn't have been this helpful. If he hadn't been stoned out of his mind when she needed him most, he would have still told her to handle the situation alone. He was never good in a crisis. He preferred to ignore them until they went away. Or he did.

Johanna helped Jocelyn get dressed. Though she pretended not to be, she was still very weak. Johanna took over, buttoning her blouse for her.

"What happened to Megan?" she asked, trying to sound casual.

"Megan?" Jocelyn looked out the window and watched two birds fly by, calling to one another.

"Yes, she wasn't there when I came back to the hotel." Johanna looked around for Jocelyn's shoes and then remembered that she hadn't had any on. Johanna debated what to do.

"Oh," Jocelyn suddenly remembered, "she said something about having a date."

Shoes were forgotten. "And she *left* you?"

Jocelyn shrugged. She felt defensive for her friend, even though the feeling of having been deserted was there. "So did you."

"Yes, but I left you with someone and I didn't intend to be gone all night. Megan was supposed to stay with you, or at least let me know that she intended to go out so I could stay with you."

"Would you have?"

She was surprised by the question and the edge in Jocelyn's voice. "Of course I would have."

"Even though you had a date?"

"Jocelyn," Johanna took the girl's hands into hers, "I didn't have a date."

"You picked him up?" Jocelyn asked incredulously.

Sometimes, Johanna felt that her daughter was growing up too fast. "No, I told you, Tommy is a friend of mine. The car broke down and, luckily for both of us," she emphasized the last part of her statement, "he just happened by. He called the tow truck and brought me back to the hotel." She looked down at Jocelyn's bare feet. "I guess that'll be all right. I'll ring for the nurse and she'll bring a wheelchair."

"A wheelchair? Why?"

"So that you can ride down to the first floor in style. Besides, you have no shoes. You were so sick, I never even stopped to think about shoes." She smoothed back the hair from her daughter's face and then brushed a kiss over the top of her head. "I love you, Jocey."

Jocelyn touched her mother's arm. "Yeah, me too."

Tommy brought them back to the hotel room and endeared himself to Jocelyn by carrying her from his car to her suite. The last time, she had barely been conscious. This time, she reveled in the deed the way only a young girl on the threshold of womanhood could.

He brought her back to her bedroom and Jocelyn did her best to flirt with him. She was definitely on the way to recovery, Johanna thought. Tommy took the time to make sure that she was comfortable and had everything she needed before he said goodbye.

"I think she's lost her heart to you," Johanna confided as she accompanied him back to the front door.

"She's a special girl." Tommy rested his hand on the doorknob. "Like her mother."

Johanna looked down, momentarily flustered. He made her forget that she was who she was and that he was a young carpenter who had no business in her life. But he was there all the same and she was glad of it.

"I don't know what to say, Tommy. Thank you seems so inadequate."

"Then don't say it."

She raised her eyes to his and he thought that he would never see blue eyes again and not think of hers.

"But you've done so much, I don't know how to repay you."

"I've already told you how, luv. Let me share the museum with you."

"All right." A giddy feeling began to build within her as soon as she consented.

It wasn't a date, she told herself again. It was just going to be an afternoon in the company of a friend. A very good friend. Nothing more.

If it was nothing more, why did her palms suddenly feel damp?

He smiled into her eyes and quickened the muscles in her stomach. "When?"

She looked over her shoulder to Jocelyn's bedroom. Johanna wasn't free to make decisions just for herself. "Call me."

"I will."

As Johanna closed the door, she had no doubts that he would.

Her contented mood sustained her as she walked into Megan's room. The girl was asleep, laying fully clothed on top of her bedspread. From the looks of it, she had had a very busy night. Johanna shook her none too gently by her shoulder.

"What?" Megan jerked up, angry words at the disturbance on her tongue. When she saw Johanna standing over her, the words faded. "Oh, I must have fallen asleep."

"So it looks." Johanna did not return her smile. "Get packed, Megan. You're leaving."

"Where are we going?"

"We're not going anywhere." Johanna opened the girl's closet and took out her suitcase. She tossed it on the bed next to her. Megan jumped back, then held her head. Her brain throbbed and her mouth felt like cotton. Old cotton. "You are. You're fired."

"Fired?" she mumbled as if she didn't comprehend the word.

"Fired. Completely and utterly. You should have been weeks ago. I was just too soft-hearted or too stupid to do it then."

"But I—" The expression that registered on Megan's face was panic.

"In case you're interested, the straw that broke the camel's back was walking out and leaving a sick child alone in a hotel room while you went out and partied the night away."

Megan tried to brazen it out. It had worked before. "I knew you'd be back."

"How wise of you." Turning on her heel, Johanna grabbed an arm load of clothes out of the closet and tossed them into the opened suitcase. "Now, if you want these in any kind of order, you'd better see to it yourself."

Megan stared down at the jumble of clothes. "I haven't got any money to fly home."

"I'll give it to you. It'll be more than worth it just to see you go." With that, Johanna walked out of the room, closing the door behind her.

She felt a lot like humming.

Chapter Seventeen

Jocelyn, for her part, was morose. "What are we going to do here, the two of us?" she wanted to know, flouncing down next to her mother on the sofa. Megan had been gone for less than a week and Jocelyn was already bored beyond words, anticipating more of the same.

When had she lost touch with her daughter, Johanna wondered. It wasn't all that long ago that they had been able to enjoy one another's company on a steady basis.

"Have fun," Johanna said brightly.

Without consciously realizing it, Jocelyn made a face at her words.

The twinge of hurt Johanna felt was quickly pushed aside. This was no time to be self-centered. "Oh, I don't know, there was a time when you thought you were having fun with me."

"There was a time when I used to think Sesame Street was heavy entertainment, too."

"I see."

Jocelyn looked contrite at the quiet sound of pain in her mother's voice. "I didn't mean that," she mumbled into her chin.

Well, that was a start. The attempted apology heartened Johanna. "Probably more than you know, but that's all right." Johanna put an arm around Jocelyn's shoulder and hugged the girl to her. "I think this is the age when you're supposed to think parents are dull."

"I am?" There was a measure of relief in Jocelyn's voice. It wasn't that she thought her mother was dull, exactly. Just not any fun.

"Absolutely. It's a phase, which is what child psychiatrists call everything they can't cure. I think you get through it when you turn twenty." Johanna raised a brow as she pretended to scrutinize Jocelyn. "Or is it thirty?" Jocelyn laughed. "Well, I guess I can't be that dull. I just made you laugh. How would you feel about taking in a movie?"

Jocelyn moved the edge of the newspaper that was spread out on the carpet. She had just been pouring over it. "Nothing to go see."

"What a shame." Johanna sighed dramatically. "All those theaters all over London and none of them playing anything. Such a waste."

"Mother," Jocelyn said impatiently.

"Daughter," Johanna mimicked.

Jocelyn got up and moved restlessly around. "You know what I mean. The movies are all dull." She began to fiddle with the curtain at the window, running the cord through her fingers as she stared out.

She looked trapped, Johanna thought. She had never felt that way when she had been twelve. At twelve, she had thought the world a wonderful place with endless possibilities. Twelve was still the time for illusions, for hope, for eagerness. How could she pass those feelings on to Jocelyn when they seemed so distant from her own life these days?

"Getting to be a rather dull world, isn't it?" Johanna

stooped to pick up the newspaper and folded it. "And you're only twelve." She dropped the newspaper on the coffee table. Jocelyn was just going to have to learn to enjoy the little things in life. It was, she firmly believed, what made everything worthwhile. "Would you like to take a stroll through Hyde Park?"

"A stroll?"

She came up behind Jocelyn and put her hands on her daughter's shoulders. "Moving feet rhythmically in front of each other. Sometimes known as walking. You do remember walking, don't you? It was invented just before the Mercedes."

Jocelyn turned and looked at her mother suspiciously. "What's at Hyde Park?"

Johanna shrugged, adjusting the shoulder of Jocelyn's oversized tee-shirt that had slipped. Rick Renfield looked up at her from the front with a lop-sided smile. "History. Green grass. Maybe a radical speech or two. That's where people go to sound off."

Mechanically, Jocelyn tugged the tee-shirt off her shoulder again. "You mean there's a special place that they have to go?"

Johanna grinned. When she was Jocelyn's age, no one could get her to wear her hair away from her face. Every generation had something, she guessed. She left Jocelyn's tee-shirt as it was.

"No, they can sound off anywhere, it's just that at Hyde Park other people are expected to pay attention. At least for a little while." She picked up her purse and moved to the door. "C'mon, it could be fun."

Jocelyn looked as if she had her doubts about that, but relented.

"Okay. I guess it's better than hanging around here."

"Spoken like a true adventurer." Johanna linked her arm through Jocelyn's.

Just as she put her hand on the doorknob, someone knocked.

"Damn," she muttered.

With Jocelyn's eyes on her, Johanna hesitated in opening the door. She wasn't expecting anyone and it was much too soon for Harry to be returning. Besides, he wouldn't have knocked. If he had lost his key, he would have shouted for her to open the door. Or pounded at the very least. Patience had ceased being Harry's long suit years ago.

"Aren't you going to open it?" Jocelyn finally asked, confused.

"I guess I have no choice." She really didn't want to see anyone. She just wanted to spend time with Jocelyn. If it was Arlene, it might be some time before they could make their escape alone.

It wasn't Arlene.

The man in the doorway was dressed in worn jeans that adhered to him like a comfortable second skin and a blue turtle neck shirt that showed off the fact that he was a physical laborer. In his wide, calloused hand he held a bouquet of white daisies.

"Tommy." Johanna felt flustered for a moment. And pleased.

Jocelyn crowded in at the door, eager to see, eager to be seen. "Who are the flowers for?"

"Both of you," Tommy replied easily. He presented the flowers to Jocelyn, although he looked at Johanna. "Mind if I come in?"

Johanna took a step back and gestured into the suite. "No, of course not."

Jocelyn stood twirling the bouquet in her hands slowly. "We were about to go out," she told Tommy matter-of-factly. But she was pleased that he had included her when he had given the flowers.

"To Hyde Park," Johanna added quickly. She told herself that she was being foolish for feeling so uncommonly flustered about Tommy's sudden appearance. He was probably just here to check on Jocelyn's health.

She knew she was grasping at straws. She also didn't know why she felt a need to do so.

A strange sort of excitement, slow and deliberate, telegraphed itself through her body.

"Hyde Park," Tommy repeated. "Haven't been there in a while. Mind if I join you?"

"How could I turn down Ivanhoe in his own native land?" Johanna laughed.

"Who's Ivanhoe?" asked Jocelyn.

Johanna filled a glass with water from the bathroom and tucked the daisies into it. "A knight who rescued ladies," she called out.

"Fair ladies," Tommy corrected. "There was a code to abide by."

Johanna crossed to the coffee table holding the impromptu vase. She could feel Tommy's eyes washing over her, saying things that couldn't be said aloud.

"I see. I take that as a lovely compliment." Johanna set down the glass filled with daisies.

Flirting. My God, she was flirting. She hadn't done that in years.

Jocelyn was taking this in as gospel. "You mean he couldn't save anyone unless they were pretty?" She frowned. "That doesn't seem fair."

Tommy laughed and Johanna thought how free, how easy laughter seemed to come to him. He shut the door behind them, then took Jocelyn by the arm as he linked his other free one with Johanna. "All damsels in distress are pretty."

Jocelyn shook her head while savoring the fact that Tommy was escorting her out just the same way he did her mother. "Now I'm really confused."

"You'll understand when you get older," Johanna promised her.

Her daughter hated that line, but because Tommy was here, the young girl smiled while she protested. "That's what you always say."

Johanna pressed for the elevator, feeling very light-hearted. She grinned at Jocelyn, but took care not to ruffle her hair. "That's because it's true."

They went together to Hyde Park where they heard some-one espousing animal rights and another man who swore that Parliament was being taken over by aliens, the kind with antennae.

Jocelyn enjoyed herself immensely. "Hey, why haven't we come here before?"

Johanna exchanged looks with Tommy. Being here with him made a difference. Being in London with him made a difference. Suddenly, the country was bright and friendly and each gloomy sky held the promise of forthcoming sun-shine. She no longer felt dejected and depressed about England or herself. "Why indeed?"

After hearing their fourth spontaneous speech, this one on the ills of the monarchy, Tommy insisted on buying them lunch. Johanna carefully dissuaded him from taking them to the hotel's restaurant. The Chelsea was known for its gourmet food and gourmet prices. Prices, she felt sure, Tommy could not afford.

Instead, they had a light lunch at a near-by outdoor cafe.

"Oh gross, what's that?" Jocelyn accused as she jabbed her finger at a line on the menu.

"You can read, Jocelyn. This isn't a foreign restaurant," Johanna murmured, looking to see what had made her daughter turn a shade of green. "Oh, kidney pie." Well, maybe Jocelyn was entitled to be a little green, Johanna reconsidered.

Jocelyn shuddered as Tommy grinned, but said nothing. "And that?"

Johanna leaned over and read. "Rob Roy's Pleasure." She looked at Tommy questioningly.

"Venison," he told her. "With chestnut puree. It's a favorite."

"Venison?" Jocelyn's eyes opened wide. "Like in deer? Like in Bambi?"

"She'll pass on Rob Roy," Johanna commented, scanning the menu. "This looks good." She chose another item, one that was lower priced.

"Don't they have any hamburgers around here?" Jocelyn moaned, dropping the menu on the table.

"My daughter, the cultural gourmet," Johanna laughed.

"I'll see what we can do," Tommy promised her.

The hamburger that Jocelyn craved was not done to her satisfaction, but then, Johanna assured Tommy, her daughter didn't like it unless it had been prepared three hours earlier and had sat under a sun lamp, waiting to be bought. "That's the way they handle fast foods back in America," Johanna explained.

Tommy frowned slightly, considering her description. "Doesn't sound very tasty."

"I know, but the worse it is, the better kids claim it tastes."

Tommy shrugged with a grin, one that Johanna found terribly endearing. "Well, to each his own."

"Exactly," Johanna agreed.

She tried to sound nonchalant, but Johanna had a definite feeling that they were skirting around something more here, like two primal animals doing a ritualistic mating dance.

Mating?

Johanna cut right through the steak on her plate and a slice slid onto her dress.

"A little water'll get it out," Tommy assured her, dabbing his own napkin in his glass. With firm, sure strokes, he rubbed on the material. Johanna felt heat climbing up her limbs to the center of her being as his hand touched her through the layers of material.

His eyes met hers and held for a moment. Her own darted nervously toward Jocelyn, but the girl was busy watching a teenage boy on a bicycle who was in turn eyeing her as he rode by slowly.

"Thank you." Johanna took the napkin from him, her

fingers trembling. She wiped the rest off herself.

My God, what was she thinking of? It had be more than nine months since Harry had touched her, since he had even *tried* to make love and that had ended disastrously. He had blamed her, saying that he had no trouble performing with anyone else.

Her fault, always her fault.

But her lack of fulfillment didn't explain the reason for her feeling this restless, edgy way around Tommy. She had never been one who needed sex. Sex was something to be coupled with love, with feeling needed and cherished. It wasn't just an exercise to be completed if the "vibrations" were right.

Her throat was suddenly dry. Johanna took a sip of her coke.

"What are you thinking about?" Tommy asked.

She nearly choked. "Why?"

"You look pensive."

"Just wondering about the future."

He smiled at her as if he knew what she was thinking, she thought nervously, then told herself to calm down and act like an adult. Perhaps that was the problem. Perhaps she was.

Tommy Reed was basically an uncomplicated man. He knew what he liked and what he didn't like. Life was too short for pretenses, although not too short for social amenities. He liked Johanna and had absolutely no doubts that he and she would come together as lovers as long as she could free herself of her inhibitions. He had no intentions of seducing her, because seduction wasn't fair. A mutual coming together was the only way to approach the very pleasurable sensation of making love. He too did not believe in sex. He believed in sharing and pleasure and kindness. And he liked Johanna very, very much and admired her as well.

"Johanna, sweetie, is that you?"

Johanna turned to look directly into Arlene's amused dark eyes. "Hello, Arlene."

Arlene presented herself in front of the threesome. She made no secret of the fact that she was appraising Tommy. And giving him very high marks. Tommy smiled back at her, which pleased her.

"Well, well, well, I see you've done very nicely for yourself."

Johanna drew her lips together. She didn't care for Arlene's inference. "This is Tommy Reed. He used to work for Harry."

Arlene tried to imagine what he would look like without his shirt. "A lot of people *used* to work for Harry."

Something in Arlene's tone alerted Johanna. "What do you mean?"

The older woman struggled to draw her eyes away from Tommy, but finally succeeded. "Haven't you heard?"

"Heard what?" Johanna pressed. She was in no mood for much of Arlene's unintentional unkindness.

"Harry's on page three of the newspaper if you'd like to see what he's been up to."

"Not in front of Jocelyn," Johanna hissed.

"Mother, I'm not a baby." The young girl stuck out her chin. But at the same time, there was a tremor in her lower lip. "You and dad aren't going to split, are you, Mom?"

She would have to tell her daughter soon enough. But not now. "Not over an article in a rag, no," Johanna said.

Her precocious daughter seemed to relax, letting the topic go. Johanna saw Tommy studying her over the rim of his glass. They had spoken of her getting a divorce and she knew that he felt she should be honest with Jocelyn. Her answer had been vague and evasive, but she couldn't deal with the pain that she would be inflicting on Jocelyn or the recriminations she knew she would receive from her. Right now, she was having trouble dealing with her own strong attraction to Tommy.

"I'll see you later, Arlene," she said quietly.

Arlene took no offense at Johanna's dismissal. Her eyes slid over Tommy slowly one last time. "My compliments, Johanna." She patted Johanna's shoulder. "Better than any one of my fantasies." She laughed at her own words as she walked away.

Chapter Eighteen

She was upset. He could tell by the way she held herself, the way her smile had tensed about the corners of her mouth. It was that woman and her bloody article that had done it, Tommy thought, resigning himself to the situation. He leaned over the table and lightly placed his hand on her shoulder.

"Would you like to go back to the hotel?" He had made plans for them for the rest of the day, but he knew that the day had been spoiled for her. It was best just to let it go for now.

For a moment, she was flustered. He had read her mind. "I—" There was no use pretending. "Yes, Tommy, if you don't mind."

"Yes, I do mind." He leaned back in the chair. "But I also understand. We'll pick it up tomorrow."

"Thank you."

He heard the gratitude in her voice. It was payment enough. "Any time, luv."

• • •

"But why can't I see the newspaper?" Jocelyn protested as soon as she and Johanna entered the hotel suite. She had barely been able to contain herself until Tommy had let them off at the hotel.

Johanna ran one hand against the border where the door met the door frame. The white enamel paint was so smooth to the touch, so perfect. The door and frame were like one. Tommy would appreciate such fine workmanship. Tommy. Her one temporary haven in this storm. He was wonderful. He was making her aware of herself again, as a person. A person who had something to offer. Who deserved to be treated well. If it weren't for him, she might be coming unglued right now. She felt so confused, so terribly impatient. She wanted things to be over, settled. Yet nothing would be for some time. And until they were, things like this article would continue to creep up and haunt them.

"Because," Johanna said, shutting the door firmly and crossing through the sitting room, "it's trash."

Stubbornly, Jocelyn reached for the newspaper under her mother's arm. "But if it's trash—"

She knew Jocelyn was consumed with curiosity, but she didn't want her exposed to the kind of things that were written in the tabloid. As long as she could shield her from it, she was determined to do it. Johanna held onto the newspaper tightly. The look on her face made Jocelyn drop her hand.

"The way trash gets perpetuated, my love, is by people reading it, paying for it, asking for more."

"Are *you* going to read it?"

There she had her. Johanna refused to lie to Jocelyn. "Yes."

"Why?" Jocelyn's hands were on her hips, impatience registered on her delicate features.

"Because I'm old enough to be able to separate fact from fiction. Because what's written here can't hurt me anymore. But it can still hurt you." She walked into her bedroom and put the newspaper away on a shelf in her closet. With a firm jerk, she slid the mirrored door shut and faced her daughter.

"How am I supposed to learn anything if you don't let me?"

Deliberately, Johanna walked out of the room. Jocelyn was forced to follow. "We'll start out with an easier object lesson, okay?"

"He's my father."

"No one ever disputed that fact, Jocelyn," Johanna said wearily, sitting down on the sofa. Except, maybe Harry when he was particularly out of control.

"I have a right to know what he's doing." Jocelyn stood in front of her, hands on hips again, legs spread wide, the picture of petulant adolescence.

"You have rights that I give you, my love." Johanna touched her cheek lightly. "Face it, until you're eighteen, you're living in a dictatorship."

Jocelyn muttered under her breath as she flounced out of the room.

Johanna hated Harry for making her go through this. Why couldn't the fool keep his private life just that? Why couldn't he exercise a little discretion with his affairs instead of flaunting them?

It wasn't until late that evening, when her daughter was asleep, that Johanna took the newspaper down from the closet shelf. She spread the paper on her bed, opening it to page three. Then she sat down to read.

A morbid curiosity drove her to it. She wasn't interested in what Harry was doing these days or with whom, although it appeared that the rest of the world was. And it wasn't the first time that her husband's infidelities and excesses had been recorded. Usually, they screamed up at her from the rack at the local supermarket. Which was why she had left the shopping to Amanda, her housekeeper, these last few years.

Johanna supposed that she was just attempting to reinforce her decision, to show herself one more time how useless it had been to waste all those years, hoping for the return of a man who no longer existed. He wasn't just buried deep within Harry, sublimated by years of drugs and frustrations and fears. He was gone. There would be no resurrection, no second coming of Harold T. Whitney. She might as well mourn his demise and go on.

But the pictures on page three did not make her mourn. They made her angry. Not for herself, but for Jocelyn. Whatever wasn't there between them any more, there was still Jocelyn to consider. How could he flaunt his infidelities this way when he had a young daughter who could read and hear? And *feel*?

She didn't blame Hollywood, or pressures or drugs. She blamed Harry. He didn't have to succumb. He didn't have to give in and take drugs. It wasn't as if he was alone. He had *made* himself alone, shutting her out when all she wanted to do was help him, to listen to his problems and to love him.

His own fault. It was all his own fault and no one else's. She was a firm believer that to a greater extent, people held their own destinies in their hands. Harry had held his and had destroyed it.

Johanna pressed her lips together. It was about time she took responsibility for hers.

Very quietly, she tore out the picture of Harry and the near nude model, folded it into tiny squares, and then tucked it away in her wallet. If, in the coming weeks and months ahead, the ensuing turmoil would cause her convictions to waver, she would just take out this picture and remind herself what she was walking away from. To remind her how low she had managed to slip.

But no more, she promised vehemently, making the vow to the glowing city that was just below her feet, outside the hotel window.

No more.

•   •   •

She was awakened by persistent knocking. Rousing her-self, she groggily looked at the clock on her night-stand and saw that it was a little past three in the morning. Who—?

Her first thought was of Tommy, but that faded just as quickly. He wouldn't come at this hour.

Harry.

Johanna fairly leaped out of bed. The comforter fell on the floor behind her but she didn't notice. Damn, why couldn't he stay away a little longer? She grabbed her ki-mono, jamming one arm into a sleeve searching for the other sleeve behind her as she quickly made her way to the door. "Who is it?"

"Santa Claus. It's three o'clock in the morning and I have jet lag. I don't want to stand in the hallway and play twenty questions, Jo."

The woman's voice, tinged with the edginess of exhaus-tion, was low, smoky.

Johanna blinked, dazed. She dragged her hand through her hair, as if that would make her think straighter. It couldn't be, and yet—

"Mary?"

She felt foolish for even thinking that her younger sister was standing on the other side of the door. Mary was half a world away, in New York, working on the new spring line for I. Magnum. But it sounded just like her, especially the choice of words.

"Okay, you win the prize. It's me. Now for God's sake, open up."

Johanna threw open the door and saw her sister, two suitcases in her hand, standing a foot away from her. Not a single hair was out of place and she looked as if she had just had a leisurely stroll down the block, not come half-way around the world in the middle of the night. But then, Mary always had style.

"What are you doing here?" It still seemed unbelievable.

"Growing roots in the hall carpet." Mary began to make her way into the suite, using the suitcases in her hand to forge a path. "Let me in."

Johanna took one of the suitcases out of her hand and moved aside simultaneously. It was either that, or get hit with a suitcase. Mary had no intention of standing out in the hallway a minute longer than she had to.

Johanna closed the door with her free hand, then followed Mary to the sofa. "Seriously, why aren't you in New York?"

Mary raised an eyebrow. "That glad to see me, eh, Johanna?"

Johanna let the suitcase drop where she stood. She put her arms around her younger sister and hugged. Hard and with a flood of sudden gratitude. Although there was only eighteen months difference, she always considered herself a lot older. She had always felt the burden of being the oldest in the family. The big sister. Mary, however, never quite saw it that way. Now it felt as if the roles had finally been reversed.

"You know better than that, Mary. I just didn't expect to see you. Especially not in my suite in London at three in the morning."

"That makes two of us." Managing to do it gracefully, Mary sank down on the sofa chair and kicked off her three inch heels one at a time. "Those damn things were invented by a man who hated women. Wouldn't wear them except they make my legs look so good." She massaged the back of one calf. "Pop's pretty worried about you, Jo," she added casually.

The tone didn't fool Johanna. She felt a stab of guilt as she perched on the arm of the sofa. Without looking at Mary, she plucked at an imaginary thread. "He sent you here?"

"He and George Tate—I. Magnum's business manager," she added when Johanna raised her head. "Time to case what the English designers are doing. I just nudged him to move up my trip, that's all."

Johanna knew better. "To three o'clock in the morning?"

"It wasn't three when I left." Mary shrugged, her long blond hair rippling on her shoulders. The London weather made it kinkier, but on Mary, Johanna thought, it looked good. On Mary, everything looked good. She was a born model. "And hey, you take what you can get."

"Aunt Mary?"

Mary turned to see her niece groggily walking out of her room, rubbing her tangled hair out of her eyes. The noise had woken her up and since Megan's departure and her father's abrupt disappearance from her life without so much as a word, the young girl was very attuned to nocturnal noises. She was afraid that her mother would leave her too, although she wouldn't admit it.

"The one and only," Mary said, opening up her arms. "Give me a hug, kid. I'm too pooped to get up myself."

Jocelyn grinned broadly as she joined her aunt on the sofa. "You didn't tell us you were coming."

"There's a reason for that. Until yesterday, I didn't know it myself. I've been away on a trip."

The smile on Mary's face told Johanna that it wasn't a trip that involved her job as a buyer. Of the three sisters, Mary was the carefree one, the one who moved with the wind and did what she pleased when she pleased. Consequences were things to be considered later. As long as she hurt no one, she was content. And a good time, she had often said, was had by all.

As Johanna had rushed into marriage, Mary had rushed into life, embracing it, savoring it, but never being mastered by it.

There was a lot to be learned from her younger sister, Johanna mused.

Johanna shifted to get more comfortable. "How long are you planning to stay?"

"Only a few days, but I thought I'd touch base with you and the kid."

She ruffled Jocelyn's hair fondly and Jocelyn didn't mind in the slightest. If she had done it, Johanna thought, amused, there would have been a high-pitched protest of "Mother," followed by an accusing glare. But Mary could do no wrong in Jocelyn's eyes and fortunately for both of them, she didn't.

"I've got to be back by Monday, Tuesday at the latest. But that gives me four days, five if I don't sleep," she said, glancing out at the dark sky beyond the window.

Mary leaned back, draping an arm on the sofa on either side of her. She looked around. Usually, by now, Harry would be out to join them, eyeing her, alternately being charming or being annoyed by her presence. She looked quizzically at Johanna. "So, where're you hiding the Boy Wonder?"

Johanna stiffened slightly, but only for Jocelyn's sake. The comment seemed to go over Jocelyn's head, or maybe she thought Mary was referring to Tommy. Johanna tugged at the sash that was loosening around her waist. "He's away on business."

A knowing look entered Mary's deep blue eyes. "I'll bet. So," she struggled to her feet. "Got a place for me to crash for a couple of hours?"

Johanna rose to join her. Jocelyn was already on her feet, next to Mary. "Harry's room."

"Been sprayed yet?" she asked as she followed her sister to the bedroom. Mary left her suitcases in her wake. Later would be time enough to carry them into the bedroom and unpack.

Johanna opened the door. The room looked oddly empty. "He didn't use it often enough to leave anything behind."

"Good enough for me."

Uninhibited, Mary began to strip off her clothes as she spoke until she was totally nude. Then she slipped into bed.

"What d'you do when it gets cold?" asked Johanna.

Mary grinned broadly. "There are other ways to keep warm."

"Blankets?" Johanna said.

"Heavy, hairy blankets," Mary answered with a chuckle. "Wake me at eight. I want to have breakfast with you two."

"Breakfast in bed?" Johanna guessed.

"What else is there, Jo?"

Johanna grinned her amusement. "Some people use restaurants."

"For lunch and dinner only," Mary sighed, already falling asleep.

It was wonderful having her sister here, Johanna thought with a smile. She always managed to make everything that much better, just by being.

Chapter Nineteen

Mary finally rose at eleven and although Johanna couldn't persuade her to go down to the hotel's restaurant for breakfast, Mary did concede to having the meal in the sitting room instead of in bed. She ordered a full course breakfast, ravenous only half an hour after waking up. It always took Johanna a full two hours before she could face the prospect of food in the morning. She had already had her token breakfast, but asked room service to bring her up a pot of coffee anyway. She nursed a cup now as she sat opposite Mary.

Having Mary arrive out of the blue the way she did gave Johanna unexpected breathing space as far as her situation with Jocelyn went. With Mary here, the tension between mother and daughter concerning Harold would lessen. Jocelyn adored Mary and her mind would revolve around having fun, not around the serious issue of parental discord.

But, having Mary here also forced Johanna to cleanse her soul. Mary wasn't a person who stood for double-talk or evasion. She didn't believe in it, not for herself nor anyone else.

"Okay, spill it," Mary instructed as she heaped raspberry jam on a muffin.

"Always so indirect and subtle." Johanna grinned as she watched her sister consume a breakfast that could fill three other people to the gills. Mary ate and ate and never seemed to gain an ounce.

"Doesn't pay," Mary murmured. She licked her index finger which had gotten a generous glob of jam when she raised the muffin to her lips.

Johanna leaned her head on her hand and watched in fascination. "You know, I'm thoroughly convinced that you have a portrait in the attic somewhere, gaining weight. You can't possibly put all that away and stay the same dress size. Either that, or you have a pet boa constrictor hiding under the table that you're feeding."

"High metabolism." Mary raised her eyes to Johanna's as she poured a second cup of coffee. "And we're not discussing me, big sister, we're discussing you."

"Boring." Johanna shifted slightly as she waved away the statement. She might have known better. Mary was nothing if not tenacious when she wanted to find out something.

"Not from what I read."

"Mary, you don't mean to tell me that you believe those stories, do you?"

"Only when they have dear Harold's name splashed all over them." Mary leveled clear blue eyes that seemed to see right through her sister. "So, have you finally come to your senses? Or was that middle-of-the-night phone call to Pop a dream he wistfully had?"

"Meaning?"

"Meaning that we all think that you should leave Harry before he destroys you, destroys her." She nodded her golden tousled head in the direction of her niece's room. "He isn't worthy of you."

"It's not like I'm a saint, Mary."

"I'd be the first to agree with you on that one." Mary laughed softly. "I know all your faults, all your shortcomings and believe me, you've never done anything to merit the kind of man Harry's become. Early Christian martyrs wearing hair shirts have done less penance than you have being married to him." She pushed the dining cart away and sat back on the sofa, pulling her legs under her. "You can come stay with me until you figure out what you want to do."

The fact that she had someone, a family, to lean on meant a great deal to Johanna. "Dad said the same thing."

"Pop meant the same thing." Mary reached out a beautifully manicured hand and placed it over her sister's. "We worry about you, Jo."

"Thanks. It helps some."

Mary studied her face. Johanna looked worn around the edges, tired. Mary could have killed Harry with her bare hands and felt nothing—except possible concern about ruining her manicure. "Any plans?"

"Healing."

"Good start."

"Aunt Mary." Jocelyn burst into the room, her eyes bright with anticipation. She was dressed in her favorite outfit, one she hoped would catch the approval of her aunt. But then, Mary rarely disapproved of anything she ever did. It was one of the reasons she liked her so much. "Are we going to go shopping like you promised?"

Mary took her hand and pulled her down beside her on the sofa. "And just when did I promise that?"

"The last time you visited us. You said the next time, you and I were on for a big shopping spree."

Mary looked over her niece's head at Johanna. "Doesn't forget a thing, does she?"

"Only when it's to her advantage to remember," Johanna said fondly.

"Okay." Mary looked at Jocelyn. "I guess I could stretch myself and do that with you, kid." She turned toward Johanna. She hoped to draw Johanna out. She felt Johanna needed to be distracted, to keep her mind off her problems once she had unburdened herself. She needed, as she had said, time to heal. Yet Mary didn't want to strong-arm her. "Want to come along and learn a few things about the fine art of shopping?"

Johanna laughed and shook her head. She stretched and shifted on the chair. She felt lethargic.

"No, I've got a few things to catch up on." Mary was already uncurling her slender frame from the sofa. Jocelyn was pulling her toward her room. "You two go and have a ball. Not too expensive a ball," Johanna said over her shoulder. "We're going to have to learn how to live on a budget soon."

"What does that mean?" Jocelyn asked Mary.

"That means that old Aunt Mary is going to foot the bill for you today, kid."

When Mary grinned like that, Johanna thought, she didn't look that much older than Jocelyn. "I can still afford to pay for what's mine," she said.

"I like spoiling her," Mary protested.

And that, Johanna knew, was the end of that. There was no arguing with Mary. She breathed a sigh of relief. It would do Jocelyn good to have a totally carefree afternoon in the company of someone Johanna trusted completely. There had always been an uneasiness when she let her go with Megan. First because she didn't know Megan very well, and then because she did.

Johanna wanted to answer a few letters, get things in order and finally think through her options one more time. This was a major decision. Once done, she knew she was burning her bridges behind her. If she walked out on Harry, asked for the divorce, that would be the end of it. He was not a man who begged. At least not where his wife was concerned. His pride wouldn't let him. She knew she had to be very, very sure before she took that final step. There would be no turning back.

She also know she had to take that final step, frightening though it was. She couldn't survive if she didn't. It was an awful thing, Johanna though, to admit that you've made such a devastating mistake, that you've wasted so much of your life because of one decision. But it was an even worse thing to ride it out to the end because you were too much of a coward to cut your losses and go.

"What's the use bandying this about, Joey? You know you have to go. It'll kill you if you don't. Everyone else's seen it. It's time you took your head out of the sand," she muttered to herself.

There was a knock on the door and she debated ignoring it, but then thought it might be room service about the cart. Preoccupied with her dilemma, she threw open the door. "What can I do for yo—Tommy?" She was both bewildered and pleased at seeing him there. He wore a green cable knit sweater that brought out a greenish tint in his eyes and a pair of faded jeans that moved with him like another layer of skin. Johanna felt a quickening of her pulse and decided it was futile to deny it.

Tommy looked at her bemused, pleased expression and judged correctly. "You forgot."

"Forgot what?"

"Our date. For the gallery. Your way of saying thanks, remember?" He grinned at her.

Her hands flew to her mouth. "Oh, I'm so sorry. It's just that my sister arrived unexpectedly last night and I guess everything else just flew out of my head." She wondered if he'd give her a raincheck.

Tommy wasn't interested in rain. "No harm done, we can still go."

She looked down at her casual outfit. She was wearing an old sweatshirt and a pair of creased slacks that needed pressing. "But I'm not dressed."

"You're wearing clothes," he pointed out.

"Yes, but—"

"There is no dress code for the gallery, luv, other than

clothes of course." He grinned and there was just the slightest hint of wickedness there. And just the slightest hint of a thrill passed through her body. "Personally, I think you look terrific."

"For the Tate Gallery?" she asked doubtfully.

"For anything."

Before she could protest further or make any other excuses, Tommy captured her hand in his. She needed coaxing, he thought, coaxing to bring out the fire he knew was inside of her. She had been on the sidelines of life for so long that she had forgotten how to participate, how to enjoy the little pleasures. They had been robbed from her. Ever so gently, he rubbed his thumb over her hand.

"I promise you, if anyone notices you at all, luv, it'll be to envy me, not to criticize your lack of proper attire."

Tommy made her feel young and impetuous again. As young as Harry had made her feel old. For a moment, just for the barest moment, her common sense wrestled with her desire to spend a carefree afternoon, dressed for the occasion or not. What would it hurt? Nothing and no one. After all, she had said she would go when he had asked. Mary had Jocelyn for the day and there was nothing to keep her chained to her room but her own stubbornness. She decided she didn't want to be stubborn.

"All right, just let me get my purse."

He grinned over his victory and she felt like giggling. She told herself that thirty-four-year-old women didn't feel like giggling unless they had had too much to drink. But she felt like giggling. And maybe, just maybe, she felt drunk as well, drunk on freedom.

The Tate Gallery stood overlooking the south bank of the River Thames, majestically hiding the fact that it was on the site of the former Millbank Prison. Now the impressive building housed a wonderful national collection of British paintings from the sixteenth century to the present, a gift to the city from Sir Henry Tate, a man of vast wealth made on the sale of sugar cubes.

Though she had never been here before, walking into the gallery was like being reunited with an old friend. She had missed being around works of art. She hadn't realized just how much until this moment. Johanna felt charged with excitement. She clutched onto Tommy's arm, her enthusiasm telegraphing itself to him. He grinned, pleased to be sharing this with her.

It had been so very long since she had haunted art galleries or museums and gazed at paintings, getting herself lost in them. Her years with Harry had been years of perpetual motion. First she had found herself caught up in a social whirl and then she was living on the edge of a hurricane, desperately just trying to hang on. There had been no time to be herself, no time to follow her own dreams. Harry's had been so much larger than hers. So large that they eventually blotted out hers completely.

Now, standing within room number nine, gazing up at the wild, vivid colors that JMW Turner had splashed on the canvas over a century ago, she was back. She was home. Her breath was almost snatched away by the beauty of *Snow Storm: Hannibal and his Army crossing the Alps*. The pending snow storm looked like a giant wave about to dash over the army.

"Do you know," she said, words crowding back into her head, thoughts, themes, colors, all vying for a spotlight, "that when Turner painted *The Slave Ship*, he had himself lashed to a ship so that he could experience the feel of the water, the terror of the sea before he painted it? He had to feel it in order to have it flow from his fingers."

Tommy liked seeing the paintings through her eyes. She was drinking all this in like a parched woman who was finally allowed to sip life-giving water. "Sounds like a man who lived life to the fullest."

"Yes." There was envy in her voice as she said it and they both heard it.

"It's never too late, Johanna," Tommy said softly.

She turned and looked up into his eyes, seeing a hundred different messages, all meant for her. "No, I guess it's not."

The man who stood a few feet away from them, jotting things down in his notebook, stopped writing.

That voice.

Was it her?

It had been fifteen years since he had last heard her speak, and yet, he was sure it was her. He looked around, tracing the source. There were several women in the immediate area and the gallery was far from hushed. Maybe he'd imagined it. Maybe—

And then he saw her, standing before the Turner painting, talking to a handsome looking man. She appeared to be with him. A spark of envy, dormant and old, filtered over him.

This was ridiculous. It was probably just someone who sounded like her. And looked like her. A bit thinner, paler, but—

It had to be her.

"Johanna?"

Another voice, deeply masculine and slightly unsure, intruded into the small world that she had spun only for a moment. She turned, vaguely recognizing the voice, wondering if another one of Harry's hangers-on had surfaced. But no one she knew would ever find time for an art gallery. It wasn't the proper place to arrange a seduction.

She turned from Tommy, still feeling a little shaken at what she saw within his eyes, shaken and frightened, wanting to reach out yet telling herself not to.

"Yes?" At first, she didn't see who was addressing her.

"Johanna Lindsey, is that you?"

She blinked, refocused and really looked at the man who called her by her maiden name. "Yes, but I—" She was about to deny any knowledge of the man before her when she stopped.

"Joshua?" she cried. "Joshua MacKenzie?" Johanna's eyes

opened wide. Delight, surprise and confusion all registered on her face at once.

Both men thought that they had never seen such a truly desirable woman in their lives.

She took both of Joshua's hands in hers and allowed herself to stare in fascination for a moment. The man who had called out to her was tall, though not as tall as Tommy, and just as casually dressed, although his hair was neater but only a little shorter.

"My God, the last time I saw you, you had long hair—"

"The suffering artist," he filled in, grinning, absolutely amazed that he should see her here after all these years. Amazed and delighted.

So many memories came crowding back into her mind. Joshua had been her friend and confidante in the days when she had dreamed of being an artist. They had attended college together. "And a lot less clothes on."

"Ouch." He pretended to wince. "My days of modeling to get by. You would remind me of that."

"Oh, I'm sorry." She turned to Tommy, suddenly realizing how rude she must have sounded. "Tommy Reed, this is a very old friend of mine, Joshua Mackenzie. Joshua and I went to school together."

The two men shook hands, nodding at one another. Within moments, they had sized one another up and decided that they liked what they saw.

"What are you *doing* here?" Johanna asked.

"I'm on a little buying trip. I own a gallery in Soho."

"London?"

"New York," he corrected.

"What about your painting career?"

"I decided that eating was a habit that was hard to give up. I'm on the other side of the easel now. Here." He dug into his pocket. "Here's my card. If you're ever in the area, I'd love to spring for a cup of coffee."

Johanna tucked the card into her purse. "Will you be staying in London long?"

He shook his head. "My last night."

"Oh." She felt a twinge of disappointment. "Are you free for lunch?"

He had someone to meet, but that could be postponed with a phone call until later. "At your service."

Johanna turned to Tommy hopefully. It had been so long since she had seen Joshua and there were of many things to catch up on. "Tommy, would you mind if we made it a threesome?

"Not at all. This way I can find out the truth about your past without prying." Tommy laughed easily.

"It may be a long lunch," Joshua promised Tommy. "C'mon, it's my treat."

With Johanna between them, they went to the gallery's restaurant.

Chapter Twenty

"**And he** proposed a day in the country?" Mary's voice went up an octave and swelled until it filled the suite. Her deep pleasure was evident in her expression as well as in her voice. But she detected a pensive look on Johanna's face. "Well, I don't see what the problem is. Go. I'll stay here with Jocelyn."

Johanna hadn't been able to sit still. She fiddled with the drapes, rearranged the throw pillows, moved a small pile of magazines from one side of the coffee table to another. Nothing seemed quite right. Like it didn't fit. Like she didn't fit. "The problem is I'm still a married woman."

Mary held up a hand to stop her before she went any further. "Jo, you're a mistreated, about-to-be-divorced woman," she reminded Johanna. "Stop this nonsense and go out and have some fun. You don't have to go to bed with him, although," a sexy smile slid over her lips, "that wouldn't be such a terrible thing from where I sit."

Everything that Mary said was true. Johanna knew it far

better than she did. She had lived through it. Maybe she was just using her status as an excuse. No, there was no maybe about it. The truth was that she was afraid, Johanna thought. Afraid of testing waters again, afraid of what she might find, or not find within herself.

"Besides, the glimpse I caught of the two of you when he left you at the door, well, I'd say you were doing pretty well for yourself."

Johanna knew that Mary was referring to the fact that Tommy had given her a simple kiss yesterday. No, it hadn't been a simple kiss, not for her. It had been a reinitiation into the rites of womanhood. She hadn't expected it, but something within her had hoped, had yearned for it to become reality. And when he had kissed her, it was light and sweet and wonderful. She still felt the gentle touch of his mouth on hers even as she sat here, talking to Mary. Yet she felt a need to deny what Mary was so obviously thinking. If she denied it, maybe nothing would happen. She wouldn't have to put her feelings on the line again.

The kiss had made her feel alive, feminine, desirable again. All the things Harry no longer did for her. Yet she was afraid of where this would lead. Actually, she was afraid of what it meant. It signalled the beginning of a new life for her. This was what it meant to be a single woman again. Still, as much as she wanted it, she felt anxious. It had been so good with Harry in the beginning. Why did that have to change? Why had *he* had to change?

What she had was a kiss from a stranger tantalizing her, making her want things. Maybe it was just deprivation speaking.

She wanted what she once had: Harry, a family, a home. She couldn't let go so easily. Yet she knew she had to. Not to grow was to whither and die. And that was what she had been doing, living with Harry. *Existing* with Harry. She had been dying. Tommy represented the future, one single step beyond where she had been.

She didn't know if she was more afraid to take that step

or not to take it. She saw Mary looking at her and realized that she had let the conversation lapse. "We're only going to spend a day in the country."

Mary raised her eyebrows and let just a hint of a smile grace her lips. "Lots of things can happen when you get back to nature."

Johanna pulled the curtain cord through her hand so hard that it stung her palm. "But not to me." She let the cord drop.

Mary leaned back on the sofa, her arms outstretched easily on either side of her. She turned her head slightly to watch her pace. "Why not you?"

Why not me? Johanna didn't want to say those were the same thoughts that were racing through her head, had been racing through them ever since Tommy linked his hand with hers and drew her out the door yesterday afternoon. "Because," she answered in frustration.

"You're going to have to come up with a better explanation than that, Jo."

She flopped down on the sofa next to her. "I don't need to come up with an explanation. I'm tired of explaining things." Mainly to myself.

"No," Mary agreed, nodding her head slowly. "You don't need to explain. You just need your head examined if you don't go."

She wanted to. Oh, she really wanted to. Her mouth softened. "You really think I should?"

Leaning over, Mary patted her hand. "Trust me on this one. And Jo."

"What?"

"Let yourself go for once."

"Go?" There was a hitch in her voice. Nerves. "Just how do you mean that?"

"Just that. Go." Mary gestured with her palms upward. "Like no one's looking over your shoulder or judging you—least of all, you."

"You know me, don't you?"

"Only too well, big sister." Mary rose and kissed Johanna's temple. "Only too well. Now it's all settled and I won't take no for an answer. You're going."

With that, Mary sauntered off to make plans for the following day with her niece. She moved with grace and ease, fluidly, as if her limbs were loosely jointed. Johanna had always envied her that grace.

Alone in the room, Johanna sat and played with the telephone, picking up the receiver and then putting it down again several times before she finally made the call to Tommy.

When a deep voice answered on the third ring, she almost hung up, then berated herself silently. Summoning courage, she asked for Tommy. Her voice cracked on the second syllable of his name. She licked her lips nervously. Her mouth felt like dust.

" 'ey, Tom, it's for you," the man called out.

Several seconds later, Johanna heard another voice, a more familiar one. "Hello?"

Now or never, Joey. "Never" seemed tempting, but then she'd have to face Mary and that wasn't tempting in the least. "Tommy, it's Johanna. I didn't want to interrupt, if you have company—"

"Company? Oh no, that's just me dad. He's staying with me for a bit. Hurt his leg he did. He likes the company of having someone around to clear his table for him."

She could tell by the smile in his voice that the relationship which existed between father and son was one of mutual love and respect. It gave her courage to go on instead of making some inane excuse for calling and hanging up.

"I, um," she hesitated. She couldn't help it, it seemed so forward of her to be calling him. She knew it wasn't the least bit sophisticated of her, but she had forgotten how to go about this sort of thing. It had been fifteen years since she had thought of herself as unattached.

Maybe she should have waited until he called and asked. But he had already asked twice before their day was up at the gallery. Once when they had gazed upon the pastoral scenes by Monet right after Joshua had left them and once at her door. It surprised her how clearly she remembered every single detail of the afternoon they had spent together. Of all the times they had spent together, she realized.

He sensed her discomfort and tried to make it easier for her. "Have you decided to come with me tomorrow?" There was enough boyishness in him to make his voice sound hopeful. "I'd love for you to come, Johanna. It's so different, so peaceful out there. I'd like to share it with you. And having someone along'll take the edge off a long drive."

"Put that way, I guess I can't say no."

"Good. I'll pick you up at seven."

"Seven?" She could just see Mary's face if someone had ever dared to ask to see her at seven in the morning. Mary only approached seven a.m. from the opposite direction, if she had been out all night. Rising that early was against her religion.

"I know it's rather early. But the Foggertys live a bit of a ways out, I'm afraid. On the bright side, once I deliver the chest of drawers, we'll get to spend the best part of the day in the country."

"Shall I pack a lunch?"

"That would be valor above and beyond the call of duty."

"You don't know what I plan to pack."

He laughed and so did she, just at the sound of his voice. And when she finally hung up half an hour later, she felt light-hearted, like a girl looking forward to a date with a beau.

But it wasn't a date, she told herself silently as she rose. It was just . . . Just.

She let it float away at that.

The countryside as they drove on the road from Cirencester into the Cotswolds was exactly as Tommy had described it: beautiful, breathtaking. Soft and lush and green. He told her that the rolling range of fertile hills used to host the most lucrative sheep farming in the world. Today, centuries later, these hills that stretched diagonally from the southeast to the northwest across Gloustershire were known for their quaint air of the past. The villages were all strictly one-street affairs built around a church or an inn or three. And always there were delightful, tiny shops nestled amid the distinctive beige limestone buildings. Tommy stopped the van in narrow streets several times so that she could stop and enjoy the beautiful simplicity of life that existed here.

She remembered Arlene's comment about wanting to run off to the Cotswolds with the leading man in Harry's movie. What would Arlene have said if she saw her now, riding off into the country with Tommy? Johanna had seen the look of lustful approval in the older woman's eyes when she had come upon them eating at the cafe.

"What are you smiling about?"

His question startled her and she did her best to appear calm. Her nerves felt as if they were close to the surface. Waiting. "Oh, I'm just remembering what someone once said to me about the Cotswold countryside."

"What was that?"

Fortunately, she remembered what else it was that Arlene had said about the Cotswolds. "That this was the country God had made when He was practicing to create Ireland."

Even as she was saying it, she suddenly wondered how Tommy would take the comparison. Many people were chauvinistic about the land they called home.

Tommy laughed quietly. "I take it your friend was Irish."

"Yes."

"They tend to exaggerate a bit, but there's no disputing the fact that it is beautiful." He looked around as he drove. "There's a lot of history that's happened here," he told her. "The cathedral contains the remains of Edward II. He was murdered in Berkeley Castle a few centuries ago."

Johanna shivered and ran her hands up and down her arms. "I'm not much on remains."

"Then we won't go." He grinned, amused. "Once I deliver this chest of drawers, would you like to pick somewhere for a picnic?"

"I'd love to." And she meant it. There had been a dozen spots that they had passed on their way that would be more than perfect for a picnic. The enthusiasm she felt was something new and exhilarating and she was eternally grateful to Tommy for generating it. The countryside was ideal for a picnic. It made her feel terribly romantic to think that she would be picnicking in a spot where once English courtiers had done the very same thing some three hundred years ago.

They drove down a long winding road until they reached a house that, to Johanna, gave new meaning to the word "cottage."

"This is adorable," Johanna whispered to Tommy.

He helped her down from the van. "Aye, that's a word for it, I suppose."

He confused her, but he did make her feel the way she had when she was nineteen and seeing the world through eyes that were innocent and eager.

Taking his hand, she stepped down and walked with him to the door. Tommy rapped gently.

The old couple who responded to Tommy's knock must have had a hundred and fifty years between them at the least. Rather than treat her as a stranger, they were enthusiastic that Tommy had brought them company.

"Sit down, sit down," the woman urged, gesturing to a chair in the kitchen. Warmth came from the hearth and Johanna felt instantly at home. "So nice of you to bring me a lady to gossip with, Tommy."

Johanna noted that the old couple held hands as they spoke. And when Mrs. Foggerty smiled, her wrinkles seemed to fade until Johanna hardly noticed them.

Love did that, Johanna thought with a pang. Love made you happy and young. She envied the couple. This was what she had once believed was in store for her when she married Harry. To grow old loving the same man, sharing the same dreams, the same joys, the way the Foggertys now shared the joy of owning the finely carved chest of drawers that Tommy delivered to them.

"Please, won't you stay for tea?" Mrs. Foggerty asked. And, without waiting for an answer, she retreated to the stove and began to brew a pot.

"Can't argue with Martha," Mr. Foggerty said. "She gets something set in her mind and there's no talking her out of it." He was a sparse little man, slightly stoop-shouldered from age, but a perfect match for his rose-cheeked wife. They seemed to look alike in the fashion of people who have spent a lifetime together. Crossing his legs, he seemed little more than thin bones held together with skin. But lively. Johanna saw it in his eyes, in his expression. His life might have been hard, but he savored his pleasures well.

They were the most unique couple, the most enchanting couple she had ever met.

"Would you mind if I sketched you?" The question surprised Johanna almost as much as it did the Foggertys. It had been years since she had felt the urge to sketch, to paint, to commit something to paper. She felt it now and was almost giddy from the sensation.

Mrs. Foggerty put her hand to her short fluffy white hair automatically. "Well, my dear, I don't know. I must look like a sight." She looked down at the apron she wore. It was creased and wrinkled. "Maybe if I changed—"

"Oh no, please." In her agitation, Johanna half rose in her chair. "You're perfect just the way you are."

"See, Martha, what've I been telling you all these years?" Foggerty laughed and drew on his pipe, trying to get it going.

"Nathaniel, hush."

Johanna could have sworn the old woman blushed. It both pleased her and tugged at her heart. Inexplicably, she felt tears gathering and felt like a fool. Drawing a deep breath, she managed to hold them at bay.

"If you have some paper and a pencil, I'd be very grateful. I—I didn't bring my materials with me."

There was no point in telling these nice people she hadn't held art supplies in her hands in over ten years. The last sketch she had drawn had been of Jocelyn as she had slept in her crib.

"Why yes, of course." Mrs. Foggerty hurried off to bring Johanna what she requested.

Johanna saw Tommy looking at her quietly. "You don't mind, do you?" she asked Tommy.

He merely smiled and shrugged expansively. "We've got the whole day. I'd like to see your handiwork. After all, it's only fair, I've shown you mine."

Johanna's eyes were drawn to the chest of drawers that he had brought in from the back of the van. Temporarily, it reposed in the kitchen until Mrs. Foggerty made up her mind which bedroom it would grace. It seemed to gleam in the corner of the room, lighting it up. It would have been a beautiful addition to any home. And Tommy had fashioned it from raw materials. He was as much of an artist in his right as she was in hers. Perhaps more, she thought.

"Don't expect too much," she told him, suddenly feeling shy. "I'm rusty. Thank you." She accepted the pencil and pad from Mrs. Foggerty.

But as Tommy watched quietly, Johanna's hand moved quickly and confidently over the empty paper, filling it with lines and shadows that became the Foggertys. More than their faces, she captured their souls, the love that shimmered between them now more strongly than it had fifty years ago, when they had first taken their vows.

"Well, if that's 'rusty' I look forward to seeing what you can do once you improve," Tommy said in admiration, taking the finished sketch from her.

"My, my, do I look that good?" Mrs. Foggerty asked, pleased, as she peered at the sketch over Tommy's shoulder.

"I sketch what I see," Johanna told her. The two women exchanged knowing looks that spoke volumes to each other. One had love, one yearned for it, yet felt she would never have it.

"I wish the same for you and your young man," Mrs. Foggerty said quietly.

Tommy saw the color rise to Johanna's cheeks. "I think we'd better be leaving now," he told the old couple, rescuing her. "We've a long way to go before we reach the city." He glanced out the window. "And it's beginning to look like rain."

So much for the picnic, Johanna thought. Perhaps it was just as well. She was feeling very vulnerable at the moment, meeting the Foggertys, finding her love of sketching once again.

"Oh, when isn't it?" Mrs. Foggerty lamented.

On impulse, Johanna pressed the sketch into the woman's wrinkled hands. "For you."

Mrs. Foggerty held the pencil sketch as if it were something very precious. She beamed down at it. "Oh, my dear, I don't know what to say."

Johanna patted the woman's hand. "Just enjoy it. I want you to have it. And thank you for letting me sketch you. It means more to me than you'll ever know."

"Ready?" Tommy asked, already on his feet.

"Ready."

They said their farewells and hurried to the van.

"That was very nice of you," Tommy said.

She shrugged, trying to appear careless about it. In truth, she felt her heart hammering. It was as if she had taken a giant step forward in her life. "It was an excellent cup of tea."

Tommy laughed.

Johanna turned and waved at the old couple as they stood, huddled beneath the eaves, waving.

The first rumble of thunder came as they drove away from the cottage.

Chapter Twenty-one

Did it bother you?"

She turned to look at him. The sky beyond the van was turning a deep, murky gray, a forewarning of the coming storm. She wondered if they'd make it back to the hotel in time. She felt uneasy about driving on these narrow country roads in the rain. To the left, far below the winding road, the river churned and lapped, its restless waves reaching toward the sky and the dark pregnant clouds that loomed there. One aspect of nature communing with another.

"Did what bother me?"

"When Mrs. Foggerty called me your young man."

Johanna looked down at her hands and shrugged, feeling a little uncomfortable. "I thought it might bother you . . ." her voice trailed off. Nerves began to rise within her, nudging, urging.

"It didn't. It doesn't."

She looked up at him, surprised. The promise she had detected in his voice once or twice before was there again.

But the promise of what? What was it he was offering her? And what was it she wanted? She wasn't sure she knew any more. But she did know she liked being with him, liked sharing the afternoon. It made her feel young, carefree. Happy. Did anyone have a right to ask for more than this?

"I'm older than you are, Tommy," she said quietly.

Her voice was barely audible. He regretted the question. She looked awkward. He should learn to think a bit more before speaking, he chastised himself. Yet he felt so comfortable with her that he didn't really feel the need to edit his words. "A couple of years don't mean very much." He turned his headlights on as the road grew darker still.

"I'm thirty-four, Tommy."

It was only a number. And it didn't fit her. "And I'm twenty-nine."

"Five years." She breathed the words out as if they were a death sentence to anything that might have been between them.

The van felt small, cozy. The light scent that she always wore filled every crevice, filled his head, his very pores. "Only makes a difference if I were two and you seven."

She laughed softly. "You're hard to resist, you know that?"

Tommy pulled the van over to the side of the road. The thunder rumbled ominously overhead as he touched her cheek gently, running his thumb along the soft hollow. His touch felt soft, so unbearably soft. Her eyes all but fluttered shut.

"Then don't try."

He breathed the words against her cheek just before he lowered his mouth to hers. Cupping the back of her head with his hand, he drew her closer.

She wasn't certain how this moment had come into being, only that it was there. When his lips touched hers, a hungry need exploded within her. The hesitation she felt was only for a moment, and then it was gone as if it never existed. Johanna wound her fingers into his hair, holding him close, drifting miles away from earth. With a mindless passion that she hadn't realized lived within her, she lost herself in the heat of his mouth as it slanted over hers.

His mouth was hard and tasted of male things that made her head swim. She held on to steady herself. When he drew back, she moaned, not wanting it to end. And then he leaned his forehead against hers as they both tried to steady their breathing.

"See? No difference at all, luv," he murmured.

With the imprint of his lips still warm on hers, she tried to back away, to cling to reality and things she knew demanded a set course of behavior. "Tommy, I really shouldn't."

"Why?" It wasn't an impatient statement. He just wanted to know. He wanted *her* to know. If there were reasons, justifiable reasons, he would back off. But he didn't think there were. His eyes held hers as he watched her search for an answer.

"I don't know." Her mind was blank. Only the need existed. The need to be held, to be cherished. To be wanted. "There were reasons, I know there were, but I just can't seem to think of them." As she spoke, as she struggled to form words, he feathered kisses along her temple and the side of her face.

"Then don't, Johanna," he urged. He took her hands in his, protecting her, drawing her to him. "Don't. Let me love you the way you were meant to be loved."

He saw the look in her eyes when they opened again, saw the fear warring with desire. She was so vulnerable, so achingly tempting. He held her hand in his and it felt small. He drew it to his lips and kissed it.

"Come," he whispered.

And she did.

She followed him to the back of the van as rain began to pelt the sides of the vehicle, echoing all around them on the lonely road. They were completely alone.

They could be the last people on earth, she thought as

she knelt down beside him on the carpeted floor. It was a soft brown, like his eyes.

"I won't hurt you, Johanna," he promised as he pressed a kiss to her shoulder. The cloth that was there burned away at his slightest touch. She felt his fingers working free the buttons of her blouse and then he was gently pushing it from her shoulders. With that single action, he stripped her soul, uncovering something very raw, very basic beneath the surface.

She could feel his body pressed against hers, his needs hard and warm and wanting. She could feel herself melting. The throbbing within her that had started earlier continued, more urgent than before. If something didn't happen soon, she was certain that she was going to explode. Yet it couldn't, dear God, she was a married woman.

"Tommy."

He heard the protest, the pain, the pleading within her voice and knew she was asking for help. She needed him to help her over this obstacle that still held her fast. He lifted his head and looked into her eyes. "Shhh." He pressed his finger to her lips. "It's all right, Johanna. It's all right."

How could hands so large be so gentle? He had worked her breasts free of her bra and was cupping the sensitive skin with his palms. She gasped, loving what was happening, yet afraid to give in totally.

"Tommy, it's not safe," she whispered, trembling against him. She wanted him to assure her that it was, that what they were doing here and now was right. That it hadn't the taint of shame to it. If he didn't make love to her soon, she was going to be utterly consumed by this horrible hunger she felt.

He gave her no empty assurances. For two people to allow their feelings to be tangled together this way was never completely safe.

"I know." He kissed the hollow of her throat. Her skin tingled, burned. All of her was instantly on fire. "You don't want to be safe anymore, do you?" The words danced along the slope of her neck, seductive, wanton. To be safe meant to retreat completely from life.

He knew, somehow, he knew. He was everything she wanted. Everything she needed at this moment. There were no strings, no tomorrows, no plans. No traps and no pain either. He just wanted to make love to her.

And she needed him.

She wanted to see his eyes, but there was little illumination within the interior of the van. The storm had wiped out the sun and left them in shades of darkness. It made the whole encounter seem that much more unreal, that much more forbiddingly wonderful. Somewhere in the distance, beyond the van, thunder rolled and lightning flashed, just as it had done time and again since the beginning. Just as it would until the end.

"No." The words escaped her lips in a breathy rush. "I don't want to be safe." And then she felt his lips cover hers, his tongue seeking out the boundaries of her mouth taking possession of all of her with a single thrust. Hungrily, she met his tongue with her own, touching, tasting, savoring. And growing more and more inflamed.

This wasn't a soft, dreamy thing. Not anymore. This was fast and real and hard. Just as he was. The bold outline of his desire pushed against her, heightening her excitement to a fever pitch. She wanted him here, now, before she had to scream out with her need.

She tugged at his shirt, pulling at it until the buttons were freed from their holes. She pushed it urgently off his shoulders, needing to touch him, to feel his warm skin beneath her fingers, to explore all that was him.

She didn't recognize herself. Had this wild passion always been there, just beneath the surface? She didn't know. She didn't care.

His hands were everywhere, stroking, taking and making her feel as if she had never been touched before. And she hadn't. Not like this. Not even that faraway first time with Harry.

"You were meant to be touched," he whispered against her ear just before he traced it with the tip of his tongue.

Johanna shivered. A moan escaped from low in her throat as his hands went underneath her skirt. There was no groping, no clumsiness. The target assured, the aim true. He was not a boy feeling his way around, but a man made to love her. Her short gasps filled the air as Tommy worked his fingers beneath the scrap of nylon, stroking, probing, touching. Possessing.

She grabbed hold of his shoulders to steady herself, afraid that she'd cry out. There was no one to hear them if she had. She buried her head against his shoulder, but one wild peak shuddered her body and she threw back her head in mounting delirium.

"Tommy, please." She wasn't certain if she was asking for him to please stop, or please go faster.

He understood her meaning far better than she. "Not yet. Not just yet."

Johanna rocked against his body, totally divorced from whoever it was that she had been when she had first met him this morning. Now she was a woman who needed to go forward, a woman who craved to go beyond the perimeters she had been so sure were permanently set within her.

Her blouse had been peeled away, exposing her firm breasts and Tommy ran his tongue over them, cradling her to his body with one hand while he gently stroked her center of femininity with the other.

She wanted to tear the rest of his clothes from his body, wanted to feel him, all of him, against her. With impatience fueling her every movement, Johanna tugged at his belt, pulling it free.

She couldn't catch her breath.

This is crazy she thought. I shouldn't be doing this. I should be back at the hotel, safe, writing letters to people, making plans.

She wanted to be here.

The only thing that existed at this moment was this aching, wondrous sensation spiraling within her body that she would have died for.

Johanna pushed his belt aside and almost broke the zipper on his jeans as she jerked it down. She heard Tommy's deep, throaty chuckle and felt it ripple along her skin.

"Easy, luv. Easy," he whispered against her skin, only managing to fan the fire rather than to smother it. "Here." He guided her hand down inside the waistband of his briefs. She was eager to comply, eager to push forward their union. Eager to touch him.

He sucked in his breath as her fingers found him. This time, the moan was his and she saw the look of vulnerability in his eyes as her hand closed. It only served to heighten her passion.

With a heady triumph, she saw his eyes half close as she moved her fingers in the same increasing rhythm that he was using on her. She wanted to excite him the way he did her. Their mutual fervor fueled the growing inferno.

And then, in an instant, he gently pushed her to the floor. He lowered his mouth to her belly, his tongue tracing a hot, moist path downward as she jerked and moved beneath his. Spasms shook her. The strokes became harder, more sweeping, his tongue plunging deeper. Johanna bit her lip hard.

With a surge of desire, Tommy deftly pulled her panties off. And then his body was over hers, his face hovering just above her own.

His eyes didn't close as he entered her. He watched her face. He wanted to memorize it, to keep this moment with him forever.

It was gentle. It was fast and furious. It was all things. A rollercoaster that took her on a ride of deep, plunging curves filled with exquisite agony. Again and again, until there was nothing left of her.

Reaching out, Johanna pulled his head down to her,

wanting his mouth on hers, wanting to bury the scream that was rising within her throat.

One explosion after another racked her body and still the pleasure continued. The ride went on. She wanted to cry, "Stop!"

She wanted it to go on until she died.

When he finally stopped, sated, neither one of them could move. Not if it meant their very lives. Not if the van was on fire.

She had had a fire of her own just now and the revelation it presented to her about herself left Johanna in awe, numb.

And grateful.

Chapter Twenty-two

Tommy had showed her the world. In the circle of his arms, within a dark, secluded van, he gave her back her self-esteem and her pride. More than that, he brought her back to life. All these last months with Harry, she began to realize now that, subconsciously, she had thought it was somehow her fault, that she was undesirable. That whatever was wrong it was because there was something missing, something lacking within her. And all the while it had been Harry. It had really been Harry. Tommy proved that to her, silently, with tenderness and a fire that only the passion of the caring could create.

Johanna lay in his arms, listening to the rhythm of the rain as it beat a timeless tune on the roof. The storm had passed and now there was only the gentle rain. Gentle and steady. Johanna felt contented, alert, yet drowsy. Wonderful. She wished, just for a moment, that time could stand still.

Tommy kissed her shoulder tenderly. "Still feel too old for me?"

With her cheek on his chest, Johanna could feel the question vibrate against her skin. She raised her head, her hair cascading down around her. "No." She smiled, tracing his lips with her fingertip.

He took her hand and kissed her outstretched finger. Johanna felt a tightening in her stomach. The renewed desire, hot and urgent, astounded her. "You were incredible, Johanna."

"Funny, I was going to say the same thing about you." She rolled over on her stomach, propped her head up on her upturned hand and looked at him. Her hair fell forward like a silken curtain on either side of her face, ends just brushing against her breasts, tempting him. "You're still Ivanhoe."

"How so?" Tommy reached out and ran his hand through her hair. Even in the dim light, it sifted through his fingers like spun gold.

"You're still doing good deeds for damsels in distress."

Was that what she thought, he wondered. That this was just some act of kindness on his part? "This was no selfless good deed, Johanna." Lightly, he ran his fingers along the hollow of her cheek, watching the pulse in her throat jump. "I think I wanted you the first moment I threw your body so unceremoniously against a wall."

Johanna stirred, unable to shut out what he was doing, how much he was affecting her. "And saved me from getting crushed."

"Saved you for myself," he corrected. He dropped a kiss on her lips. "I didn't know then that you were the boss's wife."

"If you'd known, would you have been as quick?" Her eyes teased him.

He gathered her closer to him, bringing her to his chest. Johanna rested her head against the hard muscles there, her hair fanning out and tickling him. Tommy played with the ends of her hair. Like pure gold, he thought. The word pure seemed to fit very well.

"Just as quick. You're too beautiful a woman to waste even if you belonged to someone else." Johanna caught the emphasis on the word "belonged." "Just looking at you would have been reward enough for me." Then he grinned, boyishly, with a gleam in his eyes. "Of course, this has a lot to speak for it." He raised her head until their eyes met and he kissed her.

She sighed contentedly. "We can't stay this way." Even as she said it, she wished it wasn't true.

"No," he sighed. "I suppose not."

"I promised I'd be home tonight."

He nodded. "Jocelyn."

"Yes, Jocelyn."

He sat up. Her hand glided down the rippling muscles of his chest, resting lightly there. He bent his head and kissed her again. "Then I'd better make love to you quickly this time."

She laughed, delighted, as he pulled her on top of him and then covered her mouth with his own.

Mary turned her head at the sound of Johanna's key in the lock. She was curled up on the sofa, dressed in a white silk lounging outfit and barefoot. Her small, delicate feet sported nail polish that was blood red. It matched the polish on her fingers. She and Jocelyn were nursing twin cups of hot chocolate despite the fact that it was the latter part of August. The hotel air-conditioning system was doing its part to make the evening bearable. Mary's green eyes took in everything, gliding over Tommy with approval and coming to rest on Johanna's glowing appearance.

Johanna was different. She knew it, felt it. Mary saw the change instantly. And even Jocelyn felt that something was different without understanding what or why. Johanna was lighter, more confident. Happier. It was in her eyes, her walk, her manner. Every fiber of her being had undergone a metamorphosis.

"Well, I don't think Pop's got anything to worry about anymore." Mary nodded, pleased. "You always manage to land on your feet, Jo, no matter what. C'mon, kid." She rose slowly, unconsciously stretching her body. "Let's continue talking girl talk in my room." Mary put out an arm and waited for Jocelyn to join her.

Tommy held up his hand. "Please, don't leave on my account."

"Handsome, on your account I would stay, but what we've got to talk about is strictly for female ears." Mary winked at Tommy and walked off with Jocelyn. The girl looked rather reluctant to leave.

"I like your sister." Tommy kissed Johanna lightly and put his hands on her waist. It was clear that Mary was already forgotten.

"Me too." Johanna rested her hands on his arms. She liked touching his forearms. They felt so strong, so capable, as if he could handle anything. He probably could at that, she mused.

"Soon I'd like to show you some more of my work," he told her.

Sharing this with him was touching and intimate. "I'd love to see it."

He leaned his forehead against hers and breathed in her fragrance. "Tomorrow?"

Mary would still be here tomorrow. There'd be someone to care for Jocelyn, to keep her daughter from feeling as if she were being deserted. Mentally, Johanna blessed her sister and the father who had sent her. "Tomorrow," Johanna echoed.

Tommy kissed her again before he left. Johanna savored it and every shred of the day that had gone by.

"So?" Mary asked late that night as they shared a cup of coffee together. Jocelyn had long since fallen asleep, but

Johanna had remained up in more ways than one. It didn't take a genius to know why.

"So?" Johanna questioned, her mind immediately latching on the one topic that had possessed her since she had returned home. She felt her cheeks burn, but purposely pretended ignorance on the hundred to one shot that Mary was referring to something else.

"Did you?" There was only a hint of impatience in Mary's voice.

"Did I what?" She raised her cup and drank, though there was only a drop of cold coffee left to linger over. She was stalling.

Mary set down her cup. "You did," she said with a self-satisfied grin. "Otherwise you wouldn't be talking in circles."

Johanna shifted uncomfortably. Though what she had done was wonderful, *felt* wonderful, she still wasn't comfortable about the way it might seem to others. "Mary, I don't know—"

"Ah, but I do. I know you like a book, big sister." She rose. "Don't worry, there aren't fifteen puritanical seamstresses rushing off to their machines to sew a big red 'A' on your designer clothes." Mary placed a hand on Johanna's shoulder and leaned over to kiss her cheek. "Personally, I think it's wonderful. Welcome back to life."

Johanna relaxed a little. "Is it that evident?"

Mary nodded. "Yup. You're smiling again. *Really* smiling, from the inside out. That's pretty terrific in my book. 'Night."

Johanna watched as her sister walked out of the room. She ran her fingers along her mouth. The smile was still there. And it did indeed feel wonderful.

Mary whisked Jocelyn away to a matinee at the theater and an early dinner afterward, purposely leaving the day free for Johanna. Johanna had never been more grateful to her sister than she was these last few days. She knew that her idyllic time would end very soon. Not just because Mary would go back to the States. Johanna understood that what was between Tommy and her was temporary. Beautiful, breathtaking, but temporary. They existed in two different worlds separated by an ocean and by a culture that neither would have wanted to give up for the other. It was not spoken, but it was understood.

And for the time being, for a few wonderful weeks in August, they belonged together.

Tommy brought her to his home, a tiny apartment on the first floor of a house in the center of the small town of Camden, full of stone walls and green lawns. The cobblestoned streets were alive with children and mingling, chatting people. In a funny way, teeming with life the way it was, it took her back to New York where she had once been happiest. There too she had felt the same free spirit vibrating in her and in the environment. It amused her to think how happy she managed to be in places that others might turn their noses up at.

She met his father, Stewart, a proud, handsome man in his fifties who made her forget that he was hobbling around on crutches within a few minutes of his first comment. There was nothing about Stewart to feel sorry for. He was warm, witty and she imagined that Tommy would be just like him in another twenty-five years.

"Taught him all I know, that's why he's so good," Stewart Reed told her with an openly flirtatious wink that was as safe as if it had come from her own father.

They sat around a kitchen table, talking over a round of warm beers. She thought of ambrosia and knew that the word applied not only to the drink, but to the ambience around it. There had been few times in her life that had been as rich as this. Certainly she had never experienced it at the parties Harry forced her to attend. The people there had a caricature-like quality about them. She always had the impression that she would find something else if she scratched at the veneer they showed to the world. None of them were as interesting as Stewart was, none had ever held her attention as well as he and the stories he was telling her, even though she knew by the twinkle in the man's eye that they were exaggerations.

Tommy finally rose, linking his hand with Johanna's. "C'mon, luv, let me get you away from this old windbag."

"Windbag, am I?" Stewart cried, feigning indignation. "The lady fancies a man to talk to."

"With you she's only listening," Tommy pointed out. He placed his hand on the small of Johanna's back, guiding her away from the table. "I've brought her here to see my handiwork, not my sire."

"Of the two, I'd say I was more interesting."

"Yes, I know you would." Tommy grinned as he took her out of the room.

His workshop was a small room off the kitchen. Just before he opened the door, he kissed her. Johanna looked at him with puzzled eyes.

"That's for humoring my old man," Tommy said as he opened the door.

"I wasn't aware that I was doing anything of the kind. I was being charmed right down to my shoes." Lightly, Johanna ran her hand through his wheat colored hair. It fell into his eyes, the way she found so endearing. "I see where you get it from."

Tommy grinned, pleased and embarrassed by her compliment. "Here, I wanted to show you these."

He took her hand and led her to a cradle made of ash, with roses carved into the headboard. It was lovingly polished by hand.

Johanna dropped to her knees and examined it slowly, in awe of the exquisite craftsmanship and the love that was displayed in every inch of the cradle. "It's beautiful," she said, looking up.

"No, it's good. You're beautiful."

He took her hands in his and raised her slowly to her feet. Her body brushed against his and electricity flashed again, as sure, as strong as the first time, but now she knew what was waiting for her and the urgency with which her body responded took her breath away. She wanted him here.

And then she looked over his shoulder. "Oh, what's that?"

He released her hand and turned to watch as she walked over to the window. Below the sill, catching the rays of the afternoon sun, was a hope chest he was almost finished with. It was something he was making for himself, something that he had had a need to work on.

Hesitantly, almost afraid to touch it, Johanna ran her hand over the delicate work. "It's exquisite, Tommy." She turned her face up to his. "Who's it for?" She thought of buying it, of outbidding the person it was intended for. It was so lovely, it almost made her heart ache. There was a pastoral scene carved into the lid. It reminded her of the Cotswolds. And them.

He was pleased that she liked it so much. "I'm making it for me." He crossed the room to join her. Of all the things he had made, he was proudest of this.

"Oh."

"You sound disappointed."

She was. If it was meant for him, then she wasn't free to ask if she could buy it. Not if it meant that much to him. "No, I thought that if you were making it for someone, I could offer you more money than they were paying you and buy it."

He shook his head. "It's not for sale, luv."

"No, I understand." And she did. When you put your heart into something, it was hard to part with it.

This time, when she rose, her face was upturned, waiting.

Tommy buried his hands in her hair. There was no testing of the waters this time. This time, they both knew what was waiting for them.

Johanna felt herself swimming away, leaving earth behind and linking her soul to his as she reached toward heaven. But embarrassment tethered her when she felt Tommy pulling down the zipper of her dress. She shivered, wanting him desperately. But she placed a warning hand to his chest.

"Tommy, your father—" The protest was only halfhearted.

He nuzzled her neck. His tongue made her skin quiver. The feeling shot straight through to her loins. "—Takes his nap about now and hears nothing."

Her heart was hammering hard in her ears. "Are you sure?"

"Positive."

She could feel his smile against her neck. "I knew I liked him."

"Yeah, me too."

Clothes were shed, time stood still, and love, so soft, so elusive, so fiery in its rarity, rose up once more between them, creating paradise as the sun shone on the hope chest and bathed the room in reverent hues while it set in the west.

Chapter Twenty-three

The hotel gym was nearly empty. Gleaming, state-of-the-art machines that could exercise and bring excruciating pain to just about every part of the human body stood dormant, like ill-tempered giants waiting to be awakened. For Mary's money they could go right on sleeping. She sat next to Johanna. Both were perched on stationary bicycles. Only one of them was pedaling.

"Mary, the only way to get anything out of this is to throw yourself into it." Johanna panted as she spoke. "A little sweat won't kill you." She wiped her own from her brow with the back of her hand as if to punctuate the statement.

"You sweat your way and I'll sweat mine." Mary's smile was wicked, as was the look in her eye. "Speaking of sweating, how's—Tommy, is it?"

"Yes, it's Tommy, as if you didn't have the name memorized." Johanna sounded casual, but the smile that lit her face up to a glow gave her away. "And he's fine."

Mary leaned forward on the bicycle, gripping the handlebars. But she made no effort to move the pedals. She simply rested her feet on them. "You two really seem to hit it off."

Johanna's mind wandered to that first afternoon in his van, momentarily distracting her from the mounting pain in her knee and the ache in her calves. "Right now, he's good for me, Mary."

"Right now," Mary echoed. "And how about in the future?"

Johanna shook her head a little too emphatically. "I don't make future plans anymore, not about men. I did that once and it almost killed me."

She shuddered as she remembered the scene in her bathroom, the running bath water, the razor in her hand, so close to her wrist, so close to permanently separating her from life.

Her reaction did not go unnoticed by Mary. She opened her mouth to ask Johanna what was wrong, then decided that if her sister wanted her to know, she'd tell her. There was something that flashed through her older sister's eyes which warned Mary to tread lightly here. Here was pain Johanna wasn't prepared to talk about yet. It took a long time for Johanna to open up about things that truly devastated her. The way it had taken Johanna years to finally admit that their mother had killed herself and hadn't just died.

"Sounds reasonable to me." Mary assumed a studied, careless pose. "I never make long range plans about men. There's always a more interesting one just around the next bend."

Johanna laughed, the serious moment gone. "What's the female equivalent of womanizer?"

"Manizer?" Mary arched a brow.

"I don't think so."

"Even if it were, it wouldn't apply." Mary tossed her head, her short silver blond hair dancing about her face before it settled back into place. "The term would mean I took advantage. I don't." She studied her nails and decided that she needed a manicure. Maybe she could take Jocelyn along and have them do her nails as well. The girl had bitten them down to the quick again. It was a habit that Jocelyn had developed since she last saw her. She'd have bitten her nails too if Harry had been her father, Mary thought. "I merely enjoy and know the limitations these frail creatures called men have."

Johanna glanced at the large clock that hung on the opposite wall. Five more minutes before she could stop this torture. "That sounds more like a man-hater."

"Oh, no way José." Mary shook her head again, this time with feeling. "Uh-uh, not me." She licked her lower lip and grinned.

Johanna wished she could be more like her sister. "You're the one dad should worry about, not me."

Mary waved her hand at the statement. "Me he gave up on a long time ago, dear sister. You were always his tower of strength. I was always his prodigal daughter, always coming home to the fatted calf after a mad fling." She grew thoughtfully silent for a moment, then posed prettily on the bicycle. It never hurt to be prepared. "He's your first, isn't he?"

Two more maddening minutes. "My first what?"

"Fling."

Johanna missed her rhythm and the bicycle wheel came to a squeaky halt. "I don't exactly think of it in those terms."

"Okay," Mary said gamely. "What term fits then?" Johanna, she knew, was never one to play word games with herself. Mary expected nothing less than honesty from her sister.

"It doesn't." Johanna paused, thinking. "But if it did, I guess the word healing would come to mind."

"He's a doctor?" She hadn't told her very much about Tommy. Sometimes, Johanna was too introverted for her own good.

"No, but he might as well be. He's healed me, Mary. He's made me feel whole." Johanna gave up pedaling altogether. She got off the bicycle and picked up a towel to dry herself with.

"Then why don't you go for it?"

Johanna stopped rubbing and stared at Mary. "Go for what?"

"The whole thing."

"Meaning?"

"Love, commitment. Set up housekeeping with Mr. Healer with the biceps to die for for as long as it feels right to you."

"I thought you didn't care for muscles," Johanna said, amused. At the same time, she was trying to evade her sister's suggestion.

Mary looked disdainfully at the exercise equipment as she slowly descended from her perch on top of the stationary bicycle. She really disliked regimented physical exercise. The only reason she had come along to the gym with Johanna was because she wanted to spend some time alone with her sister to talk things over.

"Just because I don't want any of my own doesn't mean I don't notice and admire them on gorgeous specimens of manhood." Mary narrowed her eyes. "And you are trying to dodge the question. Why don't you just move in with him and go on healing?"

"It's not as simple as that, Mary." Johanna avoided Mary's probing eyes, just as she was avoiding something within herself. "We're two different people."

Mary shrugged. "So? *Vive la différence.*"

Johanna draped the towel around her neck, holding on to the two ends, and sat down on a hard bench that ran along the length of the mirrored wall. "Maybe, but too much of a difference leads to problems eventually. He's wonderful, kind, sweet—"

"And as a lover?" Mary believed in getting to the heart of the matter. Johanna averted her face, but not soon enough. "You're blushing!" Mary cried, circling so that she could see Johanna's face. She sat down on her other side. Her sister's reaction delighted and surprised her at the same time. "My God, Johanna, you've been married for thirteen years and lived with Harry before that. How can you blush?"

Johanna looked over toward the stationary bicycle. "Exercise," she muttered.

"I'll bet, " Mary snorted, dismissing the flimsy excuse. "On a scale of one to ten?"

Johanna looked up and grinned. She couldn't help it. "Nineteen."

"And you're giving this up?" Mary clutched at her heart and pretended to fall backwards.

The smile faded as serious thoughts came into play. "It's not a matter of giving up."

"He has someone else?"

"No."

"You have someone else?"

"No."

Mary threw up her hands in exasperation. "Then what, for heaven's sake?"

"This is like a summer romance, Mary, an awakening. But fall is coming."

"So get warmer clothes. I'll mail you some." How could Johanna be giving up happiness after what she had been through with that slime? It didn't make any sense to Mary. Johanna was a woman who needed commitment as much as she needed air to breathe. That was the basic difference between them. Mary didn't.

Johanna shook her head. "You always did tend to oversimplify. I have to get on with my life, find out what I can do as a person, get a job—no," she amended fiercely, "get a career."

It still didn't make any sense to Mary. "Have you been sleeping with Frank Sinatra records? *I Gotta Be Me?*" she clarified when Johanna stared at her.

"No, but Frank has the right idea."

"He never had a guy like Tommy hanging around him."

"No, I imagine if he did, he'd have one of his bodyguards haul him away."

The two started to giggle and then laugh until Johanna held her sides, laughing helplessly and nearly falling off the bench.

"God, it's good seeing you again." Johanna wiped the tears away from her eyes. "I've forgotten what it's like to laugh this way. To feel this way."

"Welcome back to the real world, Johanna." Mary squeezed her shoulder affectionately. "You've been gone much too long."

"Yes," Johanna agreed, "yes, I have." She rose to her feet and looked down at Mary, who hadn't moved a muscle. "Do you want to do a few laps in the pool?"

"No, but I'll float while you lap."

"Ever the athlete."

Unfazed, Mary got to her feet. "I told you, I save myself for other indoor sports."

The door to the gym opened and closed, echoing in the large hall. They both turned and saw Jocelyn walking in quickly. Mary gestured for her niece to come over, calling out, "Over here, kid. I thought you were visiting your friend in the next suite."

Jocelyn crossed to them quickly. It was Mary who she joined, looking relieved to see her aunt. She cast nervous eyes toward her mother and Johanna instantly knew that something was wrong and it wasn't going to be an easy matter to brush off.

She put her hands on Jocelyn's shoulders. "What's the matter?"

Jocelyn swallowed and thrust a newspaper at her, the tears she had held back rising up instantly. "Is it true, Mom? Is it true?"

"Is what true, honey?" Nervous, Johanna took the paper from her. She glanced down at the front page, her mind still on her daughter's distress. "I can't tell you until I—Omigod!"

"What?" Mary circled to stand on her toes and look over Johanna's shoulder at the newspaper. "Wow!" Her immediate reaction was to put her arm around her niece as Johanna read the first few paragraphs of the story. Harry's picture took up more than a quarter of the page. He was wearing handcuffs and flanked by two policemen.

"They can't arrest daddy, can they?" Jocelyn cried, her tears spilling down her face. Arrest seemed so final, so frightening.

Johanna pressed her lips together. Harry had been arrested for possession of cocaine while entering the country.

The fool, the pompous fool.

She hated him for this, not because of any feelings she had left for him. There were none, she knew that now. It was as if a portion of her had been opened up and what had been there had just flowed out of her. There was no love, no anger for what he had done to her. But she hated him for the look in Jocelyn's eyes. How could he? How could he put himself into such a position, knowing that it would effect his daughter?

"I'm afraid they can, Jocey."

"We have to help him!" Jocelyn pleaded.

Johanna drew her close and exchanged looks with Mary over her daughter's head. To Jocelyn, Harry was still the wonderful father who brought home gifts from his travels, the father who, though he might not have time for her as often as she liked, shared secrets with her, let her do things her mother would only disapprove of. He treated her like an adult, not like a child the way her mother did. He never said no, always said give it a try, and he gave her that extra shove when she wanted it, even though she was frightened at times.

Johanna knew all this, knew the enemy she faced in Harry, knew he did it not from indulgence, but from a lack of concern as to the consequences. She had found out that it was Harry who had given Megan that marijuana joint she had smelled in Jocelyn's room the night she had almost committed suicide. Had given it to the girl knowing that she would probably share it with Jocelyn. It was like giving his permission for Jocelyn to be reckless. He did it not because he wanted her to sample life but because he didn't care.

But Jocelyn could never know that. It would hurt much too deeply.

"I was going to call our lawyer anyway," Johanna said to Jocelyn. "I'll just make the call a little earlier, that's all."

"This isn't going to change your mind, is it?" Mary's voice was low, her eyes carrying her meaning even if her words couldn't at the moment.

"No," Johanna answered, stroking Jocelyn's hair, "it's only made me realize how right I am about all of this." She looked down into Jocelyn's upturned face. "C'mon, honey, dry your eyes. We'll see what we can do to straighten out this mess."

"They shouldn't have been going through his things," Jocelyn said vehemently, her hands clenched into fists.

She couldn't let it go, not even now. "No, he shouldn't have been carrying what he was carrying," Johanna said quietly.

Jocelyn stiffened and pulled back. "You've always been against him."

"No." Johanna refused to let her daughter back away. "I've always been the one in his corner. He just never realized it, that's all. Let's go upstairs, Jocey. I've got calls to make."

Chapter Twenty-four

There was no more anger, no more pain, only pity. Johanna felt only pity for Harry. And pity on its own was a dreadful thing. It spelled the end of everything between Harry and Johanna.

It set her free.

Still, there were things to be done because of the past and because he was Jocelyn's father. She called their lawyer as soon as she read the article. Sidney Montaigne was a short, bald, overweight little man who tended to wear bow ties and vests and to think a great deal of himself. He had a right to the latter. Fussy, opinionated, sharp-tongued, he was still the best in his field. Harry paid a great deal to keep the man on retainer. And Sid, Johanna thought, was about to earn every penny of that sum.

Sid wasn't happy to receive her transatlantic call. He was one step ahead of her, having read the story, courtesy of UPI, in the morning paper. But responsibility was the cornerstone of his reputation and he had spent a long time cultivating his image. "I'll get the next flight out of LAX to Heathrow."

She could hear the displeasure in his voice. "I'll be there to meet you." And now for the bombshell. "And Sid—"

"Yes?" The single word was rimmed with impatience. Sid, a born and bred New Yorker from the Bronx, was always in a hurry and had no tolerance for people who couldn't keep up.

"Bring divorce papers with you."

Any mental calculations he was doing about the effects of the trip on his already overcrowded schedule came to an abrupt halt. "For whom?"

She could just see his expression. For some reason, it pleased her. She had never really like the man. "Guess."

"Johanna." He exhaled a loud sigh. It was the same sigh that intimidated the law clerks at the firm. Johanna was impervious to it. "This is a rotten time to make jokes in poor taste."

While Sid did not openly worship the dollar, she knew that he thought walking away from it was tantamount to being labeled certifiably insane. Fine, she thought, *you* marry Harry. I've had it. "I'm not joking, Sid. I'm very, very serious."

In his experience, women tended to run, frightened, taking the family jewels at the first hint of trouble. Sid's line of work did not make him an optimist about human nature. "Look, he'll beat this wrap, Johanna. He'll ride it out."

"Maybe, with you in his corner, but I won't be there to see it."

Another nasty divorce with its accompanying mudslinging. "Don't do anything hasty, Johanna," he counseled.

"Ten years in the making isn't anything hasty, Sid. It's slow. Damn slow." She didn't owe him an explanation, but she gave it anyway. "This isn't because of the scandal that might be whipped up. This has been a long time in coming. I was going to call you today anyway. I'd already made up my mind. That Harry was stupid enough to bring cocaine in his luggage is beside the point. That he was stupid enough to bring it into his life *is* the point. It changed him, changed him so much that I don't even know him. I don't want to know him." She lowered her voice and turned from where Jocelyn and Mary were sitting on the sofa, watching her. "And he's a bad influence on Jocelyn. I'm bailing out not just for me, but for her."

"But—"

"Don't worry, Sid. I don't want anything from him. Not a dime. All I want is Jocelyn. In exchange for that, I want him to keep away from her. Those are the terms of my settlement." Distance entered her voice. There was no one to fight her battles for her. She had to do it all alone. The independence was frightening and exhilarating at the same time. "If you don't want to handle this, I'll get someone who will."

"Calm down, Johanna, calm down." She could almost see the man mopping his bald head. He always seemed to sweat profusely when he was agitated. "I'll be there and we'll talk."

We can talk all you want, she thought. It won't change anything. "Bring the papers."

"I'll bring the papers," he promised. "Sheila will call you with my flight number and the arrangements once she makes them."

Johanna thought of talking to Sid's humorless secretary. Something else to live for. "Fine." She straightened her shoulders. There. It was out in the open now. And there was no turning back. Relief made her feel almost giddy. "I'll see you then. 'Bye." She hung up, then turned to see her sister giving her the high sign.

Johanna had no sooner placed the receiver back in the cradle than the phone started to ring. And ring. And ring. There seemed to be no end to the incoming calls. Each time she answered, there was another member of the press asking her for a statement about Harry's arrest that morning.

They wanted to know what she was thinking, what she was feeling. They wanted to photograph her and Jocelyn. They wanted to interview her at the jail. They wanted to dissect her mind, examine everything beneath a microscope for the eleven o'clock news back home. Johanna felt as if she was under siege.

When the phone rang for the twentieth time, Mary held up her hand. "I'll get this one." There was fire in her eyes as she jerked the receiver up from the cradle. "Look, you scumsucking lowlife—oh, hello."

If Johanna didn't know any better, she would have said that her sister was embarrassed. But then, Mary was never embarrassed. She was one of the lucky ones who sailed right through life without a backward glance and no regrets. Ever.

Mary put her hand over the mouthpiece. "It's Tommy. He wants to know if he can come over and be of any help. He saw the article."

"The world saw the article," Johanna muttered, weary.

She knew she was being weak. She shouldn't accept or ask for help from him. There wouldn't be any in a few days when she left for the States, destination still unknown. But she couldn't deny herself seeing Tommy one more time. She crossed over to the telephone and held out her hand. Mary gave her the receiver.

"Hello, Tommy?"

"I just saw the paper. How are you holding up?"

She smiled ruefully as she wound the cord around her finger and then let it go again. "This must have been what it was like to be a fortress about to be stormed by the Vikings."

"That bad?" It wasn't pity in his voice. It was compassion and it fortified her. And made her warm.

"That bad."

"I'll be right over." There was no arguing with his tone of voice. It was firm.

Still, she wanted to spare him. It wouldn't be long before the reporters set up camp in the lobby, or at least outside the hotel. She had seen it happen many times before. Nothing like a scandal to bring the vultures out. "Do you think you should?"

"It's my Ivanhoe training, remember? I can't turn my back on a lady in distress. Besides, I've got broad shoulders. Maybe you'll find yourself wanting to lean on them for a while."

She closed her eyes, suddenly bone weary. "Oh God, yes."

"I'll saddle up the white charger and be right over. Hang in there, Johanna."

His words were like a physical touch. She drew comfort from them. "I will. 'Bye. And thanks."

"None necessary. You know that."

"Yes, I know."

She felt a little uncertain about having Tommy come over to the hotel because of Jocelyn. Her daughter might be sensitive to having another man over, a man her mother was seeing, while her father was languishing in prison—no matter how much he might deserve it. But her worries were groundless. Jocelyn turned to Tommy like an old friend coming to the aid of the cause as soon as he walked through the door.

"Tommy." She rushed up to him. "They've got my dad. Can you help us?"

Easily, Tommy slung an arm around the small shoulders. "I'm here to give you and your Mum some moral support."

"Will that help?" the girl asked.

"I don't know." He looked at Johanna. "Will it?"

She offered him a warm, grateful smile. "It certainly wouldn't hurt." Her words were blocked out by an insistent knock on the door. She drew in a sharp breath, bracing herself for another onslaught of reporters, local and foreign.

"It's as if they smell blood and are in a feeding frenzy," she moaned.

"Let me." Tommy said calmly, his hand on the doorknob.

"You don't want to be dragged into this," Johanna warned.

The look on his face said that she couldn't talk him out of it. "What are friends for?"

What indeed, she thought. And whatever else happened between them, however this ended—and it would end soon, she knew in her heart—she'd have this to cherish. That he was her friend first and foremost.

"Give the man his lead," Mary counseled. She placed her hands on Johanna's shoulders and forced her to sit down on the sofa.

Tommy cracked the door open and instantly the commotion in the hallway roared into the room like the waters of a flash flood. Reporters with cameramen at their sides waved microphones at Tommy, clamoring to see Johanna and get her side of the story.

"Mrs. Whitney only knows what she reads in the newspapers." Tommy shouldered the door closed again.

The knocking continued, turning into urgent pounding when there was no further answer.

The hotel had had to beef up its security and was not very happy about having Harold Whitney's wife and daughter staying with them. The rooms reserved for the production company members returning from the shoot in Italy were suddenly cancelled and the manager himself came up to see her later that day to politely suggest that perhaps she would like to seek other, more secluded accommodations.

Johanna wanted to lash out at him. The obsequious little man had melted all over them when they had first arrived.

She saw Tommy grin and her nerves abated. "Why don't you go downstairs and have some of your hotel tea to soothe those jangled nerves of yours?" She stepped back as he hesitantly opened the door, then watched, pleased, as the manager fought his way out of the suite.

Mary, her luggage packed, hung back. "Come to the States with me," Mary urged.

Johanna shook her head. "Not yet. I've got to see our lawyer and tie up a few loose ends first."

Mary nodded, understanding. But she didn't have to like it. "I still hate leaving you in the middle of all this."

Johanna hugged her sister. "You might not be able to leave. Those vultures might not let you get out," she said with a sad laugh.

Mary hiked her shoulder bag higher on her shoulder. "Don't worry about me. Over half those people out there are men. I can manage." Her eyes softened as she looked at Johanna. "Take care of yourself, Jo."

They hugged one more time and then Mary swept out, luggage in hand. She was followed down the hall by several eager reporters who had staked out the area. A secondhand story was better than none.

Tommy patted the place next to him on the sofa. "You're leaving?"

Feeling awkward for the first time, Johanna nodded as she sat down.

"When?"

Deliberately she avoided his eyes. She looked over toward Jocelyn, who was sitting curled up on a love seat, trying to read. "A couple of days."

"That soon."

"School starts in a little more than a week." Johanna knotted her hands in her lap. It all sounded so lame to her ear, but he seemed to understand.

He wouldn't dwell on her departure. They had both known that there would be an end when they had started. He hooked his thumbs into the front pocket of his jeans. "Well, at the moment, it seems that you need somewhere to stay."

Johanna swallowed. Suddenly, she needed more than that. "Arlene offered—"

"They'll look there first," he guessed knowingly.

He was right. "But I don't have any—"

"Options?"

Again, she nodded, this time turning to look at him.

Tommy took her hand in both of his and just held it. "You and Jocelyn can stay with me. It'll be crowded, but they won't look there."

"They'll follow us," she pointed out, forgetting to refuse the offer.

He grinned. "If we look like us."

He was massaging her hand between his own. Her body warmed. She forced herself to concentrate on the conversation. "Meaning?"

"Why don't you call the hotel manager up here again? I think I have an idea that he might like."

She couldn't get him to elaborate any further. Playing along and eminently curious, Johanna did as he suggested. The short, stout man came within fifteen minutes. He didn't look pleased about the summons or the ongoing situation, but he had always been nothing short of polite to his guests and a lifelong habit was hard to break.

"Mrs. Whitney and her daughter would like to check out as soon as possible," Tommy told the man as soon as he walked into the suite.

The hotel manager offered the first genuine smile in over twenty-four hours. "Yes, of course."

"But they can't just walk out without being followed and harassed."

His small, alert eyes swept over Johanna. "I quite understand your dilemma, Mrs. Whitney, but I do have one of my own. The hotel cannot brook being overrun by reporters in this manner. We—"

Tommy cut him short. "We know all that. We need a bellhop sent up who is approximately my height and two chambermaids who would be around Mrs. Whitney and Miss Whitney's height and coloring."

Alistair Hornsby drew his dark brows together. "Decoys?"

Tommy grinned, shoving his hands into his back pockets. "Exactly."

Jocelyn clapped her hands together, displaying the first

excitement Johanna had seen since she brought the newspaper to her. "Like spies."

Tommy nodded. "Like spies, Jocelyn." He turned to Hornsby. "They go out first, drawing off the reporters, and then we leave, wearing their clothes."

"And the luggage—?" Montaigne asked.

"Can be sent for," Johanna answered, getting into the spirit of the thing. It almost seemed like fun, if that was possible. "Do we have your help, Mr. Hornsby?"

"Gladly," he answered. The sooner he was rid of these entertainers and their three-ring circus, the happier he was going to be.

He left quickly to make arrangements.

Chapter Twenty-five

"I feel terrible about putting you out, Tommy. Really, we can check into another hotel." Johanna looked around the small, cosy living room. After the unnerving siege by the press, it felt like a haven to her. But she didn't want to be any trouble.

Quietly, Tommy put his hand on her shoulder and turned her around to face him. The small gesture told her everything. That she was safe here for as long as she wanted to stay. "You said you were only staying in London another few days, didn't you?"

She nodded. His voice was soft, tinged with a touch of melancholy. The feeling matched her own. She wanted to distance herself from him in order to better accept the permanent separation she knew was ahead for them. But at the same time, she wanted to hug him to her, to savor the last few hours she had left, to absorb everything about them and him.

"Well, then it's really being selfish of me, not generous,

don't you see? I want to be with you as much as possible until you go." He glanced over to the kitchen where Jocelyn sat, talking to Stewart. "And my father could use the company."

She followed him as he crossed to a linen closet and removed a sheet and extra pillow. "I still feel guilty about turning you out of your own bedroom."

Tommy deposited the pillow on the sofa. "I've slept in a lot worse places than a sofa, Johanna."

"Oh?" She perched on the arm of the sofa, watching him as he went about preparing it to serve as his bed. "Tell me about them."

"Nothing very interesting. That was in my roving days." With a snap of his wrist, he sent the sheet billowing out. It whispered down to the sofa, covering it.

"Which were?" She wanted to devour every shred of information about him, more so since she knew that he would be gone out of her life soon. She wanted to be able to look back and remember.

"Right after I finished school. I traveled through Europe. I wanted to see the world to make up my mind about where I really belonged."

"And did you make up your mind?" It sounded so simple, so easy when he said it. Think and it'll come to you. But it wasn't that simple, was it? Where did she belong? She had no idea anymore.

"Yes. I belong here, doing what I'm doing. I feel at peace with that."

"You're lucky to have found your niche." There was a trace of yearning in her voice. Would she ever find her niche again? She didn't know. She wanted to believe she would, but she thought she had found it once and that had turned out to be a lie.

He stopped smoothing the sheet and framed her face with his hands. He wanted to kiss her then, kiss away the fear in her eyes, but he didn't. Her daughter was in the very next room and he knew that made Johanna uncomfortable. "You'll find your niche, Johanna. You're too strong a woman not to."

She nodded and forced a smile to her lips. She wished with all her heart that her niche might be here, with him, but she knew better. Without knowing how and why, she knew that she didn't belong here. There was something waiting for her out there. She could *feel* it. Good or bad, she had to go and find it.

And leave behind part of her heart.

Johanna rose and linked her hand with his. "It's too late to go to bed," she said. "The sun's almost ready to come up."

"Care to go for a walk?"

"I'd love it. Just give me a minute to check on Jocelyn."

Stewart had shown Jocelyn to Tommy's room while they had been talking. Johanna found her daughter already asleep in the double bed. After tucking the blanket around Jocelyn, Johanna found she couldn't resist running her hand along the intricately carved wood.

She turned to Tommy. "You do beautiful work," she whispered.

He looked down at Jocelyn's sleeping face. "So do you, Johanna."

She grinned at him. "C'mon, you promised me a walk."

Silently, they slipped out of the small apartment.

The neighborhood was sleeping as the first rays of the sun were just tickling the sky, sending out shards of rose and purple hues as forerunners to the morning. She looked down at the cobblestones beneath her feet, the sleepy streets, the charming, almost quaint rows of houses. Later the streets would be alive with vendors, with people buying and selling, making noise, going on with their lives. Right now, it was still asleep.

"It looks like a movie set," she murmured. "Not a bit like New York." Again she was compelled to make a comparison. New York had been the place she had felt really at home. It was the last place that had truly spoken to her.

Despite the ever-present noise, the endless hurry, there had been peace there. A peace she had long since lost.

"The city that never sleeps." Tommy recalled hearing that once.

"Yes, that's what they call it. There always seems to be noise around, it's never quiet at night, never still."

He was silent for a moment, studying her. "Is that where you're going?"

She turned the thought over in her mind. Suddenly, it was as if there had never been any doubt. She watched a lone car make its way up the street and then turn a corner. "Yes."

Tommy held her hand a little tighter. "What will you do?"

They crossed the street. "Get back to painting, I think. That's what I wanted to do before I married Harry. Be a starving artist." She pressed her lips together. They passed a greengrocer and she peered into the silent, dark store, seeing other things in the shadows. Seeing the future. "The idea of starving with a child, though, doesn't sound that appealing."

"You're entitled to child support, aren't you?"

Johanna looked up and saw his reflection in the store window. Their eyes met. "I don't want anything from Harry," she said vehemently. She turned and began to walk again.

A stray dog knocked down a garbage can and she jumped closer to Tommy. He gripped her hand tighter. "Easy, luv," he said soothingly. "It's not taking anything from Harry, and it's for Jocelyn, not yourself. He owes it to her, you know. And to you."

It was the logical thing, of course, but she wanted to divorce herself from everything that had to do with Harry. "No doubt of that. He owes her a lot of things. But if I had his word that he'd never contact her again, I'd gladly give up the money."

"You hate him that much?" She didn't look like a woman

who could hate. Feel yes, desire, yes, but not hate.

"No, I don't hate him." She looked down at the cobblestones. In the growing light, they took on different hues of gray. "I did, for a little while, but that's gone. I feel sorry for him if anything. But that doesn't change my feelings about his influence. I'm afraid that Jocelyn is very impressionable right now and she might follow in his footsteps. I don't want anything happening to her. She's all I have."

"No, you have you, Johanna, and a lot of people who care about you."

"Oh God, Tommy, how did all this get so tangled up?" She stopped walking and looked up at him. "How do I untangle things? How do I make them right?"

"What makes you think you're God?"

The words, softly spoken, still sounded harsh to her. "What?"

"You want to fix things you said, to make them right. But you can't. You're not supposed to. That's not your job."

She laughed disparagingly, a note of helplessness creeping in. "Just what is my job?"

He took her into his arms, heedless of anyone who might look out their window and see. "To just be Johanna. Not Harold's wife, not Jocelyn's mother, not anyone's daughter. Just Johanna." He kissed her forehead softly. "And that's more than enough."

She closed her eyes. It felt good just to be held for a few moments.

"He wants to see you, Johanna," Sid Montaigne said to her the moment that he spotted her in the crowd of people when he deplaned at Heathrow.

No hellos, no small talk. Just a delivered command. She was through with commands.

"He called you?" Of course he would, or have someone do it for her, once he had calmed down and gotten hold of himself. She had no doubts that Harry was ultimately a survivor. However much longer he could manage it.

"Yes, and he was adamant about seeing you when I told him you wanted a divorce."

Johanna stared at the lawyer. She wore her high heels, and they were eye to eye. "You told him that?"

He shrugged, his expensive wool suit whispering against his shoulders. "Why shouldn't I?"

"Because you might have spared him that until you were here. He's facing a long prison sentence, you know." Even after all he had done to her, she didn't want to twist a knife in his back. That was for people who wanted petty revenge. She just wanted to be left alone.

He took her arm and hurried her out of the area. He was carrying the only piece of luggage he would need. His brief-case held a fresh shirt and a change of underwear. He could buy anything else he needed and most likely would.

"If you're so concerned about his mental state, Johanna, why won't you see him?"

Sid had guessed her feelings correctly, Johanna thought as she led him back to the cab she had waiting. But then, the rotund little man wasn't considered a shrewd lawyer because of the way he dressed.

"Because there's nothing to talk about on that score anymore. Whatever we had between us is gone and no amount of talking or promises from him is going to bring it back. I just want to get on with my life now."

"That's pretty low, Johanna, hitting him when he's down."

Johanna stopped. She wouldn't be criticized by someone who hadn't the vaguest idea what she had been through. "He's been down for a long time, Sid. He just didn't know it. The women, the drugs, the megalomania—I've had it." She leveled a gaze at him. She wasn't about to be bullied into anything either and she knew if she let him, Sid could bulldoze her. He had done it before with other people. "Like I said earlier, if you don't want to handle this, I'll find someone who will and maybe they'll want a piece of your action."

He was quick to put a hand on her arm. "Now Johanna, don't be hasty."

She'd heard this before and knew his language. It started and ended with dollar signs. That didn't make him any the less competent. In a way, it made things simpler, more upfront. She knew exactly where he stood. He'd do the best job he could, as long as the money was there. Loyalty was something he had only to himself. But he could be bought and his expertise made the buy worthwhile. Harry had always thought so. When Harry could think.

"I thought you'd see it my way. Thank you." She slipped into the cab she had waiting for them as he held the door open for her. "I'll have the driver drop you off where they're holding Harry."

He climbed in next to her and arranged himself before speaking. "You're not coming?"

Johanna stared straight ahead as the cab driver pulled away from the curb. "No, I already told you, I won't see him. Not now, Sid. Not ever. I'm leaving the country tomorrow."

Sid took the information and digested it. "Are you going home?"

His tone didn't deceive her. He was still predominantly Harry's lawyer. His loyalty lay with the purse strings now that the divorce was coming. "No. I'm going to make a new home. You can tell Harry that when you see him. Tell him he's free to do whatever it is he wants to do with whomever or whatever he wishes. But he's not dragging me down with him anymore."

Sid leaned back and chuckled, his belly rolling under the tightly buttoned vest. She hadn't expected that of him. He rarely laughed. "Want some advice?" he asked.

"That depends."

"On what?"

She smiled. "Is it free?"

She was still one of the best damn looking women he had ever seen, Sid thought. But his appetite ran to willing, eager young women with short memories. Not strong women. "This one time."

"Okay." She thrust out her chin. "What is it?"

"Don't change your mind."

"What?" That surprised her. "I thought you said—"

"That was as Harry's lawyer. As Sid Montaigne I never understood why you hung around with that hopeless shambles of a man. I thought it was for the money, until you told me you didn't want it." He leaned forward. It was still hard to accept. "Tell me, if it wasn't for the money, why did you stay?"

She looked at him carefully and was grateful to see the prison coming into view just behind him. "You wouldn't understand, Sid. A man like you just wouldn't understand."

The cab stopped. Sid nodded, bobbing his head up and down twice. "Maybe you're right." He reached into his pocket and pulled out some pound notes. Carefully, he counted it out and handed it to the driver. "Any last words to Harry?" he asked as he stepped out onto the sidewalk.

"None that could be politely repeated." Sid nodded and began to walk off, his leather briefcase in his hand. "Oh, wait, Sid," she called. He stopped, a square little man in the middle of the sidewalk, waiting. "Tell him 'I told you so.'"

"You're a hardhearted woman, Johanna." He chuckled again.

"Thank you. I'm learning. And I had the best teachers."

With that she turned her head and leaned back in the seat, shutting Sid and Harry out of her mind completely. "124 Camden Road, please driver," she said softly.

The driver pulled down the meter one more time and guided the cab away from the sidewalk. Sid watched the cab merge into traffic and finally disappear.

Johanna never looked back once.

Chapter Twenty-six

"**But why** are we leaving?" Jocelyn pouted.

She sat on Tommy's bed, watching Johanna pack away things into an army of suitcases arranged in a circle around her, their lids opened wide like the beaks of hungry, eager baby birds waiting to be fed.

Because we're running for our lives, baby, yours and mine, Johanna thought as she went on packing.

Arlene had been prevailed upon to bring the rest of their things from the hotel's storage area. The manager had had the suite cleared the moment Johanna had stepped over the threshold. In exchange for bringing her luggage to such a "seedy little area," to quote Arlene, Johanna had told her that she was definitely divorcing Harry. Arlene couldn't wait to get back and telephone everyone she knew. Gossip was, after all, gossip and she enjoyed being the first to ferret things out. Johanna didn't bother telling her that she had already spoken to their lawyer about it.

With Harry in jail and the film on indefinite hold, it

looked as if the studio would either scrap the movie entirely or get someone else to finish it, if anyone wanted the major headache of reassembling the scattered pieces of the story. Loyalties, Johanna had learned from Arlene, were divided, but there were very few people left in Harry's camp. The hangers-on had been the first to flee, searching for a new rising star to pledge themselves to. And most of the others had families and futures to think of. Harry, it was silently agreed, did not have a future anymore. This had been the death knell. Even if he wasn't sent to jail, and odds were that he would be, the lid had been blown off the public secret. It was doubtful that his present studio, or any other major studio for that matter, would have much to do with him.

Johanna felt sorrier for him than she ever had before, but she was also just as determined to cut her losses and begin a new life away from Harry and his poisonous influence. It was something she should have done long ago.

"We're going because we can't stay here indefinitely and because I've got to get you enrolled for school right away. It starts in a few days."

That obviously wasn't enough of a reason, especially not the part about school. "But Daddy's not out yet," Jocelyn protested, tugging at the bedspread beneath, making it rumpled.

A folded pile of lingerie slipped to the floor. Johanna picked it up without comment. "Daddy might not be out for a long time, honey."

"Then we can wait."

"No, baby, we can't." Johanna was firm. "I don't expect you to understand, but I've been waiting for ten years and I can't wait any more."

Jocelyn gave her a hostile look. "You're deserting him."

He deserted me a long time ago, Johanna thought. The words were on the tip of her tongue, but what good would it do to say them? She didn't want to use Jocelyn as a rope in an emotional tug of war.

"I sent for Daddy's lawyer and he's the one who can do something—if anything." Johanna stopped packing and sat down next to Jocelyn. She put her arm around the thin shoulders. "You're going to have to face it, Jocey, daddy might have to go to prison."

"But why?"

She looked so hurt, so innocent, Johanna thought, aching for her. "Because he did something wrong."

"He wasn't hurting anyone." Jocelyn's eyes flashed angrily.

"He hurt a lot of people."

"You?" she accused spitefully.

Johanna knew the hostility was born of her own hurt. She let it go. "Me," she agreed with a sigh, "but a lot of people who were depending on him for their livelihood, for their families' livelihoods. That movie your daddy was working on put a lot of people to work, people who needed jobs. He endangered them every time he took drugs."

Stubbornly, Jocelyn persisted. "Why?"

"Because when he took them, he couldn't think clearly, because drugs robbed him of his mind, his ability to get the job done properly. Your dad didn't think of them, he just thought of himself. And now he's paying the price for it."

"That's not true!" Jocelyn jumped up. There was hot anger in her young eyes. Tears shimmered, but she refused to shed them in front of her mother. She turned and ran from the room.

Johanna closed her eyes. God, this was going to be difficult. She was leaving Harry to save herself and to save Jocelyn, but Jocelyn didn't want to be saved. She wanted to help. Johanna rubbed the bridge of her nose, wishing the headache would go away.

The bastard didn't deserve such loyalty, she thought heatedly.

It would do no good to sit here and berate him. She had work to do. And a plane to catch. Johanna rose and began packing again. It seemed incredible how many meaningless things she had accumulated and carted around. Part of her felt like throwing the whole mess down, and walking away. All of this had been bought with Harry's money and she wanted nothing more to do with him. But she didn't have the luxury to act so proud. She had Jocelyn to think of. And a new life to forge for herself.

She shivered, frightened. First steps were always frightening. But they had to be taken or else journeys would never be made, she told herself.

Tommy looked in. He saw her moving around the room quickly. He was going to miss her, he thought. More than he'd have thought possible. "How's it coming?"

Johanna turned, surprised, then smiled. She raised and lowered her shoulders helplessly. "The mechanics are getting done, but I don't know about Jocey. She wants to stay."

He walked into the room and placed himself between Johanna and the bureau. "It's only natural."

"She sees just the good in Harry." Johanna sank down on the edge of the bed, a wave of hopelessness overtaking her.

She'd get through this. He had no doubts of that. She was a strong woman. It was one of the things that attracted him to her in the first place. Strength within softness. It was a compelling combination. "That's because you've tried to shield her from his bad side for so long. You've done too good a job."

"Maybe I was wrong."

"Maybe." He sat down beside her and slipped his arm around her. Johanna leaned her head against his shoulder, content to rest there for the moment. "But a child deserves some illusions. We lose them fast enough when we grow up." He looked down at her face. Going with an impulse, he brushed her lips lightly with his own. "What were your illusions as a young girl?"

Johanna grinned, remembering. "That I was going to set the world on fire."

Her hair shimmered on his shoulder, catching the light from the window. He'd remember this afternoon long after it was gone. "You could still do that."

"Ha." But there was no cynicism in her voice. "I'd settle for just surviving."

"You'll do more than that, Johanna. You'll do more than that." He took a piece of paper out of his pocket and carefully unfolded it. "I found this in the kitchen this morning."

She knew what it was before she looked. It was the sketch she had done of him from memory. She had been unable to sleep and sitting within the warm, tiny kitchen, she had sought comfort in her skills. She looked at it now, then at him. "Do you like it?"

The sketch was of his face alone. There was pride and a touch of arrogance, softened by the trace of a smile in the corners of his mouth. "You made me look very heroic."

"You are."

He laughed. "There'd be many who'd argue with you there."

"They didn't get to know you like I did," Johanna said softly.

This would be the last time they'd be like this, talking this way. She felt an ache in her heart that she quickly shut away. She bit her lip to keep her mind away from her pain. The sun streamed in through the window and cast a spotlight around the hope chest he had been working on. It was finished. She had found him working on it late last night and that had prompted her sketch. He looked so intense on getting it done. She could admire that. She could admire a lot of things about Tommy. For a moment longer, she allowed herself to feel his heartbeat beneath her hand on his chest, feel his shoulder rise and fall gently as he drew breath. These things would see her through. "I have to leave, you know."

His arm tightened around her for only a second before he relaxed it again. "I know."

"And all this, being with you, was wonderful." She raised her head to look into his eyes, his soft, wonderful brown eyes.

"Yes, it was." He looked down into her face. She'd be gone soon. Impulse seized him. "Marry me, Johanna."

She was tempted. Oh, she was so sorely tempted, but it was wrong for them and they both knew it. The cultures, the needs, the timing, they were all wrong. "You don't mean that."

She saw through him. Knew him better than he knew himself. Still, he asked, "Don't I?"

"No." She shook her head, a sad smile on her lips. "It's just Ivanhoe riding to the rescue again." She touched his face lovingly, her fingertips tracing the pattern of his cheek. He turned her hand palm side up and kissed it. The shiver that went through her rested in her very core. "You've got several years before you can be tied down. I can feel it. Someday you'll be married, but not now and not to me."

The bittersweetness of her words made her throat ache with unshed tears. She touched his face once more, memorizing it with her fingertips, her eyes, her heart. "You're not the marrying kind yet." She saw pain rise in his eyes even as agreement joined it. "Oh Tommy, wonderful, wonderful Tommy. I knew that. I won't say that somewhere in my heart, I didn't hope that this might work."

"We can try."

"No, you'd only wind up wondering if I held you back somehow. These have been the best few weeks of my life, Tommy. You helped me grow up. I love you." She saw his eyes open wide. "Yes, I love you, but I know it wouldn't work."

And he knew it too, had known it, and was bereft because of it.

"Don't look so sad, Tommy. You've helped me more than I can ever say. You helped me heal and I'll always be grateful to you for that. You made me whole again."

He kissed her cheek softly, gently and she ached for what

couldn't be. "You were always whole, Johanna. I just made you see it, that's all."

She laughed lightly, touched. "Have it your way." She couldn't resist touching his hair, letting her fingers travel through it one more time. Words came to her that she had once been forced to read in some faraway English class light years ago. "'And when you speak of this, and you shall, be kind.'"

"Kind?" Tommy laughed, incredulous at her statement. He had never heard of *Tea and Sympathy* nor the quote, but he understood what she was saying. "I'll be proud, not kind, Johanna. Proud that once a lovely lady spent a little time with me."

He kissed her then, kissed her long and hard, with all the love they felt and all the love that would never be. When their lips parted, it was for the last time and they both knew it, even though there were promises exchanged of keeping in touch and possible visits sometime in the future. They both knew that the words were empty words that needed to be said, to be heard, to keep tears from coming. They were words that would never bear any fruit.

"I have a present for you," he said, rising.

"Oh?" It took her a moment to regain control of herself. She promised herself she wouldn't cry. He had made her happy and there was no reason to cry and ruin that. But still she felt the sting of gathering tears. She struggled to keep them back. "You shouldn't have gone to the trouble, Tommy."

"No trouble." He crossed to the hope chest and then turned to look at her. "I want you to have this."

"The chest?"

He nodded.

She didn't remember walking over to it, but she found herself on her knees before the finely carved work of art. "But Tommy, I can't. This is so beautiful, and you worked so hard on it. I saw you, last night, working on it in your workshop."

"I know. I felt you standing there. I knew you were leaving and I wanted to have it finished for you before you were gone."

Lightly, her fingers traced a rose that would live forever. "I don't know what to say."

He took her hands and raised her to her feet. "Say you'll take it. To remember me by."

She looked up into his face. As if she could ever forget. "Everything I need to remember you by is in my heart."

"You can have something in your bedroom too. I'm hanging your sketch in mine."

She laughed and leaned her head against his chest. "Thank you. With all my heart, thank you." She hugged him, glad that he couldn't see her face or her tears.

Chapter Twenty-seven

Johanna's stomach began to rebel, churning. The airplane was descending. Kennedy Airport waited in the distance to receive them. God, she hated flying. As the ground came barreling up closer and closer, Johanna wrapped her fingers around the armrests and looked straight ahead. She had flown countless times and it only got worse with each flight.

With a little luck, she wouldn't be flying again any time soon.

She hadn't called Mary to say she was coming. She didn't want anyone meeting her and Jocelyn at the airport. Not immediately. Johanna needed a little time, time to get her bearings. Time to decide what to do and where to do it. Her life lay stretched out before her like a field of tall, tangled weeds. Somewhere beneath it all was order. She had to believe in that, cling to that. There was a path there, but she had to clear away the debris first in order to find it.

And she had absolutely no idea if she could or if she was even up to it.

She *had* to be up to it. No ifs, ands, or buts.

To take her mind off the fact that the plane was swiftly approaching the airport, where hundreds of planes took off and landed every day and could very easily collide with the one she was on, Johanna glanced at Jocelyn. Her daughter was looking beyond her out of the window, a mixture of awe and apprehension on her face.

The same as me, Jocey, Johanna thought, the same as me. And not just about the landing. About our new life. Except that she couldn't admit it, couldn't afford to lean on anyone. Not anymore.

Johanna turned her face forward again. Her thoughts gathered around the immediate future. The unknown, unformed immediate future. She had to be up to facing it, tackling it and winning. She didn't have the luxury of failing. She'd be failing for two and she owed Jocelyn much better than that. Silently, she linked her fingers with her daughter's.

Jocelyn responded to the gentle pressure by squeezing back. Despite the arguing that had transpired, that was yet to transpire, they had a basically good relationship and could communicate with one another at times with just a touch. At bottom there was love.

Johanna saw the apprehension mount in Jocelyn's eyes. She forgot about her own fears. "It's going to be fine, Jocelyn."

"No, it's not. I wish we were going home," Jocelyn pouted.

Jocey'd get used to it eventually. It would just take time, Johanna told herself, hoping she was right. "This'll be home soon enough."

Jocelyn thought of the friends she missed and her own room. "Where are we going to live?"

Johanna took a deep breath. The plane landed. Her stomach lurched. "I don't know yet."

"Terrific."

"Think of it as an adventure, Jocelyn."

"Yeah." It was clear that she didn't, that she wasn't in the mood for adventures.

"Jocey." Something in Johanna's voice made Jocelyn look at her mother. "I need help here, okay?"

"You're asking me for help?" Jocelyn asked incredulously.

Maybe the burden was too much for a twelve-year-old. And then again, maybe it wasn't. Maybe Jocelyn needed to feel more of a part of her life than Johanna had allowed her to be. Protecting her, sheltering her from things had set her apart, caused a schism to form. They had to be together, to pull together to make this work. "A little cheering section wouldn't hurt, Jocey. I haven't been on my own in a long, long time."

The fact that her mother was unsure made Jocelyn nervous. "When Daddy gets out—"

Johanna hadn't told Jocelyn that she was divorcing her father and now wasn't the time to begin explaining. Not with a planeload of passengers as a backdrop. Johanna unbuckled her seatbelt, her body alert.

"Until then," she said, quickly brushing Jocelyn's words aside, "we're on our own. Just the two of us." All around them there was commotion, as people pulled out pieces of luggage from the overhead compartments and gathered their things together. Mother and daughter looked at one another. "I need you, Jocey."

Confused, a little pleased, Jocelyn nodded her head. "Okay."

It was a start.

The morning had been hectic. That in itself was unusual. As a rule, Tuesdays at the gallery were rather peaceful. It was as if the gods generously gave him a respite after the frantic pace that Mondays always seemed to demand. But today there was no respite. The gods might be sleeping, but clients weren't. Patrons had come and gone all morning. And then there had been Bruce to deal with.

Bruce Cantrell, the artist whose show was going to open this week, who Joshua had managed to calm and soothe more than once without the aid of the man's ever-present flask of alcoholic solace, was having an especially vicious attack of nerves. It wasn't the first time. The show was scheduled for Thursday evening. Joshua doubted if Bruce Cantrell would live that long, not the way he was wearing himself out. The tall, rangy, long-faced artist vacillated between sheer contempt for his future audience and absolute terror that no one would come to see the fruit of his blood, sweat and agony. He paced around the gallery, conjuring up the image of the Ancient Mariner for Joshua. Right down to the mad, glittering eyes.

Running an art gallery had its moments, Joshua thought as he poured Bruce a thick cup of coffee, his third. This wasn't one of them.

Joshua handed the mug to Bruce who curled his paint-splattered fingers around the mug, holding on as if this was a vital transfusion and he would die without it. Joshua pressed a firm hand to his shoulder and forced the man to sit down in the bright, royal blue canvas-back director's chair that was off to the side. He wanted him out of the way of the patrons. People tended to be frightened off by wild-eyed artists.

Letting out a breath, Joshua looked around the spacious gallery. It was big and bright and most important, his. Who would have thought, fifteen year ago, as he held his degree in his hand, eager to take the world by storm, that he would wind up on the other side of the easel? Then he had wanted nothing more than to paint, to create. It was food, water, air, the very life itself to him.

Well, almost, he thought ruefully, his mind drifting over the rough cobblestone of memories. There had been something more, something that had been his inspiration, his driving force. But he had lost that. Lost her. And when that happened, he lost his need to express himself on canvas in wild, passionate colors that drew out bits and pieces of his soul for the world to see. There had been no more soul left to give.

Losing her had been, he thought, his own fault. But he hadn't anything to fight with, nothing to offer, and so he had lost his inspiration. He had lost Johanna before he had ever had her.

He smiled to himself now. Across the room, his secretary caught his enigmatic smile and wondered at it. Since he had returned from his business trip abroad, she had noticed that her boss tended to drift off, daydreaming. She couldn't help wondering what had happened in London to bring about this change. Usually, he was a very sensible, straight-forward type of man. Maybe, she mused, it involved a woman.

And Johanna never even knew, Joshua thought. Never even suspected. To her, they had been just friends, sharing everything, sharing dreams, feelings, hopes. All save one. He hadn't told her. He hadn't been able to tell her what he felt. And when he finally could, she was gone, married to that man who put stars in her eyes and promised her the world.

Because he felt she deserved it and that Harry could give it to her far better than he, Joshua had let her go without a word.

How odd that he should run into her in the Tate Gallery of all places after all these years. When he had heard her voice, when he had seen her again, the years seemed to have been stripped away from him. Fifteen years, gone in a flash.

And yet they weren't gone. They had left their stamp in her eyes. The soft innocence he had always loved wasn't there any more. She had a woman's well-formed figure and a woman's maturity in her eyes, a maturity that had brought pain and sorrow with it. She had smiled at him beneath that brilliant painting of Turner's in the gallery and had talked animatedly of old times. But he had seen instantly that she wasn't happy, even though she was in her element, in an art gallery.

He had wondered about the man she was with and who he was in her life. The lunch they shared hadn't yielded enough information on that score. But for the most part, he had only thought of her. He had pressed his card into her hand, but he had little hopes that she would even keep it, much less seek him out someday. Her life, such as it was, was in Los Angeles. His was here now, nurturing frail artistic egos and immersing himself in the art community.

Joshua realized that Bruce had stopped his rambling, edgy monologue and was looking up at him with his huge, hang-dog eyes. Now they made him think a little of Rasputin, the mad Russian monk who had brought down the Russian monarchy. Bruce was a little mad himself, but harmless. Except, perhaps, to himself.

"My advice to you," Joshua began, not knowing what Bruce had just finished saying but guessing it had something to do with having to depend on ignorant yuppies standing around, eating cheese, drinking wine and making comments about his so-called visionary work, "is for you to go home and sleep until Thursday afternoon." Joshua put a fatherly hand on the man's shoulder. "Frankly, Bruce, you really look like hell."

Bruce flinched, then shrugged off the hand. "Looks aren't important."

"Maybe not," Joshua agreed amiably, "but smell is. Take a shower, okay?"

Bruce put down the mug on the black onyx top table with a thud. Coffee sloshed over the sides and onto the table. "Hey, I—"

Easily, Joshua covered the wet spot with a napkin and wiped it away, grateful that the spilled coffee was the only damage to the table. "Do it for me, okay?" Joshua urged as he took the reed-thin man by the arm and raised him to his feet.

Long legs clad in dirty brown cords unfolded. Beat-up moccasins made contact with the floor. Bruce ran a hand through hair that touched his shoulders and desperately needed to be shampooed. "Yeah, I guess I can do that."

Joshua grinned easily as he patted Bruce's back. Bones met his touch. The man needed to consume something more substantial than paint fumes, Joshua thought. "My mother thanks you, my father thanks you, my sister thanks you and I thank you."

"Huh?"

"An old line from a movie," Joshua said, waving away both the line and the puzzled look on Bruce's face. It had been from *Yankee Doodle Dandy*, a movie he had seen with Johanna. Next to art, she had loved old movies, most particularly nonsensical things where people sang their way into happily ever after.

He couldn't seem to get her out of his mind. Since he had seen her in London two weeks ago, she seemed to haunt his thoughts every time he let his guard down. The scandal involving Harry hadn't helped matters any either. He had read about it last week and had been tempted to call her and offer his help. Going with impulse, he *had* called, but his call hadn't been put through. The lines to the hotel were jammed. She was fodder for reporters, the six o'clock news and rag mongers.

He wished he could help.

He knew that he couldn't. She wasn't part of his life anymore.

That didn't keep him from wondering, though. And wishing.

"Mac?" He looked up and saw Kathy, a dark-haired woman who had a voice like a little girl, approaching him. She had already called his name twice without any acknowledgement from him. "Mrs. Regis called and wants to speak to you as soon as possible."

"Ah, wonderful Mrs. Regis." Joshua grinned. "God bless her generous heart." He began to stride toward his office.

It was thanks to Alberta Regis and her club of bored ladies with money on their hands that his gallery had gotten its start to begin with. She liked to think of herself as a patron of the arts and it had been she who had decided that the Soho region could use one more art gallery—as long as it was good and as long as she had a say-so in it. Joshua had met her quite by fortunate accident. He had had his paintings spread out on the sidewalk just as she happened to be walking by. She stopped to admire them and him. A very fulfilling and very platonic relationship had begun. Alberta Regis was in her sixties, but had the heart of a thirty-year-old and flirted outrageously. They liked each other a lot.

Joshua stopped. First things first. He turned back to Bruce. Joshua took out his wallet and pressed a fifty dollar bill into Bruce's hand. "Do me another favor, Bruce. Get yourself a decent shirt."

"I told you—"

"Looks don't mean anything, yes, I know, but I am getting kind of tired of that khaki tee-shirt of yours." The shirt was peering out from beneath an equally filthy denim jacket.

Bruce looked at the fifty in his hand. "I could buy out the army surplus store with this."

"Don't. Just get a shirt. Preferably one that fits."

Bruce left the gallery mumbling under his breath. On his way out, he nearly walked into a well-dressed woman entering the gallery.

"Hey, sorry, pretty lady." The artist grinned broadly.

"No harm done," the woman murmured, stepping around him. She was more concerned with the collision of butterflies in her stomach than with colliding with an unkempt man. That sort of thing was usual in New York. Everyone was always hurrying off in some direction, elbowing people out of the way if necessary.

Joshua turned, hearing Bruce's mumbled words of apology. And then he stood very, very still, his breath trapped in his lungs.

Johanna stood in the doorway.

Chapter Twenty-eight

Because she had stayed at the Plaza Hotel overlooking Central Park so often, Johanna was familiar with many of the staff there. When the cab driver at the airport had asked her "where to?" she heard herself saying, "Fifth Avenue and Fifty-ninth Street," the hotel's address.

Perhaps it was a need to see friendly, smiling faces before she set out completely on her own. Perhaps it was because she had always liked the hotel with its imposing European chateau ambience. She wasn't certain why, but she felt a need to check into the hotel. However much she liked it there, the stay was meant to be only temporary. The Plaza cost money and there was no longer an endless supply. Actually, there never had been an endless supply, but Harry had spent money as if there was and his lavishness had been contagious. At least for a while. The joy of buying expensive things had long since worn off. For Johanna things could never take the place of feelings.

Now she was completely on her own and she had to

figure out exactly what that meant. She knew what she wanted to do. She wanted to paint, to go back and regain the ground she had lost so long ago. She had always wanted to be an artist, from the time she could clutch a crayon in her hand and scribble her impressions of the world around her down on any free surface. There was nothing else she wanted to do. Not ever.

Except, to be Harry's wife.

But that was gone, over. That kind of commitment, as far as she was concerned, was dead.

She wanted to go back to a world she understood, a world where she could feel and be without receiving pain as payment. She needed to stabilize, to rejuvenate both physically and emotionally for Jocelyn as well as for herself. She could do it here, in the world of the art community.

But she also had to eat. As did Jocelyn. Being an artist wouldn't be something that could give her the resources she needed. Maybe someday, but bills were not paid with promises of "someday," groceries weren't bought, doctors weren't obtained, needs weren't met with the word "someday." Harry, even if she had wanted to take revenge by sticking to the letter of California law and taking half of everything, had little money that hadn't been eaten up by drugs. No doubt the house in Beverly Hills would go to cover Sid's hefty legal fees. Added to that was the fact that Harry might still go to prison and once out, might never work again. No, there was nothing Harry could give her to ease this journey she was on.

She needed a job. And she needed it now. There was, of course, the jewelry. That she had kept. It had come from Harry and it no longer meant anything to her. But she could sell it and it would go a long way to keeping her and Jocelyn comfortable for a while. Until she could get herself together.

Johanna had found the card that Joshua had handed to her in London. She had forgotten all about it and him in the hurry of making her departure plans. The siege by the reporters had thrown it all out of her head. It had surfaced quite by accident when she had been rummaging through her purse, trying to find her claim ticket for her luggage at Kennedy. She had thrown it into her purse that day she had run into him in the Tate Gallery. He represented a part of her life when things had been fresh, hopeful and the world was sweet and tender. They had been, no, still were, friends. Maybe he could help her now. She wouldn't feel uncomfortable approaching him. If nothing else, he could settle or at least reduce the anxiety that was beginning to grow within her.

At least it was worth a try.

She had called Mary an hour after she and Jocelyn had arrived at the hotel. Her sister had just walked in through the door, but her tired response had immediately brightened when she heard Johanna's voice on the line. Mary had offered to see what she could find for her at I. Magnum's, but Johanna didn't want to be a saleswoman or a window dresser, or work in customer service. They were all very good positions, she assured her sister, but she wanted to do something utilizing her own talents and skills, something that involved art, however distantly. To that end, she had told her about seeing Joshua again in London and her plans to look him up now that she was here. Mary had sounded pleased. And hopeful. Johanna had hung up, wondering if Mary knew something that she didn't.

Johanna, Mary and Jocelyn met that night and had dinner at the Plaza's Oyster Bar. The restaurant was a cross between an English pub and a fish house and reminded Johanna of Tommy. Mary had insisted on paying. The following day, leaving Jocelyn occupied in the hotel, Johanna had set out on knees that weren't altogether strong, to see Joshua.

It seemed odd to her to be looking for a job after all these years. She was, she knew, hoping that Joshua could come up with a miracle. She had absolutely no idea what she could actually do or what she was looking for. Only that she would know when she found it.

The cab ride from the hotel to the gallery brought back a flood of memories. These were streets she had once walked on, shopped on, been happy on. It had all changed and yet nothing changed. Stores were different, people were the same. The streets of New York were always crowded, so much so that it looked as if the people were gathering for some sort of parade that was about to take place. Actually, they were the parade as they marched quickly off to private destinations, jostling for space in a city that had a limited amount. The word melting pot was an old and still apt description. Hassidic Jews shared territory with women in minks, vagrants in torn coats, affluent yuppies on a break for lunch, teenagers experimenting with the latest rainbow colors for their hair. One block over from the diamond district between Fifth and Sixth avenue, a weather-beaten old man in a shabby coat so dirty that it had no color at all was hitting sticks against a stoop, playing music only he could hear.

No, it hadn't changed.

But she had.

Joshua's art gallery was located on a busy street in the Soho district, nestled between a bookstore that sold only foreign copies and a French restaurant that served only crepes. Every single crepe imaginable. The aroma reminded her that she hadn't eaten much for breakfast.

She stood outside the gallery, gathering her courage one more time. She who was so quick to grant favors hated asking for one. But there was no way around it. Time was important. And Joshua had spoken as if he knew people. Lots of people. Somewhere there was something for her.

Johanna drew a deep breath and pushed the front door, only to be practically run over by a rather unkempt man.

"Hey, sorry, pretty lady." Beneath the two-day-old stubble, he smiled, interested, at least for the moment.

She saw that his hands were smeared with indigo blue

as he reached out to steady her. She took a step back and then around him, nodding her thanks. "No harm done."

An artist. Things don't change. She found comfort in that. A lot of comfort, oddly enough. Van Gogh probably looked something like that, except that he had only one ear in which to wear an earring. She noticed that the disheveled man who almost knocked her down wore three. Two in one ear, one in another.

She had only caught her breath when she saw Joshua inside the gallery. He had told her that he owned the gallery, but he certainly didn't look it. He was dressed in a soft beige pullover and dark brown slacks that had lost their crease a long time ago. Clean, neat, but definitely not dressed to impress anyone. His hair was a bit too long, but then it always had been. It had been longer when they were going to school together.

He looked like Joshua, she thought suddenly. And yet, he looked prosperous. It was in the way he held himself more than anything. Confidence had slipped in. He hadn't had that when they were sharing dreams together fifteen years ago. He had gained it over the years. Just as she had lost it.

She didn't know what to do with her hands.

He didn't give her time to figure it out. In an instant, he had crossed to her and took both of her hands in his. Then he bent down and pretended to peer at her face. "Is it really you?" he asked.

"In the flesh." She tried to sound light.

He surveyed the trim figure she cut in her light gray, two piece suit. A vivid pink scarf was at her throat. Vivid. The word always came to mind when he thought of her. "Very little of it left."

She shrugged, a little embarrassed, more because of the reason she had come than because of the way he was looking at her. "I've lost a few pounds."

"Don't lose any more."

"Is that the artist in you speaking?"

"That's the friend. Any more and they'll have to put bricks in your pockets the next time the wind picks up." Joshua let go of her hands, though he didn't want to, and took a step back.

She laughed then, just the way she always had, and her eyes sparkled.

Her eyes had always inspired him. There were portraits of her in his loft, some painted years ago, some painted not that long ago, from memory. He had always loved her eyes.

"If there is a next time," he amended, realizing that he was making plans that he had no right to make. She was just passing through. "How long are you staying?"

She looked around and he felt the tension in her body, saw it flicker across her face. "What is it, Johanna?" He lowered his voice as he drew her aside.

She tried to laugh aside her discomfort. She had never gotten into the habit of asking favors, not even from friends. It hurt her pride to be a supplicant, but there was her daughter to think of. For a moment, she debated giving this up, pretending to have dropped by for only a friendly visit. Maybe she'd just go to an employment agency and ask them—

And then she saw the painting.

The words that had formed upon her tongue died away as she slowly moved, almost in a trance, to the painting that hung in a prominent part of the gallery. It was a seascape, full of vibrant, dark blues and grays. It was a painting of a storm at sea, or rather, a storm that threatened to break. It was the Atlantic Ocean the way it had appeared that weekend in the fall that they had spent with friends in Maine.

Johanna slowly turned to look at Joshua. "That's the painting I gave you when I left."

He remembered the day she left as clearly as if it were taking place right now. Holding the painting in his hands, he had tried to smile his thanks as he had fought back anger and hurt, neither of which, he was determined, she would see. He kept his face impassive even now. "It's the first one I hung up when I opened my gallery."

"Why didn't you hang your own painting there?" Or anywhere, she thought, scanning the immediate area. None of his paintings were on display, at least, none that she recognized. His style was like his signature. Romanticized. She felt confident that she would have been able to tell his paintings from the rest. There weren't any. Why?

"None were as good as this one."

"Can't be that good." She turned away from it. It made her uncomfortable. It brought back a wave of memories she wasn't capable of dealing with yet. "You still haven't sold it."

He grinned and shook his head. She didn't understand, he thought. "It's not for sale."

Her smile softened. Then he wasn't trying to sell it. There was a lot of friendship locked within that painting. "Then why hang it?"

"To attract patrons. That's our hundred dollar word for customers," he laughed softly. "They see this, they want to see more and maybe they'll find something they like almost as much."

She turned again to look at it. She cocked her head, as if seeing it for the first time. It was good, she mused. *She* had been good. Maybe someday wouldn't be that far off after all. "Have you had any offers?" she asked.

He laughed, knowing well the artistic ego and its need to be reassured. "Lots."

"Ever been tempted?"

He grew more serious as his eyes washed over her. "Not even once."

It was her turn to grin. Talking to Joshua was easy. It had always been easy. She didn't know why she had been afraid to come. "I need a job, Joshua," she said without preamble.

There were a hundred questions he wanted to ask, a thousand pieces of her life he wanted reconstructed for him.

But not now. She didn't need probing now. She needed peace more than he needed to hear. He could sense it. He answered the only way he knew she needed to be answered. "Come work for me."

It was too simple, too easy. And too wonderful. "Doing what?"

"I could use an assistant." Johanna glanced toward the back office and saw Kathy moving around. He saw her line of vision. "That's my secretary, Kathy. She's a ball of fire, but she doesn't know anything about art except that she likes the color blue."

Blue was her favorite color. "It's a start."

"I need more than that around here. I've got a showing Thursday evening."

"Yours?"

He shook his head. "The wild-eyed man who almost ran over you on the way out."

"He did seem preoccupied." she laughed.

"Scared out of his mind is more like it. He's going to be a basketcase by Thursday night. He can't make up his mind whether this means nothing to him or everything in the world."

"I think I know the feeling," she commiserated.

"I'll need someone to hold his hand Thursday night. Figuratively and maybe literally." He held up his hands. "As you can see, I'm not equipped for that."

His hands were large and capable and reminded her of Tommy. Artistic hands didn't have to be small and delicate to work miracles. She had seen wonderful things come from Joshua's hands, she thought, paintings with such feeling that they made her want to cry. She wanted to argue with him that he should have his painting displayed in a point of prominence, not hers, but she decided that was an argument for another time, when she had entrenched herself here.

She had already decided to take the job.

"Is he any good?" she asked.

He took her hand and led her over to three paintings he
had just hung up last night. "Here, why don't you judge
for yourself."

He watched her as she studied them, watched her for
the sheer joy of being able to look at her once again, to
have her back in his life. This time, he had already decided,
things were going to be different. He wasn't that stumbling
boy, tripping over his own feet any more.

"Mac," Kathy called, "it's Mrs. Regis again."

Joshua put a restraining hand on Johanna's shoulder.
"Stay here," he said. "I'll only be a minute and then we
can grab a bite to eat next door and negotiate."

Johanna nodded, but knew there was nothing to negotiate. Whatever he wanted to pay her, she'd take. She
needed the feel of being around an old friend, at least until
she got her bearings. She needed to feel productive. And
Joshua had always been so encouraging. He had faith in
her art even when she had wavered. It had been he who
had warned her not to throw away her talent, her gift,
when she told him that she was going to marry Harry.

She roamed around the gallery as she waited for him to
return, acquainting herself with the works. Some made her
smile, some stirred feelings, none left her untouched. He
had a good eye for choosing, she thought. He didn't need
her. But he would, she vowed. She'd make herself indispensable to him and the gallery in time.

For the first time in years, Johanna savored hope.

Chapter Twenty-nine

"This probably isn't what you're used to," Joshua said as he watched Johanna slide along the wide bench. He sat down on the chair opposite her. The tiny French restaurant was hectic and crammed, with two rows of tables set up to utilize long benches running along the wall on both sides of the room. The tables were meant for two, yet there was a feeling that everyone in the room was with everyone else. Yet since one could feel alone in a crowd, Johanna had a sense of being alone with Joshua. The constant din, the motion of patrons coming and going, of waitresses serving people around them isolated Johanna, made her feel alone. That was what she liked about New York. If you wanted, you could have it all. The absolute privacy of anonymity, provided by the masses, or the intimate company of a few good friends.

Surrounding them was the delicious aroma of an array of crepes baking in the oven at the back of the restaurant. If the word "homey" could possibly apply to a restaurant in the heart of the city, it applied to this one.

Johanna thought of the countless lunches she had endured in Beverly Hills, of the meaningless conversations she had listened to and taken part in at Spago. "No," she smiled, absently tracing the lines of a square on the red check table cloth, "it's not." She looked up, her eyes touching his. "This is much nicer."

He didn't know if she was being polite, or truthful, but her answer pleased him. "Do you want to pick up where we left off in London and continue catching up on fifteen years worth of life, or do you want me to treat you as a stunning new employee who just waltzed into my life this afternoon?"

She laughed as she sipped the water with appreciation. She had sampled water all over the world and there was nothing to compare with the water in New York. She grinned, both at the thought and at his words. "The latter?" She raised her eyebrows hopefully.

He would have rather at least a middle ground, but he had patience. Probably more than his share, he realized. That was both his blessing and his curse. "As you wish, Mrs. Whitney."

"Not that new."

He covered her hand with his own. His blue eyes softened and she saw something there, something she didn't want to see. She thought it was pity. "Johanna, it's good to see you again."

The waitress, dressed in a wide peasant skirt and blouse, approached to take their order and Johanna breathed a silent sigh of relief. She didn't want pity or affection. She wasn't entirely certain what it was she wanted. Probably just to pull her life together and make the best of the mess she found herself in. Time alone to reconstruct the phoenix and rise out of the ashes again, she thought wryly. And rise up she would, she promised herself. Stronger, this time, and never, ever allow herself to be in a position to be hurt again.

"What'll you have?" he asked as she skimmed the menu.

"I didn't know that there were so many different things they could do with crepes."

"You'd be surprised," he grinned broadly. His grin was wide and guileless, like a young boy's. There were traces of mischief there.

She remembered how infectious his grin was. It was impossible to stay depressed around Joshua. He had always made her laugh, always made her feel good about everything. Maybe, she thought, that was what had ultimately brought her here to him. To get a little of the good feelings that he could create and use them as a salve against the blackness that still existed within her. Someday, she'd be able to do it on her own. Right now, she'd use what she could.

"I'll have the ham and swiss crepes, please." She folded her menu and surrender it to the petite waitress.

"Two. And a bottle of chablis, please."

He would have eaten beef jerky right now and not noticed. He still couldn't get over the fact that she was here, sitting a few feet away from him. What had made her uproot her life? Was it the scandal? No, the Johanna he knew wasn't like that. She would have stuck with Harry through it all. It must have been Harry who had pushed her away. Yes, that would have gone along with what he had read about the man.

Unconsciously, Joshua clenched his hands into fists as they rested on the table. He had always disliked Harry, now more than ever.

Johanna saw his fingers curl into themselves and wondered what he was thinking. His expression remained unchanged. You've gotten more secretive than when I knew you, Joshua, she thought. But then, haven't we all? The thought made her feel sad.

"Is this just a temporary move?" he asked, trying to sound casual.

She shook her head slowly, the low light that filtered

through the smoky room caught fire in her hair, making it almost silver. He longed to run his hands through it. He kept them where they were and tried to relax. There would be a time for things, but it wasn't now. Now was for listening.

"This is for good." She hesitated, then reminded herself that this was Joshua she was talking to. Joshua who had never laughed at her even when others might have. "I wanted to paint again."

He nodded, pleased that she had returned to it. "I always thought you had talent."

She toyed with her glass instead of drinking. "You were always nice."

"True, but I also have a good eye for talent. That's how I came to Mrs. Regis's attention."

"Mrs. Regis?" How foolish to think that nothing had changed with Joshua. He was probably engaged, married, or on his umpteen relationship. He had always been so endearingly gregarious.

"The art gallery's prime patron."

He allowed himself a little sip of wine before he continued. Sitting here, opposite her, made his mouth dry. God, she was beautiful, even more beautiful than he had remembered. The ache he thought was long gone surfaced, demanding and urgent. It cost him a great deal to go on talking as if he wasn't sitting here, wanting her.

"Actually, if it wasn't for dear Mrs. Regis, I'd still be trying to hawk my own paintings somewhere around Washington Square. Remember, when we did that?" He did. He remembered every single detail with utmost clarity.

Her eyes lit up as the long-ago memory returned. "You told me to dress up like Alice Faye and sing *I'm Rose of Washington Square*," she said, fondly remembering when they had seen the old movie together.

"Something had to pull them in and the paintings I had weren't doing it."

"They were very good paintings," Johanna said in a voice

that was reminiscent of the past. She sounded, he thought, less world-weary for a moment, as if she had dropped the burden of the emotional luggage she was carrying. He loved her loyalty. And damn it all, he still loved her, after all this time. "The people there just had no taste, that's all."

"You always were loyal." Except when it mattered most, he thought. But then he couldn't have blamed her. She hadn't known. Would it have mattered to her if she had? Would she have stayed? It was something he intended to find out this time around.

He saw her face cloud slightly and knew somehow he had said the wrong thing.

"Yes, like a faithful puppy dog." She raised the glass to her lips and took a long, healthy sip. "That was always my shortcoming."

"Loyalty is never a shortcoming."

"It is if you use it to bury yourself, to chain yourself to something that's dead and gone."

He had promised himself not to push only a few short minutes ago. His promise only lived long enough to wait while the entrees were served and the waitress left once again. "Did he hurt you that badly?"

She tensed. Sympathy would reopen wounds and she wanted them sealed. "Joshua, I didn't come here to unload my problems—"

"Then we're no longer friends?"

"Of course we are."

"You always used to tell me what was bothering you," he said patiently.

"The things that bothered a nineteen-year-old silly girl are light years away from the woman you see here."

"You were never silly."

His smile made her feel warm and that made her uncomfortable. She didn't want warmth, she wanted only to work. Her romance with Tommy had been short, sweet and healing. But it also had its limitations. She had known the ground rules ahead of time, had known that there was no future and in knowing, couldn't make plans, couldn't make dreams that would ultimately crumble in her hand. Something in Joshua's eyes told her that she didn't have the grace of that kind of limitation here.

She switched directions. "Are you married, Joshua?"

It came out of the blue and he wondered why she was trying so hard to divert the conversation away from her. "To my work. To the gallery."

"No girlfriend in the wings?"

He thought of the women he knew, the pleasant, temporarily satisfying merges of bodies that lasted the night or the week. "No."

She kept her eyes on her plate, afraid to look into his eyes, afraid of what she would see there. "How is it that someone as wonderful as you isn't spoken for?"

"The obvious joke about 'just lucky, I guess' doesn't apply. I've always wanted a home and family."

This time, she did look up. She heard a trace of loneliness in his voice. "Yes, I know."

"But there was never anyone who qualified."

"Flunked the test, did they?" she teased.

"Something like that."

None of them were you, he added silently. It wasn't that he was obsessed with her so much as she had provided him with a guideline, a ruler that no one else he had met afterwards could match up to. Yes, she was beautiful, but it wasn't the kind of ice beauty that he had seen time and again. Hers was the kind that lingered on the mind and left a warm, pulsating appreciation. It brought sunshine into his life.

But more important than beauty, she had compassion. There wasn't a person in need that she could turn her back on, even when they were going to college. She continued to have a soft heart. He had followed her life through the magazine articles. She was always heading some charitable fund raiser. It seemed to Joshua that she looked like she could use a little charity herself right now, of a comforting nature.

"Do you have a place to stay?"

"Jocelyn and I are staying at the Plaza Hotel. Jocelyn's my—"

"Daughter, yes I know." He saw the question enter her eyes.

"I didn't introduce you in London, did I?" No, she had been with Tommy at the time. Mary had taken Jocelyn out for the day, she recalled.

"You forget, I can read."

She nodded and pushed away her plate. Her appetite was gone. "The newspaper stories."

All this was causing her pain, he thought, damning Harry to hell. "How serious is it, really? For Harry."

She wondered why he had singled it out that way. She hadn't told him about her pending divorce. He probably guessed, though. He could always read her like a book. "He could go to jail."

"For how long?"

She shrugged. "I don't know. Too long for him."

"Have you left him, Johanna?"

She raised her eyes to his and he saw the tears shimmering there. He cursed Harry for putting them there and himself for raising them.

"Yes."

"Sorry, I didn't mean to pry." Maybe, he thought, instead of cursing Harry, he should be grateful to the man for being such an ass. If he hadn't been, he wouldn't be getting this second chance to win Johanna.

She shook her head, brushing a tear away with her fingertips. "I always get sentimental over ham and swiss crepes." She mustered a grin. "Know of any vacant apartments?"

"In New York? Have you tried the obituaries?" he joked.

"Still that tough, eh?"

"Depends on what you're looking for."

"Cheap," she said quickly. "And close to the gallery."

He grinned, hoping to put the serious moments behind them, for the time being at least. "There's my apartment."

He was rewarded with a smile. "Seriously."

He snapped his fingers. "Foiled again."

"Thanks, Joshua."

"Is that a general 'thanks' or a specific one?"

"Specific." Her voice softened to a whisper. "For being here, for being my friend. For not asking too many questions."

"So much for the interrogation. Always one jump ahead of me, aren't you?"

"Never." she laughed.

"Eat your crepes and we'll see what we can do about your living arrangements."

To her surprise, she found that she was hungry again. Being around Joshua had always been good for her.

Chapter Thirty

"You know, Johanna." Joshua leaned back, sipping his wine, rolling an idea over in his mind. "I think I might have a place for you to stay after all."

She brightened. "Oh?"

"How would a loft suit you?"

Disappointment followed in the wake of hope. A loft was out of the question. "It would suit me beautifully, but that's a bit too rich for my blood these days." She hated the way that sounded, so small, so niggardly, but she had to think of costs now.

"Don't worry. You'll be able to manage fine on your salary."

"Where is the loft? Rhode Island?"

"No." Joshua finished his wine before he continued. "As it happens, the man I was visiting in London is still there. C'mon," he rose, peeling off a few bills and throwing them on the table, "let me make a phone call and see if Elton has any objections to a beautiful woman living in his loft while he's out, soaking up European influence."

He ushered her out of the restaurant, passing a buxomy redhead on the way.

The woman raked him over with her eyes before she asked, "How was it, mon chéri?"

Joshua kissed his fingers and threw the kiss to the winds. "Wonderful, as always, Veronica."

The woman beamed. "Always a pleasure, Joshua."

She looked, Johanna thought, as if she would have liked to extend her pleasure to include Joshua as the main course. She wondered if Joshua had ever been involved with the good-looking woman.

The crisp autumn air felt invigorating after the satisfying meal. Going with feeling, Johanna slipped her hand into Joshua's.

Joshua looked down at their linked hands. So natural, so right. He felt a smile growing from his very core and spreading out to include every part of him.

They walked into the gallery and Joshua had her sit down as he looked up Elton's phone number. Anticipation began to hum through her veins as she listened to Joshua talk to the transatlantic operator. Two wrong numbers and a connection that terminated in the middle followed before he finally was able to communicate with the owner of the loft. It lasted all of five minutes. Elton trusted Joshua implicitly and if Joshua vouched for Johanna, that was good enough for him. Besides, it would be nice to defray the cost of rent if at all possible.

When he hung up, Joshua turned to her, a satisfied look on his face. "The place is yours for six months. Maybe longer. Elton never estimates his time properly. He works slower than he thinks." Joshua pulled out a set of keys from the center drawer of his cluttered desk. Handing them to Johanna, he gave her an address on Broome Street.

She rolled the address over in her mind. "That's three blocks from here."

"Exactly. The only thing that Elton likes better than

painting is eating. He likes to be within smelling distance of Veronica's Restaurant. Has a passion for crepes, it seems. And Veronica has a passion for him. It works out to everyone's benefit."

She reached for her purse. "Does he want a check now—?"

"We can take care of all the details later. Details never bothered Elton. He goes for the grand picture. Besides," Joshua grinned, "I don't see you running off in the middle of the night."

Johanna thought of the address. She wouldn't have to waste any precious time commuting. That would give her more time with Jocelyn. And her painting. "This is absolutely perfect." She clapped her hands together. Hers for six months. Six months in which to get settled and find a real place of her own. It was too good to be true. She knew in her heart that coming to see Joshua was a good idea. She just hadn't realized how good.

Joshua let his eyes roam her face. Right now, she looked every bit as young as she had all those years ago. "Yes, I always thought so. It's not much and Elton wasn't the greatest at keeping house—he hated housekeepers—but it's yours for six hundred a month."

"Six hundred?" This was even better than she had hoped for. "You can't rent a phone booth for six hundred a month in New York."

"Attribute it to my persuasive charm." He sat on the edge of the desk. "Elton owes me a favor. I unloaded a particularly hideous painting of his and got a damn good price for it."

A place to stay. Somewhere she could call home. Relieved, Johanna kissed Joshua's cheek. "With you an hour and you're already indispensable in my life."

He wanted to take her hand, but didn't. "I plan to be, Johanna."

For a moment, his tone had her hesitating. "Joshua."

Slowly, the smile slipped away from her lips. "I think you should know something."

"Yes?"

"I'm dead inside."

With Joshua, it might be different she thought, then realized that she was only chasing rainbows. It was supposed to have been different with Harry and it hadn't been. It had been hideous. It was a man who had made her believe that dreams came true, he made her believe that forever could be beautiful. And it was a man who had destroyed it all. As long as Joshua stayed her friend, he wasn't really a man. She felt his reaction to her and was afraid of it. She didn't want another male-female relationship. She wanted to remain free.

"Then moving in might be hard for you," he said lightly.

She appreciated the change in tone, in topic. She was being paranoid. Joshua wouldn't want anything from her. He was just being a friend. He was being what she needed. With a laugh, she answered, "I'll manage. When do you want me to start?"

Right now. "Tomorrow too soon?"

"Not soon enough. I'll see you at—?" She had no idea when the gallery opened its doors.

"Nine'll be fine."

"Nine it is. Goodbye. And thank you."

"Don't thank me yet."

"Why not?"

He saw the apprehension enter her eyes yet. Like a horse that had been whipped, he thought. It was going to take time. And patience. "In the dictionary, under slave driver, it says, 'See Joshua.'"

She relaxed. "I can handle it."

Johanna walked out, feeling very accomplished. She had landed a job and a place to stay all in one afternoon. Since the plane had touched down yesterday, she had been worried about both things. It turned out to be so simple, Johanna felt almost guilty. It hadn't been nearly as hard as she had feared.

No, the hard part was going to be adjusting, she thought as she took a cab back to the hotel. Adjusting to making it on her own.

Johanna leaned back in the cab. The same scenery passed her window as on the trip to Soho, but this time, she didn't see. Her driver was talking steadily, something about the baseball play-offs, but she wasn't listening. The afternoon had left her in a state of wild euphoria. Thank God for Joshua, she thought. He had made the solution to almost all her problems seem so simple.

"We're moving," she announced to Jocelyn breathlessly as she swept into the suite.

Jocelyn scrambled up on the sofa, rising up to her knees. "To California?" she asked excitedly.

"To Soho."

"Where's that?"

"You'll find out, my love. You'll find out. Oh, it's going to be wonderful."

"For you," the girl grumbled, sitting down on her heels on the sofa.

Johanna cupped Jocelyn's chin in her hand and raised it until their eyes met. "For us," she corrected.

There was no dampening her enthusiasm. She had a job, an apartment, a future. Everything was going to be just fine.

They checked out of the hotel within the hour and arrived at their new home. On the trip over, Jocelyn had grown progressively more morose about the prospect of actually living in New York, away from her friends, away from the sunshine, to reside in a city she considered "gross."

Jocelyn stood in the doorway and looked around critically, unwilling to move, as if taking a step into the apartment would bind her to stay. It was a huge room. It was only one room.

"Where's the rest of the rooms?"

"This is it."

"What a dump!"

Johanna deposited the remainder of her suitcases just inside the door, too tired to do anything more. "Auditions for Bette Davis are being held next Thursday, not today, kid."

Jocelyn stared at her. "Huh?"

Johanna dismissed the question with a shake of her head. "You had to be there. Before your time, Jocey."

Jocelyn glared. "So's this place."

It needed help, that was true. Joshua's friend might have been kind and a successful artist, but as a housekeeper, he left much to be desired. Such as a vacuum, a dust rag and all the cleaning essentials that would have helped to make the loft liveable. Still, the place was tremendous and more than she had hoped for.

Jocelyn refused to enter. "Are you sure we won't catch anything if we stay here?"

Johanna spared her one look, then went back to planning things out. "No, but we will if we linger out on the street."

"Why can't we go back to the hotel?"

She deposited one suitcase on the huge round bed in the center of the room. That would have to be moved, she decided. At least while she lived here. "I checked us out."

"Check us back in again."

"Hotels cost money, my love, and though I know you have no concept of it at all, it takes a lot to afford the Plaza Hotel."

Sensing defeat, Jocelyn took one tentative step inside the apartment. "What does this place cost, ninety-nine cents?"

Johanna laughed and shook her head. "Spoken like a true spoiled child of the eighties."

"I wanna go home."

"This is home," she said firmly.

Jocelyn was determined to hate it and she did. "This is a dump."

"You've already done that line." Johanna took a few essentials out of the suitcase.

"Please, Mom?" Jocelyn placed her hand on her mother's shoulder in mute supplication.

"Honey." Johanna turned, taking her into her arms. "I know this is a big adjustment for you. It's no picnic for me either."

"Then why are we doing it?"

"Because we have to." She kissed the top of Jocelyn's head.

"Why can't we go back to Beverly Hills and wait for Dad?"

"Dad's going to be gone for a long time, honey." Johanna ran her hand through her daughter's silver blond hair. "And I've got to earn a living."

"You can't earn one there?"

It was too difficult to explain and she was too tired. Maybe it was the coward's way out, but for now she'd take it. "No. It has to be here. I've already got a job and Aunt Mary knows of this great private school that you can go to."

"School?" Jocelyn pulled away, hostility building in her voice. "I have to face school here, too?"

She dug deep for patience. "Why not? They have schools in New York."

"Oh God, Mom, new people—" Jocelyn looked absolutely horrified. She covered her mouth with her hands and looked as if she was going to be sick.

Johanna knew what it meant to be the new kid on the block. It wasn't easy. "They only stay new until you meet them." Easy for me to say, Johanna thought.

Jocelyn sank down on the circular bed. "They'll hate me."

"Why? I don't think you're horrible."

"You're my mother. You're supposed to say that."

"Nope." Johanna sat down beside her. "Nowhere in the

mother manual does it say I have to say that. It says I have to feed you and clothe you until age eighteen, but nowhere does it say I have to say that you're not hateable."

"Is that a real word?"

"Not to my knowledge."

They laughed for a moment, the way they had when the world wasn't quite so tense, quite so frightening all around them.

Johanna rose. There were lots of suitcases to unpack and things to get in order. She felt a little overwhelmed. "What do you say we do first?"

Jocelyn looked around. "Move."

"Next suggestion?"

There was a knock on the door. "Answer the door?" she guessed.

Johanna looked at the door, a quiver of anxiety running through her. "No one knows we're here. I haven't had time to tell Mary."

Jocelyn was already running to the door and about to open it. Johanna crossed over her like a shot, covering her hand with her own.

"No!"

"Don't people in New York answer their doors?" Jocelyn asked with the innocence that came from having people shield her from everything that was ugly and evil.

"Not to strangers," Johanna hissed, turning to the peephole. All she saw was the side of a very broad shoulder.

"They do if they want to have a pizza," the voice on the other side of the door answered.

Jocelyn gave her mother a quizzical look.

"Joshua?" Johanna asked uncertainly.

"The pizza is burning a hole in my hand, Johanna. Open the door."

She unlocked the bottom lock and threw the door wide open. "What are you doing here?"

"You found me out. I moonlight as a pizza delivery man

and the people who called the order in weren't home, so here." He held the pizza aloft.

Joshua made his way to the tiny kitchen table and placed the large box down. Shaking the sting from his fingers, he turned to the girl who was opening the box eagerly. "You must be Jocelyn."

"Yes."

"I'm Joshua MacKenzie. Most people call me Mac."

"My mother calls you Joshua."

"Your mother isn't like most people," he said with a grin.

"Is that a criticism?" Johanna asked.

"That is an observation. Hungry?"

"The word starving comes more to mind." She looked around. "Plates?"

"Right over here." He led the way to an overhead cabinet and took out three plates, two small, one large. None matching. "Like I said, Elton doesn't care much for details."

She glanced at the sparse, mismatched furniture in the open area. "So I see."

"I thought this might do until you found something better."

Johanna shook her head as she pulled the pizza pieces apart. A streamer of mozzarella cheese followed the piece she gave Joshua.

"This apartment is terrific, Joshua. I'm more than grateful."

Jocelyn mumbled something into her piece as she chewed.

Johanna gave her a sharp look. "So is Jocelyn."

"Yeah, I can tell," he laughed.

Chapter Thirty-one

Joshua checked his watch. If Bruce didn't hurry, he was going to be late for his own show. It wouldn't be the first time an artist had succumbed to a case of devastating nerves.

He glanced over to where Johanna was fussing over a table that held a crystal punch bowl, a collection of tiny crystal cups and appetizers from a catering service that Veronica had recommended. A cousin in the business as it turned out. But his thoughts weren't on Veronica or the caterers. Or even on Bruce and the show any more. They all centered on Johanna. She was wearing a simple blue sheath that matched her eyes, hinted at the allure of her body and stirred feelings within him that made him wish they were alone in his apartment instead of inside the gallery, waiting for a crowd of people to arrive.

Because all the details pertaining to the show and the anticipated patrons had been taken care of hours ago, Joshua allowed himself the luxury of just drinking in her presence for a few moments. He crossed the highly polished oak floor and placed his hand over hers.

"You fuss anymore over that setting and you'll be worn out before anyone shows up to use it. Hey." He glanced down at their joined hands in surprise. "Your hands are like ice, Johanna."

She turned and offered him a quick, nervous smile. "I know."

"Nervous?" He couldn't believe it.

She nodded. "Maybe just a little."

"Why? This is just a little show in a tiny gallery tucked in between a foreign bookstore and a French restaurant that hasn't replaced its tablecloths in three years. It's really no big deal. You've been photographed going to premiers in Paris and Rome, dancing with celebrities from all four corners of the world at those parties Harry was so fond of taking you to."

Johanna raised a brow in surprise. He was rather well-informed on the details of her past life. "What makes you think I wasn't nervous then?"

Her response intrigued him. "Were you?"

"I never felt really comfortable there. I always thought of myself as Johanna Lindsey from Sunrise Falls, Connecticut."

He was tempted to push a curl from her cheek, but didn't. It would only make him want to touch her even more. "Apparently no one else did."

"How would you know?" Her tension was dissipating, as it always had whenever she talked to Joshua. He had that sort of calming effect on her and she blessed him for it now.

"I followed your life in photographic spreads, magazine stories, lines in gossip columns in the leading newspapers. Every one I could get my hands on."

"What, no grocery store tabloids?" She grinned, wondering if he was teasing her.

"I wanted news, Johanna, not trash."

He was serious. Her smile faded and the lines about her mouth tightened slightly. It would have made a difference in her life, knowing he cared what happened to her. Knowing there was someone from the past she could touch base with. "If you were that curious, why didn't you answer my letters, Joshua? Why didn't you ever write?"

And say what? *That I missed you more than I thought possible? That I wanted you to leave that son-of-a-bitch and come live with me?*

It had taken Joshua a long time to work her out of his system. Now, looking down into her face, it was as if that time had never been, as if he had never succeeded, not even for a moment. He had only fooled himself, masked his need so effectively from himself that he thought he had succeeded. But only thought. Writing to her would have prolonged the pain, the loss.

He shrugged. "I'm not much on letter writing, Johanna. One of my many faults."

She laughed just as the bell on the door sounded. Bruce came in, moving disjointedly with long, looping strides. Johanna thought that he looked as if his knees wouldn't support him. He was wearing a new shirt, just as Joshua had requested. It was a deep purple that made both of them wince a little.

"Artistic license," Johanna whispered.

"Should be revoked," Joshua commented. Then he glanced toward the rear of the gallery and its private stairway. "Want to look in on Jocelyn one last time before the fun starts?"

Jocelyn was safely tucked away in the apartment that Joshua maintained above the gallery. Mary had been unavailable for the evening and Joshua had been quick to ease Johanna's concern about leaving Jocelyn alone at night. His apartment was only a shout away from the gallery, he told her. That had won her over and pleased Jocelyn as well. She was too old for something so demeaning as a "babysitter" to look after her.

Johanna was tempted, but refrained from going upstairs. Jocelyn wanted desperately to savor a measure of independence. Having a mother look in on her every ten minutes didn't mesh with that desire. Johanna shook her head. "I left her watching her favorite movie, surrounded with three kinds of junk food. She'll be fine."

"Then I'd better see to our vividly attired artist." He began to cross to Bruce who was crushing out a cigarette with one hand as he felt his pocket for his pack with the other.

"Joshua."

She sounded so serious that for just a moment he hoped she would say something he wanted to hear.

"Yes?"

"Thank you."

Her smile hit him like a fist to his stomach. Fine way for a grown man to react, he upbraided himself. It didn't ease the pain. Or the want. "Nothing to thank me for."

"You don't even know why."

"Doesn't matter." He winked and held her hand a little too long. He could only mask his intensity just so far.

He always made her feel so good, she thought, so safe, so secure. Why hadn't she come here sooner? She could have spared herself so much pain. She could have resumed her career and —

No, there was no use in feeling regrets for what should have been. It hadn't been then, but it could be. She was lucky to be here at the gallery now.

The front door bell sent a melodic chime through the gallery, heralding the first wave of patrons.

"Time to be professional," Joshua said, letting go of her hand.

She let go of his reluctantly. Holding it had made her feel more confident, gave her strength. She had forgotten how much she had depended on Joshua's friendship to see her through back in the old days.

"See if you can keep Bruce propped up for at least part of the evening, will you?"

"I'll do my best," she promised.

She watched Joshua walk over to the door and greet a party of four people with the warmth that meant they were old friends or at least patrons of long standing. With her eye for fashion, she assessed the outfit that Joshua was wearing. Neatly pressed gray slacks, a blue shirt opened at the throat and a blue blazer. Black loafers finished the outfit. Harry would have never dressed so casually at a function. He believed in appearances. Joshua, she thought, believed in substance.

She realized how much she had missed the world of art. How much she had missed Joshua and his friendship.

"Got a cigarette?"

She turned to look up into Bruce's eyes. He looked like a man who was struggling to stay inside his skin. Flight looked like a very viable option.

"No, how about an *hors d'oeuvre?*"

"Only if I can smoke it."

"I like your paintings," she said easily.

Bruce forgot how uncomfortable the new shirt felt. "You do?"

Easily, Johanna linked her arm through Bruce's and led him over to one of the paintings that was prominently displayed. "Oh yes. Now this one over here, I'm afraid I have to admit, has me a little confused. Maybe you could explain it to me." Bruce walked off with her like a mouse following the Pied Piper.

Johanna smiled to herself. Nothing set an artist at ease as much as talking about his own work. She ought to know.

Joshua watched Johanna out of the corner of his eye as he spoke amiably to the people milling around the gallery. A smile of admiration was on his lips. He wondered if she knew just how charming she was, or how stunning. The gallery was quickly filling with an impressive crowd of people who had come by invitation only. Mrs. Regis's friends, socialites and people of prominence whom he had come to know. There were women wearing jewels that could have bought and sold the entire gallery with change to spare. None could compare to the simple elegance that Johanna possessed. She would have radiated it had she entered the gallery barefoot, wearing rags.

No doubt about it, Joshua thought as someone tapped his shoulder. He had it bad. And this time, he intended on doing something about it.

She took to it like a duck to water. It wasn't until that moment, as she stood talking to the Peruvian couple who had admired the almost savage pathos in Bruce's *New York at Sunrise*, in which he depicted a child of the streets staring with rounded eyes at the opulence of the city's skyscrapers as they stretched upward before him that, she realized just how much she missed all this. Looking at the painting, she could almost feel the hunger, the hopelessness depicted in the old eyes set in a young face. It was with feeling and verve that she praised Bruce's talents and discreetly encouraged the couple to purchase the painting now, while they still could.

"He's going to be an important artist," she assured them.

It was enough. They went to find Joshua to make arrangements for its sale.

"I should have answered one of your letters a long time ago and offered you a job then," Joshua said to her two hours later. "You're a regular whirlwind." Of the thirty paintings on display, twenty-one had been sold and another three had options on them. "I thought Californians were supposed to be laid-back."

She grinned. "I've always been a misplaced New Yorker at heart, I guess. This was fun."

And it was. It was the first such party that she had enjoyed in she couldn't remember how long.

"Hey, you were right," Bruce declared, carrying over a bottle of champagne and three glasses. "They really liked them."

Johanna saw the relief in the man's eyes. Pride was a horrible thing to put on the line. She had experience in that.

Joshua took two of the glasses and handed one to Johanna. He waited for Bruce to pour. "I told you you were good."

"I knew I was good and you knew I was good, but they didn't." He gestured out toward the front of the gallery. The large bay window looked out on the darkened streets and the populace that lived just beyond.

"Apparently," Johanna said, taking a sip, her eyes on his face, "now they do."

Bruce beamed at her, literally beamed. "I like your lady," he told Joshua, raising his glass high to toast Johanna.

The smile on Johanna's lips tightened. The quick, minute movement was not lost on Joshua. He didn't dwell on the hurt.

"Johanna is her own lady." Joshua raised his glass to her as well. "A shining free spirit whom I had the good fortune of going to school with."

"No shi—" Bruce coughed. "No foolin'?"

Johanna nearly choked on her champagne trying to stifle her laughter. It had been a long time since anyone tried to amend their language on her account. Harry's crowd spoke in only expletives, using them to fill in any temporary verbal void that came their way. "No, no fooling," she answered.

"Well," Joshua looked at his watch, "I think we should call it a night."

"Hey, I feel like really celebrating." With the show finally over, Bruce had gotten his second wind, a far more invigorating wind than the one he had when he first walked in the door tonight. "How about going out and painting the town?"

Joshua put his arm around Johanna's shoulders. "Nope. I'm afraid you have to count me out this time, Bruce. Some of us get up early to work."

"And I have a daughter to bring home," Johanna suddenly remembered. "Do you mind?" she asked Joshua as she started toward the back of the gallery.

"I'll go with you." He looked over his shoulder at the artist. "Bruce, just pull the door shut when you leave. The lock's already set."

Bruce merely nodded, tucking an unopened bottle of champagne under his arm. He stuffed a few remaining *hors d'oeuvres* into his pocket before he made his way to the front door.

Jocelyn had fallen asleep on the couch. An empty blue light shone from the set. The VCR had rewound itself and the cassette protruded out of the machine like a wide tongue.

"I'll drive you two home," Joshua offered.

"It's only three blocks." She protested only for form's sake, then reminded herself that this was Joshua and no formality was necessary.

He nodded toward Jocelyn. "She doesn't look up to walking. And you must be exhausted."

He was right, as usual. "Yes, I am, just a little. But happy. Very, very happy."

Like a man on a very restricted diet, he allowed himself only one touch as he slid the back of his knuckles along her cheek. He saw a slight flicker in her eyes that he thought she was unaware of. Fear. He tightened his control, his need to ask why, why she should be afraid of him. "I'm glad. You deserve to be."

Johanna shut off the television set. "We'd better get her home," she murmured.

She was running, he thought. He wondered if it was from him or herself. The need to know burned within him, but he banked it down. He had to give her time to readjust, time to fully trust him.

He lifted the young girl into his arms. Jocelyn went on sleeping. "Let's go. My car's in the parking lot behind the gallery."

Chapter Thirty-two

It was Jocelyn's first day at school and Johanna tried to keep that fact uppermost in her mind that morning, but other thoughts kept crowding in. They were making it difficult to keep her role as the sympathetic mother clear-cut. Mother was also a woman, a woman with a problem. She was having trouble with her emotions, with the path her feelings were taking. They were ganging up on her, surfacing, and it was all Joshua's fault even though he might not know it. Joshua had been more than kind. But his kindness stirred something within her that she didn't want roused. Not now, not ever. The girl in her, the girl who had fallen in love at nineteen and dreamed of living happily ever after, still yearned for commitment. But the woman who had endured a marriage of recriminations and deceit knew that commitment was tantamount to a death sentence. To commit to a man would only mean that you began waiting for the inevitable death of love.

She wanted Joshua to stay a friend, nothing more. But

he was entrenching himself in her life, taking an interest in every aspect that concerned her and Jocelyn and he was making it so easy to lean, to relax, to dream again.

But she knew she couldn't. She'd been there before and she had vowed that she would never let that happen to her again.

Yet the more she relaxed, the more tense she became. She was a living, breathing paradox.

She looked across the tiny table at Jocelyn. Her daughter had barely touched her breakfast. Normally, Jocelyn ate everything in sight.

Nerves, Johanna thought. Poor thing. She reached over and put her hand over Jocelyn's and squeezed. "It'll be all right, honey."

Jocelyn wanted desperately to be blase, but all there was to draw on was terror. "No, it won't."

Johanna remembered first days and her heart ached for her daughter. "Everyone's always nervous the first day at school."

"What do they have to be nervous about?" Jocelyn complained. "They all know each other."

"How do you know that? There might be a lot of new people coming in." Johanna put her coffee cup in the sink, where it would remain until she had a chance to deal with it. Housework had acquired a fairly low priority in her life these days. She searched for the right words, something that would make her daughter feel better. "This isn't a small town, honey, where everyone knows everyone else. People move around a lot in New York."

Jocelyn looked unconvinced as she toyed with oatmeal that had grown cold and hard.

Johanna eyed the mess. She wouldn't have eaten that on a bet. But Jocelyn had always loved oatmeal. Until now. "I borrowed Joshua's car so I could drive you over."

Jocelyn remained unimpressed. She pushed her breakfast away. "You like him, huh?"

In order to have something to do with her hands as she

mulled over the right way to address the question, Johanna swept away the bowl of dried oatmeal and deposited that in the sink as well. "Joshua's a friend from a long time ago." It didn't answer her daughter's question, but then, she didn't think she could answer the question, not honestly. She didn't want to, not even to herself.

Jocelyn played with the button on her vest. "He seems pretty nice."

A smile rose to Johanna's lips. "Yes, he is."

"Think he'd let me work at the gallery?" Jocelyn asked suddenly. Hope sprang into her eyes with a half-formed thought.

Johanna was about to ruffle her hair, then stopped, her hand still up in the air. Jocelyn had mumbled a blue streak over brushing her hair just right this morning. Johanna dropped her hand to her side and stuck it in her dress pocket. "You're a little young."

"He wouldn't have to pay much."

Why did it hurt so much to be young, Johanna thought. Not so long ago, she was this same insecure girl, wandering off to college in the big city. And then, she remembered, she had met Joshua and she wasn't lonely any more. "If you mean in place of school, the answer is no. You're too young. They'd send me off to jail."

Jocelyn's eyes lost their momentary light. "Just thought I'd ask." She drifted off into her own little world as she looked out the window. "Did you know he had paintings of you?" she asked out of the blue.

"Who?"

"Joshua."

Johanna walked over to face her. "What do you mean, paintings of me?"

"In his apartment. I saw them the night you worked late at the show. I kind of found them leaning against the wall in his bedroom."

Paintings? Paintings of her? He had been painting her? Her pulse quickened and then stayed at that high rate. No, it wasn't what she thought. She wouldn't romanticize it any further than the truth. Joshua has always said she had great lines for a model. It was as simple as that. "What were you doing in his bedroom?"

The thin shoulders beneath the vest shrugged. "I was kind of, you know, bored, so I explored."

"What else did you explore, young lady?"

Jocelyn made a face. Johanna felt a touch of guilt for interrogating Jocelyn when the girl was really so nervous. "Nothing."

"Let's go," Johanna linked her fingers with Jocelyn's. Icy hand met icy hand. She was nervous for Jocelyn as well. Jocelyn's eyes held a question in them. "Mothers get nervous for kids, too. C'mon, before traffic gets heavy." For the time being, she locked away the information that Jocelyn had given her.

A bright royal blue sweater was carelessly tossed over Jocelyn's shoulders, its sleeves knotted about her neck the way she had seen a friend in L.A. wear it. "If I'm lucky, there'll be gridlock."

"Let's go, optimist." Johanna shut the door behind them.

Johanna had chosen the private school on Lexington and Third because she had hoped for a better environment for her daughter. Jocelyn was used to a certain lifestyle and while Johanna didn't condone elitism, she had to admit that the idea of sending Jocelyn off to a public school in New York City frightened her. From what she read in the newspapers, the element there was just what she was trying to get Jocelyn away from: drugs and easy sex begun too early. Knowing that it was next to impossible, she still wanted to try and protect her daughter as much as possible.

As she dropped her off at the imposing double front doors, Johanna prayed that Jocelyn would like the Rosewood Academy.

"Want company?" Joshua asked.

Johanna whirled around, dropping the album of prints

she was holding. Joshua made a grab for it. Together they rescued the book from crashing to the ground. "Thank you," she murmured, feeling clumsy and foolish. She let Joshua take possession of the gilt-edged album that featured some of the paintings the gallery had to offer. "What did you say?"

"I asked if you wanted company." He set the book down on the black onyx tabletop. "You've been looking at your watch every five minutes for over an hour. I figure it's almost time to pick up Jocelyn. I thought that you might want company."

Yes, she wanted company, and yet, she knew it was a mistake to get so accustomed to having him around all the time, to keep enjoying his company. She sought refuge in a simple ploy. "But the gallery—" Johanna gestured around as if it were another entity that needed constant watching.

"Kathy can take care of anything that comes up this afternoon. Besides," he pointed out, whispering the news to her, "in case you haven't noticed, it's like a morgue in here today. Might as well take advantage of slack time." He grinned.

"What do you mean?" Because he beckoned, she followed him to the back office.

Joshua took out her purse from the bottom drawer of the desk and held it up before her. "Haven't you ever wanted to play hooky?"

Yes, oh yes, from everything. "Not recently." Johanna accepted her purse.

"You don't lie very well, Johanna. I can see it in your eyes. You're a born hooky player." He ushered her out into the gallery. "Kathy," he called out.

The young woman came around the corner, pushing her glasses up on her nose. "Yes, Mac?"

"I'm taking off with Johanna to pick up her daughter. I'm not sure when I'll be back. Keep the home fires burning, okay?"

"Sure thing." Kathy sighed as she watched them leave.

Romance always made her sigh and she could spot one a mile away.

Joshua was certainly laid-back about work, Johanna thought as she sat down in the passenger side. How unlike Harry he was. All Harry could ever think of was "better," every movie always had to be better than the last one. He had always been trying to make a bigger blockbuster, reaching out toward sensationalism at the cost of substance.

"A penny for your thoughts," Joshua said as he guided the car out of its narrow parking spot.

Instinctively, she knew he didn't want to hear that she was thinking about Harry, even fleetingly. "Do you always just take off?"

"No, sometimes I work around the clock." He stopped the car, waiting for an opening in the flow of traffic on the street. Waiting was an art one developed while driving in New York. "Then I reward myself." He saw his chance and took it, squeezing his car in behind a cab. A horn blasted behind him. He didn't seem to notice. They had merged into the slow, endless stream of traffic. "Otherwise, the gallery would own me instead of the other way around."

She sat back. "You have a point."

"I always have a point," he told her and was rewarded by the sound of her soft laughter. It echoed around him in the car. It was good to see her smiling again. These photos he had seen of her in the various magazines, the smile always seemed artificial, as if it had been pasted on just for the moment. He had always wondered if she was happy. Now he knew.

He also realized that he should have fought to make her stay when she had told him about her intentions. There was no time like the present to make up for the past.

"How does Rockefeller Center sound to you?" he asked suddenly.

"In reference to what?" She looked up in the rearview mirror and watched a car stop just inches away from their bumper as the light turned red in front of them.

"Dinner."

Johanna's mind swung around to the conversation. "I, um—"

There was fear there. Always that little flash of fear. "With Jocelyn."

She let out a breath. "You want Jocelyn to come with us?"

"Why not?" he asked easily. The car moved forward again as the light turned green. A pedestrian darted by quickly, trying to make it across. "The fact is, she doesn't eat with her hands and only rests her elbow on the table when she thinks you're not watching."

"Joshua, you don't have to be this nice to me."

"Why?"

Because you're melting me, that's why. Because my daughter says you have paintings in your bedroom with my face on them and I'm afraid to think about what that means. For both of us. "If you have something else to do—"

He pretended to turn the matter over in his mind for a full two seconds. "Not a thing I can think of. How about it?"

"Let me ask Jocelyn. She might just want to go home and kick the furniture."

He laughed. He knew the feeling. "That happy about going to school, huh?"

"I almost had to drag her. The last time I had to do that, she was in kindergarten. I think they still have her heel marks in the cement back there." Johanna grinned fondly. All of her most memorable flashes from the past involved Jocelyn. Only Jocelyn. "She can be very stubborn when she wants to be."

He leaned over and touched her chin as he braked at yet another red light. Miss one, you miss them all, he thought. "Wonder where she gets it from."

"I'm very easygoing."

"Ha."

"What do you mean, 'ha?' "

He shifted his foot to the accelerator as they inched further along. "Don't forget, I sat next to you on the debating team." It was then he had fallen in love with her passion. It was evident in every word when she argued for a point she believed in. He had always wondered what that passion would feel like, directed toward him.

"It's hard arguing with someone who knows all your skeletons."

"Not all, Johanna." He said it so mildly, Johanna looked at him for a moment.

No, not all. But I will, he promised himself. And when I do, we're going to find a way to make you forget them and not be afraid to live again.

There was no parking allowed in front of the school. Joshua double parked next to a light blue mustang across the street.

"Here, you get out and wait for her. I'll circle the block." He glanced at the traffic that was thickening on the street. "Easier said than done," he murmured with a sigh.

By the time the three of them were together again, it was half an hour later. Jocelyn looked thoroughly miserable about the day she had spent.

"I don't want to go back," she informed her mother as she sat in the back seat her arms folded defiantly in front of her. Her new textbooks had been dumped unceremoniously on the floor. Jocelyn rested her heels on them in absolute contempt.

"That bad, eh?" Joshua asked. He glanced to his right and saw the distressed look on Johanna's face.

"They were awful. Somebody said I had an accent. Can you imagine? Me? They're the ones with an accent." She glared out the window at the streets as they drove by. "I hate it here."

Johanna opened her mouth, but it was Joshua who said, "Give it time."

"Why?"

"It might grow on you," he suggested.

"Yeah, like a fungus."

He turned to look at her for a split second. "Got homework?"

"No. Just covering my books and things. Why?"

"Well, I thought that if you didn't have any homework, we might stop at the Strand after dinner. There's a new Rick Renfield movie opening tonight."

He glanced in the rearview mirror and saw her eyes open wide.

She leaned forward, grasping the seat with her hand. "Can we, Mom?" Can we?"

Johanna looked at Joshua. "I think you've earned yourself a friend for life," she said in a stage whisper. Joshua saw the gratitude in her eyes. "How did you know she liked Renfield?"

"He was plastered all over the tee-shirt she was wearing the night of Bruce's exhibition at the gallery. I figure you don't wear a man's face on your body if you hate him."

But you might wear his emblem on your soul even though you hate him, Johanna thought.

"Mom?" Jocelyn squealed impatiently.

"What?"

"You didn't say we could."

"I think even if I said no, I'd be out-voted. Drive on, James."

Joshua touched two fingers to his temple in an elaborate salute. "Yes, ma'am."

Jocelyn clapped her hands and laughed, school, ostracism and homesickness temporarily forgotten.

Chapter Thirty-three

She had been holding her breath. Figuratively, perhaps, but the tension that had caused it was very real. She hadn't realized just how real until she started slowly releasing it. She had left London four weeks ago and had managed to slowly pull the fragments of her life together. Harry had not contested her request for a divorce. He was too busy filing appeals. The court had found him guilty and had sentenced him to eighteen months in a British prison. For all intents and purposes, he was out of her life.

Starting over again was very difficult. She knew it would be. Being a single parent without the cushion of a house-keeper, the help of charge cards whose bills didn't have to be dreaded at the end of each month, was decidedly much more difficult. For the last eight years, she had already considered herself to be a single parent. Harry had never been there for any of the traumas, any of the important things that mattered to a growing child. She had shouldered it all, made excuses and been there for Jocelyn in every way she knew how. But she had never had to worry about the financial end before. And she hadn't had to worry about not being there. Now, with a full-time job, she wasn't there as much as Jocelyn needed. With Jocelyn entering a new school and needing more than her share of understanding, Johanna, smarting from the irreversible step she had taken, needed understanding herself. It hadn't been easy turning her back on Harry. Even as she boarded the plane, there was still a glimmer inside of her that cried out for her to stay, that maybe, just maybe, tomorrow would bring a change.

The eternal optimist. She had had to bury that part of her. And in so doing, she had eliminated hope from her soul. The kind of hope that went with romance. She could only pray that the rest of her life would proceed on an even keel. She wanted nothing more than to raise her daughter and pursue a career in art. If her mind occasionally strayed to other things, she ignored the yearnings and chalked it up to normal physical responses that had to be curbed. She was, after all, human. But that wasn't an excuse to slip, to let her guard down.

She found that while she liked working at Joshua's gallery, it had its drawbacks. Mainly Joshua. She liked him too much for her own good. He had changed since she had known him in college. All his good points had intensified and where once he had boyish charm, now he was attractive in a very manly sort of way. The kind of attraction that addressed itself to all her nerve endings, to the part of her that never stopped being a woman who needed to be loved. It had taken her only a few days to realize that. Somewhere in between his helping her settle into her apartment, training her at work and taking Jocelyn out after her first day at school, Johanna had realized that she could be very, very attracted to Joshua.

More than that, she was afraid that she was.

So much so that she hesitated when he invited her to attend the theater with him. He had only two tickets this time. She couldn't take Jocelyn along as her convenient shield as she had on their outing to Rockefeller Center and to the movies.

Joshua slipped the two tickets back into his shirt pocket. He was smiling easily, but his eyes told her that he saw more than she wanted him to. Johanna wished for a room full of patrons, but not a single one crossed the threshold to come to her rescue. The gallery was empty this morning. Even Kathy was busy with billing statements in the back room.

"I know you haven't seen the play because it just opened last week." Just then, Kathy approached with a letter for him to sign, then, assessing the situation, backed away discreetly. "And as I remember, you were always a sucker for musicals."

She bit her lower lip. Lying never came easily to her. It didn't now. "Still am."

"So, what's the problem?" He leaned a hip against the table where she had spread out the latest prints they had received for the gallery's album.

Her hand trembled slightly and she silently called herself an idiot. What was there to be afraid of? This was Joshua, just Joshua.

Still, her heart hammered harder than it was supposed to around an old friend. She raised her eyes to his. "I don't know if this is such a good idea, Joshua."

He saw the doubt there, the hesitation. That she was wavering from her staunch position as his friend gave him hope. "I think it's an excellent idea."

She pressed her lips together. "But—"

"And, as your boss, I'm insisting that you attend."

She couldn't suppress a grin that came to her lips. "That's called harassment."

He raised and lowered his brows comically and flickered an imaginary cigar. "You ain't seen nothing' yet."

"That was Al Jolson's line, not Groucho Marx," she corrected.

Because he had a need, he touched her shoulder beneath the guise of friendship. "See, I need you with me to keep me straight on this kind of thing. This play is about heaven actually being an old vaudeville house and I don't know one comic from another. Besides, it's lonely going by yourself."

"Oh, and you can't get a date, right?" she teased.

He looked into her eyes again. "Right." His voice had dropped and his expression was very serious. "I seem to be striking out rather miserably."

"On the contrary, I think you're doing rather well."

"Then you'll go?"

"Then I'll go." The words had come out of their own volition, telling her that whatever she might say to the contrary, even to herself, she wanted to go out with Joshua, wanted to test herself. Or perhaps, just perhaps, enjoy an evening out with an old friend.

That was a long shot, but she clutched at it.

The problem with the loft was that there wasn't that much privacy. Since Johanna and Jocelyn shared the sleeping area, Jocelyn considered it as much hers as her mother's and planted herself there now to watch her critically as Johanna got ready.

"What's on your mind, Jocey?" Hastily, she slipped on earrings that had been a present from her father on her twenty-first birthday.

"Is this a date, Mom?"

It was hard to tell from Jocelyn's tone of voice if she approved or disapproved, but Johanna played it safe. For both of them. "Don't be silly. I'm going out to see a play with Joshua. He's taken the two of us out often enough, hasn't he?"

"Yeah." Jocelyn leaned back on the bed, looking at her with suspicious, accusing eyes. "How come I'm not going this time?"

"Because, kid, it's a school night," Mary said, coming

into the tiny alcove that Johanna had partitioned off. She looked around critically. "Boy, this certainly can't support a lot of traffic, can it?" She gestured toward the opening in the curtain. "Let's go, kid, and leave your mother to her make-up." With one arm around her niece's shoulder, Mary turned back and pointed to Johanna's lids. "A little longer on the lashes, Jo. It's sexier."

"I don't want to be sexy. I just want to see," Johanna called after her departing figure.

But she did, she realized as she looked back into the vanity mirror. She did want to be sexy, if only to prove to herself that she still could be. Was she vain because she wanted to hear a man's compliment, see a man turn his head to look at her? No, it was only natural to want to feel like a woman once in a while, she thought, fastening the other small diamond teardrop to her ears. Even Mother Teresa must have had those kind of feelings once, she speculated. And she was a far cry from Mother Teresa.

Tonight, just for tonight, she'd pretend that she wasn't who she was, pretend that she was just a woman out on a date in the company of a very handsome, attentive man.

So why did you tell Jocelyn it wasn't a date? she asked herself, looking into the mirror. The answer was too confusing, so she let it go. With a sigh, she pushed the partition aside and walked out.

Mary surveyed the figure that Johanna cut in her light blue dress. "You'll knock him dead."

"I don't want to knock him dead." For the third time, Johanna checked the contents of her clutch purse. Nerves again.

Mary grinned, knowing. "Then can I have him?" She watched her sister's face for the reaction she knew to be hidden within.

Because she knew what Mary was up to, Johanna maintained a very cool demeanor. "I'll let him know you put in a bid for ownership." Johanna put her keys into her purse, then snapped it closed. "Get your homework done, Jocelyn and then you can watch television."

Jocelyn looked at her sullenly from beneath hooded eyes and nodded.

"She'll be an angel, won't you kid?" Mary raised one brow in jest. There was enough truth behind the words for both to know that Mary would brook no less than what she asked for.

Jocelyn grinned in response and curled up on the sofa with a book in her hands.

Johanna wished she could manage Jocelyn the way Mary could. Nothing ever seemed to ruffle Mary. Mary wouldn't have stood for the things Harry had done and he would have either had to straighten up or that would have been the end of it. None of this hanging on, hoping for better times for her sister. She envied her that trait. Still, she had Jocelyn and that meant the world to her, even though they were going through a period of readjustment just now. She knew it was part of being twelve and a female. Johanna only hoped she'd be able to survive it from the opposite end this time.

The doorbell rang just as Johanna picked up her purse. Nerves jangled again and were banished in an instant. This was Joshua, remember? Just Joshua.

With a quick intake of breath, Johanna opened the door.

Just Joshua, huh? So why did he look so damn handsome in his light gray suit? And where had her eyes been all those years ago?

Tonight, she looked different than the other times, Joshua thought. Her hair, always so beautiful free, was swept up on her head, with tendrils falling at her temples. A goddess done up in a blue ribbon, he thought. But he didn't want her to be a goddess. Goddesses couldn't be touched and he wanted to touch her, to caress her and make her his.

Soon, very soon, he promised himself. This time, it would be different.

"I believe the expression is 'Wow!'"

The look in his eyes was enough to make her blush.

"If you stand drooling in the doorway, you're going to miss the curtain," Mary warned, peering at Joshua from behind Johanna's shoulder.

"Hi, Mary." He glanced at her, then looked back at Johanna, wondering how in God's name he was going to go through the evening without succumbing to instincts that were far older than polite manners. "Hello, Jocelyn," he said, only because he knew that Jocelyn had to be nearby. He saw no one but Johanna.

"We'll exchange pleasantries some other time. Now go, you two," Mary warned. "The theater isn't around the corner."

"Mary's got the bossy streak in our family," Johanna said. She felt both pleased and unsettled over the same range of anticipations that were thundering through her.

"Nice to know." Joshua put his arm around Johanna to usher her out. He winked at Mary and Jocelyn over her head as he closed the door behind them.

Without the buffer of her sister and daughter, Johanna felt a wave of apprehension wash over her and told herself she was being silly.

The wave died down, but didn't ebb away completely.

"So, aren't you glad you came?" he asked.

She nodded. Yes, she was. The show had been wonderful and she couldn't remember when she had enjoyed going to the theater so much. Dinner at the small, cosy restaurant Joshua had taken her to was simple, yet delicious and they had talked of old times. How could she have been afraid to come with him? she wondered. What was she afraid of? She laughed at herself.

He waved for a cab and was instantly answered by two that pulled up directly in front of them.

"Your choice," he said.

She laughed. "The one with the little old driver."

But as she climbed in, she listened to the address that Joshua gave the driver.

"That's not home."

"Who said we're going home?"

"I just assumed—" She fumbled. "It's late."

He looked down intently at her feet.

"What are you doing?"

"Checking you out for glass slippers."

She flushed. "I just meant that we both have to go to work tomorrow—"

"I'll give you a note," he promised. "I happen to know that your boss is a very understanding guy. And he has a soft spot in his heart for blue-eyed blondes who have the good sense to like his paintings. Besides, I have it on the best authority that he might be just a little late coming in tomorrow himself. He's out on a date with a bewitching woman even as we speak."

She settled back with a laugh. "No arguing with you, is there?"

His hand closed over hers. "Glad you're learning."

She wondered if he could feel her palm growing damp.

The driver pulled up a few blocks later in front of a hansom cab. "This'll do fine," Joshua told him. He handed the man money, then stepped out of the cab. He extended his hand toward Johanna, waiting.

"Joshua, what are you doing?"

"We," he corrected. "What are *we* doing."

She took his hand, curling her fingers around it and holding on as she slipped from the cab. It was chilly tonight. She pulled her oversized shawl closer around her shoulders. "Okay, what are we going?"

"Going for a drive in a hansom cab." He hurried her along the avenue, guiding her to a cluster of men in top hats seated in open horse-drawn carriages.

Johanna blinked, walking briskly to keep up with the pace he set. "Why?"

"Because it's there. Because I think it's romantic and I've

always wanted to do it with the right woman."

He felt the tension enter her body immediately. "She isn't me."

He stopped a few feet away from the first carriage. "I'll be the judge of that." He saw a flicker of fear in her eyes. "Johanna, are you afraid of me?"

"No," she said a bit too quickly, looking away.

"Then it's you."

She jerked her head up. "What?"

"You're afraid of you," he said simply, turning toward the first driver. He nodded his head and the old man straightened, taking a firmer hold of his horse's reins. "Don't worry. I won't let you have your way with me. Unless, of course," he helped her up into the carriage, "you intend to use brute force."

The driver gave him a funny look before he turned around and flicked his whip far above the horse's head. Johanna clutched to the seat. The leather felt old, cracked.

"You can relax any time now. I don't think anyone will mug us," Joshua assured her.

"I wasn't thinking about muggers."

"What were you thinking about?"

She licked her lower lip, searching for an answer.

"Don't do that," he told her.

"Why?"

"Because," he said, his face a scant inch away from hers, "it makes me want to do this." Cupping her chin in his hand, he lowered his mouth to hers.

Johanna stiffened, then something within her let go, even while she argued with herself to hang on. And then suddenly she was, hanging on for dear life as she wove her fingers into his hair and parted her lips in unconscious invitation.

Joshua took it slow, very, very slow. He knew that his footing could slip at any moment and then he would have to retrace his steps again. He didn't know if his control could last out a second journey to this small triumph.

Chapter Thirty-four

Johanna's entire body felt tense, rigid, excited. She had to think about breathing. Her hands were trembling. Instead of being in her lap, they were holding onto the lapels of his jacket as if they had a life of their own. With concentrated effort, she forced her fingers to relax, letting go of Joshua's jacket. Her heart was hammering in her ears. He toyed with a tendril at her temple and it made her feel warm. And frightened, very, very frightened.

"Joshua, please."

"Please yes or please no?" He saw the fear again and humor left his eyes. Harry shimmered beside him like a specter he couldn't best. "Johanna, for God's sake, let go."

She shook her head. "I can't. I made a mistake once and I'm scared to death—"

"That it'll happen again?" She nodded. "I'm not Harry, Johanna."

"I know that." She looked away.

"Do you?" He took her chin and turned her head toward

him so that she had to look into his eyes. "Do you really?"

She took a deep breath. There was no hiding things from
him. He knew her too well. "Fear isn't logical, Joshua. It
just is."

"But it's illogical to let it ruin any chance for happiness.
Our chance for happiness. You kissed me back, Johanna."
There had been feeling in her kiss. It wasn't perfunctory.

A small smile played on her lips. "Reflexes. A stone
would have kissed you back."

"I'll take that as a compliment—and a start." He glided
his fingers along her cheek. "I could kill him."

He meant it. The words were said quietly, but there was
no mistaking the intent, the heat, the rage. Johanna stared
at him, stunned. She had never known him to express anger
before. "What?"

"He took the light out of your eyes, Johanna. He doesn't
deserve to live."

She shrugged. "Maybe it was both our fault."

Damn the man, damn him for making her feel some sort
of misguided loyalty to him. She might tell herself that she
and Harry were equally to blame for what had happened,
but Joshua knew better.

"You don't believe that." He said it more for himself
than for her.

"No, I don't. I was just trying to be—"

"Noble?" he suggested.

"Stupid," she answered honestly. She stared out into the
inky night. The park looked solemn at night, solemn and
quiet. All she heard was the sound of the horse's hooves
as they made contact with the ground.

"Yes, that's a good word for it," Joshua agreed after a
beat.

She turned, surprised. "What?"

Though he wanted to slip his arm around her, go on
holding her and just absorbing the night sounds, he faced
her. "Johanna, I'm not an idiot. I know that what I read
about Harry in the papers isn't gospel, but seeing you tells

me that there was a lot of truth in the articles. He hurt you. A lot. It's going to take time for you to heal. I understand that. Now you understand that I care."

She looked out again, wishing she were someone else, wishing she wasn't afraid. But there was no changing what she was. "You're rushing me."

"Fifteen years is not rushing."

"Fifteen years?" That didn't make any sense. That was when she had first met Harry. "I don't understand."

"That was just the trouble. You didn't." He took her hand, not to force her to commit, but just because he needed to touch her, to maintain contact as he spoke. "I was head over heels in love with you from the time you knocked over my easel that first day in art."

"I dropped paint all over your shoes," she remembered, a grin rising to her lips. "They were absolutely ruined."

"That's not the only thing you ruined. You ruined me for any other woman."

My God, he was serious. And she hadn't known. All this time, and she hadn't known. She thought about the paintings Jocelyn said he had in his bedroom. Paintings of her. It all made sense now.

"But I didn't do anything, Joshua."

"Oh, now there you're wrong. Your size six shoes waltzed into my heart with that first flash of your quirky little smile." He touched the corner of her mouth that always lifted higher than the other side when she smiled. "Besides, you liked my painting."

"Guilt," she quipped, at a loss for an answer to what he was telling her.

"I prefer to think it was taste."

Another time, another place, it would have worked. But she was tired, used, disillusioned. "Joshua, I can't give you what you want."

"Tell me you don't feel anything for me."

She looked down at her hands. He was making this hard. "I don't feel anything for you."

"Look at me when you say it."

She raised her head. "I—" She faltered. "Joshua, please, you don't understand."

"I do." He wove his arms around her. "More than you'll ever know."

He kissed her again and all the neat little arguments faded into the recesses of her mind. She didn't think why it couldn't work, she didn't think that it might. She just didn't think at all and let herself feel just for this moment in time.

The wave was powerful, pushing her over the edge. He pulled all the air out of her lungs until she heard herself gasping. It felt as if she was savoring the substance of life itself in his kiss.

But she knew she wasn't. It just didn't work that way. She had been painfully taught that.

There was an attraction between them, she couldn't deny it. But this was different from the way it had been with Tommy. With Tommy she had known that there was a limit, an end in sight, and so she didn't have to be afraid of it. It was understood. Here, Joshua wouldn't be satisfied with just a casual affair, even if she could be. She was afraid that he'd ask her for more than she could give. She didn't want to lose the friend by turning away the lover, but she was going to have to.

She pulled back, though her fingers still clutched at his shirt, for warmth, for steadiness. "I need time."

She was shaken. Even in the dim light, he could see the look of smoky desire in her eyes. He'd wait this out. "Okay, nobody ever said I wasn't fair."

She touched his face. "Joshua."

He turned her hand over until her palm was up and his kissed it. "Let's go home before I remember that promises made in hansom cabs are non-binding on Thursday nights."

She rested her head against his shoulder, wishing she was free to feel. If she were, she would snatch up Joshua and run for the hills.

But she wasn't free. Fear of failure, of repetition held her prisoner. Once she had loved Harry utterly and completely, with no restrictions. That love had wilted and died within her hand as she watched, despite everything she did to keep it alive.

She couldn't bear to have that happen twice. And so she locked her heart away.

Or told herself she did.

"Want to invite me in for a nightcap?" he asked. When she didn't respond immediately, he went on. "Hot chocolate? Cold chocolate? A glass of water?"

She laughed. She couldn't help herself. "You're easily pleased, aren't you?"

"What have I been trying to tell you?" He put his arms around her, drawing her against his body. "I'm only fussy in my choice of paintings and women."

She meant to put her hands between them and somehow managed to put them around his neck instead. For the friend, she told herself, only the friend who was so dear to her.

But it was the man who frightened the hell out of her even as he intrigued and tantalized her.

She wanted to protest, to tell him no. Logically, she wanted to do that. But her emotional need to be held, cherished, won out and she tilted her head back to reach his lips.

Joshua groaned as he drank in the overpowering sweetness he found there. Over and over, his mouth slanted over hers, bruising her lips, bruising her soul, making the ache within them both reach out and pull. Hard.

Her head swam as the world dipped into darkness and disappeared. There was nothing and no one, except for Joshua. His hands tightened on her, holding her against him. He didn't caress, didn't possess. And yet, by not doing any of it, he did. Just by touching his mouth to hers, just by enfolding her in his arms, he branded her, took possession while she fiercely wanted to retain ownership.

She wanted him. She knew she couldn't have him. It just wouldn't work. It never did. The fact had her nearly sobbing.

"Pleasant dreams," he whispered against her ear.

"Your cold water?" she asked, surprised that he was leaving.

"I've decided to wear it—as soon as possible." He winked and then was gone.

Johanna nearly slid down against the closed door. His kiss left her weak and wanting. She needed a cold shower of her own. And a good dose of common sense.

"Home kind of early, aren't you?" Mary asked as Johanna let herself in.

"Early?" She glanced at her watch. It was almost two in the morning. "The play was over hours ago. We had a late dinner and a ride around Central Park in a hansom cab."

Mary curled her toes beneath her on the sofa, her head resting on the arm, her eyes bright. "And?"

Johanna let her purse drop to the sofa a moment before she did. "He brought me home."

"His?"

Johanna looked at her sister curiously. "No, mine."

Mary blew out a breath, curbing annoyance and disappointment. "I think you need pointers."

Everyone seemed to know what was best for her, except her. "I think you need to go to bed."

Mary rose, a knowing smile on her lips as she looked her sister up and down. Johanna was definitely tense. The evidence was in her shoulders, in the way she moved. In the way she spoke. "Ditto."

"I am." She took the pins out of her hair and shook it free. God, her neck ached. *She* ached.

With her hands braced on the back of the sofa, Mary leaned over so that her face was level with Johanna's. "I don't mean your own."

"Mary," Johanna sighed, "I don't need a love life."

"Bull—" Mary bit off the rest of the word. "Fleas don't need a love life, people do."

Johanna kicked off her shoes and leaned back, her eyes closed. Maybe if she kept them that way, Mary would take the hint. "Thank you, Dr. Ruth."

When it came to hints, Mary chose the ones she took and the ones she ignored. "Just because Harry was a bastard doesn't mean that everyone is."

That sounded exactly like something Joshua had said to her earlier. She opened one eye and looked up at her sister. "Joshua been cuing you your lines?"

"I always liked Joshua."

"Fine, I make you a present of him."

"Would that I could, dear sister, would that I could, but the man is already in love." She saw the way her sister's eyes opened wide. "With you, you idiot."

Johanna rose stiffly, her shoes dangling from her hand. "You're crazy."

"No, but you are if you let this opportunity slip through your fingers."

"There *is* no opportunity."

"No, not if you shut your mind to it."

If she fell asleep instantly, it still wouldn't be enough to see her through the next day. "It's too late to argue, Mary."

"Good. I hereby declare this argument over. I won." She kissed her sister's cheek. "Now, get out of my bedroom." She waved her hand around the immediate area that surrounded the sofa. "I'll see you in the morning." She yawned and curled up on the sofa.

Johanna shook her head. "Everyone's against me."

Mary opened one eye. "There you're wrong. Everyone's for you. You just have to stop being the battered wife long enough to realize that."

Johanna whirled around. "Harry never beat me." That he had hit her once and that it had sealed her resolution to leave him was something she was determined to keep to herself.

"There are other forms of being battered than being used as a physical punching bag," Mary informed her sleepily. "I'm too tired for another sparring match, Jo. I won the first argument and that's that. You get the prize—Joshua." She yawned and stretched.

"Thanks. I'm sure he'll be thrilled to hear that." She began unbuttoning her dress. Something distant wondered what it would be like to be undressed by Joshua. That was Mary's doing, she thought, quickly shutting away the thought. If Mary would stop suggesting that—

Oh God, who was she kidding? It was of her own doing.

"I bet he will," Mary chuckled just before she drifted off to sleep.

Johanna gave up and went off to bed. It wasn't her, she thought. It was everyone else.

Tonight had been wonderful, but it was over and she was back to reality. And reality was that she was not about to let her heart lead the way again. She couldn't withstand the inevitable heartache and disappointment that would come. And there wasn't just herself to think of. There was Jocelyn. She stood next to her daughter's bed and looked at the sleeping girl.

Jocelyn slept fitfully and her blanket was bunched over to one side, with her leg dangling over it. Johanna eased the blanket over her and tucked it around her daughter, then smiled, lightly pushing the hair from the girl's face. This was all the love she had room for in her heart. And it was enough.

Unconsciously she put her hand to her lips, then realized what she was doing. As if she had been burned, she dropped her hand quickly to her side.

Chapter Thirty-five

The pallet felt rough in her hand, but not awkward. It was as if it belonged there, even after all these years. The smell of the paints made her high. Not the high Harry had sought so desperately. A joyful high, the kind of high only gotten on thoughts lined with happiness.

She remembered the fear with which she had faced the empty canvas. Was it still there? Did she still have something to give, something to feel?

Yes. Thank God, yes.

Why had she walked away from this and stayed away so long? It was hard to believe, to even attempt to justify. It didn't matter. She was back. She added a dab of brown to the pallet and blended the color with what she had until she was satisfied.

Lifting a brush, she used it as an extension of her soul. It met the canvas and set her free.

It was an odd feeling. Her life was falling into place, and by the same token, it wasn't. Each day, she felt a little more stable, a little more sure-footed on the road of life. Her work was exciting and there was a joy in working at the gallery that had been missing in her life. She was meeting artists and people involved in the art community. Joshua took her along with him to various auctions in search of the right acquisitions. He had impressed her at Sotheby's, displaying just the right amount of restraint, yet cunning. The painting they came away with was one by a lesser known artist who was just approaching his zenith. In his own, subtle, easygoing manner, Joshua was far more dynamic than Harry ever was.

Joshua.

He had done his best to put her at ease. She blessed him for that. There was no pressure. He seemed satisfied to give her space, although every so often, a look or comment would give him away. She was thankful he didn't push because she had been afraid that she would have to leave the gallery. She was afraid of repeating her mistake. She didn't realize that Joshua was fighting for what he wanted in the only way he knew how. He loved her and wanted her. But he saw her fear and knew that it would take time to conquer. So he used time as a tool, even though it cost him.

Even Jocelyn was beginning to settle down a little, she thought with a smile as she studied the canvas she was working on. It was a simple still life of a bouquet of fading flowers. Against the vase was a small porcelain doll, its bright yellow ribbon undone. A shoe was missing. The end of summer. Still, it was more than she had done with paints in years.

She frowned, her mind shifting from her painting to her life like a pendulum. There were waters closing in on her that she refused to test and yet was drawn to, almost hypnotically. Certainly against her conscious will.

She tried to shut out the seductive call and yet couldn't. Wanted to ignore it and yet desperately needed to believe that it existed. Existed for her. That there was still love out there that was possible, love that was true, supportive, that didn't eat away at you like a deadly acid until there was nothing left. She felt like a woman condemned to torture, to self-inflicted torture.

Johanna added one splash of red to a petal.

She was too frightened to take the risk. Once was more than enough to have her heart cut out of her. Tommy had healed rents that had been in her, made her feel like a woman again, made her realize that she was desirable. Tommy was a walk on a soft misty spring day. What Joshua represented was forever. But she knew that nothing lasted forever. Except disappointment.

Leaves fell, dried and brown, about the vase and against the doll.

"So this is what you do on your lunch break."

She spun around, startled. The tube of light blue paint she had been squeezing on her pallet emitted a little arc of color that dribbled down her index finger.

"You don't have to look as if you've been caught trying to steal the crown jewels, Johanna."

He had walked into the tiny back room and looked with a critic's eye at the painting she was working on so diligently. In it he saw the pain she tried so often to conceal from him. There was a time that all her paintings bore a burst of hope and happiness within them.

It wasn't until he spoke that she realized how much his approval meant to her. She had always painted to share feelings, not to hide them.

"This is nice. A little depressing, but very nice." He owed her the truth and they both knew he wouldn't lie, not about something so important to her. "Done without the benefit of the required artistic northern skylight." He grinned, remembering how they had both vowed to live in lofts and nothing mattered except for the position of the incoming sun.

As he spoke, he took out his handkerchief from his back pocket and wiped off her finger. The gesture, small, perhaps to some insignificant, seemed unbearably intimate to Johanna. She raised her eyes and looked at him, her breath stopped in her throat.

No, she wouldn't, she told herself, she wouldn't let herself go. If this couldn't be casual, it couldn't be at all.

Self-consciously, she drew back her hand.

Joshua pretended he hadn't seen the flicker of desire, followed by an equal spark of wariness in her eyes. With studied carelessness, he put the hankerchief away. "When did you start this?"

She shrugged. "A week ago." She knew what he was going to say.

"If you wanted to paint, I could have let you use my apartment during lunch. There is a good window there that lets in the afternoon sun."

"I didn't know how far I'd get. It was just a whim." And she wanted to do it on her own, without anyone knowing. That was why she kept it hidden here. She had to know if she could still bring things to life with a stroke of a brush. If she had failed, she wanted to make sure that no one else knew, especially not Joshua.

"No." He studied it. "I don't think so. This isn't just a whim, Johanna. This is your destiny. Something tells me that your days as my assistant are numbered."

She looked up sharply. "You're firing me?"

"I think being elevated to the rightful place as artist when the time comes is usually thought of as being promoted, not fired."

He was being too good to her again. It made her vulnerable, put her at a disadvantage. She needed to stand firm, be firm. Nervously, she glanced at her watch. "I'd better be getting back."

"No hurry. The gallery's not that busy this afternoon and whatever comes up, Kathy or I can handle. If it gets hectic, I'll call you. Why don't you go on? You can use my loft—"

"No."

Why couldn't she accept what he offered? "I won't come up to seduce you, Johanna," he said softly.

"That's not what I meant," she answered quickly, then paused. "Well, maybe it was."

He took her hands in his. "Sometime soon, Johanna, we're going to have to talk."

"There isn't much to say."

"Oh, I think there's quite a lot to say." Instead of leaving, he pulled up a chair and straddled it. "Have you been to the museum yet?"

She knew he meant the Museum of Modern Art. As students, they had spent many a rainy afternoon hanging out there, absorbing, criticizing, planning where their art work would someday hang. It seemed light years away from the person she was today.

"No."

"Why?"

"I haven't found the time."

He got up. "Consider it found. They've finished pouring fifty-five million dollars into renovations. The museum is now twice as big as when you were last there. You have to see it to believe what they've done."

He was rushing her again, rushing her in a direction she wanted to go in, but was afraid. "But I—"

He wouldn't let her say no. "We'll make a day of it. The theater there is showing a musical trilogy I think you might find interesting."

"But I—"

Joshua curbed his annoyance at her reaction. She had stayed with Harry even though the man put her through hell. Here he was being kind to her, being infinitely patient and yet she kept backing away. He felt the sting of jealousy prick him. It was an effort to rein in his temper. But he did.

"*Kiss Me Kate, Kismet* and *Showboat.*" He dug into his pocket and produced tickets. "Tickets for three, Johanna.

It's time Jocelyn got a little taste of what her mother's all about."

"Do you have an endless supply of tickets coming out of that pocket?" She laughed, remembering the tickets to the play.

"There's lots of things about me you don't know." He grinned. And he intended for her to get to know all of them in time.

She stared at the tickets. It was too much to resist. And it would be the three of them. Safety in numbers. She smiled at him as she picked up the pallet again. "You're too good to me, Joshua."

"We'll work something out," he winked.

That was exactly what she was afraid of.

"Now get back to work." He pointed at the painting. "Maybe we'll have an exhibition of your paintings sooner than either of us think."

He made it all sound so simple, as if wishes and dreams could come true if you only tried. She almost believed him. Except, that she had been there and found that they couldn't. Still, it was nice to dream once in a while and if he didn't mind...

Johanna picked up the brush and began to paint again. Unconsciously she began to hum a song from one of the movies Joshua had mentioned.

"Museums are boring," Jocelyn protested Saturday morning as Johanna tried to get her to hurry up. "I don't want to go."

Johanna hadn't counted on opposition. "Just give it a chance."

"Why?"

"Because it's culture. Because it's something I care about. Because you might surprise yourself and actually like it. Joshua's taking us. And afterward, he said we could go to Rumplemeyer's."

"What's that?"

"A place where they serve ice cream to die for."

Jocelyn bit her lower lip, weakening.

Johanna knew she was getting to her. "Did you have other plans?"

"I was going to see Darcy and her boyfriend." Jocelyn shoved her hands into the back pockets of her torn jeans and rocked on her heels.

"Darcy?" The name was unfamiliar. Jocelyn had a friend and she hadn't even told her about the girl. Johanna knew it was all part of growing up, but she felt left out. Silly, she chided herself. At least Jocelyn was making friends. That meant that not everyone in her classes were "know-it-all nerds" the way she had initially described the group to her mother.

"Just somebody in my class."

"And she has a boyfriend?"

"Sure, what's wrong with that?"

Plenty, Johanna wanted to say, but knew she couldn't. Jocelyn already looked too defensive. It was hard always having to pick your words just so. "I was just surprised, that's all. I don't generally picture twelve-year-olds with boyfriends." She slipped on a bright red dress and buckled it at her waist.

"Darcy's thirteen."

Johanna stepped into her shoes. "Oh well, that makes all the difference in the world. Hurry up, Jocey, he'll be here any minute."

Jocelyn tried to be nonchalant, but Johanna noticed that the girl did get a move on. Johanna tried not to let her smile show.

It was a homecoming. The museum, large, a bit over-whelming on first sight, greeted her like an old friend. Johanna felt as if the years hadn't happened, as if she was stepping through a time warp, back to her youth, back to days where passion for art mattered most of all. She squeezed Joshua's hand without even realizing it in a gesture of happiness and gratitude. This, she knew, was where she belonged. She should have never left New York City, never left this atmosphere. It was where she could thrive and grow.

"Are we going to spend the afternoon looking at dumb paintings?" Jocelyn wanted to know, trailing behind them, scowling.

"She does the bored heiress well," Joshua remarked to Johanna in a stage whisper. He turned to Jocelyn. "No, there're film clips here, books, sculptures, photographs, movies—"

"Movies?" Jocelyn came to life. "In a museum?" She glanced around, defying him to show her a trace of a movie theater.

"Only the finest." Casually, Joshua put his arm around Jocelyn's shoulders and steering her toward a particular wing that he and Johanna had haunted. "Let me show you a few paintings that blew my mind when I was a little older than you and then we'll see if we can find ourselves some seats in the theater."

"Well, if I gotta," Jocelyn muttered.

He crooked a finger under her chin so that she looked up at him. "Humor me."

"Okay." Jocelyn grinned at Joshua good-naturedly. "For you."

Johanna could only look on in admiration. Joshua turned and put his hand out for her to hurry up. "C'mon, Johanna, you're holding up the show."

."Yeah, move it, Mom," Jocelyn said impatiently.

"Someday you have to show me how you do that trick," Johanna whispered to him, taking his hand.

"I fully intend to, Johanna. I fully intend to."

She had the feeling he was promising her something she hadn't asked for.

Johanna wanted to reach out and touch the painting before her with its swirls of color and contrasts. She wanted to run her fingertips along the rough peaks and textures made by the paint. It was like a sailor walking the beach after years of being landlocked. It seemed unreal until contact was made.

Hesitantly, she reached out and touched a corner of the frame. It was enough.

"Mom," Jocelyn hissed, surprised.

"Shhh," Joshua put his finger to his lips. "Be on the lookout for the guard."

"But you're not supposed to touch them—are you?"

Johanna shook her head. "No, you're not. But I needed to. Just this once."

"All clear to make our getaway." Joshua put his arm around her shoulders. Then he looked into her eyes for a moment before he led her away. "One need out of the way, others to be met and fulfilled."

"Joshua—" she began.

"The movie theater awaits, ladies." He held out the crook of his elbow to Jocelyn who took it with a grin. "Ready?" he asked Johanna.

Johanna let out a long sigh. He was impossible. And impossibly irresistible. She didn't know how much longer she could hold out before she stepped into the pool of quicksand that her emotions were leading her into.

"Ready," she answered.

Joshua raised his eyebrows.

"For the theater," she added.

He merely laughed aloud.

On their way out of the room, they passed a guard who looked at them suspiciously. Joshua began to whistle as Jocelyn giggled.

Chapter Thirty-six

She saw trouble in Jocelyn's eyes the minute she walked into the loft. In the same instant, she knew it was about Harry. A newspaper lay on the dining table. One of the pages was torn in half, as if in anger.

"Why didn't you *tell* me?" Jocelyn shouted, scrambling to her feet as Johanna closed the door behind her.

Playing for time, trying to steady herself for what she instinctively knew was coming, what she had been dreading and avoiding even when she knew she shouldn't, Johanna slowly pulled her shoulders straight. "Don't shout at me, Jocelyn. Tell you what?"

Jocelyn crumbled up both halves of the newspaper and threw them on the floor. "That you were divorcing my father."

It was here, the scene she didn't want played out, more dreadful in reality than in her mind. But there was no hiding from it anymore.

Johanna licked her lips and let her purse drop to the floor

beside the door. "Because I was afraid. I couldn't find the right words to make you understand."

"So you let me read it in a *newspaper*?" the girl shrieked. "What's all this garbage you're always trying to shove down my throat about our being honest with one another?"

"I didn't lie," Johanna said helplessly. "I just didn't say anything."

"*That's lying!*"

"No, that's being a coward. I didn't want to see the look in your eyes that I'm seeing." She tried to take Jocelyn by the shoulders, but the girl pulled away. "Jocelyn, I'm not the heavy here."

Hurt and anger flashed in Jocelyn's eyes. So accusing. So like Harry's eyes, Johanna thought. "You never even gave him a chance."

Jocelyn's display of anger cracked Johanna's resolve to remain calm. This wasn't fair. "I gave him *every* chance, dammit."

Johanna pressed her hand to her mouth. She didn't want to shout at Jocelyn, didn't want to turn her even further away. But her words hurt. It hurt to have her daughter turn on her this way. Why was she being so protective of her father? Why wasn't she more understanding of her position? Why was it Harry who got her loyalty? Where was Harry when she was sick, or needed someone? Where was Harry for the school plays, the parties? Why didn't she think of that? "What's this allure he has for you? He was never there for you. Me. I was. Whether it was popular or not, I was always there for you."

Jocelyn glared at her, not hearing the words. Her parents were divorcing and she had been ignored, lied to with silence. Rage bubbled through her, seeking an outlet. She wanted to lash out, to hurt someone. Only Johanna was there. "Thanks a lot."

Johanna felt betrayed. Hot, angry tears stung at her eyes but she refused to let them fall. "Maybe it's my fault for not telling you about him, but I wanted you to have a few illusions about your father."

Jocelyn raised her chin, her eyes daring her to say something against Harry.

Johanna took a deep breath. There was no need to avenge herself at the cost of the father Jocelyn thought she had. "Look, I don't want to argue about this now. It has nothing to do with you."

"It has *everything* to do with me," Jocelyn cried impotently. "You're my parents."

"And we'll go on being your parents. That doesn't change." Again, she tried to touch Jocelyn, but was held back by the angry look in her daughter's eyes. "Your father and I are getting a divorce because we don't get along any more. I can't help him, I can't do anything for him except make him angry. That's not an atmosphere in which to raise a child or continue a marriage."

"So you just left him," Jocelyn accused. "When he was in trouble. When he was in *jail*."

Restless, Johanna paced around the large room. "Baby, he was in trouble a long time before I left him."

Her words did nothing to change the look on Jocelyn's face. It was pointless to argue now. The wound too raw, the cut too deep. Johanna felt helpless. She had to fight this feeling. It had the potential of overwhelming her, of making her incapable of dealing with the difficult period of time that loomed ahead. "I have to go back to the gallery for a couple of hours. I just stopped in to check on you. Get your homework done and we'll take in a movie tonight." She hesitated, waiting to see a reaction to her suggestion. Nothing. "Okay?"

Jocelyn refused to look up at her mother. "I don't feel like taking in a movie."

"Okay."

Johanna prayed that time would heal this. She wasn't sure how to deal with Jocelyn and it terrified her. She had lost Harry and in losing him to his devils, had lost a part of herself. She couldn't face the prospect of losing Jocelyn as well. Anger began to overcome fear. This was Harry's fault. He had almost destroyed her once and now, thousands of miles away, he was doing it again. His tentacles were reaching her again. She couldn't lose her daughter. She couldn't.

Perhaps this was one of those times that discretion was the better part of valor. She had to just leave Jocelyn alone for a while, let her come to her senses. Johanna ruefully admitted to herself that this was more of a cop-out than a studied response to the situation, but she didn't know what else to do. There was no turning back. "All right, when I come back, we'll just stay home and talk."

"I want to go live with Dad."

Johanna swung around, her hand on the door. "No!" The word sprang to her lips like a reflex. She almost said, "You're part of the reason I left him," but stopped herself in time.

"Why?"

"Because he's in prison."

"When he gets out."

Her knees felt weak. "We'll talk about it then. See you later."

Only a silent glare met her words. Johanna left. If she stayed, she knew that the hurt she felt would erupt and words might be said that would be regretted later. Jocelyn had to be treated with kid gloves at this time even if the kindness was not returned.

When Johanna came home an hour and a half later, the loft was empty. Telling herself not to panic, Johanna called Jocelyn's best friend at school, Darcy. And then the next name in her little book. And the next. Each time the response was the same. No one had seen Jocelyn since school. When Johanna called Mary, there was no answer at her sister's apartment.

It was then that the icy panic finally set in.

Having nowhere else to turn, she went to the only one she could. Johanna ran the three blocks back to the gallery. It was closed, but the doorbell on the side connected to Joshua's apartment as well. She leaned on the button, praying that he was there and hadn't gone out somewhere. She should have called him rather than just run down, but she wasn't thinking logically anymore. It was hard to pull her thoughts together at all.

Joshua crossed through the white-walled gallery, wondering what in God's name was so urgent. When he saw Johanna, his expression softened. "Hey, if you wanted to come over all you had to do was—Johanna, what's wrong?" He took hold of her by the shoulders. "You're shaking."

"It's Jocelyn. She's gone."

"Gone?" He ushered her inside and closed the door behind her. One lone fluorescent lamp provided light for the gallery. At any other time, it might have seemed romantic. Now it was just eerie. "What do you mean, 'gone?'"

"She's run away." As soon as she said it aloud, tears began to fall.

"Did she leave a note?"

Johanna shook her head. She brushed back her tears with the heel of her hand. "But we had an argument. She found out about the divorce."

"Found out?" He was stunned. How could she not have discussed something so important with Jocelyn? "You mean you didn't tell her?"

She shook her head, wishing she could go back and change things. "No, I couldn't. I just—she read it in the newspaper and exploded at me. I told her we'd talk when I came back from the gallery. But she's gone."

The main thing was to stay calm. He wouldn't let himself think of what could happen to a young girl alone in New York at night. "Have you called—?"

"Everyone. Nobody's seen her. And Mary's not home."

Shrugging away from his hold, Johanna moved like a caged panther, wanting to escape, not knowing which direction to take. She whirled around, her hands on her mouth to keep the sob back.

"Oh God, Joshua, she's just a baby. Do you realize what could happen to her out here? I should have moved back to Beverly Hills." Tears streamed down her cheeks but she didn't bother to wipe them away this time. All she could think of was Jocelyn.

Joshua took out the bottle of brandy he kept in his office and poured her a drink, but she shook her head. He pressed it into her hands anyway. "Drink this." His voice was firm. "You need to get a hold of yourself." He wanted to hold her, to tell her that it was going to be all right, but at the moment, he wasn't sure it would be himself.

He watched as she tilted her head back and took a long sip. "None of her friends have seen her?"

She shook her head, afraid to trust her voice. The alcohol burned going down. It was a shock to her system. But he was right, it did seem to steady her. She took in a deep, ragged breath. "I called them all. It's not a long list."

"Maybe one of them was lying to cover for her." He saw hope flash in her eyes, that and gratitude at his words. "Kids have been known to lie. Do you have addresses to go with the numbers?"

"In her book."

"Let's go back and get it."

She nodded numbly, only slightly aware that he was holding her hand.

When she handed him the book, Joshua quickly glanced through the names and addresses, then pocketed it. "Okay, I'll go and check them out in person. You stay here."

She grabbed at his sleeve as he turned to go. "But I'll go insane just waiting."

He wanted to take her with him, to erase the worry from her eyes. But logic prevailed. "If she comes back, or calls, you'll want to be here."

He was right. She wanted to go with him and search and

stay here and wait, anything that would bring Jocelyn back faster. She couldn't do both, and if she went with Joshua, her mind would be busy, but she might miss Jocelyn's call. "I'll stay here."

Because they both needed it, Joshua kissed her lightly and held her for a moment. "I'll give you a call as soon as I find her." He squeezed her hand before he left. "We *will* find her, Johanna. I promise you that."

He only hoped he could deliver.

Johanna paced around the loft, trying to keep from climbing the walls. Once the phone rang, but it was just a wrong number. Her heart had hammered in her throat a full five minutes after she had hung up. She tried to get herself to calm down, but things kept flashing through her mind, horrible things she kept pushing away before the thoughts were totally formed. Jocelyn was going to be fine, just as Joshua had promised. She was just doing this to torture her. She was safe at one of her friend's homes and they had lied to her when she had called.

Her eyes strayed to the hope chest beneath the window. Tommy's gift. It had been delivered just yesterday. She took a deep breath, trying to get hold of herself. Maybe if she had stayed in London with Tommy, none of this would have happened.

No, it would have. Staying in London wouldn't have been right. What she had with Tommy had represented an interlude, not a way of life. She had to stop torturing herself with paths not taken.

Joshua would bring her home, just as he promised. But why wasn't he calling? She stared anxiously at the white phone hanging on the wall next to the stove.

Because he hadn't found her. Because she wasn't at any of the addresses in the book. Because something had happened to her.

Oh God!

It was all her fault. She should have stuck it out with Harry. Even hell was better than this.

She squeezed her eyes shut and willed herself to calm down. "At this rate, Joshua's going to walk through that door with Jocelyn, and you'll be a certifiable basketcase. She'll be fine, just fine," she sobbed. "And then I'll kill her for doing this to me."

She sat down on the sofa and tucked her arms around herself. Johanna began to rock, trying to contain the hysteria that was threatening to overtake her. She couldn't let go, she couldn't. If something had happened to Jocelyn, she was going to need a clear head to deal with it. Crying like this wasn't going to get her anywhere. It wasn't going to help find Jocelyn.

Unable to sit still, she was up on her feet again, walking to the window. Two stories below, cars moved up and down the avenue as people milled around on the streets. People. So many people. She dragged her hands through her hair. How could Joshua find one lone girl amid so many?

She wanted to call Mary, to call her father. To talk to someone, to hear something besides the sound of her own voice, her own heart pounding in her ears. But if she telephoned, she would be tying up the line and Jocelyn might be trying to call her.

At that moment, her heart went out to every parent who had ever had a runaway child, or a child snatched away from them.

Why wasn't he calling, dammit!?

The phone rang and she collided with the coffee table in her haste to reach it. She knocked over the plant she had been tending to so painstakingly. Dirt spilled everywhere. Johanna didn't notice. The only thing on her mind was the telephone.

Please let it be Joshua. Please let him have found her. Oh, please.

"Yes?" she cried breathlessly.

"I found her." When only silence met his declaration, Joshua became concerned. "Johanna?"

She gulped in snatches of air. "Where? Is she all right? Was she—?" She couldn't make herself say the last word. If Jocelyn was hurt, if anything had happened to the girl because of her own cowardice, she'd never forgive herself.

"She's at Mary's. Mary found her waiting in the hall for her."

"Mary? But why didn't she call me?"

"She tried, but every time she did, she couldn't get past the dial tone. Her phone's out. I'm calling from a booth on the corner. She didn't want to leave Jocelyn to call you until she had calmed her down. By then I showed up."

Thank you, God.

With her back against the wall, Johanna slid down to the floor, her legs unable to support her any longer. "Oh Joshua."

He heard the relief, the fear drain from her. "I know. It's okay, honey. She's asleep and I think it's best if she stays with Mary tonight. We can come and pick her up in the morning."

She nodded numbly and then realized that he couldn't see. "Fine."

"She's going to be all right, Johanna. Are you?"

"Now. I—Joshua, could you—?"

He heard the need in her voice. He had intended to come back anyway. She had been through hell and now that it was over, he wanted to be there for her, just to hold her if that was all she needed.

"I'll be right over," he promised.

Chapter Thirty-seven

When she opened the door to him, he saw the tear streaks still fresh on her cheeks. Without saying a word, he reached out and brushed them gently away. Johanna mustered a smile and shut the door behind him. A long sigh escaped her lips as she turned toward him.

"Joshua, I can't begin to tell you how grateful I am to you."

"Then don't try." Words weren't necessary, not those words. He could read them in her eyes.

"I have to," she insisted. "I have to talk to an adult. I've been talking to myself for three hours and you know how I can go on. I nearly drove myself crazy." The abrupt flow of words stopped and she flung herself into his arms, pressing her head against his chest and holding on to his arms. "Oh God, Joshua, I was so frightened, so frightened. I kept envisioning all sorts of things happening to her and—"

"Shh." He stroked her head, his fingers caressing her

silky hair. "It's all over now, Johanna. I should have brought you with me."

"No, no." She looked up at him, still holding on. "You were right. If she had come home on her own, wanting to talk and I hadn't been here, I wouldn't have forgiven myself."

He liked the way she felt against him, soft, supple, feminine. "She loves you very much."

"Did she say that?"

He wanted to lie, to tell her yes, but he had lied once, a long time ago. And it had cost him her. He was through with lies. "She didn't have to. It was in her eyes."

She found that she could grin. "Oh, you read eyes now too?"

"Didn't you know? I've been reading eyes for a long time now. A hobby." He brushed a strand of hair away from her cheek.

Vulnerable, she felt incredibly vulnerable. The pending excitement, the electricity that was just out of reach, licked at her from all sides. All she had to do was take a step toward it.

She took it.

"And what do mine say?"

She knew what she was doing, Joshua thought. Whatever lies she would tell herself later, she knew. "I'm not sure. I have to get in closer."

"Myopic?"

"Just came on suddenly."

His breath touched her lips a moment before he did, preparing her, anointing her. She raised herself up on her toes just slightly as she molded her body to his, feeling the heat flare from his loins to hers. His need for her, hard and hot, was there and suddenly, she wanted nothing more than to forget everything but this passion that was igniting within her. Her lips parted, inviting him in, to taste, to sample. To possess.

Joshua held her tightly in his arms, deepening the kiss

slowly, taking time, holding himself back when all he wanted to do was make love to her, here, now, on the floor, breathlessly and passionately until exhaustion claimed them both. He had wanted this so much for so long that now that it was finally happening, it seemed unreal. If he rushed, he might frighten her, make her back away or he might wake up and discover it was all only a dream. He wanted to savor this as much as he wanted to plunge himself into her and enjoy her.

But even now, he wanted to give her the gift of time, so he went slow, calling on all the control he had in his possession, stretching it tightly to its very limits and then asking a little more of himself for her. For Johanna.

Once the waltz had started, she found that she didn't want it to end. She knew all the arguments against this. She had been over them in her head a hundred times. She would give herself and inevitably have something taken away. She knew all the pitfalls that lay ahead, the trap that would spring and hold her prisoner, but she didn't care. Not now, not this moment. All she wanted was to be held and to hold. To touch and be touched. Whatever penalties there were to be paid, she'd pay them. Tomorrow. When dawn came. But for now, with morning still hours away, she wanted to be his.

The vulnerability that was ripped open tonight had made her open to attack by her own feelings. There was no use hiding from them or from the way she felt about Joshua. If she still believed in happily ever after, Joshua would have met all the conditions.

But things didn't happen that way. She knew and still she wanted him.

He made love to her with his mouth. His lips roamed her face, touching her eyelids, her cheeks, her forehead, her throat with an endless chain of kisses that reduced her limbs to liquid and heated the very core of her being. As with the return to the museum, she felt as if she had suddenly come home, as if her soul had been searching for only this and had finally come to it, after journey's end. Only the tiny part of her mind that was still functioning knew it was an illusion

But for tonight, the illusion was enough.

Johanna tangled her fingers in his hair as he cupped her head back. Shards of desire shattered all through her as he did nothing more than kiss her over and over again. With impatience, she tugged at his shirt. A button popped off, pinging against a glass on the coffee table before coming to rest on the rug.

Her very touch made it hard for him to keep his restraint in tact. He was only flesh and blood and the best of intentions could be easily burnt away by passion. "Careful," he murmured against her skin, "I'm not much at sewing buttons back."

"I'll do it," she promised, tugging at the others. "I'll sew them all on."

"Oh God, Johanna, you have no idea how long I've waited for you to say that."

She felt his smile along the hollow of her throat. "Even now, you can make me laugh."

"Laughter's good for you," he whispered, caressing her, letting his mouth glide down lower on her skin. "I'm good for you."

And he was. Oh, he was, she thought, groping to pull the shirt off his shoulders. She nearly shredded it as she pushed it down his arms.

"You're ahead," he told her, his voice thick. "My turn."

With slow, deliberate movements, he worked the zipper of her dress down her back. Johanna shivered as she felt its descent until he came to a halt well past her waist. With both hands on her back, he parted the material like two halves of a book and rested the pages on her arms. The dress floated down to the floor and she stood in a soft blue teddy that made him ache in its transparency.

"Part of me wants to undress you totally, the other part,

the artist in me, wants to just worship here and now. God, you are beautiful, Johanna."

He made her feel soft, feminine. He made her feel as beautiful as he said she was. Every pulse in her body throbbed. Yet somehow she found words. They had always been able to communicate. She clung to that, that difference. Could that be the key? "Which part wins?"

Mischief entered his gray blue eyes. "This is one work of art I really want to get into."

A giggle broke loose and it made the kiss that followed all the sweeter, all the warmer. Secrets were there, their secrets. Secrets they shared now and before. He spanned her waist with his hands, pulling her to his body as his mouth pulled away all the secrets she had kept from him, all her hurts and pain.

Her hands curled against his chest, her fingertips gliding along the light matting of soft brown hair, her body heating at such a rapid rate that it stunned her. Even with Harry, it had never been like this, never this quick, this wild. And yet this sweet.

It was past the time for words, for banter, for niceties. Needs and wants, so long denied, took over. The teddy whispered to the floor beside the dress. He lowered his head and touched her nipples with his tongue, sensitizing the skin along the way. She moaned, digging her fingers deeper into his hair and arching her body. She needed this, wanted this, loved this.

Loved him.

God help her, she was doing it again. She was falling in love with Joshua, perhaps had always been in love with Joshua, and there was nothing she could do about it to stop it.

Nor did she want to. Perhaps tomorrow, but not tonight. Tonight she would burn away her sorrow, her bridges, and all the consequences that lay ahead. Tonight, she only wanted to be loved and to make love with Joshua.

He shed the remainder of his clothes impatiently, tossing

them aside. Rather than carrying her to the bed, he gently guided her to the white rug beneath their feet. The time for patience, for slow, languid steps had gone. The kisses grew more passionate, more caring, and they found that they bruised each other's lips without feeling the pain. Only the ecstasy. The only thing that mattered was quenching the fire that burned between them.

Her hands roamed his body. She wanted to touch every part of him, to pull his essence into herself. To absorb him and this moment, to pretend, for a little while, that it was all right. That somewhere down the line, her heart wouldn't break. She heard his groan as her long, delicate fingers left their mark on his bronzed skin.

It took every shred of control not to give in to the urgency that savaged his body. He wanted to plunge into her, to make her his now, finally, after all these years, but even now, his breath ragged in his throat, his heart hammering at every pulse point, he held himself in check, pleasuring her. First, always first. Her satisfaction before his because it *was* his. He wanted to give her the joy that he was feeling and knew that at the very least, he could give her the jubilance of being loved.

When his tongue glided down her body, teasing her skin, she tensed and arched and kept her cries muffled within her throat. It became unbearable to hold back. As his tongue reached the moist, inner core of her feelings, she felt a scream mounting, begging for release, just as her pleasure begged for it. The first crest tossed her like a skiff in the wind, first up, then down, then up again. She dug her nails into the rug, searching for a hold as his mouth worked indescribable wonders, making her rediscover her body, her wants, herself. She was moist and hot and aching for him.

"Joshua, please."

The words were forced through a throat so dry she could bearly speak. She held out her arms to him and felt his hot body along every inch of hers as he slowly pulled himself up over her. It was skin against skin, flesh against flesh, need against need. Never had she experienced such excitement, such pleasure.

He framed her face in his hands for a moment and looked down at her. Her eyes were smoky, clouded with desire. She had never appeared more beautiful to him. He wanted to tell her then that he loved her, had always loved her and would go on loving her until there was no breath left in his body.

But it was too soon for words like that, too soon for her and he knew it. It saddened him even now. But it would come soon, he promised himself. For now, he would content himself that he had her body. Her love was something he was willing to wait for.

His mouth covered hers and he drove himself into her. The cry she gave echoed into his mouth as they both moved to a rhythm that had been preordained since the beginning of time. She didn't know who set the pace, or if it was something they both escalated within each other. He had begun slowly, moving his hips just a little. Her response had become more intense, more demanding, spurring him on, until they both went spiraling faster and faster, bringing each other up higher and higher until they met again on the final plateau.

A low moan echoed between them. It might have been hers. It might have been his. Neither knew.

Spent, satisfied, their skins damp against one another, they lay within the shelter their arms created and let their breathing slow to a peaceful, easy sigh. He shifted his weight only slightly, to keep the burden from her. But he couldn't bear to pull himself away from her completely. Not yet.

Johanna keep her arms encircled around him for a long time, afraid that if she let her arms drop, if she let go, the rest would go, too. And the joy, the fulfillment, the sense of peace she felt within her was far too precious to release just yet.

When he finally moved, she gave a small cry of protest,

like a child about to be chased away from the only shelter she had ever known. He moved her over until her head rested on his shoulder and he could cradle her against him. She felt safe, protected and this was another gift he gave to her.

They stayed like that a long time, each not wanting to move, not wanting to talk. Not wanting to break the spell of the moment, even though there was so much to say, so many feelings to explore.

Finally, she fell asleep.

Joshua listened to her breathe evenly and thought how wonderful a sound that was.

Chapter Thirty-eight

It had been a long time since Johanna had woken up in a man's arms. Her mind still fuzzy with sleep, she was slow to open her eyes, not wanting to let go of the delicious sensation that enveloped her body and warmed it. With a sigh, she snuggled in closer. When she finally did open her eyes, she felt slightly disoriented. There was a man's hand wrapped tightly about her breasts. And then it all came back to her in abrupt waves. Jocelyn. Running away. Joshua.

Joshua!

She jerked and turned her head toward him.

He was awake. He had been for some time, but had been reluctant to move, not wanting to disturb her. He liked watching her sleep. She looked innocent, sweet. Untroubled.

Joshua ran his fingers along her lips. "Good morning." He saw the startled look that had entered her eyes as sleep quickly faded. He was determined not to let her withdraw from him. "Sleep well?"

She felt awkward, embarrassed. She knew she shouldn't. She hadn't been last night. But her feelings about him, about the relationship that seemed to be swallowing her up so quickly, were too strong for her to be at ease. She didn't know where to look. She didn't know what to do. He was naked beneath the sheet, as was she. Heat radiated through her. There was less than a hair's breath between them. Her heart began to hammer as she tried to think of something to say. Her mind was a total blank.

"Yes, I—"

"You were beautiful last night."

She pulled at the sheet, wanting to cover herself. The warm glow within her was at odds with an attack of raging embarrassment.

Joshua put his hand lightly on hers, a gentle protest at her belated modesty. "Don't hide from me, Johanna."

She knew that he wasn't just referring to the sheet. He meant more. He had seen it in her eyes. Her fear of involvement. Her fear of being hurt again. Was she so transparent? Well, if she was, then he'd already know and understand her reasons. "Joshua, I can't give you what you want."

Firmly, he uncurled her hand from the sheet and waited until it relaxed beneath his. "Yes, you can."

He was going to make her cry. She didn't want to lose what she had felt last night, but she couldn't let herself believe that it was more than a wonderful illusion, a scene that had been played out and was now over. To believe more would be putting herself on the line again. But, oh God, she did so want to believe. "I don't believe in happy ever after."

He smoothed the hair back from her face. "Try."

Struggling, she found strength from somewhere. "No. I can't face any more problems or heartache. I'm sorry, but

I've been through all that once before. I won't do that to myself again. I won't risk it."

He thought he was going to lose his patience. How was he going to convince her? He cursed Harry's soul to hell. He was still there between them, even in bed, a specter Joshua couldn't exorcise. But he would. By God, he'd find a way.

"Without risk, what is there?"

This time, she did pull the sheet up higher, tucking it above her breasts. She didn't look at him. "I have my work, my daughter."

"Work is a poor substitute to take to bed with you at night, Johanna." Wanting to drag her mouth to his again, he satisfied himself with merely touching her face with his fingertips. "And Jocelyn will be on her own soon enough. Then what'll you have?"

When he touched her like that, it was hard to think, to remember. "I'll join a volunteer group." She dragged her hand through her hair and let it fall heavily. "What do you *want* from me?"

"No more than I know you're capable of giving, Johanna."

She shook her head, fighting back tears. She wanted to, God knew she wanted to. But fear held her captive.

It would do no good to press. What he won could easily be lost. "We'll take it slow. One day at a time and see where it goes." He kissed the tip of her nose. "I'm not about to develop fangs and grow hairy at a full moon, Johanna. What you see," he spread his arms, "is what you get."

It was certainly a lot, she thought, a smile slipping to her lips. She had never realized just how well built he was. She had known him once, worked with him now, and hadn't realized that there were hard muscles beneath the jeans and pullovers. He was magnificent.

But that didn't alter the situation.

"You're making it awfully hard for me to stand firm, Joshua."

He caressed her cheek, his touch unbearably gentle. "I plan to make it damn impossible, Johanna." His lips feathered lightly across hers, his tongue outlining them softly. "Damn impossible."

"Oh God," she groaned, her body leaning into his. Her arms went around his neck and the sheet tangled between them before he kicked it away.

This time, the lovemaking was slower, richer, deeper than it had been. This time, they both knew the extent of the ecstasy that waited for them. And yet it was a surprise all over again. The wealth of feeling they evoked from one another overwhelmed them both. He had loved her, been in love with her for years and now fell total victim to her. In trying to ensnare the woman, he was that much more hopelessly caught himself.

Colors flashed beneath her closed eyes, such colors that her breath was snatched away. Her head swam and the joy that jumped through her veins made it inconceivable that anyone had ever felt this before or would ever again.

She found that she was the eager one as her body heated instantly at his kiss. This time she wanted to catch the brass ring quickly in her hands.

But Joshua wouldn't let her. "Enjoy," he murmured against her throat. "We have all the time in the world. We have forever."

If only she could believe that. If only it were true.

How could anyone feel like this and still function, she wondered, still think? She was in a daze, and yet somehow aware of every single sensation that he brought to her, like a fresh bouquet of meadow flowers. A rainbow.

Her blood felt hot as he suckled at her breast. She entwined her fingers into his hair, pressing him against her, urging him on. His tongue just barely grazed her navel. Spasms seized her stomach as anticipation quivered throughout her body.

She even fooled herself into thinking that it would be different this time.

For a time.

When Johanna went to pick up Jocelyn, Joshua insisted on coming along with her. She knew that she should face her daughter alone and yet was grateful for the moral support he provided.

"I like bringing a friend into the enemy camp," she laughed nervously as they walked into the stylish co-op where Mary lived on Second Avenue.

He nodded at the security guard as they walked to the elevator. "Jocelyn doesn't think of you as the enemy."

Johanna punched the button, her only outward sign of tension. "She's not too crazy about me right now."

He kissed her temple. "That'll pass. I'm crazy enough about you for both of us."

She clutched the words to her breast as they entered the elevator. The way he said "us" to include Jocelyn made her heart swell. If Harry had never entered her life, she knew that there would be no measuring the joy she could be capable of feeling. She would blindly go into this relationship, thinking it absolutely perfect. But Harry had entered, had been the one whom she had fashioned dreams around, only to have them crushed by the very person she trusted so implicitly.

Once burned, twice leery, she thought. And so weary.

Mary answered the door on the first ring. "C'mon in, you two. Jocelyn's waiting." She stepped back, vaguely gesturing into her apartment.

The gray clay-tiled foyer echoed her footsteps. "How is she?" Johanna asked, dropping her voice.

Mary shut the door. "Scared."

Adrenaline jumped, pumping hard through her veins. "Did anything—?"

Mary placed a gentling hand on her sister's arm. "No,

nothing like that. Nothing happened to her last night while she was wandering around."

Linking arms with Johanna, Mary stepped down into the sunken living room. The apartment had large windows that offered a breathtaking view of the city. The high ceiling, sparse furnishings and light-colored walls made the room look much larger than it was.

"Then why—?"

"I think you'd better hash this out yourselves." Mary let her go and turned toward Joshua. "So, handsome, can I interest you in a glass of orange juice?"

"With pulp?"

Mary's smile was brilliant. It reminded him of Johanna's. "Is there any other kind?" She guided him toward the door on the extreme left side, leaving Johanna standing in the living room, looking down at Jocelyn.

The girl sat on the sofa, her legs pulled up under her, her face averted. She looked small, lost, defiant.

Johanna felt hurt. How could Jocelyn do this to her? How could she have put her through this? She wanted to yell, to shake her, to cry. She knew that none of this would work. Slowly, she approached Jocelyn and saw her stiffen and become even more aloof-looking than she already was. For a moment, Johanna hesitated, then sat down beside her daughter.

Jocelyn's pride and fear gave way to the need to be held, comforted. She raised her eyes to her mother's face, waiting. Hoping.

"You scared me to death, Jocey. I thought something had happened to you."

"Would it have mattered?" the small voice asked, thick with tears that were held back.

Johanna took hold of Jocelyn's shoulders and stared at her face. "Are you crazy? Of *course* it would have mattered. You are the only, only thing, the only *person*," she corrected herself, "that matters in my life. I love you, Jocelyn."

Jocelyn pressed her lips together and nodded her head,

her eyes shimmering with tears. It was what she needed to hear.

With care, Johanna pulled her close. Jocelyn put her head on her mother's shoulder, needing the contact. "Why did you run away from me?"

"I wanted to go before you left me, too."

Johanna raised her head to look into Jocelyn's face. "Too?"

Jocelyn swallowed. The lump in her throat was enormous. "Like you left Dad."

"Oh, honey," she cried, stroking Jocelyn's hair that was wet with her tears. "I left Dad because he wasn't the man I married and because I was afraid that if I stayed, he'd destroy us."

"And if I changed?" There was a challenge and a plea in her voice.

Johanna hugged her daughter close and kissed the top of her head. "I'd fight like hell to make you unchanged."

"Promise?"

She laughed, with tears falling freely down her cheeks. She didn't bother brushing them aside, but let them fall. "Promise."

Mother and daughter hugged and cried, and washed away the residue of the battle with tears.

"Well," Joshua said, reentering the room, "is everything okay?"

Jocelyn nodded. She dug the heels of her hands into her eyes, quickly brushing aside tears. She didn't want to be caught crying in front of Joshua.

He crossed to them and ruffled Jocelyn's hair, pretending not to see the tear-streaked cheeks or swollen eyes. "Good move, Jocelyn. You made her get a few gray hairs."

Johanna's hand automatically moved to her head. "I did not." She knew he was teasing, but couldn't resist playing along.

"Mothers always get gray hair when their kids run off." He sat down next to Jocelyn. The look on his face was serious, though not stern. His meaning was clear. There would be no lectures from him and no repeat performances from her. "You mother doesn't look too hot in gray." He took a sip of orange juice, finishing the glass. "Clear?"

Jocelyn nodded.

"Okay." He braced his hands on his knees and rose. "Let's all go out for breakfast. My treat."

Mary was already pulling her ermine jacket from the closet in the foyer. "Don't let this one get away, Jo." She and Joshua exchanged grins.

Johanna felt a quavering in her stomach as she got up. She remembered Joshua's words to her this morning and told herself that it was the only way to go. One day at a time. What she had rebuilt within her was frail, hanging on by a thread. She had gotten back her self-esteem and found that she could make it on her own. She didn't want to jeopardize all that by pledging her heart in a relationship that would one day blow up in her face.

Yet not pledging her heart would eventually cost her Joshua.

Silently, she linked her hand with Jocelyn's and followed the others out the door.

Damned if she did and damned if she didn't.

Chapter Thirty-nine

October threaded its way quickly into November. The weather, for New York, was mild. There was no cold snap and snow seemed a long way off.

It was hard, Johanna thought, watching the kite inch its way up into the brilliant blue sky, on a day like today to imagine that winter and Christmas were just around the corner, although the stores were certainly prepared for it. Bright decorations and holiday merchandise were highly visible. Garland and brilliant Christmas lights were everywhere, entangled between the street signs, greeting the citizenry and reminding people that for a few short weeks at the tail end of the calendar, everyone was supposed to love everyone else.

Joshua, she noticed, pleased, had gotten caught up in the season and had given in to the race to celebrate Christmas earlier and longer. Two weeks shy of Thanksgiving and he had Kathy hang mistletoe in the gallery. Johanna knew there was an ulterior motive behind that. One she cherished.

It gave her an excuse to kiss him.

She loved being kissed by him, she thought. Power, passion, gentleness, they were all there whenever his lips touched hers. And standing beneath the mistletoe, she was safe. She could shrug off her willingness to be kissed, to be bathed in the sensations that were created, by saying that it was all in keeping with the Christmas season. And she could pretend that the feelings behind the kisses that were exchanged were nothing more serious or binding than her just getting caught up in the spirit of the holidays.

A group of children moved past them, huddled together like a gaggle of geese, their teacher at the head and several harried mothers in attendance at the sides and the end. They were evidently headed for the zoo, Johanna thought. That would probably be Joshua's next stop.

She turned and grinned at him now. He was lying face-up a few feet away from her, propped up on his elbows, totally engrossed in what he was doing. The concentration he was displaying could have been the kind merited by a major undertaking. Joshua was flying a kite.

He was dressed in a cream-colored fisherman's sweater and his ever-present jeans. His dark hair tousled, he looked like a boy on a holiday. Leaning back on his elbows, his long legs stretched out before him on the grass, he held the kite string in a steady hand. Jocelyn was next to him, purely fascinated.

"I can't believe you never did this," he said to Jocelyn. "How could you be twelve and never have flown a kite?"

"I don't think we have any in Beverly Hills," she said with an absent shrug of her shoulders. Her eyes danced as they followed the kite's path. It was climbing higher and higher, flirting with the wind.

"Another reason not to live in southern California," Joshua murmured.

"Don't you like southern California?" Jocelyn asked, curious.

"I like seasons." He spoke to her the way he would to an adult. It never occurred to him to talk down to her. "Leaves that turn color before they crunch under my shoes. I like snow."

"We have snow. It's just in the mountains," Jocelyn volunteered.

"I know, but I'm lazy. I don't like to have to drive to see a snowfall. I like looking outside my window." He grinned at her as he looked her way. "They close schools here when it snows too hard."

"They do?" It was evident that she was very close to being completely won over.

"Sometimes," Johanna put in. "But only when it snows very hard and it's several feet deep." She saw that Jocelyn was barely listening. Her eyes were on Joshua and the bobbing kite. Johanna couldn't help smiling. "Besides, we're already playing hooky today."

Joshua leaned back to look at her. "We're *all* playing hooky," he reminded Johanna. His eyes skimmed over her body familiarly, touching it and seeing beneath the heavy lavender sweater and neatly creased slacks.

Johanna warmed under his gaze and shifted slightly.

"I didn't know adults played hooky." Jocelyn's voice broke the spell.

"Worst offenders," he said seriously, playing out the line to the kite.

"To fly kites?" Jocelyn wanted to know.

He grinned. "Sometimes. Sometimes just to spend an afternoon with two gorgeous women."

Jocelyn liked the fact that he had said two women instead of two girls.

Someone walked by with a portable radio. Rather than having music from a rock group blaring at them, the radio's owner was playing a tape of Beethoven.

"Oh, yuck," Jocelyn muttered.

"Don't much care for classical music, eh?" Joshua laughed.

"It's the pits."

"Oh, I don't know." Joshua considered her statement. "If it wasn't for Beethoven, the Beatles might have had a problem."

"The beetles?" Jocelyn looked at him. "Who're the beetles?"

Johanna and Joshua exchanged looks. "Ouch, I think I feel old," Johanna said.

"Never." He patted her thigh with his free hand. The gesture was fleeting, but intimate. He turned his attention to Jocelyn. "They're the guys who made it easy for The New Kids On The Block to do their thing on stage."

Jocelyn came to life. "Really?"

"I have it on the best authority."

Jocelyn looked after the funny little man as he moved away, his music fading away with him. "Hey, how about that?"

"You know," Johanna said in a lowered voice, "you have her eating out of your hand."

"How about her mother?"

She found his eyes difficult to resist. She found him difficult to resist. "As long as it's not fattening," she said.

"I'm guaranteed low-calorie." He winked at her. It was a decidedly wicked and sexy wink.

When the wind picked up, Joshua took a vote and they decided to retire the kite for the day while it was still in one piece.

They went to the zoo next, just as Johanna predicted. The wind helped clear away the smells and Jocelyn was in seventh heaven.

"She loves animals," Johanna confided as they walked behind the girl. Jocelyn tried to be everywhere at once, seeing everything.

"I know."

She looked at Joshua. "Is there anything you don't know?"

"Yes," he said meaningfully.

Johanna turned away and pretended to look at the antics of a spider monkey as he climbed up to the top of his black iron-bar cage. "I've been thinking of getting her a pet for Christmas. Think your friend would mind if I had a puppy in his loft?"

"It couldn't do more harm than some of the friends he's had over there on occasion." Joshua laughed. "What kind of a puppy did you have in mind?"

"I haven't decided yet. Something small. I like tea cup poodles myself." A woman with three children, all heading in different directions, rushed by Johanna, making a grab for the nearest one.

Joshua side-stepped the woman and he shook his head. "Nope. Too hyper. Strictly a Beverly Hills-type dog."

She was amused at the way he seemed to divide the country between good—New York—and bad—Beverly Hills. "Oh? What would you suggest?"

"I don't know. Let me think on it."

"You have until a week before Christmas."

"I hope I have longer than that."

"Jocelyn, don't wander too far ahead," she called after her daughter, using it as an excuse to curtail the direction the conversation was going.

They had slept together only that one time when Jocelyn had run away. Johanna made certain that there were no more times alone like that, no more solitary moments when temptations got the better of her. To her relief, and just possibly her regret, he had gone along without protest, even though she could tell that he wasn't happy about it. She wanted no more thoughts of happiness, that kind of happiness, clouding her mind. She knew what she had to do, how she had to live. If it was shutting love out, so be it. It was also shutting out pain of a magnitude that she couldn't endure twice.

Yet when he had appeared on her doorstep that morning, kite in hand, she couldn't find it in her heart to turn him away. Even if she had, Jocelyn would have begged until she agreed. Work and school were forgotten. Dangers lurking in the dark, in soft kisses and light touches, were forgotten. The day was made to be enjoyed.

They spent another two hours at the zoo. Though it was by no means a large zoo, hardly meriting the title when compared to the zoos that Johanna had taken Jocelyn to, there was something very special about sharing the afternoon this way. He bought them hot dogs at a stand and Jocelyn swore she had never eaten anything tastier.

"And for dessert," he announced, producing a crackerjack box from his jacket pocket.

"Those'll break your teeth," Johanna warned.

"Where's your sense of adventure, Johanna?" he teased, opening the box and pouring some carmel covered kernels into Jocelyn's outstretched, cupped hands. He took some himself and then eyed Johanna.

"Well, I might as well go to the dentist with you two." She reached into the box.

"What a sport, eh, Jocey?"

"It takes her a little time to get used to change," Jocelyn told him matter-of-factly.

"Out of the mouths of babes," he murmured, tossing up a kernel and catching it in his mouth.

"Hey, do that again," Jocelyn urged.

"Don't encourage him, Jocey."

"I love an audience." He winked at Jocelyn. "Hey, what's this?" He looked into the box, moving some of the kernels around.

"What?" Jocelyn asked eagerly. She stood on her toes, trying to look into the box.

"Well, you know, if I remember correctly, these things used to have a prize in each box," he told her.

"Does this one?" Jocelyn wanted to know. She had more

than her share of expensive toys, but somehow the promise of a mysterious trinket outweighed them.

"Yes." But rather than give it to Jocelyn, he handed the box to Johanna. "This one seems to have your mother's name on it."

Johanna stared at the box, dumbfounded. "Mine?"

"Open it, Mom. Let's see," Jocelyn urged, clapping her hands together.

Johanna eyed Joshua for a moment, then looked into the box. There was a small box within it. Cautiously, she drew it out. It was a ring box. Her breath caught in her throat as she opened it. A single perfect diamond mounted on a silver wishbone setting caught the sunlight and formed a rainbow of colors that spilled out onto her hand.

"Hey, wow! Do you think you can get another box like that for me?" Jocelyn asked Joshua, her eyes huge.

"I don't think so," Joshua answered quietly, watching Johanna's face. "This is a one-of-a-kind box."

Johanna raised her eyes to his. He saw wariness there again and he swore inwardly. He blamed himself, though. He should have never let her go all those years before. But all he had to work with was the present. And he intended to make the present work.

"Well, Jo?" he asked softly.

She closed the box, her face impassive as icy panic seized hold of her heart. She thrust the ring back to him, her hand trembling slightly, but he refused to take it. It was a major effort to keep the anger he felt from his face. She let the ring box fall back into the crackerjack box that he was still holding.

"I think we'd better go home," Johanna said quietly. Her throat felt as if it was closing up, as if she couldn't breathe. "It's getting cold,"

"Whatever you say."

Chapter Forty

"**She said** what?" Joshua's voice echoed in the empty gallery. It was eight-thirty and more than an hour away from opening. It was further away than that as far as Joshua was concerned.

Kathy blinked. She'd never seen Joshua more than mildly annoyed. She had thought that the message she passed on when he walked in would make him frown. She didn't think it would make him shout. Her boss, she decided, had it very, very bad.

"Johanna called in," Kathy repeated patiently, "and said that she was taking the next three days off. She said that if you wanted to fire her, she'd understand."

His hands curled into fists, but he refrained from hitting the desk. Just barely. "What I want to do is take her over my knee and spank her."

"Isn't that a little excessive for taking three days off?" Kathy asked mildly, not bothering to hide her knowing grin. She hadn't been blind to what had been happening between her boss and the classy blonde he had hired. As far as she was concerned, it was about time someone rattled his cage. Kathy Connors firmly believed that everyone belonged married with children of their own. That was true equality as far as she was concerned.

Joshua made a few quick calculations. "Kathy, can you hold down the fort for a while?"

"Haven't I always?"

He kissed her cheek quickly. "Atta girl."

Kathy ran her fingers along her cheek. "Do that again and I'll forget I'm a married woman."

He was already out the door, but he spared her a moment. "Why are the best ones always taken?"

"Ha!" She waved him out the door. "Go get her!" she ordered.

"I'm going to try, Kathy." He closed the door behind him and stepped out into the street. "I'm damn well going to try."

He tried the loft first.

Two minutes worth of ringing and calling her name had him bringing out the spare key that Elton had left with him before he went to Europe. It was to be used in emergencies and this, as far as Joshua was concerned, was a full-fledged emergency.

The loft was empty. And her suitcases, the ones he teased her about dragging all around the world, he thought bitterly, were gone. Though a few things remained in the loft, most notably the carved hope chest she kept by the window, he had the sinking feeling that she was gone for good.

He sat down on the white sofa, his hands clenched into fists.

Not again, he thought. Not again.

"Jo, what are you doing here?"

"Hi, Dad, can we come in?" Johanna asked, offering a weak smile.

James Lindsey, a small, spare man with kindly eyes and

a gentle smile, threw open the door and then his arms. Though they were all practically the same height, he drew both his daughter and granddaughter into the circle of his arms.

"God, it's so good to see my girls again." He allowed himself a moment just to drink in the sight of the two of them. Jocelyn had gotten taller, prettier, a lot like her mother. Johanna was thinner than he liked seeing her, but the worn look he had expected to see wasn't there. Just a certain leeriness in her eyes. "What a wonderful surprise."

"Are you going to work, Grandpa?" Jocelyn let her suitcase drop on the hardwood floor that bore the indelible scuff marks of three young girls growing up.

"Oh." He looked down at the white smock that peeked out from beneath his dark topcoat. "That's right. I am." He drew in his shallow cheeks as he thought the situation through. This was Wednesday. The young assistant pharmacist who had been with him since late July didn't work on Wednesdays.

Johanna touched her father's downy smooth cheek fondly. She knew he was thinking of the drugstore, of his responsibility. He was very predictable. And very dear. "We'll be here when you get back. You need a home-cooked meal."

The store could wait a few minutes. He closed the door behind Jocelyn. "You didn't come all this way because you were worried about my stomach, Joey." He effectively turned so that Jocelyn was cut off and couldn't hear his next sentence. She was already roaming about the cozy family room and out of earshot. "Some kind of trouble because of Harry?"

"In a way."

The answer was too evasive. "In what way?"

Johanna patted his shoulder as she opened the door. "We'll talk when you come home. It's nothing that won't keep," she assured him.

Reluctantly, and only because there was no one to take

his place today, James Lindsey left. A thirty-five-year-old habit was a hard thing to turn your back on. But he worried. That was his right as a father. As a father, he also knew that Johanna would tell him things when she was ready to and not before.

As soon as her father was gone, Johanna turned to Jocelyn. She tried to sound breezy. "C'mon." She picked up a suitcase. "We'll use my old room." Johanna led the way to the staircase.

Jocelyn trudged behind her, dragging one of the suitcases. "I love Grandpa, Mom, but I still don't see why we had to come here all of a sudden. My teacher—"

"I'll write a note to Mrs. Olsen," Johanna promised. "I just had to get away, honey, to think." She stopped at the landing. Her room was the first on the left. The door was opened. For a moment, as she stepped inside, she felt seventeen again. Young and alive. The world was full of promise.

Just the way it was when she had laid in Joshua's arms.

"About the crackerjack prize?" Jocelyn asked quietly.

Johanna smiled sadly, turning around. "About the crackerjack prize," she echoed, tugging at a strand of her daughter's hair. "How d'you get to be so smart?"

"I got it from my mother," Jocelyn answered off-handedly as she pulled her suitcase further into the room. Then she looked over her shoulder at Johanna and grinned broadly.

Johanna laughed. "Go, get settled in."

"How about you?" Jocelyn asked.

"I'm going out behind the house."

The back of the house faced a wooded area. The first fifty feet constituted her father's backyard, the rest belonged to Connecticut, but she and her sisters had always thought of it as permanently on loan to them. They had played many games of hide-and-seek, had breathtaking adventures and had shared long, lazy summer days there.

The weatherbeaten swing still hung from a branch of the old sycamore tree. She felt a pang when she saw it. She used to sit and swing for hours, daydreaming. The distance from those days to now was almost insurmountable. And yet it could be crossed by just a few steps. If only she could take them, dare to take them.

Johanna went to the swing to sit, to remember, to look for an answer.

Most of all, to look for peace.

Life had been so much simpler when she used to swing here, she thought, gingerly dropping her weight onto the wooden board. It creaked and groaned, but held. She wrapped her hands around the rough hemp that tied the swing to the tree. The cold air made her cheeks red and nipped at her hands, but she refused to put her gloves on. She wanted to feel things, at least these things.

Other things, she was afraid to feel. She knew it and was ashamed. Joshua would make a wonderful father for Jocelyn. The girl was so taken with him. And in her heart, Johanna felt—no, *knew*—that he wouldn't fail her, wouldn't fail either one of them, not the way Harry had.

And yet. . . .

And yet, she couldn't make herself take that long, frightening final step. What if it all went sour again?

From the recesses of her mind, an image of the Foggertys came to her, old, stooped, still holding hands. Still living and in love. Sometimes things worked. Sometimes, she thought, a kernel of hope beginning to form, love did win out and stay.

Johanna leaned her head against one of the ropes of the swing and let out a soft sigh.

"If you wanted to swing, there was a park not far from the gallery."

She jumped to her feet as she swung around. "Joshua! How did you get here?" How could he have gotten here so fast?

"By driving like a bat out of hell for the last two hours. I've had two hours to get over being angry." He took a measured step toward her. "Two hours isn't enough."

She looked at the ground, unable to meet the accusation in his eyes. "What are you doing here?"

Joshua crossed the sloped distance that separated them. He had been watching her for a few minutes. "I could ask you the same thing. You were supposed to come into work today."

Overhead she heard geese calling to one another, flying in formation. They were late, she thought. But determined. "I called Kathy."

He came and stood next to her. The swing separated them. It wasn't the only thing. "She told me."

The formation faded to a speck in the sky, their sound fading with them. She looked into his face, seeing things that made her feel guilty. "But I didn't tell her where I was going. How did you—?"

"I have a great ally in your sister. She thought you might be here." He took hold of one of the ropes. It was either that, or touch her. And this last bit of distance she had to cross herself. He had come as far as he could. The rest was up to her. "She also thinks you should have your head examined for passing me up. Modesty not withstanding, so do I."

"Joshua, I don't know—"

"Yes, you *do* know and that's what frightened the hell out of you." He wound his fingers around the cords. "Do you honestly think I'd force you to do something against your will?"

"No."

"You love me," he said, his voice softening. "I've seen it in your eyes, felt it in your kiss. Why won't you marry me?"

"I don't want to ruin it." The excuse sounded so feeble. But it was also true. What she had with Joshua was precious, but it was the "before" stage. Marriage changed people, changed promises. She didn't want him to change. She thought of the Foggertys again and felt torn.

"That's a bad joke, Johanna."

"My marriage was a bad joke."

"And are you trying to tell me that on the basis of that one mistake, you're ready to rule out love from your life forever?"

"It's not that simple," she argued, but even as she did, something within her was gaining strength, rising up against her and uniting with Joshua.

"It *is* that simple. I'm not offering you paradise or a perfect world, but I damn well know that I can love you a hell of a lot better than that neurotic, cocaine-snorting freak."

"He wasn't always that way." But in her heart, she knew Joshua was right.

"No, but he was weak. He was always weak."

"I—"

"If he wasn't, he wouldn't have given in so quickly. And he'd have never let you go."

Joshua deserved the truth. "He didn't know I was divorcing him."

She tried to turn away, but he wouldn't let her. She was through turning from him, he thought, taking hold of her shoulders. "I'm not talking about the divorce. I'm talking about years before. He let go of something precious, of your love, because of his lust for acclaim. Well, I don't need anyone telling me I'm great. I'm happy with what and who I am. There's only one thing missing in my life." Johanna opened her eyes wide, waiting. "You," he whispered.

Her resistance was dissipating, crumbling to dust. And subconsciously, she was glad. Without realizing it, she pulled the swing aside and stepped forward. "Oh Joshua, I want so much—"

"Then do it, Johanna. Do it. For me. For Jocelyn. For us." He took her into his arms. "I promised you I'd never hurt you and I won't. But damn it, I can't let you out of my life twice, Johanna. It's not fair. You can't do that to me."

She turned her face up to his. "You love me." It *was* as simple as that.

"No, I collect women whose first initial matches mine. Yes, I love you, you idiot. I've loved you from the first moment I saw you. And, though I tried to bury you after you left, to forget you ever existed, I've loved you all these years. That's why there's never been any other woman who mattered in my life. None of them were ever you." He threaded his fingers through her hair and framed her face. "Marry me, Johanna. Marry me and you'll never regret it. At least not for the first hundred years. After that, we'll see."

She'd been a fool, running all this time from the past. The scars she bore would only heal if she let them. That meant not picking at them, not remembering. And she knew Joshua could make her forget. He was already doing it. "You do make me laugh."

"Not all the time, I hope." His lips were so close to hers she could taste them, but he didn't kiss her. He waited.

She thought of the last time he had made love to her. Too long. It was too long ago. Suddenly, she ached for him with such fierceness, she was afraid she couldn't control it. "No, not all the time."

The low, whispered reply told him everything he needed to know. "Then you'll marry me?" Before she could answer, he kissed her, long and hard until they were both breathless and desperate for air, desperate for each other.

She dug her fingers into the soft leather of the jacket he wore, leaving imprints. "Do I have a choice?"

He grinned, then nuzzled her throat. He felt her pulse leap up. For him. Only for him. "Yes. But it doesn't count if it's the wrong one."

She pretended to sigh, then laughed, feeling free, really free. It was as if everything that had hurt had been suddenly washed away, as if it hadn't existed. It mystified her, but she wouldn't examine it. She had been examining life far too long and not living it to the fullest. That was going to stop as of this moment. "Then I guess there's no use fighting it."

"Nope," he teased her lips with his own, bending her body into his, "none at all."

The sun came out just before he kissed her again, bathing them both in its light. Johanna snatched up the covenant and held on with both hands.

This time, she knew, it would be forever.

MARIE FERRARELLA is the author of forty-one novels. She lives in California with her husband and two children.

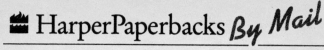

☰ HarperPaperbacks *By Mail*

Ambition—
Julie Burchill—
Young, gorgeous, sensuous Susan Street is not satisfied with being deputy editor of the newspaper. She wants it all, and she'll do it all to fight her way to the top and fulfill her lust for success.

The Snow Leopard of Shanghai—*Erin Pizzey—*
From the Russian Revolution to China's Cultural Revolution, from the splendor of the Orient to the sins of a Shanghai brothel, here is the breathtaking story of the extraordinary life of an unforgettable woman.

Champagne—
Nicola Thorne—
Ablaze with the glamor and lust of a glittering industry, fired by the passions of the rich and beautiful, this is the sizzling story of one woman's sudden thrust into jet-set power in a vast international empire.

Kiss & Tell—
Trudi Pacter—
Kate Kennedy rises from the ashes of abused passion to become queen of the glittering, ruthless world of celebrity journalism. But should she risk her hard-won career for what might be the love of a lifetime?

Aspen Affair—
Burt Hirschfeld—
Glittering, chilling, erotic, and suspenseful, Aspen Affair carries you up to the rarified world of icy wealth and decadent pleasures—then down to the dark side of the beautiful people who can never get enough.

Elements of Chance—
Barbara Wilkins—
When charismatic billionaire Victor Penn apparently dies in a plane crash, his beautiful widow Valarie is suddenly torn from her privileged world. Alone for the first time, she is caught in a web of rivalries, betrayal, and murder.